THE WELL OF STARS

THE WELL OF STARS

ROBERT REED

TOR®

A Tom Doherty Associates Book
New York

THE WELL OF STARS

Copyright © 2004, 2005 by Robert Reed

A slightly different version of this novel was published in England in 2004
by Orbit, an imprint of Time Warner Books UK.

This book is printed on acid-free paper.

Edited by James Frenkel

A Tor Book
Published by Tom Doherty Associates, LLC
175 Fifth Avenue
New York, NY 10010

www.tor.com

Tor® is a registered trademark of Tom Doherty Associates, LLC.

Library of Congress Cataloging-in-Publication Data

Reed, Robert.
    The well of stars / Robert Reed.—1st ed.
       p. cm.
    "A Tom Doherty Associates book."
    ISBN 0-765-30860-6 (alk. paper)
    EAN 978-0765-30860-3
    1. Space ships—Fiction.   2. Life on other planets—Fiction.   I. Title.

 PS3568.E3696W45 2005
 813'.54—dc22

                                                        2004058861

First Edition: April 2005

Printed in the United States of America

0 9 8 7 6 5 4 3 2 1

TO MY WIFE, LESLIE RENEE

THE GREAT SHIP

I have no voice that explains where I began, no mouth to tell why I was imagined or how I was assembled, and I have no idea who deserves thanks for my simple existence, assuming that thanks are appropriate. I recall absolutely nothing about my exceptionally murky origins . . . but I know well that for a long cold while I was perfectly mute and only slightly more conscious than stone, sliding through the emptiest, blackest reaches of space, my only persistent thought telling me that I was to do nothing but wait . . . wait for something wondrous, or something awful . . . wait for some little event or a knowing voice that would help answer those questions that I could barely ask of myself. . . .

For aeons and a day, I felt remarkably, painfully tiny. Drifting through the cosmos, I imagined myself as a substantial but otherwise ordinary species of cosmic dust. Compared to the vastness, I was nothing. How could I believe otherwise? Unobserved, I passed through intricate walls woven from newborn galaxies—magnificent hot swirls of suns and glowing dust, each revolving around some little black prick of collapsed Creation—and among that splendor, I was simply a nameless speck, a twist of random grit moving at an almost feeble speed, my interior unlit and profoundly cold, my leading face battered and slowly eroded by the endless rain of lesser dusts.

Through space and through time, I drifted.

Galaxies grew scarce, and the void was deeper and ever colder . . . and when I might have believed that I would never touch sunlight again . . . when my fate seemed to be blackness and the endless silence . . . I found myself falling toward a modest disk of stars and dust and little living worlds. . . .

By chance, a young species—the human species—noticed me while I was still descending through the outskirts of their Milky Way. Brave as fools and bold as gods, they built an armada of swift little ships and raced out to meet me, and to my utter amazement, I discovered that I was enormous—bigger than worlds, massive and enduring, and in their spellbound eyes, beautiful.

Humans were the first species to walk upon my face, and with a quick and efficient thoroughness, they explored my hollow places. To prove my considerable worth, they fought a little war to retain their hold on me. According to law and practicality, I was salvage, and I was theirs. In careful stages, they began to wake me, rousing my ancient reactors, my vast engines and life-support systems, repairing the damage left by my long, long sleep. And they gave me my first true voice—in a fashion. A thousand mouths were grafted on to me. Radio dishes and powerful lasers, neutrino beacons and spinning masses of degenerate matter endowed me with the power to shout at every approaching sun and all the living worlds. "Here I am," I would announce. "See me! Study me! Know me, then come visit me!" In a multitude of languages, my new mouths claimed, "I hunger for your company, your friendship, and your infinite trust." I asked, "Are you, like so many technological species, a functional immortal?" Then I promised, "For a fair fee, I will carry your ageless and precious soul to a distant world. Or in half a million years, after circumnavigating the Milky Way, I will bring you home again. Can you imagine a greater, more ennobling adventure than to journey once around our galaxy? Or for a still greater payment, I can become your permanent home—a vast, ever-changing realm offering more novelty and sheer wonder than any other body in Creation." Then with a barker's teasing laugh, I would ask, "What kind of immortal would you be if you didn't wish for such a splendid, endless fate . . . ?"

Like every proud child, I spoke obsessively about myself. Addressing species that I had never met, I defined my terms and described my dimensions, my depths, and my laudable talents. I was lovely igneous stone and ancient iron buttressed with hyperfiber bones, and my skin was a thick armor of high-grade hyperfiber capable of shrugging off the impacts of interstellar gravel and full-bodied comets. I was swimming through the Milky Way at one-third the velocity of unencumbered light. My engines were as big as moons, and I was bigger than most of my patrons' home worlds: twenty Earth masses, and fifty thousand kilometers in diameter, with a hull covering nearly eight billion square kilometers. But my skin was nothing compared to my spongelike meat. Whoever built me had the foresight to give me endless arrays of wide caverns and neat tunnels, underground seas and chambers too numerous to be counted. I could conjure up any climate, replicate any odd biosphere. To travelers who appreciate robust numbers, I spat out an impressive figure. "Twenty trillion cubic kilometers." That was the combined volume of my hollow places. On a simple world such as the Earth—a world I will never see, except perhaps in passing—there are barely 200 million square kilometers of living space. Life exists in two dimensions, not three; trees and buildings reach only so high. Only the top fringe of the ocean and the little zones by the rifting plates are productive habitats. "Not with me," I said with a seamless arrogance. My new voice was designed to sound prideful, sharp, and confident. "With me, every little room is a potential paradise. I can give you the perfect illusion of any sunlight and the exact atmosphere that you find most pleasant, unless you need a hard vacuum, which I can achieve just as easily. I can manufacture soils to fit the most delicate chemistry and fluids enough to slake any thirst, and by an assortment of means, you can wander through my public areas—my shops and auditoriums, religious sites and scenic vistas—unless it is your preference to live entirely by yourself, which is your right. If solitude is your nature, I will honor your noble choice.

"I accept all species," I claimed. Which was true, to a degree. I would welcome every sentient soul, but my ageless human captains always retained the final word. My voice never entirely mentioned the possibility that travelers could come some great distance, and at no small risk to themselves, only to be informed that they could not afford passage, or less likely, that they were deemed too unstable or too dangerous to be allowed to live among my more docile passengers.

Always, always, I sang endless praises of my human caretakers. They were my captains, my engineers, my guiding hands and crafty fingers. They owned me, I admitted with a voice that couldn't have sounded more thrilled. Better than any other species, the humans knew my depths, understood my potentials, and were fully prepared to hold tight to me until the end of Creation.

Perhaps I believed those boastful words, but my truest feelings remained secret, even from myself.

I am rich in many things, but particularly in those things that are unknown.

Washen was one of the first children born inside me, and that earliest little portion of her considerable life was spent in a modest house overlooking one of my warm blue seas. Her loving parents were engineers, by training and by deepest conviction, meaning that not only did they know how to build every possible structure and every conceivable machine, they also possessed the clear unsentimental and pragmatic outlook of true engineers: the universe—their universe—was rich with an elegant beauty, known elements and reliable forces playing against each other in ancient, proven ways. If there were questions of consequence needing to be solved—a dubious possibility, at best—then those questions didn't involve people of their particular caliber. Engineering was a finished profession. The galaxy was adorned with many wise old species that long ago had mastered Nature's basic tricks. Humans were virtual newcomers. With nothing but science and intuition to guide them, human engineers had managed to teach themselves how to build lasers and fusion reactors and bioceramic materials. Given time, they might have invented much of the rest of what was possible. But during their twenty-first century, a moonbound observatory glanced at a particularly rich portion of the sky, for a few perfect moments, intercepting a tight-beamed broadcast from a distant civilization that was bound for an even more distant world.

Inside that dense and highly structured burst of blue light were enough tricks and fancies to fuel a dozen intellectual revolutions. Hyperfiber was perhaps the greatest of the alien gifts. Built from deceptively ordinary materials, it was a lightweight and potentially immortal substance that could endure almost any abuse, and do so while shouldering almost any burden.

There were many reasons not to expect to find a great ship wandering on the fringes of the Milky Way. But no competent engineer was surprised to learn that my skin and bones were composed of hyperfiber. What else would a godly power employ in such an enormous construction? Perhaps my particular hyperfiber was a better grade than what people and most other species had cultured in the past, or even in the brilliant present. And yes, the scale and perfection of my spherical body demanded resources and quality controls that not even a thousand worlds working together could achieve. But nothing about me seemed genuinely impossible, much less threatening to the status quo. Yes, I was grand and highly unlikely, and marvelous, and enigmatic, but I still resided firmly in the grasp of an engineer's venerable, often-proved theories.

When Washen was a young girl, her parents helped first culture the finer grades of hyperfiber, using my hull's armor as their inspiration. They taught themselves to do the magic in sufficient quantities to patch my old craters and the occasional deep wound. Their house was littered with scraps and useless shards—failed experiments brought home from the factories—and sometimes Washen would pick up one of the bright pieces, staring at her own reflection. She was a slender girl, a pretty girl, a little tall for her age, her black hair worn long and oftentimes damp from swimming in the sea. Even though she was the offspring of deeply committed engineers, she lacked their narrow curiosity. One day while sitting at the breakfast table and staring at a ball of sweet new hyperfiber, she suddenly inquired, "Where did this come from?"

Her father was a handsome man, young-faced but in his second millennium of life, and even on his most poetic day, he was a literal soul. With a calm, studied voice, he explained what was obvious and essential. A nanoscale foundation was laid down in the factory. Each atom had to be doctored before it was set in its perfect space, aligned with its neighbors, then every quark allowed to find its perfect resonance. Then if a certain standard was achieved, the entire batch was turned into a quasi fluid, thick and gray and ready to fill molds or one of the ancient craters scattered across the ship's hull. The material's final grade depended on subtle, oftentimes invisible, factors. Unfair as it seemed, luck played a powerful role. But he didn't wish to bore his daughter with dense technical terms. Using a few convoluted sentences, he had answered her question, adding, "That's where this comes from," as he gestured at a mirror-faced ball barely bigger than the hand that was holding it.

Washen nodded agreeably. Her question had been answered, if not in the manner she had hoped. There was no reason to act rude or complain. No, she realized the best course was to turn in her chair, turn and smile, and ask her mother the same essential question.

"Where did we get this?"

Washen's mother had different gifts, different strengths. She was very much an engineer, but she possessed a more rarefied appreciation for theory and high mathematics. Quietly and with a seamless patience, the woman explained. "We call it hyperfiber for good straightforward reasons. The name refers to the hyperdimensions that we can't actually see. Dimensions other than up or over or back. Dimensions other than time, which isn't a true dimension anyway. You see, it takes eleven dimensions to build the universe. Or thirteen. Or twelve. The exact number depends on which Theory of All you happen to subscribe to. But in every important way, the answers are the same. Some of these invisible dimensions are enormous and others are quite tiny, and what you are holding there . . . that very tiny piece of hyperfiber . . . well, its fibers stretch into these other dimensions, both physically and through deep subtle forces. . . ."

The full lecture continued for a long while. The woman could be pleasantly loquacious, and Washen accepted her mother's nature just as she accepted the fact that she couldn't understand what was being said. But she nodded politely. She sometimes smiled. When bored, she looked at her own skeptical reflection. Perhaps she had thought her question was very simple, and it plainly wasn't simple, and how could she make herself understood?

"When you strike a piece of hyperfiber," her mother continued, "the impact forces don't spread just through our three dimensions, no. They dissipate through all eleven of them. Or thirteen. Or twelve. Or twenty-three. There are approximately seven distinct universal theories. Your father and I like the eleven-dimension theory, but all give the same conclusion: Even when hyperfiber fractures, a quantum echo lingers in the upper-dimensional realms. What you're holding there . . . it's really a much larger object than you can see. It extends out into every corner of the universe, in all of its manifestations, and even if you could grind that ball down to dust, the ball remains intact. If only as a theory, of course. As a delicious mathematical concept existing in the shadow realms—"

"No," the young girl blurted, finally interrupting.

Offended, her mother stiffly asked, "What is the matter, dear?"

"What's wrong?" the old man growled. "Darling, you're talking nonsense, that's what's the matter. The girl's barely half-grown, and what are you doing? Jabbering about quantum mechanics and ghostly physics . . . !"

"I know she's young."

"Hell," he said. "Your song barely makes sense to me. And I passed the same classes you passed."

"You didn't have my grades," her mother countered.

"Who remembers that?" he snarled. "Besides you, I mean."

There was an ugly, much-practiced pause, then a gnawing discomfort. It was unseemly to argue in front of a child, even one of your own. The two old people stared at each other, making their apologies with the tiniest of winks, and into that silence came the stubborn voice of someone demanding an answer to her insistent little question.

"Where did this come from?" Washen repeated.

Then she explained, "I don't mean how we cook it up, or why it works. I just want to know where we got it in the first place."

"Oh," her parents said, with a shared voice.

"Hyperfiber was a gift," Father replied. "An accidental gift from an alien civilization."

"The Sag-7 signal gave us the essential recipe," Mother added.

Washen shook her head.

"I know that much," she promised. "That's history, and I got that in school, plenty of times already."

With genuine confusion, her parents asked what she really meant.

Washen concentrated, her chocolate-colored eyes revealing a seriousness not usually found in someone so young. "I want to know: How did the Sag-7 learn to make hyperfiber?"

They found an answer. It took a long moment to use their nexuses, dredging up arcane details from data files carried all the way from Earth. According to histories composed by a wide array of species, an even older alien species—one of the first to evolve in the once-youthful Milky Way galaxy—had cultured the first bright bits of hyperfiber. And before they went extinct, many millions of years ago, that species had shared their secret with the now venerable Sag-7.

But even that explanation didn't seem to answer her question. Washen shook her head, her strong mouth working while her deep dark eyes stared at the bauble in her hands.

"But who taught that first species?" she asked.

Nobody could say. Maybe nobody had taught them, her parents confided. The long-vanished aliens must have found the great stuff for themselves, which really wasn't all that incredible.

"But were they first?" Washen wanted to know.

What did she mean?

"The very first," she persisted. "In the universe, I mean."

The obvious answer presented itself. Neither of the engineers, nor any of the consider-

able experts on board, could do more than guess at my true age. But I was at least as old as the Earth, and perhaps much older. "It could have been the ship's builders," Washen's mother offered with a shrug and a little laugh. "Maybe they were first in Creation to culture hyperfiber."

She and her husband had been married for most of a thousand years. Their feuds and little fights served as a mortar, as relentless as gravity, helping to keep them securely and forever locked together. As soon as her husband saw the flaw, he snarled, "That's ridiculous. Think of the odds! That the builders were the very first, and that they happened to send their empty ship toward our little galaxy . . . and then out of the 2.2 million estimated intelligent species in the Milky Way, we just happened to be the first to come along and take possession of their prize . . . !"

The complaint served no purpose except to send his wife's mind drifting down a new avenue.

While she pondered, the old man turned to his daughter. "We don't know who was first, Washen. Does that answer your question?"

For endless reasons, it did not. It could not. Yet the young girl nodded, setting the round scrap on the table, and after a moment of perfect balance, it began to roll away from everyone. Over the edge it fell, hitting the floor with the softest ping. Then with a charm that would eventually lead billions of souls, Washen lied, telling her parents, "Yes, sir. Yes, ma'am. And thank you very, very much for your help."

For more than a hundred thousand millennia, I had a great voice, and never once did I show any doubt in the words and images that I offered to the universe. My captains led flawlessly, or nearly so. The Master Captain was the image of a wise ruler—a nourishing queen, or at least a pragmatic and occasionally forgiving despot. My voice beckoned, and a multitude of species and odd souls rode little starships out to join me. My voice lured them, and the humans were enriched in myriad ways: with fresh technologies, cultural hybridizations, and trading pacts, plus fat grants that gave them worlds and asteroids to terraform and colonize, or to mine down to dust if they wished.

And then came Marrow.

Unknown to the captains, an entire world was hiding inside me. A living world, as it happened. The first examples of native life ever found inside me—forests and fungi and a multitude of pseudoinsect species—had thrived on this Mars-sized globe, undetected for many thousands of years. And deep inside Marrow lay other surprises. There was a cargo. Or perhaps, a passenger. Some willful entity, ancient and mysterious, imprisoned in my core and apparently dangerous, and according to a few voices, important beyond all measure.

I wasn't just an empty ship after all.

A few of the captains journeyed to Marrow, in secret. There they were marooned, and with the scarce resources on hand, they built an entirely new civilization. Then over the course of the next centuries they lost control of everything they had built. Their children and grandchildren spoke of Builders and the Bleak. One was worshiped, the other loathed. But which was which? Who gave them visions and faith? What power born at the beginning of the universe was responsible, telling the self-named Waywards to climb up to the Great Ship and take back what had always been theirs . . . ?

There was a swift and devastating war, and my voice suddenly fell silent.

The Waywards' conquest failed—just by a little ways, it collapsed—and the worst of my newest wounds were repaired. But my proud and loud and long-reaching voice remained silent. My carefully plotted course through the galaxy had been changed. Passing near an aging sun, then its sister, a massive black hole, my trajectory was twisted, sending me plunging on a course that in just a few thousand years would carry me out of the Milky Way, back into the cold, empty reaches of space.

With my other tongues gone, I could hear my true voice again.

Warnings whispered to me.

Urges tugged, too subtle for anyone else to feel.

Fear lay in my bones. My fear, or another's? I didn't know. I didn't dare guess. Out of wisdom or simple exhaustion—is there any difference?—I decided not to make distinctions.

Anyone's fear means there could well be a reason to be scared.

I have always been, as I am now. Terrified. And I shall always be this way, I imagine.

One

"So where is this holy site?" Pamir asked.

The two of them had just emerged from an unmarked cap-car. Washen paused, bright black eyes fighting the glare of a sun that was not real. "Out on the rocks," she reported, gesturing at a long spine of basalt that reached into the blue sea. She was a tall and elegant woman, and lovely, and her smile was quick and full of a shackled but genuine pride. "The chairs are waiting for us."

"I see them fine, but that's not what I'm asking."

"What's your question?"

"Your original home," Pamir explained, impatience lurking in his rough, low voice. "You've only mentioned it a few thousand times. We're close enough to walk. Since we have time, maybe you could show me your childhood abode."

Why not? thought Washen.

Yet for the next moment or two, she fumbled for her bearings. Centuries had passed since her last visit, and the city had changed its appearance in her absence. Entire streets had been moved or repaved, and the buildings surrounding them were either remodeled or obliterated. Unless, of course, everything was exactly the same as her last visit, and she was simply being forgetful. After more than a thousand centuries of life, not even the brightest person, on her finest day, could remember more than a fraction of everything she had seen and everything that she had done.

The easy response to the confusion was to ask a buried nexus for an address and map. But Washen resisted the temptation, and after waiting for an inspiration that never quite arrived, she started to walk, leading her companion along a likely avenue while hoping it would lead to the correct hilltop.

The cavern surrounding them was a modest-sized bubble tucked inside a vein of black basalt, strands and girders of buried hyperfiber holding the ceiling and distant walls securely in place. When first mapped by the survey teams, this entire volume was filled with water ice dirtied with nitrogen frost and veins of methane. Because of the cavern's relatively small dimensions—barely a thousand kilometers long and half as wide at its widest—and because it was close to the ship's bridge and Port Alpha, this was among the first habitats to be terraformed. Coaxing half a dozen nearby reactors out of their ancient sleep, the engineering corps had gradually warmed the ice to where it was an obedient, if still chilled, fluid. Then the cavern was drained. As an experiment, every drop of fluid was filtered twice and analyzed with an array of sensors, and like everywhere else on board the ship, not a single credible trace of past life was uncovered. The water was far from pure. In the ancient ice were traces of minerals and salts and a few molecules of simple organics. But missing were the telltale fragments of lipid membranes, the persistent twists of DNA or RNA, or any cell that could not be tied directly to any human being or one of her escaped bacteria.

Giant pumps and siphons were scattered throughout the ship, presumably intended for this one function. With a command, the machines began lifting the water back into the cavern, and when it was half-filled, the engineers stopped the pumping and sealed the drainage holes. Other teams began tinkering with the environmental controls, establishing a day-and-night cycle and a sequence of seasons, modeling a climate that was dubbed Mediterranean. The new ocean was salted just enough, then laced with iron. A bright blue sky was painted with holo projectors, and at night, blackness and a scattering of ancient constellations wheeled overhead. Then an array of simple microbes and planktons was released in the wind, and the rare patches of flat ground were slathered with black soils made from hydrocarbon stocks. Fish and squid were pulled from arks originally brought from Earth, rugged oaks and olive trees grew on the black shores, and a tidy few species of birds suddenly seemed to be everywhere. The ship's first city was built on this ground, housing the engineers and other crew members who had come on the starships. Twenty-two other patches of ground and shallow water were designated for future settlements. But even after more than a thousand centuries, only half of those planned cities had so much as a few houses standing on the reserved sites. The ship's enormity had absorbed the vast bulk of development. With more caverns than passengers, why not live in your own private paradise? Besides, since this was the first little corner of the ship to be terraformed, people better suited to repairing starship engines had done the hurried work. Every other sea seemed more elegant or beautiful or odd or special. At least that was the snobbish opinion carried by most of the passengers. But not Washen. She had grown up along this rocky black shoreline. Even now, uncertain about her bearings, she found it very easy to remember sweet moments and those long, long days when she was a child in a world with very few children, busily living her life in what was the Great Ship's finest city.

The rising avenue was a wide lane, basalt pavers set in the traditional quasi-crystal pattern, red buckyfiber mortars pressed between them, and the lane was lined with stout oak trees that might be two hundred years old, or twenty thousand. To the left, the blue sea quietly rolled into the rocks and the increasingly high cliffs. On their right, houses and little businesses created the comfortable mood of a genuine neighborhood. The occasional resident saw Washen and Pamir passing, and too late, they would emerge into the dappled light. Had they really seen whom they thought they saw? Were these the two captains who had defeated the Waywards? Word spread up ahead and along the tributary lanes. Humans and other species hurried outdoors, waiting to see the spectacle of two people dressed in their mirrored uniforms, walking side by side up the most average of streets. No one could believe her luck. Were they holo projections? No, apparently not. One fearless little boy approached, showing a big smile before asking, "Are you really the First Chair, madam?"

"I am," Washen replied.

"And you're the Second Chair, sir?"

"I suppose," Pamir rumbled.

The two captains had recently become Submasters. The precise reasons for their promotions were complex and a little sordid and inevitably quite sad. But to a boy's mind, the story was obvious. The Waywards were evil and dangerous souls who had risen up from that secret world, Marrow. Washen and Pamir had done heroic deeds, beating back their enemies, and their new epaulets had been earned by their bravery and undiluted loyalty to the Great Ship. The Master Captain herself, with nothing in her heart but gratitude, had bestowed these high offices on their proven, glorious shoulders, and now everyone should sleep easy through the night.

"You're here for the meeting," the boy told them.

He was walking beside Washen. They made an unusual pair—the small boy with short straight hair and a stocky build, and the tall, willowy woman with the pretty face and the basalt black hair worn in a tight bun. Washen nodded and glanced down at her companion, and with a false nonchalance, she asked, "Do you live nearby?"

"Up there," he replied, waving at the hill rising before them.

"Hunting for a local guide?" Pamir teased.

Washen conspicuously ignored him.

With pride, the boy announced, "This is the oldest city on the Great Ship. That's why we call it Alpha City. Or the First City. Or just Alpha."

"I know," Washen purred.

"The Master Captain always holds her most important meetings out there, on those big rocks out there."

"So I understand."

"Have you ever been to one of those meetings?"

Washen shook her head. "I don't believe so. But there's always the chance that I don't remember."

"So why walk up this way?"

"That's a wonderful question," Washen allowed.

"Because we're lost," Pamir offered, remaining a step behind the First Chair and her new best friend.

Other pedestrians laughed with a nervous glee, but the boy seemed to disapprove of their mood. He frowned for a moment, then he decided to warn Washen, "There's nothing important up here. Nothing at all."

"Is that what you think?"

Was this some kind of trap? The boy concentrated before repeating his warning. "It's an old neighborhood. The houses can't be torn down, unless they happen to fall down. And they can't fall down, because everybody is supposed to keep them strong."

"Because this is an historic district," Washen explained. She winked at the boy. "The first people to board the ship built those houses. That makes them important. And one or two captains were born up there, as I understand it."

The boy seemed genuinely surprised. "Which captains?"

"Just some little ones," Washen said.

"I'm going to be a captain," her new friend announced. Then he glanced up at Washen with a sudden wariness, and finding something agreeable in her expression, he looked back at the Second Chair. "I'm going to be a captain soon. Very soon."

Pamir was a tall, imposing man. Unhandsome and typically surly, he had little interest in charm or false smiles. His heavy rough-hewn face was perfectly capable of frowning at any crew member or passenger, at any time and for the smallest good reason. But this was a child, and perhaps Pamir's new uniform and rank helped him to behave. Whatever the reason, he decided to avoid the bald truth. "Maybe you will be a captain," he replied simply. "I wish you all the luck."

Then through a private, heavily shielded nexus, he said to Washen, "If there's still a ship to rule, that is."

EVEN IN THE midst of a seemingly ordinary walk, the Submasters were busy watching over the routine and the remarkable. Buried nexuses made it possible, and their rank made escape from their duties almost impossible. The ship's giant engines were being repaired and refurbished in a crash program. Security teams still were hunting for the last of the Waywards. Passengers and the crew had to be encouraged and kept informed, and that required a multitude of media campaigns, each tailored for a given species and the quirky local cultures. And always, rumors had to be exposed and killed in very public ways. If any hazard terrified Washen most, it was the capacity for a simple story to ripple through the public consciousness, mutating and swelling in importance as it spread out from whatever misunderstanding or half-truth had given it birth. Right now, as she strolled calmly into the ancient neighborhood, she was dealing with a persistent bit of nonsense: The captains and their families were preparing to abandon the Great Ship. It was a rumor that began the very minute the Waywards were defeated, and despite every attempt to prove it wrong, the lie continued to find life.

Today, the abandonment story was being told by an obscure species using a language of elaborate scent markers and fluorescent urines. As soon as the trouble was noticed, a team of AIs and xenobiologists began working on a countercampaign and the means of delivering it. Washen was alerted, and while walking on the narrowing road, she examined and canceled half a dozen plans. "Too much," was her general assessment. "A light touch," she demanded. "Get a captain to pee the truth in public," she suggested; and then she looked up, surprised and more than a little pleased to find a familiar scene greeting her.

A grove of ageless oaks and walnuts covered a piece of land just large enough to appear endless from the edges. The heavy interlocking limbs and thick green leaves produced a shade so compelling that only a few Lipanian murkshrubs managed to survive on the stony black ground. The single break in the canopy was above and alongside one low-built house. Obviously conceived by engineers, the structure was solid and balanced and slightly drab, fashioned from carved basalt and cultured diamond. Martian trusses and Roman arches lent strength and an accidental elegance, and the false sunshine poured over it, granting it a false brilliance. The front door stood shut—a thick white door made of smart plastics and brass flourishes—and for a little while, it seemed as if no one was at home. Washen gave a greeting, but she couldn't hear the door calling to the inhabitants, and it certainly didn't speak to her. Perhaps the house was abandoned, she thought. If it were empty, she would buy it. She had time enough to make that decision and briefly imagine living here again, then to suffer the first tugs of regret. She didn't belong in this place. The girl who had lived here once was gone, and it was a foolish thing to wish for.

The boy was still hovering nearby. She turned to him, asking, "Whose home is this?"

"It's somebody's," he blurted with authority.

Then a face appeared behind one of the diamond windows, and Washen felt a giddy, almost intoxicating sense of relief.

"See?" the boy added.

But the face vanished with a strange swiftness, and the door remained closed and silent. With his patience spent, Pamir stepped up and used a heavy fist, pounding until a set of locks turned liquid and flowed into the jamb. The door opened grudgingly. The peering face belonged to a little human woman. She now appeared in the gap, and with a whispery little voice said, "Yes, sir. Yes, madam. What is wrong?"

"Nothing's wrong," Washen insisted. "I used to live here, that's all."

The boy gave a low laugh and ran off to tell what he had just learned.

"And if it's no trouble," the Submaster continued, "I'd love the opportunity for a quick tour, please."

A hard pain struck the woman. Several hundred of her neighbors and presumed friends were standing back in the shadows, watching everything. She stared out at them, a grimace slipping loose for a moment. Then she buried her rage, and with a soggy voice muttered, "I can't stop you from looking."

Her discomfort was contagious. Washen flinched, and said, "I know this is an imposition, ma'am. And if you tell us, 'Go away,' we most certainly will."

That promise startled the woman. She took a deep breath, and her face turned, whispering a few words to someone unseen. And then because she couldn't believe Washen—because no little passenger could stand in the way of a Submaster—she dropped her head in resignation and slowly backed away from the door, allowing the two great captains to step inside.

By law, the structure's interior had to maintain certain historic standards. And for her trouble, the resident was granted some fat financial benefits. Washen naturally assumed that the standards weren't being maintained. That would almost explain the woman's brittleness. But if there were discrepancies, they were subtle ones. Without tapping the old data banks, Washen couldn't find anything worse than a few little rooms that had been remodeled to make several kinds of alien guests feel comfortable.

The house covered only a hectare of ground, and the walking tour took a matter of minutes. She and Pamir strolled through entertainment rooms and social rooms and an old-fashioned library, complete with glass books and paper books sealed behind sheer diamond screens. An indoor pond triggered memories. "I learned to swim in there," Washen mentioned. Then she showed Pamir each of the three rooms that she had claimed for herself, at various stages of her childhood, the last one as far from her parents' room as possible. Finally, they entered the big ancient kitchen where a person, if she was so moved, could cook without the aid of robots or smart-meals. Stoves big enough to feed a brigade stood against one long wall, ignored but ready. Pots and tubs made of steel and hyperfiber hung from copper pipes lashed to the high ceiling. And in the middle of the room, sitting before a simple wooden table, was a stranger. He was a smallish man taking a last deep sip of a thick hot narcotic drink. When the Submasters entered the room, he moaned. When they looked at him, he threw his glass down and sobbed, then dropped his face, nose mashed against the yellow wood. The half-covered mouth offered a squeak before muttering, "Forgive me."

The woman stood in a different doorway. In the yard, squinting through the windows, were maybe half a hundred curious neighbors.

"I'm very sorry," the little man whispered.

Pamir laughed.

Softly but furiously, he asked, "After what you've done? Why shouldn't we just kick you to pieces?"

The man trembled, saying nothing.

Washen settled into a facing chair. Her expression was distracted, but she heard enough to say, "Tell us," as she cupped her hands before her. Holding nothing, she stared at her hands, and said, "The entire story. Tell us."

The man made his confession in what seemed like a single breath. He was a lifelong technician who had worked in the Alpha port, and when the Waywards came, he had abandoned his post. He went into hiding. He bought a new face and body, then the war came and went, and he decided to change his face twice more, building a new identity that should have been perfect. But it obviously hadn't been. He was staying here with his sister, which must have been his mistake. But it wasn't the security troops that had found him, no. Who could imagine it? The First Chair and Second Chair had both come here, which meant that for some incredible reason he must be regarded as an enormous criminal.

Pamir smiled, loving the whole string of coincidences that had conspired to produce this very unexpected moment.

But Washen barely noticed. Her cupped hands pulled apart, dropping the nothingness that they had held, and she watched the nothingness roll off the tabletop, her head tipped to one side, as if listening for an echo nearly as old as herself.

"Stand," Pamir commanded.

The technician jumped to his feet and almost fell over.

"Sober up," the Second Chair advised. "And then return to your post. Today. If you can do those two things—sobriety and work—and if you can remember how to do your work, I'll speak to the Master Captain about clemency. Is that understood?"

"You would do that for me?"

"I'm not doing this for you. This is for the ship's own good." With his nexuses and his personal authority, Pamir had both identified this woman and tracked down her missing brother, and he was already wiping the record clean. Technicians were precious, particularly today. The man hadn't joined the Waywards, which was a fat plus. And besides, it would make this moment considerably less funny if he had the criminal thrown into the brig.

"Thank you," said the grateful technician. "Sir. Madam."

With the scrape of wood against tiles, Washen pushed back her chair and stood again. If she had heard a word in the last couple minutes, she didn't mention it. Instead, she adjusted the tilt of her mirrored hat, and with a distant little smile, she asked, "How long have you lived here?"

The woman swallowed, then confessed, "For the last seventeen centuries. Madam."

Washen nodded.

After a moment's consideration, she said, "That's ten times longer than I lived here." Then Washen smiled, and winked. "This is your house now. Do what you want with it. Remodel it. Tear it down and build another. Whatever you wish to do, you may."

"Madam—?"

"But if you find anything interesting . . . anything that seems old and odd . . . please, send it to me, please?"

Two

HUMANS BEGAN AS perishable apes, but aeons ago they infused their bodies with synthetic genes and bioceramic minds, creating souls more durable than the exposed face of any simple rock. This basaltic hill was a prime example. Since the first day of her rule, the Master Captain and her highest officers had met on this ground, and during that tenure the shoreline had eroded noticeably, the original black boulders gnawed down to mere stones that quietly rolled off into the patient surf. What began as a proud high hill seemed rather less impressive today, and much the same might be said of the Master Captain. To the eye, she looked as everyone would expect—massive and queenly and cold-faced—but her enemies had grievously injured her during the Wayward War. Her body was only recently reborn, golden flesh and tough bone reconstituted beneath her comatose head. Newly minted nexuses had been implanted, her body swelling in response, linking her mind to the widest possible array of systems and sensors. In narrow terms of schematics, she was the same as she had always been. Yet despite her very narrow survival—indeed, because she was fortunate to be alive at all—she had been changed. Transformed, even. The Master sat on the traditional black chair, high-backed and thickly varnished, carved from a single piece of polished kallan teak; but except for a veneer of authority and moral certitude, this was an entirely different person. Reconstituted from the brink of nothingness, she had been reinvented in a thousand ways. And even more important, virtually every one of her Submasters was new to the office, and oftentimes new to the ranks of the captains. Most were human, yes. But not all, and who would have imagined such a thing? A pair of fierce harum-scarums sat on convenient boulders. Dressed in a water suit, a gillbaby stood at mock attention, while a little fef and a Janusian hermaphrodite amiably traded stories of the war. Three decorated members of the AI corps were scattered among the organics, each buried inside a rubbery face and humanoid body. Aliens and machines now wore the mirrored uniforms of captains, each displaying the epaulets of the highest offices—an honor won when they helped defeat the Waywards. But stranger even than their appearance was their mood: In every past meeting, the Master had set the tone and defined the heart of every discussion. Her orders were usually cast beforehand, and sitting on this hilltop was meant to be a tidy dance of ego and pride and enduring traditions. Yet on this bright warm illusion of a day, the reborn Master appeared just a little bit unsure of herself. While her officers talked among themselves, often in non-human languages, her vast hands clung to one another, and her new face turned almost transparent, blank eyes gazing off into the distance while a voice that could just be heard above the quiet surf asked nobody in particular—with a distinctly nervous honesty asked nobody in particular—"Where are my first two Chairs?"

"Approaching," one of the new Submasters offered. "Washen took a wrong turn, it seems."

The officer was a Remora named Conrad. Barely human, in other words. The Remoras lived on the ship's hull, their bodies permanently encased in lifesuits woven from hyperfiber. Surrounded by vacuum and raw radiations, they were subjected to endless mutations and odd cancers, but not only did the Remoras accept the damage, they used it. Each mutation was an act of Creation, full of potentials and possibilities. To the good Remora, the body was a ripe and holy vessel meant to be reshaped without end—a perfect canvas on which endless brushstrokes of gaudy paints could be applied at will.

Conrad's single eye looked human, but it rode a muscular stalk, allowing it to pivot as he winked at his associates, joking, "It's not a good sign, having your First Chair lose her way."

The Master stared at him while saying nothing.

"Perhaps," one of the AIs sang out. "Begin without them?"

The golden woman shook her massive head, and from a position of utter weakness, she had to say, "No, we'll wait. We have to wait."

Everything was different now.

Everything.

THE TWO MISSING officers walked a narrow trail, working their way toward the black point of rocks. Pamir's grin betrayed a rare good humor. He nodded at the security troops standing watch, and with a sly grin, he asked, "What would you guess? If we walked into every house in this city, how many deserters would we trip over?"

Washen remained silent, concentrating on other matters.

"Ten or twelve no-goods," Pamir offered. Then with a genuine laugh, he added, "It's always been easy, vanishing."

"Should we make it more difficult?" she inquired.

Pamir had considerable experience with desertion. A great portion of his life aboard the ship had been spent hiding, in one fashion or another. Only a general amnesty had coaxed him out of his self-imposed exile. Given the chance, he would be the first to admit that his rise to the Second Chair's post was astronomically more unlikely than finding a little criminal making himself drunk inside Washen's childhood kitchen.

"Perhaps disappearing should be more difficult," he offered. Then with a breezy laugh, he added, "If only to cull out the amateurs."

They were still smiling when they reached the crest of the hill. The Master remained sitting while the other high officers stood. Washen offered a smile and a curt nod, saying, "Madam. All. My apologies. Shall we begin?"

The Master bristled silently.

In truth, this had always been Washen's intention. By arriving late, just this once, she would show her colleagues the new order. The Master couldn't complain about her tardiness. Washen and Pamir had saved both her life and her command, and she ruled today only because they had decided to allow her golden round face—that very familiar face—to continue to speak for the Great Ship.

"Welcome," said that face.

Humans nodded, and everyone repeated the word, "Welcome."

Washen, then Pamir occupied the final two chairs, flanking the Master Captain.

"We'll begin with reports," the golden face continued. "Conrad? Please."

The epaulets of the Remora's new rank had been fastened to his hyperfiber shoulders. The single stalked eye stared out through the diamond faceplate, glancing at each of his equally anointed colleagues. Then with a wide, elastic mouth, he described the state of the ship's hull. "It's shit," he assured them. "We took a huge pounding after the lasers and shields went down. We've got some awful craters to patch, and the shields and lasers are barely at half strength. And because our telescopes and other sensors were pounded to dust, we're flying close to blind now. It'll take years to rebuild our eyes, and decades more to patch the craters properly. Except for the monster crater, which could eat up a full century of hard work."

At the height of the war, after the shields and lasers had abruptly failed, a fat comet had collided with the ship, and at one-third lightspeed, ice and tar and frigid stone had turned into a bubble of white-hot plasma, those wild energies absorbed by the hull until the hyperfiber had no choice but to melt, forming a temporary lake that splashed outward in a kilometer-high wave.

"We've got a genuine mess," Conrad declared. "The comet struck on top of an old scar. Our biggest scar, as it happens. Where some moon-sized something hit, maybe five billion years ago. Although you know how tough it is to measure anything about hyperfiber. Its age, or when it was damaged. Anyway, my ancestors patched that old crater as fast as humanly possible, with the best grades of hyperfiber available . . . and because of our lousy luck, this new blast seems to have made the old damage worse . . ."

"Are we risking a breach?" the Master inquired.

"If a Kuiper-class body hit at a greater velocity, at the very worst angle, yes. There's a small but ugly possibility of a hole punched clear through the hull."

But it was a minuscule risk. Through his nexuses, Conrad fed his full report to the others, and for a few moments, he allowed them to ponder his rough estimates and his hand-drawn, surprisingly lovely maps. The new crater was a tiny ring compared to its ancient predecessor, but it overlapped the central blast zone, fractures reaching deep inside the hull, compounding a host of subtle weaknesses made in some ancient, faraway place.

"Of course work could be done faster," Conrad promised. "But Remoras don't have the hands anymore." The war had decimated their ranks, and if anyone had managed to forget, he reminded them now. "It's going to take thousands of years and a lot of babies before we match our old demographics. And maybe a million years before we forget these last few days."

The Master remained silent, angered by his tone but forbidden to say so.

Washen turned to another of the new Submasters. "Aasleen," she said. "Perhaps you have something to offer here."

Aasleen had been placed in charge of the entire engineer corps. She was one of the captains who had gone to Marrow, and unlike some, she had remained loyal to the ship. Rising to her feet, she showed the humans a warm smile, gave the harum-scarums a well-received glare, and spoke for a little while about the sorry state of certain engines and the various reactors that supplied power to billions of passengers and crew. Then with a genuine affection, she reminded them, "We are, however, sitting inside a marvel, an ingenious mix of design and craftsmanship. Whoever the Builders were, they created a machine that seems meant to be repaired, refurbished, and when necessary, remodeled. I can have every reactor in full service inside eight months and the engines within eighteen. Then my engineers can start helping the Remoras."

As a rule, Remoras accepted no aid from outsiders. The hull was their realm and their responsibility, and their only home, which was why it was a surprise to hear Conrad mutter, "Any good hand would be a blessing."

Just how badly damaged was the hull?

Silently, with a renewed paranoia, the other Submasters began reexamining the report. And lifting her tail, the little fef happily said, "My species will help. Many hands at the ready!"

The single eye closed, and opened.

"Of course," said the Remora. "And thank you."

Days ago, Washen had met alone with her chief engineer, Conrad, and the fef. This little moment was the outcome of reason and blunt commands delivered during that earlier meeting. The hull was weakened slightly and would remain vulnerable for decades, regardless what was decided today. But the hull was not the point. Washen wanted to build cooperation among these diverse souls and establish what would serve as her personal authority, and she had to achieve both goals while honoring the best of their hoary traditions.

The mood improved, at least a little bit.

With an appreciative nod, Washen invited the Master to speak again.

"Security," said the reborn woman. "I'd like to hear its report now."

One of the harum-scarums held that critical station. His name was Osmium— a massive and utterly imposing biped sitting comfortably on a rough lump of gray-black stone. Speaking loudly through his breathing mouth, he described the ongoing hunt for the last of their enemies and the reestablishment of a trusted security corps, pausing long enough for his eating mouth to consume an odd blond nut pulled from a leather sack set on a long-toed foot. Then with a low, gravelly voice, he announced, "I want the ban on new passengers to hold. And I want the authority to do what is necessary to give that ban a gizzard."

Nothing bothered the Master more than having this particular species sitting in her inner circle. Harum-scarums were a difficult species, prone to violence and simple childish grudges. True, they were instrumental in saving the ship. But they were too fierce, too easily angered, and if anything, too much like the worst elements of human beings. She preferred nearly every other species before them. She could even embrace the idea of AIs joining the ranks of captains. But when her new security chief asked for more authority, the Master felt a keen appreciation. A genuine bond. She and the alien both understood what was important: that for as long as there had been a universe, nothing mattered as much as power.

"But there won't be any new passengers," the other harum-scarum remarked, sharply disagreeing with her colleague. "We are off course. Our ship has suffered civil insurrections and considerable damage, and in a few thousand years, we might leave the galaxy entirely. Unless he was an idiot, why would any simple traveler put his precious flesh at risk with us now?"

"Agreed," the Master said.

Washen remained silent.

The Master nearly looked at her First Chair. Then with a visible tightening of her shoulders, she added, "Yet in the same vein, I think we should loosen our restrictions on emigrants. If a passenger wishes to leave us, and if we can come to an agreeable financial resolution, then perhaps a critical exception or two might be allowed."

Pamir leaned forward.

"Madam," he said, that single word dripping with an unusual respect. Then in the next breath, he explained, "Yesterday, I took a census of both passengers and crew—by an assortment of means, I counted everyone. We have more than a hundred billion souls on board. Depending on your definition of sentience, there might be many more than a hundred billion." The heavy face nodded, eyes squinting. "I counted minds with my census, and I tried to ascertain the general moods of those minds—"

"Measured how?" the Master inquired.

"Sloppily," he admitted. "I commissioned three different polls by three different species. I charted consumer interest in various escape entertainments and psychoactive drugs, plus the foot traffic in mating parlors. But most important, I asked for opinions. I prepared a holo of myself, and in the course of an hour, I interviewed nearly a million residents. And each of these studies came to the same ugly conclusion. We've got a lot of scared and angry souls, and most of our hundred billion would leap off the ship tomorrow. Or today. Although they would have preferred to have left years ago . . . before anybody ever heard about Marrow or the damned Waywards . . ."

There was a brief, tense pause.

Then one of the AIs spoke, reminding everyone, "But we lack the starships." Behind the rubbery face lay a tiny consciousness—a quantum-computing mind smaller than the tip of a finger—and with that day's face, it gave precise figures about the starships on hand and their limited capacities. Machine souls were the tiniest passengers, but even if they were packed like so much mindless sand, not even their ranks would be able safely to escape.

"Thank you," the Master interrupted. "We don't have enough lifeboats. We're aware of that hard fact, and thank you."

Had it said something wrong? No, it couldn't find any factual errors. And none of the other Submasters were offering new information either. The AI threw back its false shoulders, and with a little too much humanity, it began to pout.

"Some of us have already escaped," Pamir continued. "After the war and our dive past the old star . . . when it looked as if the ship was going to collide with the black hole . . . there was a small exodus. By my count, we're missing two streakships and thirteen slow taxis—maybe fifty thousand passengers in all—plus another eleven or twelve or thirteen hundred souls riding inside emergency blisters." Blisters were sacks of hyperfiber launched from the open hull. Possessing only alarm beacons and minimal recycke systems, they relied on their initial trajectory and the benevolence of others. "The blister cowards are screwed," Pamir reported. "We're crossing an empty stretch of space, in terms of friendly ports. If they could have fled before we changed course, they might have been all right. In another hundred years or so, we would have entered a thickly settled region. But most of those poor bastards left with some variation on our present trajectory. The wrong trajectory." Streakships could twist their vectors, and with patience, even a slow taxi could eventually make it to someplace important. "But there aren't fifty suns in the likely sweep path," he continued. "M-class dwarfs, mostly. We know of six worlds with technological life. Four terraformed, two native-born. Maybe some have the resources to reach out and grab a few blisters. Maybe. But the prospect of applying a major fraction of their economy to save a motley collection of refugees . . . well, I know about luck and a little something about kindness, and there isn't enough of either to save more than none of those crazy shits . . ."

Pamir fell silent, leaning forward in his chair. The sturdy wood creaked as the back legs lifted off the bare rock. Then with a quiet but massive urgency, he told his audience, "We need every last one of the remaining starships. Seventeen thousand-plus sitting in berths inside our ports, as my good colleague has reminded us. And as soon as it's practical, we should build more ships. Faster, bigger, and better ships, if that's possible. And we should never allow anyone to leave, for any sum—unless we can guarantee that the vessel eventually returns to us. Bearing critical cargo, if possible." He shook his homely face, reminding them, "We've managed an ugly eighty-degree turn around the red giant and black hole, and now we're charging into districts we do not know. That we never bothered to care about. In not too many centuries—if we cannot or will not return to our old course—we'll cross into intergalactic space. Few suns, the occasional world, and next to no civilizations out there to help us." His eyes narrowed, and with a shaman's keen intensity, he said, "Don't ask me why. I don't know why. But I've got this feeling, this sense—"

"That we need every starship," the Master offered.

"In part," Pamir replied. "But I was thinking more about the passengers. Some of them, or all of them . . . we're going to be glad that we've got so many of them, before this mess is over . . ."

EACH SUBMASTER was free to speak his mind, and most did, and votes were cast while the three supreme officers made the final choices. By the time the subject was exhausted, the day was done. The illusory sun was touching the sea's far shores, and the night birds were flying, and two critical decisions had been locked into the ship's codes: a nearly total ban on emigration, plus the conscription of every private vessel capable of long-distance travel. To entities accustomed to great spans of changeless time, this had been a very busy day. Gazing out at the sun with both of her/his faces, the Janusian asked, "What follows now? After these next few suns, what waits?"

There was the obvious answer. Submasters and captains and even many of the passengers understood what lay across the ship's path. But the Janusian was asking larger, more complex questions. "What follows?" was an opening to predict the future. "What waits?" was a plea for someone, anyone, to define those things that were inevitable.

Washen triggered one of her nexuses, and a chart appeared before them. The Great Ship was a carefully defined point falling through a mist of little suns. The suns and their various worlds had been mapped, while the sunless worlds between and the occasional primordial black hole wore navigational labels. The starry mist was relatively brief, barely seventy light-years thick, and beyond those suns stood the smooth, vast, and perfectly black face of a nebula. The nebula was a conglomerate of cold gases and lazy dust, ice particles and perhaps a few half-born suns. Before the Waywards, the occasional brief survey had peered inside that deep frigid blackness, finding traces of odd heat and soft radio voices—the hallmarks of high technologies busily at work.

Washen avoided the obvious. If the ship fired its working engines tonight and for the next two hundred years, their course wouldn't change any important distance. They would pass by every sun at too great a distance for a useful flyby, the nebula would eventually engulf them all the same, and then with their fuel nearly exhausted, they would have no choice but to plunge through the black dusts and opaque gases. The wiser course would be greedily to hold on to their hydrogen oceans while repairing their shields and lasers, and always make plans, then make more plans, and finally scrap all of those wise contingencies, inviting new ideas to push aside the obvious and useless.

Washen said none of that.

For a long moment, she made no sound. Rising to her feet—an imposing woman who had always had more grace than strength; the consummate captain wearing a mirrored uniform seemingly designed for her before anyone else—she looked out across the open water, thinking back to a childhood spent on this little shore. Some feeble half memory nipped at her. For the second time today, she was thinking about her parents. The three of them sitting together, talking. About what? She still couldn't recall the subject, and probably never would. Let it go, she kept telling herself. Then with her face and stance and wise silence, she looked at each of her companions, a genuine fondness preceding the smile that came before she said, "Whatever happens."

Then just as suddenly, she paused.

Even the aliens and the swift-minded machines felt curious, waiting patiently for the next word or little gesture.

"Whatever happens," she repeated. Then with a nod, she said, "It will be an endless surprise, I think. And hopefully, a sweet surprise."

A warm reassurance rippled through her audience.

Everyone who was sitting began to rise.

Except for the Master Captain. She remained planted upon her chair, her golden face taking a quick measure of her new Submasters. A figurehead now, she still managed a massive dignity, and with a whisper of her old self, she cleared her throat, demanding the full attention of others.

"A proposal," she said. "May I?"

Washen immediately turned toward her. "Yes, madam."

The Master climbed out of her black chair, her feet apart to hold her body steady. "Each of us should imagine ten distinct futures," she suggested, her bulk dwarfing even the harum-scarums. "Ten possible and awful futures, well-defined and thoroughly simulated. Then as an exercise, we will trade our futures, and before the next Master's banquet, each of us needs to save our ship ten times."

With an appreciative nod, Washen said, "Yes, madam."

"As an exercise," the ancient woman repeated. "That's all I intend here."

"Of course."

Then with a charm that hadn't been seen in aeons, the Master admitted, "I know what I am now. Full well, I understand my new role here. And while I don't enjoy it, I most definitely deserve it." The ageless face grinned, sadness mixed with an almost childlike resignation. "But please, if you will, Washen? Would you allow me the tiny honor of declaring this meeting complete . . . please . . . ?"

Three

IN HIS DREAMS, he was always the walker. He would find himself strolling past odd shops and entertainment emporiums, cafes and apartments, the avenue decorated with alien skies and the occasional exotic tree or sessile animal planted in solitary steel pots, or sometimes many of them planted in elaborate groves designed to seem just a little wild and pleasantly mysterious. At the border of every district was an alien statue carved from marble or light, and with a human voice it would say, "Careful, sir. You are about to enter a different atmosphere." In life, the demon doors produced a slight and mostly ignorable tingle. But in his dreams the doors were heavy cold curtains clinging like a statically charged cloth to his restless body. He had to push his way through the invisible barrier, and suddenly the air was thick and oven-hot, or it was mountaintop thin and cold enough to blister his lungs. Yet he wouldn't stop, and somewhere in the next few hundred steps his dream body would adapt to the new environment. Then came more shops to visit and new aliens to watch—by the hundreds and by the thousands, the endless avenue jammed with their vast and tiny and always odd and wondrous bodies— and in the midst of that chaos, he would spy friends sitting around a little table, eating exotic fare while chatting amiably. In every dream, he approached the table and smiled. He could feel his face grinning while his heart beat harder. He would hear his own voice above the mayhem, saying to these dear lost friends, "Hello."

A moment would pass, then another. Finally, one of the friends would look up—usually a human friend, oftentimes a former lover—and what might or might not be a smile would precede the mouthing of his name.

During his long tenure aboard the ship, the man had possessed half a hundred identities. Or more to the point, those identities had possessed him. There was no guessing which name would be used now. People who never knew him by one name would use it regardless, and to his great distress, he realized that everyone at the table could peer inside his soul, cutting loose every secret. He felt transparent. He was simple and obvious and quite helpless. O'Layle was his final name, but none of his dream-friends ever used that appellation. Even his most recent lover would refer to him as someone officially dead and lost, then with a warm hand, she might touch him on the back of his suddenly cool hand, the smile falling into an easy scorn as a slow loveless voice asked, "Don't you feel foolish now?"

Very foolish, yes.

"We survived," she would proclaim. "It looked bad for a little while, but we managed to avoid obliteration. We clipped the fringes of that dying sun, but that's all. A touch. Little more than a kiss, really. And then we missed the black hole entirely, and now everyone is safe and happy again."

Good for you, he would say.

"What about you?" His final lover was little older than a child, and she was pretty in a thousand ways, and as happens with youngsters, she had been intrigued by his life of petty crime and low-grade corruption. "Are you still alive?"

I am very much alive, O'Layle would claim.

"Not to me." Then with a casual scorn, she would laugh. Her hand would retreat, and her beautiful eyes—bright cold white eyes set in a dark brown face— would turn away from him. To other friends and ex-lovers, she would say, "This man is very much dead."

"The fool," another would spit.

"Idiot coward," a third might add with conviction.

Then everybody sitting around the table stopped hearing O'Layle. He would sit among them, speaking to them, explaining his good smart reasons for everything. And then he would scream at them, fiercely defending what he had done.

The Waywards had appeared suddenly, and just as quickly, they were defeated and gone. But the Great Ship had been pushed toward catastrophe, with everybody sure to be killed when the monster trapped at Marrow's core was set free.

Every rational soul had panicked. O'Layle reminded his companions that each of them had imagined the worst, and in those next minutes and hours, the worst had seemed inevitable. Everybody here had done their frantic best to escape, but with the fighting and damage, and the general martial law, the rest of them had failed. O'Layle was the lucky exception. Though it wasn't exactly luck that bought him passage to the open hull, nor did good fortune give him that little escape blister and enough momentum to carry him off into the deep and cold and relatively safe depths of space.

With a sadness that was mostly genuine, he would tell his ex-lover, "I couldn't take you with me."

She would pretend not to hear him.

"How could I take you? The blister's tiny, and your mass would have doomed both of us."

In his dreams, his arguments sounded logical and noble, and he was always surprised when the sweet young face glanced in his direction, those white eyes growing hot as a matching voice spat, "Fucking coward." Then she would stand abruptly, and everybody at the little table would rise. Each might glance at O'Layle, using expressions laced with scorn and hatred and sometimes a pained pity. Then they would leave him sitting alone, and he would hear his own sorry voice explaining why he was the most reasonable and practical creature in the galaxy.

"Just to do what I did . . . it took every resource I had! The contacts. The ridiculous bribes. I had to slip past the security patrols, get myself up to the launch site. Most were broke before they even got on top of the hull. And even then, there were more of us than there were blisters, and the crew in charge of the whole operation just laughed at us, saying, 'Guess what? There's going to be a surcharge.' Which I'd halfway expected, and I was ready. Faster than others, I could transfer the last of my money into ghost accounts, and what did I get for a lifetime's savings? A tiny, tiny blister. A hyperfiber ball barely two meters in radius. With an iron collar around its waist, and me strapped inside it, and I was plopped down on one of the only magrails to survive the war. We were on the backside of the ship. Did I mention that? On the ship's stern, with the red sun already behind us, the black hole still over the horizon. They set my blister on the little rail, and I draped an old crush-web over my body, and they started to accelerate me. A huge, bone-snapping acceleration. 'We'll send you toward a nice living world,' the voice in my head promised. Then I died. I became a comatose pulp lying beneath the crush-web, and unknown to me, there was a power surge. A hiccup. I found out later. I wasn't even a thousand kilometers into the launch cycle, and there was a

sudden disruption . . . and you well know, you can't do anything wrong at the beginning of an engineless voyage, or your chances of getting to your destination
fall away to nothing . . .

"I would have aborted, if I'd known. But by then I was a wet smear and a blind
brain held together by the web.

"Then after another seven thousand kilometers, I roared out into the shadow
of the ship, and my blister was released from the rail, my iron collar fell off, and my
body slowly, slowly began putting itself back together. I've never been so dead before. It took days just to remake my bones, my organs and skin. When I was conscious again, the first thing I did was look out through my little diamond
windows. The black hole had fallen behind, and I was free. I watched the ship. I
watched you. Honestly, I hoped you would survive. Why wouldn't I want the best
for all of you? My thousands of good friends, and of course I was thrilled when
you changed course just enough . . . for days and days, I watched you fighting . . .
a gray ball getting smaller and duller . . . slower than me by a long ways and with
a slightly different trajectory . . . and then I couldn't see you anymore, except inside my head . . ."

The dream always ended there. O'Layle would stop explaining himself, and as
he glanced up and down the avenue, he discovered that he was alone. Not only
had his friends vanished, but the multitudes of strangers had evaporated, too, and
the air had turned stale and dark, and there were no more shops or little forests to
enjoy. The ship was as empty as the moment it was discovered, a palpable loneli-
ness hanging over the vastness, making it almost easy for the man to open his eyes,
looking at the tiny but comforting space that was his world.

O'LAYLE'S WORLD WAS a blister of moderate-grade hyperfiber punctuated with
little diamond eyes—a nearly perfect sphere enclosing layers of recycling equipment and automated beacons, finger reactors and streamlined libraries, plus a
minimal navigational system and a single holo projector. Damp air lay at the
hollow center, and a naked human body was the only substantial inhabitant.
O'Layle's minimal diet had triggered an assortment of lifeboat genes, reducing
his metabolism to the bare minimum. One little meal every other day was
ample, and he cleared his bowels less than once each week. Sleep filled sixteen
hours out of his typical day, and his waking time was spent reading projected
books and speaking quietly to himself, or he did nothing but contemplate his
circumstances and the elaborate path that had brought him to this place. Then
on those rare moments when he could coax himself into a halfway buoyant
mood, O'Layle would use the diamond eyes, peering out into the increasingly
black universe.

More than anything, O'Layle was amazed how quickly he had adapted to his
new and extremely tiny life. Before this, he was a comfortable if not quite wealthy
human, and if every day had seemed like every other, at least the mornings

brought the possibility of doing one or two or a thousand entirely new things. The ship was a wonderland of diversions and raw surprise. Sitting in any public avenue, he could watch inhabitants from a fat fraction of the galaxy as they strolled past. Or rolled past. Or glided overhead on long, powerful wings. And if he wished, he could spend the day exploring the Great Ship. There were endless caverns laced with rivers and deep cold lakes, and dozens of genuine oceans, and because there were so many passengers busily making homes for themselves, the caverns and big rooms were changing every few centuries. Every wandering would feel new and strange, and memorable, and why hadn't he done more of that when he had the chance?

Because there was always time, he had believed. Tomorrow was an endless parade, and he was comfortable where he sat, and so why go to so much sweaty trouble today?

It was a mistaken assumption, yes.

A long life thoroughly wasted.

But still, O'Layle couldn't remain angry or forlorn. Against so many odds, the ship had survived, and he was alive, too. Both of them had won, at least temporarily. And wasn't there a small but genuine chance of being saved? Perhaps he might even one day return to the ship and rejoin his circle of friends and lovers— provided that enough time had passed for them to forgive his abandonment, or at least forget their own rage. Then he would have a spectacular story to share. How many souls had ever traveled between the stars alone, inside a tiny cocoon of hyperfiber, with no companion but their own tiny soul?

The chance of that future—survival followed by redemption—was fantastically small. On the brink of impossible, frankly. His tiny lifeboat had no engines, thus there was no way to adjust its course. Its launch had been hurried and flawed, and the navigational equipment was consistent in its expert pessimism. O'Layle would miss his target sun by almost a tenth of a light-year, which was a considerable distance. Someone would have to be listening for his beacon, and that same someone would need to launch their own ship at a fantastic velocity. His lifeboat lacked engines, but it had the momentum of the Great Ship plus the punch that had been delivered by the electromagnetic rail. He was streaking through the heavens at nearly half lightspeed, which would be a challenge for the best startravelers to match. Even if he had remained on course, few could have caught him, and fewer still would have bothered. His passage through any solar system would take less than a long morning, unless it ended with his fiery impact against someone's suddenly boiling sea.

O'Layle originally wished for an impact course. That would make him a threat, which would force the natives to deal with his presence, in one fashion or another. But eventually he settled on a less aggressive and possibly more compelling scheme: In his first twenty months on board the blister, he had reworked the beacon's endless message. What began as a general plea for help delivered in a thousand popular languages was now an elaborate set of promises and lies, implications and subtle miscues.

"I am a very important person," he told the stars.

In honest terms, he described the ship that he had abandoned—its majesty and great age and the powerful display of technologies aboard—and then with a rugged assurance, he painted himself as being one of the very best experts about the Great Ship. "I have explored it in full," he lied. "And I was a member of the crew for the last long while. I am a qualified engineer possessing a robust working knowledge of the ship's enormous engines and its reactors and the various means by which the highest-grade hyperfiber can be produced in planetary quantities."

His fable gained a backbone through the use of little details—the harvest of a long life spent sharing tables with wiser, more informed souls. In particular, he borrowed from a human named Perri—an expert explorer who was said to know the ship better than even the captains knew it, and who had walked or floated or flown through as much as one or two percent of the ship's considerable volume.

"It is a wonder, my ship," he proclaimed.

"I want to show it to you," he told the silent stars. "Come help me, and I will give you everything that I know about this ancient wonder."

Would that be enough bait?

For another few months, he thought so. But then the doubts began to gnaw, and after some considerable reflection, he decided to build on those rather pedestrian lies. During his last few hours on board the ship—in the midst of the panic and the desperate fight to save it—a wild rumor had found its way to O'Layle. By then, everybody knew about the secret world buried at the center of the ship, but inside Marrow were more secrets. Greater mysteries, claimed the fresh rumors. In fact, according to a onetime lover who had recently spoken with Perri, there was the distinct and momentous possibility that the Great Ship had been built to entomb something from the very beginnings of the universe. Something tiny, but powerful. Something with a soul and intentions and the capacity to reach out of its abode, influencing the thoughts of the lesser souls within its ethereal grasp.

O'Layle borrowed parts of that very odd rumor.

But he decided to downplay the entity's malicious nature. His unseen audience needed to feel curiosity, not fear.

For more years, the beacon's central message was about the ancient and powerful soul riding aboard the ship—the ship he knew so well. And that was why O'Layle could entertain a genuine optimism about his prospects. Alien or human, every sentient organism was inflicted by a measure of greed. His long, comfortable life had been spent using that innate quality, slaking his own considerable thirsts. Perhaps the creatures living on the first world wouldn't respond, but there would be plenty of opportunities in the future. He would spend another few thousand years inside the galaxy or on its fringes . . . there was no way to know how many worlds would hear his pleas and promises . . . and surely someone would launch an armada to save the little man who could deliver the Great Ship to them . . . !

How likely this was, O'Layle couldn't guess.

But the plan gave him hope, and hope became a habit, and the habit brought a kind of rugged happiness that made it possible for him to open the diamond eyes on an irregular basis, inviting the glories of the universe to trickle down inside his very tiny world.

In darkness, O'Layle saw nothing but stars and the blackness between. Relativistic velocities made the retreating suns turn redder than normal, and there was some distortion. But in most ways, he saw nothing too strange and nothing in any great hurry to change. Before him were few visible suns, blued by their approaching velocity, and beyond lay the deep black mass of dust and gas that blocked an increasingly huge portion of the sky. Pass through the nebula, and there were some thick bands of stars. His navigational charts promised as much. If he could just pierce the cloud of dust and gas without suffering a significant collision, then everything seemed possible.

Even salvation.

"I am important," he told the universe. "And I know about things far more important than me."

The beacon's tiny voice sang and sang.

And then came the day when O'Layle awoke from his usual dreams, and after a tidy little meal of cold, heavily sugared fats, and after a sip of distilled water and squirt of urine into the appropriate orifice, he told the diamond eyes to open.

"Show me the universe," he whispered.

But instead of the stars and the nebula, he saw something else entirely, and for a very long while he just drifted in the middle of his tiny world, startled and puzzled, laughing in that nervous, almost joyous, way people use when they feel as if they should be scared, but really, they can't quite tell why.

Four

WASHEN WAS FAILING, spinning wildly downward into a perfect blackness, silent and boundless. This was a dream, and an old dream at that, and after a few moments of acceleration, she tried to yank herself awake. But even then, she felt her body plunging into the coal black depths. Long legs kicked while arms lashed out, reflexively clutching for handholds. Then the sheets took hold of her, reassuring with their firm embrace and instant warmth, and possessed by that narrow clarity that comes after sleep, Washen realized that she was lying in her own bed, safe as safe could be, and that she was far from being alone.

But if Pamir noticed her unseemly little episode, he had the good manners or the sturdy indifference to pretend sleep. He lay in his customary pose—naked on top of the sheets, on his back, hands tucked firmly behind his head. Something in that simple posture betrayed an innate defiance, or perhaps a brute indifference. Any sort of enemy might lurk in this darkness, but he proclaimed with his body that he truly did not care.

Quietly, Washen gasped.

Wishing for any distraction, she triggered a service nexus, and her apartment delivered to her bedside a chilled glass of water and another of pawpaw juice.

The bedroom was a substantial chamber, the floor tiled with slowly changing views teased out of the Mandelbrot fractal, the surrounding black brick wall rising toward a high domelike ceiling. Dimly illuminated, the ceiling displayed a present-time view delivered from the ship's armored prow. Blue-shifted light and the relentless shimmer of the shields had been carefully scrubbed away. What remained was a ring of stars that lay at the bottom of the ceiling—the eye able to peer hundreds of light-years through the heart of the Milky Way. But directly above were far fewer suns, most of them rather small and all of them close by, and beyond those points of light was a different species of blackness, deeper and much stronger, possessing a palpable mass and a distinct chill that any experienced starfarer would recognize at a glance.

Washen did more than glance at the nebula.

Carefully, she sat up. She allowed her sheets to wick away her perspiration, and her pillows built a little chair against which she could sit and sip at her cold water, then the juice.

Enormous telescopes had once stood near the ship's prow—great fields of eyes probing the space to come. But when the Remoras fought the Waywards, they needed a trap. They had lured their enemies out onto the ship's leading face, then destroyed the lasers and shields, bringing down a rain of dust and comets that obliterated an entire army, plus every mirror and each of the hundred-kilometer dishes. The entire system had to be built again from nothing, including support facilities and key upgrades. This was eighteen years after the war's end, and only now were enough eyes and ears ready to give the First Chair an honest view of what was to come.

Through her nexuses, Washen changed the sky.

The nebula was black for two basic reasons. Enough gas and cold dust were spread out before them to build almost a thousand suns. And even more important, barely a handful of dwarf suns were scattered across a roughly spherical volume some twelve light-years in diameter. Without illumination from within, the cloud was blacker and even colder than it might normally be. If the nebula followed the typical history of such structures, it was on the brink of collapsing into dozens and perhaps hundreds of high-density regions, forming nurseries where stars and brown dwarfs coalesced over the next million little years, followed by an array of new worlds that happily danced with one another and battered each other, violence and mayhem carving new solar systems out of the rawest beginnings.

Centuries ago, when the ship was still firmly on course and untroubled, cursory studies had been made. An officious name was given to the nebula—numbers and letters defining its position, apparent size, and year of discovery. Charts of mass distributions and temperature gradients, plus models projecting a range of likely futures, were accumulated and routinely stored in ship libraries. But the nebula was neither an obstacle nor a likely ground for recruiting new passengers. The occasional hint of life and high technologies might have intrigued some experts, but not the captains. On at least five occasions, the Master had diminished the priority of the work, arguing with conviction and not a small amount of good sense, "We're approaching a rendezvous with a black hole. That's where our focus belongs. Not in some little storm cloud sitting on someone else's horizon."

Even now, Washen couldn't fault the Master's decision. How could a rational mind act on the very remote possibility that this place had importance? Black holes were dangerous for many compelling reasons, particularly those massive black holes living beside aging suns. How could any decent mind dedicated to the service of the Great Ship imagine things going horribly wrong, and going wrong in the precise pattern necessary to put this ship where it was today, on a collision course with a star nursery?

"Infrared," Washen ordered, specifying frequencies and the resolution.

What looked like a normal dark nebula remained normal by most measures. The bulk of its enormous mass was really quite thin and very cold, composed of molecular hydrogen and helium gas, with tiny flecks of hydrocarbons and silicates and the occasional odd buckyball or two. On average, the cloud was a superior vacuum, and if not harmless, at least endurable. But inside it were pinpricks of heat. The largest heat sources were as big as worlds, and the smallest to date seemed no larger than a major comet. From the radiant signature, it was obvious that the bodies wore elaborate insulation—clinging to precious heat, or perhaps supplying some measure of camouflage. Scattered between the warm bodies were much smaller, much brighter heat sources, each betraying the presence of a fusion engine. Those ships were neither particularly large nor powerful. But if those warm bodies were settlements—little worlds unto themselves—then the unremarkable ships were exactly what one would expect from local trade and slow, patient migrations.

Against the vastness of the Milky Way, the nebula was a fleck of blackness. But when you summed up the volume of warm living space that might exist inside a volume some twelve light-years on a side . . . well, the numbers were quite simply staggering . . .

"Microwave," she ordered, picking her frequencies moment by moment.

When water molecules radiated energy, they had a specific signature, and inside every normal nebula was an abundance of water. But not in this case, it seemed.

Barely a third of the expected moisture was visible, and its distribution was highly unusual. When the Submasters examined the recent maps, Aasleen saw the obvious. "Like rivers in space," she observed. "Look. Ice particles are being collected and shepherded into specific regions. Here, and here, and this knot over here." The woman had giggled out loud, like a child. "Dopplers give us velocities. Look! The rivers are flowing toward the interior, but not toward the same exact points."

"How is this done?" the Master had inquired.

"Carefully," Aasleen reported, admiration mixed with the humor in her voice. "Whoever's doing this, they're not being aggressive or energy-intensive. Otherwise, we'd see more heat and other big telltales."

Washen had imagined trillions of comets, each the size of a closed fist. "Microchines," she suggested. "Landing on each little world, and then building a tiny mass-launcher—"

"Probably not," Aasleen interrupted. "There'd be too much dust flying, and pumping energy into each ball of ice would make a second mess."

"What then?" the Master pressed.

But the chief engineer needed another few moments to make a string of enormous, exacting calculations. Then with her imagination and a long life rich with experience, she devised a simple answer.

"Microchines, yes," she said with a genuine appreciation. "But what they do . . . they sit on the surface and generate an electrical charge. Give your pebble or dust mote a robust negative charge, say. Then whoever oversees this business . . . this construction project . . . well, they use static charges to push and pull their little bricks wherever they want them. Which is here and here, and these places over there. Do you see? Estimate the volume of these presumed worlds, and compare that figure to the water that seems to be missing from the nebula. They're not equal, but they're close to equal. And if you assume that they've been gathering up all the dust and asteroids and whatever else is available—"

"How long?" Pamir had asked. "The project to date . . . from what you can tell . . . how much time has it taken?"

"At this morning's rate?" Aasleen used a fingertip, drawing figures on the dark brown palm of her hand. "Ten or fifteen or maybe twenty million years."

But nebulas didn't persist that long. Either they collapsed into new stars, or nearby supernovae blew them apart.

"Maybe our neighbors worked faster in the past," Aasleen conceded. Then she nodded, adding, "What we're seeing . . . it could be the tail of a long building project. With these tools and tricks, and the kinds of populations that we can envision . . ." A look of delighted awe came into her face, eyes shining while a low voice said, "My goodness. You know, now that I think about it, this might not be a natural nebula."

That earned a sturdy silence from the others.

Finally, Washen asked, "What do you mean? Their engineers have stabilized it somehow? Staving off its collapse, maybe?"

"Maybe," Aasleen replied.

Then with a nervous laugh, she added, "Or maybe I mean something considerably bigger than that."

"Neutrinos," Washen told her nexus.

Her ceiling erupted into a fierce white glare. What had been a dark cloud was suddenly a kind of ghostly fire—a great if extremely diffuse rain of subatomic particles emerging at the speed of light, particles born inside the fusion furnaces keeping millions of sunless worlds as warm as bathwater.

"Dim it," she ordered.

But Pamir had felt the light, and with a low grunt, he rolled onto his side, facing her now, one broad arm tossed over his tightly closed eyes.

In the false light of the neutrinos, Washen looked at her lover. He was a huge man blessed with a naturally powerful build, and even in sleep, he carried himself with a tangible indifference to things that most people would consider important. Rank meant little to him. Making him assume the post as Second Chair had proved difficult, and if Pamir enjoyed his newfound authority, he was careful not to show it. A modern person could affect his appearance in nearly infinite ways, and this man wore his own peculiar homeliness without self-doubt or special importance. Yet in every circumstance, he believed in work and serving the ship, and there wasn't one captain in the ranks who would risk as much as Pamir to care for the passengers, defending them as well as the enormous crew.

With a wet gasp, the man began to dream. Under his lids, the eyes jumped back and forth, and with a shameless ease, his penis began to stiffen, the vivid dark blood pooling inside a structure older than the species. That thought drew Washen into thinking about people in general: Why was it that with all the tools and tricks at their disposal, people still looked like people? Artificial genetics and bioceramic materials were discovered ages ago, yet in most cases, people had applied these extraordinary technologies to enhance their traditional bodies. They made themselves immortal, and also, immortally human. And it wasn't just human beings. Harum-scarums were a considerably older species, scattered across thousands of light-years and a wide array of worlds, yet they cherished their ancient appearance and most of their instincts. The majority of the passengers were the same. Reach a certain point in development, and the sentient species ceased to change. When you could look and act in any fashion, you tended to gravitate toward familiar bodies and old manners, leading lives that you willingly let carry you for the next million years.

Washen reached for the ancient penis. But her hand stopped short, and with a whisper, she said, "Radio. Laser light. Any artificial signal."

The ceiling took on a new appearance.

As expected, the nebula was riddled with modulated noise. Tightly focused beams and weak lasers jumped from little world to little world. What they could see from the Great Ship was the occasional trace of leakage—millions of brief examples collected over the last several years. And what they had learned from this vast puddle of data was nothing. Or nearly nothing. What lived inside the nebula used deeply encrypted tools for every kind of chatter, and that secrecy, taken alone, might be a clue. A harbinger.

The nebula had its official designation. But every species seemed to have its own name for that dark and cold and rather mysterious smear. Some passengers used any of twenty common labels: The Cloud. The Deep Dark. The Dust. And on a few occasions, The Face of God. But a name employed by the Master Captain, almost in passing, had been accepted by the captains, and as the years passed, it was gaining favor elsewhere.

"When I was a very young girl," the Master said at her most recent banquet, "there was an artifact in the possession of one of my relatives." Standing before a silent and increasingly alien audience, she had recounted an age very close to the beginnings of human civilization. "My grandfather had this antique sitting on his desk. It was a very simple container. Heavy glass upon which sat a silver lid. A fancy object, perhaps, but not ornate. A couple centuries old already, which made it seem deliciously ancient to me. Inside that little basin was an intense and thick black ink derived from the excretions of a certain sea creature. A beautiful animal with a close resemblance to several of our honored passengers." The woman had grinned at some portion of that memory, or perhaps just to show her audience that she could feel sentimental about her long-ago childhood. "What humans would do, back in ancient times . . . they would grip a metal-and-wood tool in one hand, dipping it into the ink, and with that they would compose some of the oldest, finest works in our literature . . .

"That artifact was called an inkwell," she continued. "A little bath of potential from which great and hopeful things were born . . ."

AGAIN PAMIR ROLLED onto his back, his dream ending.

For a while, with a haphazard discipline, Washen attempted to fall back to sleep. The inkwell and its neighboring suns lay overhead again, looking much as a motionless human eye would see them, and she soon reached that point where thousands of years of habit and every inborn reflex were coaxing her back into a light, dream-stirred sleep. But it didn't last. She was awake again, suddenly and utterly, her mind tripping over another one of her endless obsessions.

Silently, she sat up in bed.

Without an audible sound, she told her nexuses what she wanted. Immersion eyes were all-spectrum cameras tied into AI overseers that could never blink.

Nearly twenty thousand kilometers beneath her apartment was a single immersion eye. Between it and her was a sealed, secured channel. No one but Washen could connect with it on a whim, and perhaps no one else could care half as much. In an instant, she and her bed as well as her blissfully ignorant partner were stuck to a surface of high-grade hyperfiber, and above her was an entire world held suspended from the chamber walls by an ethereal array of mighty buttresses.

Marrow.

The war had left it badly mauled, but alive. Eighteen years later, the planet's atmosphere was still choked with dust and ash, and the vacuum above was gradually growing dark, some kind of night approaching within the next couple centuries. Directly beneath the tiny eye, where the once great Hazz City had stood, an ocean of molten iron and nickel still bubbled and spat at the sky. But there was solid ground elsewhere, and liquid water. The immersion eye could see the telltale signs of photosynthesis and oxygen metabolisms. Waywards had survived, in some battered fashion, along with the native life-forms, enduring and strange in their own right. More than Washen could let on, she missed that odd world. She had lived there for better than forty-six centuries. Those people were her own desperate grandchildren, and she was their absent grandmother who had set her allegiance to the surrounding ship, leaving them to weather these horrors by themselves.

Washen was still crying when Pamir woke.

The whisper from a nexus told him it was morning. The urging of ancient biorhythms made him ready for his day. His grunt was soft and disgusted. Looking up, he said, "if you want, I could cut out your heart. Would that make you feel better?"

"You might as well."

"The Waywards picked that war with us," he reminded her. Then with a glowering expression, he added, "Besides, this is where you belong. For the moment, you can't help anyone as much as you can help us."

"You're nice to say that."

"I'm never nice," he countered, laughing.

"You're a mean old shit," she said.

"Absolutely!"

"Except you aren't," she remarked. Then with her own warning glower, she said, "We each have our weakness. Marrow is mine. And yours is you."

"I'm not as tough as I pretend. Is that it?"

With a thought, she severed the com-line. Now there was nothing above them but a dome of polished green olivine stained over the last thousand centuries, the dampness of Washen's breath doing most of the damage.

With an easy fondness, she took hold of Pamir's morning erection.

"When a species gains total control over its body and its mortality," she began, "it typically improves its sexual organs. But it never, ever edits them out. Hearts, on occasion. Limbs, sometimes. But never has a man been born—"

"Who willingly surrenders his prick," Pamir said, finishing the old truism: "Ever wonder why?"

"Never," he replied with a perfect honesty. "Not once, ever. Never. And no."

Five

EXCERPTS FROM TIGHT-BEAM broadcast received 119.55 post-Wwar—Origin K-class sun 8.2 light-years from the Inkwell—Apparent source Streakship *Calamus*, Acting Captain Lorkin (Former rank: Tech-agent, Class-C)—Security status of transmission: For the perusal of Master, Submasters only; zero exceptions.

AN OPEN LETTER:

Until this evening, we honestly did not know your fate, Good Master. None of us could imagine anything but the worst for you and our good colleagues, what with the Wayward invasion and subsequent conquest of the ship, and the suicidal fight between Waywards and Remoras . . . a battle that threatened every vessel berthed at Port Denali, I should add . . . and then our subsequent maneuvers around the dying and dead suns, placing considerable resources and valuable property in mortal danger . . . Naturally my crew and I had no choice but to save whatever lives and property we could. Thankfully, we were able to pluck nearly one hundred passengers from the mayhem, along with myself and 311 handpicked crew members . . . at a time when the reconquest of the ship seemed quite impossible, I should add . . . and naturally, afterward, we were thrilled to see the Great Ship survive both its close approach with the red giant and its dance with the black hole . . . but until this evening, while conversing with our new friends, the Pak'kin, we never imagined that your forces, Good Master, had actually won the war, regaining full control over the helm and all the facilities within our wondrous home . . .

Congratulations to you from all on board the *Calamus* . . . !

HOLO IMAGE:

Captain Lorkin posed for the cameras, accompanied by his officers and current hosts. It was a nighttime image, the rare stars hovering above the distant horizon, only the Inkwell filling the heart of the sky. The humans wore new uniforms grown for this single occasion, the tailoring reminiscent of various military cultures, with tall boots and wide belts on which hung overly ornate sidearms. Lorkin's chest was decorated with colored ribbons and important jewels, implying many selfless actions and examples of intense bravery. He smiled, after a fashion. But his officers seemed less determined about their pleasure. The image captured one of them—a young-faced woman—closely watching the Pak'kin squatting beside her. It was a rock-colored creature, roughly cone-shaped with many legs and thick, short, jointed arms, plus dozens of orifices scattered haphazardly across its body. The officer's expression might be described as disgusted, perhaps even appalled. A single detail in one holo—one image among thousands squirted home to the Great Ship—yet much was implied. The woman did not like her hosts. She was suspicious and perhaps even scared. Indeed, none of the humans could easily hide their constant discomfort, both with the environment and the Pak'kin. To cope with the world's extremely high gravity, they employed an assortment of mechanical braces worn beneath their uniforms. To cope with the dense atmosphere, they had met the aliens on a very high mountaintop. In an apparent bid of friendship, gifts had been exchanged. The humans brought examples of hyperfiber—random scraps of battered ship armor, mostly. The local Pak'kin, knowing next to nothing about their guests, gave a pheromone-laced oil that was promised to give its wearers access to their particular hive.

Olfactory files attached to this image proved what the expert eye would suspect: The Pak'kin possessed a horrible, choking odor. Also, orbital images and cursory sensor data proved that no portion of the world was habitable by humans. The atmosphere was thick and hot and extraordinarily dry. Cataclysms during the world's formative years had either denied it water or removed the seas it had managed to collect. Old oceans and a thick carbon dioxide atmosphere could have been peeled away by a collision with another world. That would explain the world's substantial mass and how it had avoided runaway greenhouse events: The nitrogen–oxygen atmosphere lacked the heat-retention capacities. Life formed in one of several tiny seas, or perhaps inside a persistent hot spring. With water scarce, the local biosphere evolved as mechanical systems wrapped around tiny aqueous vacuoles where key reactions occurred.

The Pak'kin were hive-born pseudomachines. With poor eyes and spectacular noses, they lived at the bottom of an enormous gravity well. They possessed certain critical technologies, including radios and fusion reactors; but without the urge or muscular capacity to launch large vessels, their presence in space was limited to a few tiny probes.

Return to the tired, scared people. Walking inside the holo, approaching them to the limits of resolution, any observant soul could see the cumulative erosions caused by travel and endless fear. Acting Captain Lorkin was a prime example. He smiled, and for as long as that image exists, he will continue to part his lips and show his teeth to the circling cameras. But he had lost weight since abandoning his post and the Great Ship. Worse still, his flesh and the deep centers of his eyes showed the telltale signs of inadequate nourishment. A significant event had recently stolen away his right leg. It had regenerated, but not with the usual thoroughness. Even wearing high-gravity braces, Lorkin tilted conspicuously to one side.

Between the scraps of battered hyperfiber and the physical state of the crew, an obvious conclusion presented itself: The *Calamus* had suffered some kind of near-crippling damage. One or several bolides had struck it, and with inadequate supplies on board and a crew composed of low ensigns and techs untrained for this kind of voyage, the ship may well have been crippled. What's more, the shuttle waiting in the background—the squat, muscular vessel that had brought them to the surface—had been designed for this single flight. Equipment harvested from every onboard shuttle had been lumped together, huge stocks of fuel had been burned, and Lorkin had risked everything to stand on this barren mountaintop, meeting with this new and rather peculiar species.

AN OPEN LETTER (continued):
As I have said, I learned tonight that you survived the terrible war, Master . . . I cannot be more pleased, and thankful . . .

Our hosts also mentioned broadcasts coming from the Great Ship. Most of the transmissions predate the war, but the last several appear to be narrow-beamed signals meant only for their eyes. (More properly, for their noses. Their language is quite intricate, and because of a lack of expertise on our little ship, plus our limited translators, comprehension has been difficult for both species.) As a friendly gesture, they showed us your most recent broadcast, and we have confirmed their basic conclusions. The Great Ship will pass within a light-year of their world before plunging on into the heart of a dark nebula. You desire information. In exchange for knowledge, you wish to learn everything possible about the nebula's inhabitants. Which is perfectly reasonable, Master. And let me assure you, speaking for my crew and our passengers, each of us wishes to help in every way possible.

But first, let me say this much.

I am responsible for my many mistakes. Everyone aboard the *Calamus* has made errors of judgment, and all of us are infinitely sorry for our failures. But when you consider the circumstances of our leaving and the simple fact that we have several dozen passengers of quality who are desperate to return to their apartments and old lives . . . well, I cannot drop to my knees and cower, Master. I am forced to beg across many light-years, admitting to you that I am weak and sorry; but in all circumstances, Good Master, I have strived to do what is best. A different officer might hold back his knowledge about the nebula. The Inkwell, as you call it. But using what I have learned as a bargaining chip . . . well, that would be wrong, and I won't fall for the temptation.

Simply stated, we need help to come home again. Our streakship is empty of fuel and seriously damaged, and the mood on board is less than comfortable. I trust you, Master. Send a mission to retrieve us. And to show my own good intentions and my genuine faith in your kindness, I will tell you all that I have learned about the dark nebula and its citizens.

SHIP'S LOG (excerpts, presumably edited):

A beautiful disappointment, our first potential refuge has been. An M-class sun with three massive jupiters and an assortment of moons, it looked inviting in our best charts. With ample volatiles and a native intelligence broadcasting strong, highly modulated radio signals, we assumed we could find fuel and technical aid. But we didn't make contact with the local species until we were on the fringes of the solar system. They live on the cold watery moon of the largest jupiter. Their technologies are few and development is slow, hamstrung by a lack of metals and stone. Rather like cetaceans, but larger and with far slower metabolisms, they produce the radio signals with their own vast bodies, choruses of them working together. Not having a xenobiologist on board, our interpretations are little better than informed guesses, but it seems there is a religious component to their radio voices. They hear the long radio broadcasts coming from the three local gas giants and their sun—the natural noise generated by magnetic fields and solar flares—and they assume that these celestial bodies are gods, and the gods are speaking to them . . . and if enough little voices can speak in tandem, then the gods will listen to them . . .

But if the planets and sun are deities, then the black nebula is the Mother Ocean that blesses the universe with her bounty. ("It's the best explanation we could decide upon"—Lorkin added later, with a scribbling hand.) In some long-ago past, the Mother Ocean visited their world with Her body. Their descriptions sound like a starship. The aliens aboard were as large as the natives, or larger. Or perhaps they were secondary ships departing from the main body. Either way, they were finned and perhaps warm-blooded . . . they knew how to speak to the natives . . . but in most cases, they chose to say nothing . . .

The visitors seem to have planted the idea that the nebula is an ocean and a god, and that She washes the universe with her bounty. Until then, the locals had assumed that the blackness was just a hole in their otherwise god-rich sky . . .

We could have visited the cold cetaceans, but our streakship is meant for fast transit and fully equipped ports of call. An icy moon would have supplied us with limitless fuel, but our machine shops are minimal and our shuttles small. I have decided to pass through the system, using the sun to help slingshot us on a new, more promising trajectory . . . a second system closer to the nebula, where the cetaceans claim to have heard voices rather like their own . . .

The K-class sun has no worlds, only a loose assemblage of asteroids and comets left over from an impoverished dust cloud. Settlers from a machine species have claimed every rock larger than a human fist, attaching beacons and at least one species of booby-trap. In culture and language, they seem to be related to the 449-Ables, but since they won't meet with us, much less allow close examinations, we can only make sloppy guesses about their origins . . .

They claim to know nothing about the nebula. They say it does not interest them, that they possess all of the room and resources they need right here, for now and the next ten billion years . . . which is a fair estimate, considering that to date they have retroformed only half a thousand scattered bolides . . .

But my first officer has voiced doubts about their attitude.

We passed through the system last night, borrowing momentum from the sun to acquire a new course. Neither my first officer nor I could sleep. "Remember when we were approaching?" she asked. "When they first noticed us, I mean. We made a burn and gave our little 'Hello . . . '"

"What about it?" I asked.

"Remember? What did their first transmission show us?"

An elaborate, highly detailed picture was sent to us. (I'm including the image, of course. Perhaps you can make more out of this, Master.) From what I can tell, the picture shows us that the local residents possess no starships. They were tiny machines, and scarce, and by a thousand measures, utterly harmless. They had no intention of launching toward the nebula. Again and again, they referred to us as being "great thinking silicon"—apparently a common 449-Able reference to intelligent machinery—and they seemed to mention an old treaty, a sworn agreement, or maybe a desperate promise . . .

"I don't think it was a treaty," my first officer told me. "Treaties are drawn up between near equals. To me, they sounded as if they were little guys begging the nebula to let them survive."

"That doesn't make sense," I argued. "We weren't coming from the direction of the nebula."

"Yeah, but we seem to be heading toward it," she reminded me. "At two-thirds the speed of light, which might be an alarming sight to somebody who spends a lot of their time being scared . . ."

Today, we caught a stray broadcast from a G-class sun twenty light-years removed from us . . . from the far side of the nebula, apparently . . .

A highly intelligent species—a sessile species from a world with a dense wet atmosphere—was trying to communicate with someone inside the dust cloud. For thirty seconds, we were traveling inside their much-weakened com-laser. We captured just a portion of their message. (Broadcast included.) They seem to be giving thanks for some small charity or favor . . . and when they are not saying, "Thank you," they are begging for a response . . .

In one image, they show themselves rooted beside a second species. The nebula inhabitants, perhaps? Both species appear sessile, as it happens . . . like giant hydras, with very much the same body design . . . But their neighbors—the ones who are now refusing to answer their pleas—seem at least ten times larger than them . . .

Approaching the new world, the Pak'kin seemed to assume that we were a starship returning to the nebula. One nest after another sent us greetings, wishing us a successful voyage home. Even from fringes of their solar system, we could see that their world was enormous and very dry. Again, we found another weak candidate for a port of call. But on the outskirts of the system, a stony little comet smashed our armor, its shards gutting us in a hundred places, and after making rough repairs, I have just told my first officer, "We've got to stop here."

We have no choice.

Our main antennae will have to be rebuilt from scraps and scavenged pieces of our shuttle com-systems. We will be in a blackout state until finally moving into a high orbit around the Pak'kin world. My first officer suggests that we pretend to be from the nebula. "In this neighborhood," she points out, "everybody seems to respect whoever lives inside that black cloud." She says, "We should fake it, and we might win favors. You never know until you try."

But I have made a different choice.

"We come from the Great Ship," I have told her, and everyone, "we don't have any reason to lie. In fact, I think we can use our home ship to our advantage. An artifact bigger than most worlds, and older than any sun . . . How can a cloud of cold black soot appear any more impressive than us . . . ?"

As THE *CALAMUS* transmissions were being replayed, the Submasters were scattered around the ship, in secure immersion tanks, each sitting inside the same holo image showing the landing party and the Pak'kin. It made for a very crowded mountaintop.

"Now look this way," Pamir instructed, using a blue laser to guide everyone's eyes. "Past Lorkin and his crew. Past their ugly-ass little shuttle. You see? Out where the cameras weren't really pointing . . . do you see that . . . ?"

Washen thought she could see it, yes. Where light and shadow had been captured by the peripheral edges of the lenses, she could see bodies. They were even lower-built than the Pak'kins sent as the delegation, perhaps they were more powerful, and there were too many of them to count. And each cone-shaped body seemed to carry some type of weaponry.

"No, I'm talking about something else," warned Pamir.

The holo was received just three days ago, and he had done the initial analysis. Until moments ago, nobody else knew what he had found.

"But who are these others?" the Master inquired, her image sitting with the invisible cameras, her puzzled voice twisting the conversation back to the obvious. "Are they soldiers from the local hive? Or another hive?"

"One or the other, madam," Pamir replied.

Washen walked through the image of Lorkin and then his first officer and lover. Alone, she strolled to the edge of the holo, observing what seemed to be the low, gravity-smashed peak of a second mountain standing on the very brink of sight. Strong limbs or machinery had eaten into the peak's bare stone. An image had been created, and at first glance, it was a Pak'kin. A nest queen, apparently. But the proportions were a little wrong, and she understood biomechanics well enough to appreciate that this enormous figure portrayed a creature that was not at all Pak'kin. But whatever the species, myth or alien, it had so impressed the natives that they had spent centuries and fortunes to reproduce its vastness and majesty.

"Has there been another transmission?" asked Osmium.

Washen glanced at the head of security.

Pamir shook his head, a grim smile dissolving with a heavy shrug. "They promised a second transmission in thirty hours," he said to the harum-scarum. "But that deadline came and went thirty hours ago." Then he walked through the Pak'kin dignitaries, telling everyone, "We did manage to catch two little squawks of modulated noise before the scheduled broadcast. Then our largest mirror field spotted what might have been the detonation of a nuclear charge above the Pak'kin home world."

"These are dead faces," Aasleen remarked, looking straight into Lorkin's famished eyes.

"Obviously," the Master declared.

Then with a survivor's instincts, she added, "They should have lied about their origins. Given themselves a stronger position to bargain from. If someone thinks you're a god, you'd better let them believe it." She broke into a wild laugh, knowing that grim lesson from her own spectacular life. "Lorkin's first officer had the only good set of instincts," she argued. "It's a shame we can't bring her back. A little prison stay as an example, then give her a small commission—"

"But what lives inside the Inkwell?" half a dozen Submasters asked, their faces gazing up at the vast Inkwell.

Just the *Calamus* signal had mentioned four candidate species: a giant cetacean, and a thinking machine, and a giant hydra, and perhaps some sort of Pak'kin queen. And that was in addition to transmissions filtering in from other far-flung worlds. Dozens more species had been described as originating from somewhere inside the Inkwell. Each description was suspiciously similar to the species offering the testimony; but in every case, the nebula's inhabitants had been physically larger, and always made a lasting impression on their neighbors.

Washen wasn't certain they yet had any clue about what was waiting ahead of them. She walked back through the holo to join her colleagues, but unlike the rest of them, she stared down at her feet.

"We're running out of time," she muttered.

Eyes focused on the barren alien rock, she reminded everyone, "We've got less than a hundred years to get ready . . . and we still don't have any clear idea what we're getting ready for . . ."

Six

SHE WAS TINY and boyish and by most measures quite plain. Her hair was long and spiderweb-thin, her skin an impoverished yellow left thin and smooth by life. Eyes the color of roiled water were much too large for the narrow, sharp-boned face, while her mouth was a thin, inexpressive line almost lost beneath the simple long nose. Yet those big eyes had a watchful quality and an obvious intelligence, the slight body possessed a surprising strength, and on those rare occasions when she spoke, she had a musical and memorable if somewhat sad little voice.

"Hello," she quietly sang out.

Half a dozen harum-scarums were sitting together, enjoying a communal meal in a small open-air cafe that catered to predators. Six mouths chewed while the other six quietly gossiped. The remnants of the shared meal lay in the middle of their table, assorted bones and hooves and a long black skull still lashed together with fat pearly ligaments. Five of the diners glanced at the newcomer. Even sitting, they were considerably taller than the little human—grayish bipeds with thick hides and spikes jutting from their elbows—and with a smooth, malicious ease, the nearest alien remarked, "A monkey girl for dessert. What a fine treat!"

Four of her companions laughed at the insult.

"Here, monkey girl," she continued, shoving a long hand between the human's sticklike legs. "Let me help you onto our table."

Any other human would have screamed and galloped off. Or wept. Or shown some other equally offensive reaction. But this human simply went limp, as if she anticipated the hand and hard words, and with an amused glint in her doelike eyes, she clung to the long forearm, a whispery little voice begging, "Please help me, please?"

What could the harum-scarum do?

Match the creature's bluster with your own bluster, naturally.

The woman threw the little human into the middle of the table. Passersby stopped and stared at the odd scene, alarm mixed with curiosity. But when the tiny human refused to flinch or beg, the harum-scarum had no choice but to stand tall and tear off one of the legs of the creature's simple brown trousers. The bare flesh beneath barely covered the sticklike bones. Even for a human, the creature was scrawny, sickly-looking, and unappetizing. Suppressing her revulsion, the harum-scarum began to insert a knobby foot into her eating mouth, followed by the ankle and shin and the big pale lump of a knee.

Even as the pressure of teeth and the muscular throat gripped tight, the human smiled at her assailant.

And it wasn't a human smile, either.

The human mouth was a dirty orifice, air and food sloppily mixed into a gruesome shared mush. Yet somehow that thin and exceedingly alien opening had acquired the scornful, belittling expression of a harum-scarum. Even as her bare leg was being squeezed hard, a thousand teeth dimpling the helpless skin, there was a real and unnerving sense that this alien—this stupid ape—almost welcomed the miseries to come.

With a deep retching sound, the harum-scarum threw up her dessert.

But the game wasn't finished. The human continued to lie beside the stripped carcass, and with a mocking delight, she offered her bare leg to each of the diners. With her own throat, without the aid of any translator, she said, "Please," in their native tongue. Somehow she managed to make the appropriate deep grunt, mocking one after another with a brazenness that appalled most of her audience.

"I am nothing," she told them, in nearly perfect harum-scarum.

"I am a baby," she whined. "A newcomer to space and the stars. Human, I am. Undeserving of my fortune. And you—you are ten million years older than I—and I am barely worthy to serve as your meat's own meat."

Throughout the whole performance, the sixth harum-scarum remained silent. When the bare leg was offered to him, he said nothing, staring at the little alien with a face scrubbed free of emotion. His companions assumed that he was furious, but unlike the rest of them, he couldn't afford to show his rage. He was considerably older than they, and he was a hero from the recent war, and for reasons political and proper, he had been welcomed into the ranks of the ship's captains, then swiftly promoted to become one of the very few Submasters.

"Osmium," the human said, reading the name riding on the bright uniform. Then with a laugh, she mocked him. "Have you ever wished to? Eat a little human whole, maybe? I would be honored to feel my bones shatter in your brave throat, my flesh boiled away by your brave acids, my remnants shit out of your glorious ass . . . I would feel like such a fortunate little girl . . . !"

At last, the Submaster reacted.

With a wet cough, the offered foot was thrown out of his eating mouth. Then the other mouth broke into a deep, deeply amused laugh, and displaying a casual respect that took his companions by surprise, Osmium said, "Hello, friend," in the human language.

"Hello, Mere."

———

MERE WAS INVITED to sit with them. Without explanation, Osmium gave her an equal status, their table reconfiguring itself, the hexagon growing a matching seventh side. Then with barely two glances at the tiny soul beside him, he turned to the woman across the table, saying, "What you were telling us? Continue with your confession, please . . ."

"I am not a coward," the woman replied. "I am brave enough to be honest, and honesty only sounds cowardly."

"You wish to leave the ship," Osmium pressed.

"How else can I say it?" She glanced at the human, disgust mixed with a grudging respect. Harum-scarums had been flying between the stars before this creature jumped down from the trees. Yet humans were first to find the Great Ship. Humans claimed the artifact first and managed to hold it, and according to the chaotic but mostly honored legal codes of their galaxy—The Fire of Fires, they called the galaxy—the Great Ship would remain with the humans until the end of time.

"I was born on this vessel," she reminded Osmium.

Except for the Submaster, all of the harum-scarums were born somewhere nearby.

"I grew up inside these avenues and rooms and caverns," she continued.

"And you love the Great Ship," Osmium offered.

"How can anyone not love her birthplace?"

The little human seemed to flinch. But she said nothing, those wide dark eyes endlessly absorbing her surroundings.

"I love this ship, and I treasure my life, and I have always believed that I would live my next trillion breaths here."

"Of course," Osmium growled.

"But this," the woman rumbled. "This new direction of ours. This accidental, supremely pointless trajectory. How can I hold my enthusiasm for an endless voyage into the deepest, emptiest realms of Creation?"

Osmium said nothing.

Mere sat beside him, her chair tall enough to lift her eyes up to the level of their thick, heavily armored necks. She seemed to understand every word, and she noticed gestures and swift expressions that other species wouldn't perceive, and in the midst of everything, she watched the carcass on the platter begin to move slowly, ligaments yanking at the black skeleton as the creature—a little river-bear—remembered that it was still alive.

Humans ate cultured meat or occasionally killed specially bred animals, pretending to be carnivores. But harum-scarums had more respect for life. Millions of years ago, they had infused their domesticated animals with the same life-prolonging technologies they used on themselves, and as they traveled through space, they took their treasured animals with them, eating them down to a minimal last morsel before reconjuring them inside special vats.

For an instant, Mere seemed disgusted by the sight of those flopping, bloodied bones. But her voice was calm when she pointed out, "There is a ban on emigration. And this man here is authorized to forcefully stop anyone who tests that ban."

"Every soul makes its choices," the woman countered.

Mere nodded, human fashion.

With a simple contempt, she said, "Kill yourself. Then you'll be set free."

Suicide was an unthinkable abomination, but the woman refused to take offense. Quietly, she pointed out, "My opinion is not only mine. But where I wield enough strength to accept disagreeable fates, there are lesser creatures on board who grow desperate. The farther they fall toward the Inkwell, the closer they are to panic."

The cafe was in a bright avenue of white granite, wide but not so wide that the walls were lost with the distance. Above them, the gently arched ceiling was built from raw hyperfiber decorated with globes and gelatinous ribs filled with ultrathermic bacteria. The glow of the microbes supplied the steady blue-white light. Even when the avenue was less than crowded, it was a loud place. Today, thousands of creatures were strolling or rolling or sometimes drifting overhead on broad wings. Every form of mouth and speaking anus made a steady white chatter, and to an experienced ear, there was a persistent discord to the mayhem. Thousands of years of seamlessly pleasant travel had come to an end. During the last quick century, the wealthiest souls from a multitude of worlds found themselves unsure about the most secure of commodities—the future. If souls weren't afraid, something would be wrong. Yet what they were feeling wasn't just the tiny reasonable worries brought on by an unexpected change to the ship's course. It was also the Wayward War. It was also the sudden discovery of an entire world hidden in the midst of what was supposed a fully explored ship. And it was the rumors of an ancient cargo, and an evil force or forces called the Bleak . . . and there was the pernicious fear that the Waywards would recover someday and attack once again. "What worth is there in a captain's assurances?" the voices asked. Plainly, the humans didn't know their vessel half as well as they had promised, and to souls who had thousands and millions of years left to live, this had become a daunting and endlessly sobering situation.

"I fought for the captains," said the harum-scarum woman. With an honest, well-deserved boast, she said, "I was brave. I did important things. And I murdered a few of the Waywards, too."

The human said nothing.

"All five of us helped in the fight, Osmium. We deserve the chance to construct our own ship—with our own moneys and time and tools. Why shouldn't we be allowed to travel where we wish? Or if it is our choice, in the end, remain on board?"

"Where would you go?" Mere asked.

"Anywhere," the woman replied.

The tiny woman shook her head, human fashion. "We've left your colonies behind. And mine, too. The orbital mechanics are pretty gruesome. A little starship with very few passengers won't be able to turn around. And even if the ship could make the maneuver, then it very likely dies during the long voyage. Impacts and recyke failures are just two miserable possibilities. Which leaves you searching for an alien world and the hope of finding sanctuary there." She paused, then said, "How about the Pak'kin?"

Everyone knew the story of the *Calamus*. The Submasters had let the truth slip free, most certainly as a warning to anyone who thought of making any wild leaps to freedom.

"What about the Inkwell?" the harum-scarum countered. "I have heard plenty of rumors, each one claiming there is life inside that cloud. Life and little worlds full of light and heat, and water, and perhaps other treasures, too."

"You cannot," Mere remarked. With what looked like genuine sorrow, she said, "Even if you could find the aliens, you don't have the skills. The sense. The magic necessary to make those very strange organisms think of you as their friend. And even if you did have that rare magic, how happy would you be to live aeons among such strange souls . . . ?"

Then she gestured, sticklike arms reaching out, as if trying to embrace the multitude around them.

The harum-scarum had no worthwhile response. She sat motionless, her mind fixed on a series of equally disgusting images. Life among the humans was barely tolerable, and these baby apes were not nearly as awful as most of these other intelligent species. Perhaps for the first time, the woman appreciated just what kind of doom would hang upon her if she actually abandoned the ship, now or in any conceivable future.

Mere rose abruptly.

To Osmium she said a few quiet words, using the human tongue. Then with an expression of utter contrition, she reminded the others, "It is not any kind of weakness, of course. This need that you feel . . . this love of your own kind . . . a species-hunger telling you to sacrifice everything to keep close to your own little flavor of life . . ."

THE PECULIAR LITTLE human gave a two-stomp salute and left. Their table quickly absorbed its extra side, and after a few dismissive insults, everyone sat quietly, watching the carcass flinch and writhe.

Osmium conspicuously said nothing.

Finally one of the other men remarked, "I have never met a monkey woman quite like that one."

Again, Osmium was silent.

The woman who had bluffed and lost now looked at the Submaster, and with a transparent frustration, she said, "All right, I will beg. Tell us about that little creature, if you would."

For a long while, the old harum-scarum gazed across the avenue. Eventually he spotted a massive black sphere rolling in the distance. Inside that insulated contraption, safely entombed, was a creature rarely seen by passengers or crew. Jellyjells, humans had dubbed them. Organic crystals formed frail bones and a slow but relentless mind, and overlying both was a gelatinous body composed of complex fats dissolved in liquid methane. On the ship, the jellyjells lived in their own little sea, frigid and sluggish. They were ancient and rich, and on the fringes of half a thousand solar systems, they were rather common. But their customs and nature seemed extraordinarily strange to hot-blooded creatures like the harum-scarums. Watching the black sphere tumble out of sight, Osmium asked, "Why did the captains allow them on board?"

"The aliens paid enough," the woman replied testily. "In empty worlds, in technologies. In those things cherished by monkeys."

The Submaster made a rude sound with his eating mouth.

Another woman used a nexus, and with a sudden expertise, she attacked his question. "Their home world was old and stable, and very simple," she explained. "Organic rain fed a few species of plankton that fed the jellyjells. There were no other multicellular species in their universe. Until they moved into space, they never interacted with other species, much less anything intelligent. They barely imagined creatures such as us were possible, much less important."

"They have some difficulties in their past," Osmium allowed. "Feuds. Long wars. And ugly extinctions for certain rivals."

His little audience glanced down the avenue.

With a gesture both fond and self-conscious, Osmium touched his uniform. "You don't appreciate this. Until you stand inside one of these mirrored suits, you are powerless to understand: Every day, the captains must decide what is best for the ship. Every moment, small and mammoth choices are made. What passengers do we allow aboard? And which species are turned away? Who is too dangerous or too demanding, or too disruptive, or simply too hard to judge fairly?" His broad armored hand floated above its own reflection, fingers and thumbs slowly closing into a jagged fist. "A species offers us a fortune to come on board, but will that be enough? As a captain, I must consider that difficult question. And always, my first loyalty is to the Great Ship."

The others stirred uneasily. Did their old friend mean what he said? Incredible as it seemed, they couldn't smell duplicity or any other politics at work.

"A strange and potentially dangerous species approaches me. I am offered worlds and technologies and everything else that I deem valuable. But will I place my ship and passengers in jeopardy by accepting these newcomers?"

Quietly, he asked, "To whom do I turn?"

Then with a flash of humor, he said, "Mere," and opened his fist, the big hand dropping into his lap.

"You don't realize this," he assured. "But that creature who was just sitting here . . . she is genuinely famous among the ranks of the captains." Osmium looked at each of their doubting faces. "Famous, and highly respected, too."

"What does the little monster do?" asked the woman.

"With jellyjells . . . with a wide assortment of species, cold and hot . . . she goes to live among them for a long while . . ."

"Ah," said another woman. "An emissary."

"Hardly," Osmium countered. "Diplomats travel in full view. As emissaries, they meet with officials and queens, tyrants and presidents. What they see is what they are shown, and if they are very talented, they see a little more. But telling the captains, 'We can absorb this new species' . . . well, that's not their responsibility or their burden, or at least it shouldn't be . . ."

"She's a scientist," a young man speculated. "Some kind of cultural exobiologist, I would think."

"Again, hardly." His eating mouth spat another foul sound, and at the same moment, he explained, "Thousands of years ago, riding inside a shielded and very swift little ship, Mere visited the jellyjells' home world. To breed, they lay eggs on shallow ridges under the methane. In secret, she studied their breeding and the eggs, then the creatures that hatched from the eggs. When the babies were old enough, and important enough, she created a duplicate of one of them, inserting her own shielded and heavily insulated mind into the new body, and like the rest of her litter mates, she slowly swam out into the great cold sea."

Disgust and fascination held sway over his little audience.

"They are a physically slow species," he reminded them. "It took her contrived body several centuries to mature. Yet because she knew how to act and how to speak, Mere avoided detection and serious suspicion." With a mocking laugh, he asked, "How many of you would live just one day in those circumstances? Bathed in liquid methane. Your bodies so much slime reaching out to harvest the thin crop of plankton. A minute of that life, and which one of us wouldn't go mad?"

No one spoke.

"Mere lived among the jellyjells," he continued, "and when the time came, she slipped back to her hidden ship. She returned to the Great Ship. The Master Captain's original First Chair, the old bitch Miocene, didn't want any part of these aliens. The expert arguments about the jellyjells described them as treacherous xenophobes with a capacity for murdering entire species. But despite every smart warning and all the rational fears, Mere managed to convince the Master Captain that these cold creatures had learned and matured, becoming flexible enough and confident enough to dress up in a cold little pond and go for a roll down a public avenue."

The faces began to look at one another, plainly impressed.

But Osmium wasn't satisfied. With a steady, level voice, he listed several dozen species, famous and obscure, that Mere had lived among and who were aboard today because her respected voice had said, "Trust them."

If this was true, the variety of monsters that she had lived with was astonishing. Spectacular, and numbing.

Then the Submaster offered a shorter list of species. When the angry woman admitted that she didn't know those names, he replied, "Of course. Mere lived with them, too. Lived as them, on occasion. And she found good compelling reasons to refuse them passage."

"A talented little creature," one of the men conceded.

"But why her?" another man asked. "Among the multitude of humans, how did she gain this rare talent?"

"That," Osmium replied, "is quite a story."

"Stop," the angry woman interrupted. "Before you tell the story—"

"If I tell it," he warned.

"First, I want to know something else. Now."

The Submaster waited with a keen anticipation.

"You've been a captain for barely twelve decades," she pointed out. "You're still learning your own little job, and I doubt if you know much about the history of your new profession. Which makes me wonder why you are the expert. Where did you learn about a creature that the rest of us didn't hear about until today?"

With both of his mouths, Osmium smiled.

Then with a deep and honest pleasure, he explained, "Before you were born . . . before any of you were prophecies written on your parents' seed . . . I spent a few happy centuries as the husband of that strange little human being . . ."

Seven

As A BOY, Locke had always been quiet and thoughtful. The only child produced by two of the most ambitious captains, he had inherited something about their appearance and a blend of their keen intelligence but nothing of their innate desire to lead others. On a diet of Marrow nuts and grilled insects, he had grown into a moderate-sized young man, healthy in every measurable way, but distinctly and forever different. He was strong and smoothly graceful. He had his father's eyes, busy and bright and always intense. He had much of his mother's face and seamless confidence. But he had absolutely no interest in controlling any group or manipulating any cause, no matter how worthwhile. After much consideration, his mother had decided that it wasn't an absence of ability; genetic shuffling hadn't stolen away any inborn talent, and he didn't lack for an education in the art of inspiring other souls. No, it was simply that Locke easily saw great and noble causes that to others, including his parents, were abstract and perhaps a little questionable—ethereal realms where dream and theory danced together along chains of infinite and infinitely perplexing equations.

As a young man, Locke fell in love with the Waywards' beliefs. One of their major tenets was that in the remote past, when the universe was tiny and young, there were the Builders who created the Great Ship, and the Bleak who had tried to steal it. Then both died away, for a time. The universe was left as a sterile realm, expanding outward, with the ship wandering through the deepest, coldest reaches of space. Then the Bleak were reincarnated, and they found the ship and took it for themselves. Humans were the Bleak, claimed the Waywards. Unless of course you happened to be one of the humans conceived on Marrow, which made you into the Builders reborn, and how could it not be your duty and sole purpose to reclaim the Great Ship, taking it for yourself and your magnificent ancestors?

As a loyal follower of a lofty cause, Locke lived as a Wayward. But there came a horrible moment when impossible choices had to be made: His mother was in mortal danger, and the only possible way to save her was to kill her assailant. With much grief but absolutely no hesitation, Locke murdered his own father. Then he marked his mother's burial site with her own silver watch. And afterward, he managed to look as if he was still the loyal Wayward. But Locke was a guilt-ridden son, and whenever he stared at his faith, he saw its flaws and cruel failures. Then he found a second chance to help his surviving parent, and not only did he do everything possible to help her, he also turned his back on the Waywards.

Of course Washen was his mother.

In the days following the war, there was lazy talk about allowing Locke to join the ranks of the captains. Washen said it, as did Aasleen and a few of the other survivors of that mission to Marrow. But as Pamir pointedly warned, the young man still looked like a Wayward, and he spoke like one, and he had served their peculiar cause for centuries without complaint. Besides, how would it help the ship if the First Chair began grooming her once-traitorous baby for some lofty, undeserved position?

"Do you think he isn't qualified?" Washen asked, her voice tight and a little prickly. "If he isn't, say so."

"I thought I just did." Pamir laughed.

But it was Locke himself who put an end to the possibility. With a shrug and a gentle tone, he said, "Mother." Then the busy dreamy eyes looked off into the distance, and he confessed to her, and to himself, "I don't have the barest skills to be any kind of captain. And even worse, I don't have a flicker of the fire that I would need."

Washen was injured, and in ways she hadn't imagined, she was impressed by his honesty and relieved to be free of her own motherly ambitions. Quietly, she asked Locke, "What do you have a fire for?"

Shrugging amiably, he said, "I'm usually clever, and in narrow ways, I can be very smart. Plus I see things from odd angles. And since I just abandoned the only belief system that meant anything to me for my entire life, my mind is temporarily free and empty."

How would such a loss feel? Washen could only imagine that kind of devastation of purpose and place.

But Locke felt blessed instead.

"I am empty," he repeated. "Rudderless, and lost. My soul is desperate to find something new to believe in. Something worthy, this time. Everywhere I look, I can almost see things that are great and true."

"What things?"

With a casual ease, he said, "Here's a notion, Mother." Then with the most unremarkable words, he calmly asked if the Builders had constructed just this ship. Or maybe they had fashioned the universe, and the Great Ship was just another little mystery nestled inside an endless series of concentric hulls.

The purpose and meanings of the ship was a subject of relentless debate. A team of AIs had been built and educated to think about nothing else, and after nearly a thousand centuries of hard thought, they had come up with nothing substantial. But Locke's little notion interested them quite a lot. The Waywards and their myths also held a certain fascination. A final decision was obvious enough that the machines and both humans came to the same inevitable conclusion. "Join them," Washen urged her son. "Learn what you need about physics, cosmology, the high mathematics. Help them when you can. Or work on your own, if you'd rather."

"That's what I'm doing now," Locke reported, with a narrow, somewhat wary smile. "Learning and working on my own, mostly."

"Since when?" Washen sputtered.

"Since that day when we looked down on Marrow."

One last time, just before the entranceway was sealed with fresh hyperfiber, they had traveled to the ship's core.

"I didn't know this," Washen confessed. "Why didn't I know?"

"You've been terribly busy, Mother."

True enough.

"You're usually distracted," he observed.

"And very tired," she added. "But really, we have to make a point of talking to each other. From now on!"

BUT THE FIRST CHAIR had always been a busy post, even in easy times. The War was finished, but there were immense repairs begging to be made. Like never before, there were civil concerns and economic barricades. A multitude of passengers had to be calmed and educated, and when necessary, kept distracted. A battered and suspicious crew had to be retrained and reenergized, and an entirely reconfigured army of captains had to be watched over, learning their stations and the subtleties that no school could prepare them to see, much less master. And always, there was the tireless need to make ready for the Inkwell, which would be followed by the next leg of the voyage. As a barrier, a cold nebula offered an endless array of hazards. Dust and the intermittent comet would test the ship's shields and lasers. Even the most benign course would swamp their defenses, and the hull would again be battered until it was pocked and unlovely and a little bit weakened. That was why Washen decided to keep the repair missions at work, even when every system had been made fully operational again. On her authority, new lasers and enhanced shields were being constructed and deployed, and great fields of mirrors were scanning deeper into the Inkwell every moment. But even if they could conquer the crude monsters of nature—mindless ice and stone and the occasional sunless world—there were the simple and inescapable questions about who or what lived inside that cold black mass and what, if anything, they might want from the ship.

Washen was consumed by her work. With an army of nexuses to help, she manipulated grand plans and careful long-term schemes, always striving to make them play well with one another. To protect her sanity, she slept, but only in bites and little breaths, and only when Pamir or Aasleen fell into the breach. Seeing her son was a rare business, and for a long time she assumed that the long gaps were the fault of her office or some lack of discipline in her own self. But what else could she do? A relaxed dinner with Locke meant that she would have to plan the next major burn in a different hour, which meant delaying two meetings with the fef and the Remoras, and that meant that she would have to postpone her speech of comfort and well-wishing to one of the resident species until a less appropriate time, or she would simply have to go without sleep again, draining herself even more than she had anticipated. Speaking with Locke was too hard. Sometimes she didn't see him for several years at a time. Yes, they traded messages and holos, usually once every week. But no technology had ever matched the intimacy and power of a relaxed supper. And when that meal arrived, often after a long absence, the entire evening could be spent just fighting to pick up the threads from their last dinner.

If they met in her quarters, the meal was simple but elegant—a gift from one of the local communities, perhaps. Human-prepared or otherwise, but always familiar to Washen. But if they met in Locke's quarters, they ate grilled hammerwings and sweet lava nuts and other Marrow treasures. Her son had cultured those species from samples brought up by the would-be conquerors. In a private cavern several kilometers long and almost as wide, he had built a tiny but authentic model of Marrow, complete with molten iron spills and a sky gradually growing dark. His diet and the sky kept him looking like a Wayward, with the smoky gray skin and a slightly famished cast to the eyes. But at least in his mother's presence, he dressed like a law-abiding passenger, in simple trousers and a light shirt. And when possible, Washen left her uniform elsewhere, matching his casual tastes—a touch of detail from the relentless and deft administrator.

Too often, she spoke about her work and its biggest problems.

When Locke stared off into the distance, watching a fat hammerwing flying against the illusionary sky, she would stop herself. In midsentence, if necessary. Then with a sorrowful honesty, she would say, "Sorry."

At first, Locke would nod, and say, "No, it's all right."

Then Washen would insist, "I want to hear about your work. What are you doing now?"

But after a few decades of graceless niceties, her son decided simply to leap past her weak apology as well as the rest of the traditional noise. Washen would be recounting what she believed to be an interesting story, perhaps about an obscure species and how she had handled them in a dangerous moment . . . and in midsentence, Locke would blurt out, "My work is going well."

It was his signal, and after a few more decades, Washen stopped feeling insulted or embarrassed.

"I'm still learning about the science and mathematics," her son would explain. He had enjoyed a thorough education as a boy on Marrow, but those were harsh times, and on Marrow, children and their society had no clear picture of the greater universe. "I've still got a long way to go," his confession went. "And that's just until I can match what the AIs know by pure instinct. Doing any significant work . . . well, that might never happen. Who can say?"

"But you're learning," she would remind him.

Locke would nod and smile amiably, pleased to have his discipline recognized. Then he might tell his mother a long, convoluted story about some odd feature in one of the six essential Theories of All. In common usage, there was just the single Theory. Robust and remarkably simple, it seemed to explain everything of substance about the universe, from its tiny birth to its endless inflation, from the relatively quiet present and into the gathering darkness, with its bitter cold and the eventual, inevitable death. Only certain rarefied specialists bothered with the incongruities and wilder details: What was the basic nature of the superuniverse? Was time real or an illusion? Were the parallel existences genuine, or were they just mathematical conveniences? And was there anyplace inside this conundrum for something that might be labeled "the soul"?

Out of simple convenience, those detailed and often contrary theories had been lumped into six equal categories, or species, or little hills.

As the daughter of engineers, and then as the trained captain of a starship, Washen had been promised that each of those theories was as valid as any other, and just as trivial. There was no available means to test them against one another, at least not inside this universe. But their lofty and deeply clever mathematics always pointed to the same conclusion. Washen was traveling through an existence that was inevitable—a tail of reality riding on the end of every great equation. The only factor that mattered to a captain was which of her passengers believed in which of the six theories. Each had its attractions and inducements, as well as its disagreeable points. Most species embraced whatever vision of All would make them sleep easiest or live best or accept their own hard existences with the least complaint. What they believed was a window on their nature, and sometimes when Locke spoke about one of the theories, she would mention, in passing, "The Galloon don't believe in time, either," or with a tisk-tisking tone, she would warn Locke, "The harum-scarums despise the idea of parallel realities. There's only one existence, and of course they have to be at the middle of it."

Locke would nod patiently, perhaps showing a little grin. He didn't particularly care about the aesthetics of any species, including his own. What he was striving for was to sit on a high point and look at the terrain without prejudice, seeing everything that there was to see.

During one of the little lunches, more than ten decades after the Wayward War, he launched into a description of a new mathematics. At first, Washen listened intently and felt certain that she understood the heart of it. But at some point during the monologue, she realized that she hadn't any clue about what the sounds striking her ears could possibly mean. As always, Locke had given her files to examine—lessons and illustrations produced from his own notes and elaborate papers—and she linked herself to the day's files, burrowing deep, then coming up again like a drowning woman bursting out of a cold bottomless sea.

"What are you talking about?" she blurted.

But her son had ceased talking, probably several minutes ago.

"I don't understand any of this," she confessed. Complained. And then with a self-deprecating laugh, she said, "Throw me a line, darling. Would you?"

"A line?" The image didn't make immediate sense to him.

Finally, a dim old memory tickled her mind. Washen said, "Wait," before her son could offer an explanation. "I remember now."

"What?"

"My mother, and a few teachers . . . they would sometimes mention . . . what was it . . . ?" She closed her dark eyes, concentrating. "A seventh Theory of All. Very obscure, and trivial . . . nobody ever actually believes in it . . ."

Locke's response was a gentle shrug and a nod.

"I don't know anything about the seventh Theory," she said again, begging for any help.

But Locke could only shrug, admitting, "I don't know much more than you." Then after a long pause, he added, "It is a disgusting set of equations. Really, even the AIs—my teachers, my colleagues—they despise that seventh solution to everything. It's that ugly, that sad. If it wasn't fascinating, I doubt if they'd ever look at it twice."

THREE DECADES LATER, in the midst of another lunch, Washen again asked, "How are the lessons going?"

He smiled broadly, which was a little odd.

Then with a shrug of his shoulders, he mentioned, "I'm actually accomplishing a little work now. Nothing important. But at least I'm building a framework for everything that I'll accomplish in the next million years."

He meant it. When he spoke of such an enormous period of time, he did it with a pure and withering expertise. Better than almost anyone, Locke understood that frightening span of time. And with a devotion that only fanatics and madmen could embrace, he accepted his doom with a deep, pure, and utterly happy smile.

Finally, Washen asked, "What work are you doing?"

"Something small," he said.

She waited.

"I made a list," he reported. And of all things, he produced the huge wing of a copperfly—the first parchment used by the captains when they were marooned long ago on Marrow. "A little list."

"Good," she offered.

He unfolded the wing along its natural seams, bending it so that only his eyes could see words written by his own hand.

"What sort of list?" she inquired.

"Just some obvious questions," he replied.

"Such as?"

"Obvious questions," he repeated. He had his father's energetic eyes, but his silences reminded Washen of her own mother. Every few years, Washen again realized that Locke and his grandmother were rather similar creatures. Except that the old woman had been swallowed up by the exacting, impatient business of engineering— a rigid realm of perfect knowledge drawn across a thoroughly defined existence.

"What is obvious?" she pressed.

He said, "I'm sure you've asked these questions yourself. Probably thousands of times, I would think."

"Show me."

He considered the request, but then the hands began to refold the tough ruddy wing. "Not now."

"A glimpse, maybe?"

He shook his head, stowing the wing out of sight.

"Really," she pressed, "I would love to see what you've asked."

But her son was woven from sterner stuff. With a gentle shake of the head, he repeated, "You've asked these questions yourself. And if you haven't . . . well, Mother, then seeing them now isn't going to help much, is it . . . ?"

Eight

"AT LAST COUNT," said Pamir. And then he said nothing else, glancing toward Washen and the Master Captain before gazing out at the rest of his audience, his expression shifting from a veneer of professional focus into what seemed to be a rugged little smile. His big soul wore a matching voice, and after that pause was finished, he remarked, "But there is no last count. Or any first count, as it happens. Our data are so imprecise and subjective, our basis for opinions so badly defined, that if you wanted to fix a number to what we know, you're misleading yourself. Or you're some species of fool."

That declaration brought a sturdy silence, forcing others to peer into elaborate files that they had already digested, sometimes for more than a decade.

Washen knew exactly what Pamir planned to say, yet she felt the same surprise that she saw in the other faces. Years of expert research were being discounted, at least for this moment. It was a shock, and it made an old soul nervous, and to hide an anxious grin, she firmly clenched her jaw.

But the Master Captain nodded appreciatively. Sitting between her First and Second Chairs, she said, "Exactly," and an instant later, with a polish resulting from ages of determined practice, she steered the meeting back onto its expected rail. "But perhaps, Submaster Pamir. Perhaps you might give us a brief and tidy summary of these imprecise, subjective, and very foolish numbers."

"Of course, madam. Of course."

The room was not large, the furnishings were minimal, and until less than an hour ago, this space had been just an anonymous bubble tucked inside the bottom reaches of the ship's hull. Random protocols had chosen the room from a hundred thousand candidates. The audience had been ordered to come to the ship's bridge, and except for the top three captains, each had his journey interrupted by a single security officer wearing civilian garb. The officers brought them here, and until the meeting was finished and its participants had dispersed, the same officers were to remain inside an adjacent room, every last one of their nexuses disabled for the duration.

Secrecy was a reasonable precaution. But more to the point, secrecy was terribly easy to accomplish, which was why the Master had insisted on taking these effortless precautions.

"Besides," she had argued, "my experience is that if you dress someone up in the pomp and circumstance of deep secrets, he will have no choice but to consider himself as essential to some critical undertaking. Which isn't a bad thing. Making the soul feel as if it matters . . . well, that almost always helps you . . ."

Washen remembered the conversation, then Pamir's voice brought her back to the present.

With a firm but impressed voice, Pamir explained, "At last count, we have 306 separate accounts of life inside the Inkwell. Yes, that's two more accounts than you have in your files. Which is part of the reason we're here today. A good fat part, yes."

Faces stared him, a little anxious as they waited.

"About the other 304 accounts. Records. Legends, and what have you." He shrugged. "The commonality is the variation. We've always noticed that. How every species living near the Inkwell has a murky but distinctly individual vision of what lives inside the nebula. Plus this tendency, this odd reflex . . . of picturing their neighbor as being simply a larger, grander version of themselves."

The room was furnished with chairs grown for this occasion and a long table adorned with uneaten and entirely ignored foods. Beside the longest wall was a simple squidskin pane into which Pamir poured a variety of images. There were towering machines and beetly giants and ruby-colored lizards and apish creatures plainly evolved for zero-gee conditions, plus a wide assortment of starships from the Inkwell, and little shuttles, and probes too small to carry more than a lone human heart. To date, the Great Ship had collected accounts from a volume fifty light-years to a side. And even more impressive, the oldest accounts had been supplied not by witnesses or their descendants, but through the stolid work of paleo-scientists—researchers digging into buried homes and bunkers on worlds formerly inhabited by technological species. On three occasions, they uncovered files or stone-etched records, copies of which had been sent to the Great Ship in good faith; and according to the scientists who discovered the relics, each was at least as old as the human species.

"The pattern holds," Pamir assured. "Whatever lives inside the nebula, it shows itself to others as being rather like themselves."

Examples continued to parade across the squidskin.

"And this holds for the 305th example, too." Pamir triggered a deeply encrypted file, and the screen went blank except for a lone sun, ruddy and extremely small. "This M-class dwarf is a little less than two light-years from the outer margin of the dust. But unlike most of the local suns, it's cutting rapidly through the galactic plane."

Their perspective leaped closer. These images had been built year by year, a great rain of photons gathered and condensed by the giant mirrors, then refined by an army of single-minded AIs and gifted navigators. Not only had they drawn out every conceivable detail, they had also reached back along the star's course, pinpointing where the wandering mass had emerged from the black dust, and before that, where it had probably first burrowed into the Inkwell's body.

"It was a glancing collision," Pamir observed. "We still can see the dust roiling about. Where the sun reemerged into open space, for instance. Here."

From the audience, a male voice said, "Sir?"

Pamir was staring at the various images, the rough face concentrating with the same intensity shown by every other face. It was as if he had never seen these files. It was as if he was interested and completely at a loss for any opinion, and there was a brief pause where it seemed as if he hadn't heard the voice calling to him. But he had heard it. And without looking away from the squidskin, he calmly said, "Perri. What is it?"

Sitting in the front row of chairs was a boyish-faced man of no particular age. Perri was something of a minor celebrity. It was said, with good reason, that he knew the ship better than anyone but those who built it. He certainly knew its passageways and habitats better than any other living passenger, and probably more than anyone in the captains' ranks, too. He was smart and effortlessly charming. Among his detractors, who were many, there were those who claimed that Perri was nothing but a cheap thrill-seeker and a slippery manipulator. But when the Waywards appeared, he and his wife joined the rebellion. While his detractors hid or joined the enemy ranks, the self-taught expert on every function of the ship had proved instrumental in its salvation.

"That little sun has only the one planet," Perri remarked.

Pamir answered with a crisp, half-distracted nod.

"But of course, that could be tied to its velocity. I'm assuming some kind of near collision in its past. Maybe an ejection from a multistar system."

Again, the Submaster nodded.

"Which would have stripped away any other planets, I suppose. But what I'm seeing here, at first glance . . ."

His voice trailed away.

"By all means," Washen prodded.

The young face grinned, pleased to have the First Chair watching him. Then he gripped the hand of his wife—a beautiful, ancient woman named Quee Lee—and with a half laugh, he mentioned, "That's an oddly ordinary orbit for a single world. If there were other worlds in the past, I mean. And if they were stripped free of this little sun during some old mayhem."

Pamir grinned slightly. "Too far out, you mean?"

"And too circular," Perri added. "I'd expect something more elliptical. A scarred orbit, I'd want to see."

Again, the circumspect nod.

"And what about moons? It looks like some kind of gas giant. What is it? A jovian mass?"

"Nearly," said Pamir.

"Wouldn't it have retained at least its closer moons? But I don't see anything like that. Or rings. Just the one pretty sun and her faraway husband."

Quee Lee laughed softly, squeezing at the hand.

"There's other ways to accelerate an entire sun," Perri continued. "This could be ancient momentum stolen from its nursery. Seven or eight billion years ago, judging by the metal loads and the core profiles."

"Eight-point-two billion years old," Washen offered.

"Or it's from outside our galaxy. From one of those dwarf galaxies that splashed into the Milky Way, and over the last few billion years have shattered and fallen back into us again." He shrugged, and after a moment said, "Huh."

Quee Lee tugged on his arm. "What is it?"

"There's still another place where this planet looks wrong."

The observation wasn't his alone. Several other voices had already started to whisper about some of the more recent, more thorough observations.

"Too much helium," he declared. "By a long ways, I'd say."

Estimates were muttered; guesses were generated. The audience had enough experts present to come up with all kinds of explanations, a few of which might actually kiss what was true.

"An old gas giant should have pulled most of its helium into its core," he continued. "And those temperature profiles . . . well, they look awfully high. Which means something could have stirred up its interior, maybe. Brought the old helium rising to the surface again. Although that's a pretty cumbersome way to get this effect."

The Master had taken a mild interest in Perri. With a rumble, she said, "Name another, more elegant method."

"Nobody lifted the helium," he replied. "Instead, I'm guessing that they just stole away a fair fraction of the resident hydrogen." When he looked at the Master's golden face, Perri almost giggled. "But you know that already, madam. Sure you do. You just want to see what we can accomplish, stumbling over this little puzzle for ourselves."

Again, voices made guesses. Most of them approached the best, most recent estimates. The jovian mass had originally been half again larger, but some compelling force or bullying hand had peeled away the outermost layers of the atmosphere.

Quee Lee finally asked the obvious question:

"What is this 305th message? Does someone live on this gas giant? Or somewhere nearby?"

"As far as we can observe," said Pamir, "the system is utterly sterile."

Then after a deep breath, he added, "What we have found is something else entirely. Something we've been carrying with us for thousands of years now. An old transmission buried inside a million bottled transmissions—in an historical archive given to us to help pay for a few hundred passengers. The transmission was a distant radio squawk originating on a superterran world. The species had just developed high technologies. The transmission was typical of these sorts of things: a picture of themselves and their home, the sun and neighboring planets, and their relative position in the galaxy." The dusty data emerged beside the most recent images of the dead jupiter. "Nobody noticed. Until a few years ago, nobody even thought to look for this kind of clue. And you'll see why nobody imagined drawing a link between this sun and that old whisper. There were six planets, including the living one. And the gas giant had a big family of moons.

And even the sun itself was more massive than what we see today. Which implies that the same force that carried off the missing hydrogen also dismantled every other world. Every asteroid, and the entire cometary belt. And whatever that force was, it even managed to take a big spade to the red sun, digging out enough gas and plasma to make another world or two."

The room was silent, and respectful.

"A few hundred years before their sun entered the Inkwell, the vanished species broadcast their first message. They aimed at a likely sun, which was uninhabited, but the signal continued on for another few hundred light-years, and it was noticed at least once, and recorded, and we captains were shrewd enough or lucky enough to accept that kind of useless knowledge as a partial payment for some of our new passengers."

Perri asked, "What do the aliens say about the Inkwell?"

"Nothing," Pamir replied.

Then with a cold face and a wisp of anger, he added, "No, I may be misleading you. When I say that we have a 305th message, I mean that we don't have anything. Just silence. Just five worlds missing, plus a sentient species that's gone extinct, with no trace of any of these precious things after they passed through that damned cloud."

PAMIR SAT ON his chair, one long leg thrown over the other.

After a moment, Washen rose, and with a relaxed smile, she said, "I'm sure you know enough to guess our general plan. Each of you has at least one skill that makes you valuable. Many of you have served the ship as ambassadors or xenobiologists. Others have different talents, and hopefully, new perspectives." She nodded in Perri's direction before adding, "There is a mission first planned long ago. From a much larger pool of potential candidates, we've chosen you. Just in the last few days, as it happens. Your participation is asked for but not demanded. But I will tell you: If you decide to stay on-board the ship, you must move to secure quarters until this mission is finished or until we've lost all interest in this undertaking."

Several dozen faces nodded in weak agreement.

The squidscreen brightened with a flash. Suddenly everyone was staring at the interior of a sealed and heavily guarded berth inside Port Alpha. Filling the berth was a set of enormous engines, fusion rockets spiked with antimatter and the power yields increased by every possible trick of hyperfiber containment and quantum manipulations. The engines were attached to cavernous fuel tanks ready to hold millions of tons of metallic hydrogen, and above the giant tanks was what passed for the streakship's prow—a blunt but elegant arch of high-grade hyperfiber, designed to be reconfigured at will, then braced in twenty different ways to protect the ship from every impact. If there were living quarters, they were invisible, tucked between the fat tanks in a slot that looked too tiny to give anyone more than the barest legroom.

Washen summarized the ship's history. She listed five past missions and every one of its important successes, and because there has never been a crew without a feel for luck or its absence, she failed to mention the little tragedies that had kept two other missions from being total successes.

"Over the last nine decades," she continued, "this particular streakship has been refitted and repaired. What isn't new is nearly new, or better than new. There probably aren't three vessels of this mass that can move any faster. Not in this galaxy, at least. At better than two-thirds the speed of light, you will be able to beat us to the Inkwell by more than ten years. Critical years, I should add."

After a moment, Washen said, "Questions."

Hands rose high.

One woman asked, "Who's our captain?"

"I am." Pamir gave a half nod. "I've got experience in small starships, and I can represent the ship with full authority."

It was momentous news. The idea that the Second Chair would leave on any mission underscored its importance. Unless this was a demotion, of course. Pamir was a stubborn soul, and in the universe of gossip, he was always butting heads with the Master Captain.

Washen pointed at a fresh hand. "Yes, Quee Lee?"

The woman smiled politely, then with an honest distaste, she mentioned, "We seem to be a rather narrow group."

Judging by the nods, the question swirled in every head.

She was a beautiful woman, Asian in the old ways, born on the ancient Earth in times that no one else could remember. Quee Lee lifted her gaze as if finding something of interest in the ceiling, and she said to nobody in particular, "All of us are human."

Washen and Pamir conspicuously said nothing.

The Master rose to her feet in a slow, powerful motion that ended with a deep sigh and a shake of the head. Snowy white hair framed the rounded face. The face acquired a less honest disgust, as if some deep voice were reminding her that these were new times, and she needed to bow to the newborn conventions.

"It was our decision," she reported. "For good solid reasons, the three of us decided to send only a single species."

Nobody spoke.

While the Master rose, Washen had sat back down again. Now she looked at the others, saying with the crisp voice of an order, "Ask it."

They hesitated.

"We told you," she continued. "Three hundred and six messages, to date. Which means that there's still one communication that we haven't quite managed to tell you about."

Again, she said, "Ask it."

"Okay," Perri said. "Where did this last message come from?"

Washen hesitated.

It was the Master Captain's right and honor to announce, "The message came directly from the Inkwell. Of course."

Silence descended.

Then she added, "What we have received is a brief greeting, plus a chart giving us the safest course to one of the nearest warm worlds—"

"Who are they?" Perri interrupted.

The breach in etiquette went unmentioned. Quietly, the Master warned, "We don't know anything that is certain. Not about what lives inside the ink, we don't. But the face that it showed us, and the body . . . well, she looked rather like a human person . . . as odd or ordinary as that sounds . . ."

Nine

WHOEVER THE BUILDERS had been and whatever their high purpose, they possessed a considerable fondness for rivers. The ship's rock-and-hyperfiber crust was laced with intricate long caverns and winding tunnels perfectly suited for the simple purpose of letting methane or ammonia, silicones or liquid water flow free across their floors, pooling now and again to create the lakes and little seas, then pouring over some brink or lip before continuing on their poetic journey. The first explorers found abundant stores of ready ice, muscular reactors to supply heat, and banks of environmental controls to salt and sweeten the molten treasures. Pumps and attached conduits waited at the bottom of every deep hole, having no obvious purpose but to lift those rivers high again. On occasion, two or more caverns joined together, entirely different chemistries mixing, life-forms from opposite ends of the galaxy suddenly sharing the same narrow channel. One great room welcomed a dozen major rivers, plus at least thirty lesser streams. It was a round room beneath a high-domed ceiling of mirrored hyperfiber, the nearly flat floor made of gravel and river mud and great expanses of tired water. At eighty kilometers in diameter, the room was vast enough to feel worldly, particularly at its center. The dying rivers gradually spread out and merged, becoming a single flow bearing down on a simple hyperfiber throat—a seemingly bottomless pit set at the precise center of the room, one fat kilometer wide and leading into a maze of pumps and busy filters. Engineers had constructed a series of platforms around the hole, and billions of passengers and crew had taken the time to stand on one of those vantage points, watching an ocean's worth of water plunge into a blackness, screaming as it fell, the thunder loud enough to kill a human's ears, leaving him or her deaf for as long as an hour after each little visit.

Washen went away happy and deaf. Her only company on the platform had been a school of gillbabies who barely noticed the spectacle below. Far more remarkable was the sight of the First Chair, and one after another, in ways less than subtle, they had conspired to make sonar images of themselves standing beside her famous sound-wake.

Washen left her admirers, a little cap-car swiftly carrying her upstream. Low patches of soggy ground and tangled marshland emerged from the slowing, shallowing waters. Individual rivers defined themselves, each of the large flows shackled by banks of dried mud and determined tufts of vegetation. Every wood had its color, its distinct and illuminating shape. Life from dozens of worlds lived together in this great room. Every day, one or two rivers would flood, spilling out into their neighbors' channels. Dry places would be swept bare, new seeds germinating from the raw mud. A novel current would cut a hundred new holes, then fill the old holes with suffocating silts, while odd fish and things not at all like fish would colonize the fresh deep water. In the entire galaxy, there was probably no little place with so many species pushed so close together. Every day, the local ecology shifted ten times, and little species went extinct, and new species were brought down on rivers that could be ten thousand kilometers long, and in the quiet backwaters, by means natural and otherwise, new and entirely novel species would slip into existence.

Upon one of the taller, more stable banks, where a spine of bluish trees stood above an earthly green tangle of corn, someone had constructed a tiny cabin. Even though she knew its approximate location, Washen could not see the cabin on her first pass. She smiled without smiling—a tight, uncomfortable grin betraying a long-building unease—then she turned, coming back again and setting down on the most distant available slip of brown goo and Timothy grass.

Washen sat inside her cap-car, one hand holding the other. When her ears began to heal—when she could hear the squawks and opera songs of birds—she climbed out, stretched for a moment, and began to walk. After a little while, she could hear her boots making the mud squish and the soft rumbling of the falls, twenty kilometers from this nameless place and dampened by antinoise baffles, yet still, astonishingly loud. Then she heard the closer waters moving over flat banks of warm muck. A great long reef of titanium shells lay on her right, and to the left, in a different kind of water, a whale-sized fish lay in the chocolate shallows, basking in the illusory sun.

The cabin was tiny and artfully placed. Washen didn't notice it until she saw the woman sitting in the open door. A tiny and apparently frail creature, by all signs, she seemed to be sleeping. Her chair was some kind of puffer fish, inflated before death and probably not too uncomfortable to sit on, and her clothes were simple and rugged, dyed the same silvery blue of the sky to help her hide from the fish that she hunted for food.

As close to silent as possible, Washen crept forward.

Like a portrait painted in some impoverished age, the sleeping woman sat motionless. Washen thought of a peasant girl, half-starved and possibly dying of some ancient blight. With every step, the creature looked less human. She was so small and emaciated, and her skin had a thinness that Washen had never seen in another person. Stare hard at her face, and the skull seemed to emerge. And it was only the thinnest sketch of a skull, tiny teeth, and big eye sockets—human always, but in a thousand subtle ways, wrong.

Again, Washen took a step.

The woman did not stir. She didn't even seem to inhale, which meant that she had been holding her breath, waiting to speak. The thin, wide, and wise mouth parted slightly, and the words leaked out before the eyelids finally rose.

"Is it time?" she asked. "Already?"

"Yes, Mere," said Washen, her own voice sounding a little bit sorry in ears rebuilt just moments ago.

WHEN THE SHIP was barely two hundred centuries into its voyage—when Washen was a midlevel captain finally beginning to show her promise—the original First Chair came to her with an assignment.

"I am honored," Washen declared.

"That's foolish to say, and a little funny," Miocene replied. "You don't know what I will ask you to do."

But in her entire life, Washen had spoken to this great woman only at the Master's banquet, and then only in the most glancing fashion. She felt honored, and she refused to backtrack from her declaration. "If I can help the ship, in any way, madam. In any little fashion."

"Perhaps you should help me," Miocene rumbled. A tall, narrow-faced soul famous for her personal drive and her unmatched talents as the Master's best hand, she said, "I have a problem. Not a large problem, but rather difficult. I require a captain who can give an honest impression, and afterward, my request will remain with the three of us."

"The three of us?"

"Or just you and me." The woman laughed without real humor, adding, "Everything depends on your decision. Unless I don't particularly like what you decide."

The less-than-large problem involved a peculiar starship. It was tiny and powerful—one of the original streakships, according to its designation—but it was also poorly maintained and heavily damaged. Someone with minimal talents had repaired it and refueled its powerful engines. The ship's AI had also suffered crippling abuse, leaving it stupid and almost entirely ignorant about its own past. According to the fragmentary logs, the little ship was meant to ferry a group of wealthy colonists to the Great Ship. Indeed, there were more than twenty names with empty apartments still waiting for their arrival, paid for by a transfer of wealth from a very distant human world. But the names and the people attached had never reached their destination. According to the AI, a chunk of cometary material had breached the hyperfiber armor, exploding into a bubble of super-heated plasmas and radiation, shrapnel scattering backward at better than half the speed of light.

Everyone on board the ship was instantly killed.

But as it happened, one of the women was a little bit pregnant—an embryo sleeping in suspended animation inside her patient uterus. It was a common tradition among colonists: arrive at your new home with a child ready to be born. The intended mother died, but while searching for survivors, the brutalized AI discovered a single entity still alive, barely, entombed inside a mangled, now-headless corpse.

Using its last autodoc, the AI managed to coax the corpse back into a mindless life, saving the embryo. With most of its intellect stripped away and no clear instructions, the machine decided to do its best to help its only companion. A few months later, the girl was born inside a tiny volume of warm, barely breathable air, and she grew up on a diet of recycled meats and bone meal, nothing to drink but tainted water and sometimes her own diluted urine. The AI couldn't directly communicate with her. It was too mangled and far too busy keeping the derelict ship functioning. Save for the slowly changing stars visible through the diamond ports, there was nothing to see. The girl grew up in an abysmally impoverished environment, suffering constantly, nothing to touch but the close cold walls and her own miserable self. So she did what was natural: in many ways, and for every good reason, the poor creature fell into a deep and simple insanity.

The comet's impact had pushed the starship off course. Moving faster than the Great Ship, it slipped past unnoticed, its arrow-straight trajectory carrying it deeper into the galaxy, past countless suns before it moved back out to a place rather near the ship's future course.

According to this very unlikely account, the AI pilot found a pair of close-orbit suns and the living world that revolved around both; and after some lovely or very lucky navigation, it managed to burn the last of its fuel, bleeding off most of its momentum, then jettisoning its lone passenger, sending her down onto the world's largest continent.

With an immortal's constitution, the woman survived both the impact and several temporary deaths. Then for the next few thousand years, she lived among the resident aliens—small humanoids called the Tila. In the early years, she was worshiped as a god. The Tila taught her their language and culture, and she played an occasional role in their development. During her long life, she watched as her foster species built their civilization, gradually learning about the universe and their world and the two suns that kissed one another in their bright beautiful sky.

"So how did you acquire your name?" Washen asked, during the first interview. She said the name twice: first as the Tila supposedly had, then as a human might. "Mere," she said. "It means small. Tiny, and unremarkable."

"I am," the tiny woman said of herself. "Small. Tiny. And not all that remarkable."

Tutors had taught this little creature the human tongue. But Mere spoke the alien language with much more skill and an unconscious ease, and she moved her limbs in ways no human ever did. She could have been raised by another species. There were a few examples on record, although nothing as lengthy or as unplanned as Mere's supposed life.

"You say you were a god to them," Washen pointed out. "Why would anyone name their god Mere?"

"Because I wasn't much of a deity, they learned. Soon enough."

A considerable sadness showed in her face and body, but the expressions weren't quite like what a normal human would display. Starvation at birth and an alien diet of odd amino acids and the wrong minerals could conceivably produce a body like hers. But Miocene's fear, and now Washen's fear, was that this was not a genuine human, but instead another kind of creature wearing some elaborate camouflage. Washen's assignment was to discern what was true, or at least to give her best guess. This little whiff of a body and the soul inside . . . were they really as simple and strange as they pretended to be?

Perhaps Mere understood the importance of the interview. Or maybe she wanted to lend her false story another set of telling details. Either way, she promised the young captain, "The Tila think quite differently from the way you think."

"Do they?"

"And I think rather differently from the way you or they think. I don't have a Tilan brain. I don't have its skills. But judging by everything that the other giant woman said to me—"

"Miocene?"

"I think that you . . . meaning your species . . . I think humans entertain some odd little notions about the universe."

"Little?" Washen laughed softly. "What do you mean?"

"Everything that is possible," said Mere in a flat, certain voice, "is inevitable. Everything that can happen has no choice but to occur."

"Is that what the Tilan believe?"

"It's what they know, and it's my firm, sure belief." The big eyes gazed off into the far corners of the room. A prison cell, really, but infinitely more comfortable than the tiny habitat that somebody had added to her battered old starship. "The Tilan mind is very sensitive to the quantum effects of the universe. Every motion they make, every little thing that they see, is shrouded in a cloud of possibility. Life moves in all directions at once. Life always persists, in at least one thread of reality. And the universe—the real universe—encompasses too many realities to count."

"But I know that," Washen remarked, almost casually. Then with a quiet calculated laugh, she added, "We have several theories of the universe. Two or three of them believe in the many-worlds scenario."

Mere laughed at her—Tilan fashion. Then with a tone dismissive in both languages, she said, "You have the mathematics. But do you believe the great equations?"

"Believe in them how?"

"Do you apply them to all aspects of your life?"

"No," Washen had to say.

"Does any human that you know . . . or any other organism, for that matter . . . do any of them believe in this infinite realm . . . ?"

"On occasion. Yes."

"That's worse than never," was the little woman's verdict. Then after a long, thoughtful silence, she said, "We had two suns. Close enough that they touched one another, like lovers."

It happened on occasion. Twin stars were born close together, spinning fast around their common center of gravity.

"Our suns were too close," she whispered.

Washen waited, saying nothing.

"I watched it," Mere remarked. "With thousands of years to fill, I could study the suns' intricate motions. I could measure the changes coming. There was a great drought on my world, and then after that, a long period of endless rains. The twin suns were dancing too close, their atmospheres touching, and their momentum was changing."

"A chaotic situation," Washen allowed. "There are harmonic circumstances, and gravity waves. Sometimes the suns can hang apart for long times, then quite suddenly, in the course of a few centuries—"

"My world was dying."

For the first time, Washen moved liked a Tilan might. Miocene had built a small vocabulary of meaningful gestures, and now she used one of them in a bid to show understanding and compassion.

The motion pleased the strange little woman. She sighed, smiled like a Tilan, then like a human, and with a quiet little voice, she reported, "My people attempted to save themselves. There were plans to build colonies on the outer worlds, and there were larger plans to pull our world into a wider orbit. But then they heard the signals from this ship. They saw your invitations to join the voyage around the galaxy. You were already past us, but they'd found my old starship moving like a comet around our suns, and after generating a series of entirely random events—allowing the many-worlds to decide everyone's inevitable fate—they decided to forgo all of their great projects."

Washen watched the big sorry eyes.

"They refitted the starship. But instead of using it to help save themselves, they put me on board and pointed me toward you. Because I was the same species as you. Because they were thankful for the little help that I had given them. Because in this one thin river of an existence, they wanted me to reach my intended destination. At long last."

"You came willingly?" Washen asked.

"No." Mere made the confession with anger and a wrenching grief. "No, I am not that good at being Tilan. I wish I had been. But no."

Washen nodded, and waited.

After a little while, Mere said, "I fought them. I fought as hard as I could. But they shattered both of my legs and both of my arms, and while I was helpless . . . while my body was healing itself, and my ship was preparing to leave . . . they said to me, 'Don't be selfish, Mere. It isn't your right. It isn't even possible. Even if we wish, we can't destroy any little portion of our destiny.'"

THE INTERIOR OF the cabin was a single room, comfortably snug and minimally furnished. Mere served her guest a small meal of cold fish and an unnamed tea that left both of their mouths stained a vivid sour purple. Conversation came and went. When they spoke, they usually concerned themselves with trivial matters: the weather on the delta; the whereabouts of an odd species; the burdens in being the new First Chair. And then after a longer pause, Washen looked at her hostess with a mixture of sorrow and compassion, promising her, "If you would rather, stay home. I can ask someone else to do this. If you want, recommend somebody. You know the candidates better than I do."

Mere rose and walked over to the only window, looking out across the flat tired water. Then touching the window frame, she caused the river to vanish. Even sitting, Washen was tall enough to see another river pushing through an entirely different time, and the barest glimpse told her enough.

Tila.

Ages ago, Miocene had approached a young captain. "I want to know what you think about this strange little creature," she had explained. "Learn whatever you can. Believe or dismiss what you want of her stories. Then come to me and give me your final report."

"I believe her," was Washen's verdict.

Miocene seemed to nod agreeably. But then she asked, "What do you believe?"

"Mere is human. She was born in horrific conditions. The first few thousand years of life were intellectually and emotionally impoverished, then she suddenly found herself surrounded by aliens. Which is why she doesn't seem entirely human. She isn't. The Tila did their best, I suppose . . . but her half-starved brain didn't finish a normal, healthy development—"

"I never bothered," Miocene remarked. "Did you look for the Tila?"

"Of course."

"What did you find?"

Washen hesitated for a moment. "Back along her ship's course," she admitted, "there is a solar system. But there is only one sun. Two smaller suns coalesced sometime in the last few decades, and what remains is very hot and blue. And what would have been the Tilan home world is now a superheated Venus-class world."

"And did you show her this news?"

"Yes."

Miocene squinted at a point just above Washen's head. "What was her response?"

"Misery," said Washen. "Despair. But also, a kind of resignation."

"Because her homeland died in just this one little existence," the Submaster offered. "She's human, but she's Tilan, too. Wouldn't you say so?"

In the present, Washen muttered a few words under her breath.

Mere turned, and with a smile that took both of them by surprise, she asked, "What are you thinking about, madam?"

"The past," Washen allowed. "I'm talking to a dead woman."

Mere seemed to understand. She nodded and took one last long look at the vanished river. Then she touched the frame again, causing the window to rapidly jump from one alien world to another.

"Why wouldn't I accept this assignment?" she inquired, her tone more amused than offended. "And how could I ask anyone else to take my place? This is my river to navigate to the best of my ability. My destiny to live through and die inside."

Washen didn't reply.

For a moment, she was standing with Miocene again. Again, she was explaining, "The woman is exactly who she seems to be. Human or Tila, I believe her. And she isn't any kind of threat to the ship, either."

Miocene had laughed with a harsh, amused tone.

"Of course she's no threat," the woman cackled. "We can watch her. We can let her sit in prison forever or kick her back into space. My dear. You misunderstood your assignment."

Appalled, Washen asked, "What was my assignment?"

"To assess her abilities," Miocene reported, subtly changing the original wording. "She isn't human, or Tilan either. Have you noticed? Maybe it's the starved brain, or maybe it's her very peculiar upbringing. But she seems remarkably plastic when it comes to behaviors, and thoughts."

Miocene had already digested Washen's final report, or she had come to the same conclusions.

"What I want to know is this," the original First Chair had said. "Can we find some way for that odd little creature to help our wonderful ship?"

IN THE PRESENT, Washen stood beside Mere, laying a warm hand on the bony little shoulder.

"I've infiltrated dozens of worlds," the tiny creature muttered. "Have you ever been disappointed in my work?"

"Never," Washen admitted. Then with the next breath, she mentioned, "But this isn't a simple world, and we know almost nothing going in."

Mere shrugged and giggled.

"Every day, we die," she reminded Washen. Then she reached up, patting the hand that was set on her shoulder. "And every day, against incredible odds, we find a thousand ways to live."

Ten

A DOZEN LASERS threw their malevolent best at the target. Born to defend the ship against collisions, their purpose was to shatter and melt, pulverize and dissolve objects as large as small moons. More than adequate for this tiny assignment, they focused their rage on a single body that was moving overhead in a long lazy orbit. What they hit was a mass of Ganymede ice—a highly compressed form of solid water waiting inside an elegantly shaped cone of woven diamond. The first fierce blasts compressed, then superheated the exposed surface. By carefully changing the sequences and frequencies of the coherent light, the lasers created an endless explosion of plasma and white-hot steam, plus a bone-busting acceleration as the thrust increased and the target's mass fell away. The streakship rode on the tip of the diamond cone. The assisted launch saved fuel and coddled the high-output engines. Without question, it made for a spectacular show, which was not a small matter with the crew and passengers watching. According to popular opinion, this was the most important emissary mission in the last hundred thousand years. Representatives of the Great Ship were bound for the Inkwell and its mysterious inhabitants. So important was this adventure that the Master's own Second Chair was in command. Speaking from his seat on the little ship's bridge, almost smothered beneath a silky crush-web, Pamir grunted the word, "Done," as the last of the water exploded into space. Then a second onslaught of light arrived—new frequencies battering and boiling the diamond cone, delivering another potent push—and afterward, he said, "Done," again, that sketch of cultured jewelry evaporating in his wake, a cooling mist of ionized carbon lending its mass to the cause.

For a little while, the streakship coasted ahead at a fat fraction of lightspeed. Pamir and his AIs made triple sure that they had cleared the debris field. Sometimes in the chaotic mayhem of high-velocity impacts, shards of the diamond or ice could be kicked out ahead. Disasters were unlikely, but why invite any chance? Once the appropriate checks had been made, Pamir told both his small crew and vast audience, "Light the torch." And an instant later, with a clean and fiercely hot and nearly invisible blast, the swift ship started to gain velocity again, yanking itself up toward better than two-thirds lightspeed.

The Inkwell lay ahead. A black splash against the far-off stars had become a great ocean, bottomless and vast. More than three light-years of nearly empty space lay between them and the margins of the nebula. But even at their incredible velocity, the emissaries wouldn't reach their final destination until the Great Ship was approaching the first waves of dust and cold gas. They were plunging toward a target that was barely visible, trusting their own thin armor and defenses as well as the decency of unknown souls.

Whenever the Master spoke in public, she reminded her audience, "Nebulas are not clouds. They aren't as dense as the thinnest air, even. In fact, according to the course that we've mapped for ourselves, the Inkwell isn't going to be a tenth as difficult as diving through someone's Oort cloud."

Once Pamir was gone, the Master gave a good smart speech. She had written it herself, without input from Washen or her acting Second Chair. Every public channel was hers, and her performance was both perfect and minimal. Aasleen was the acting Second Chair. Sitting on the bridge with Washen, the chief engineer grinned with pleasure and astonishment. "I couldn't do this," she admitted. "This kind of purposeful sweet noise. I couldn't make it. Not so that humans would believe me, I couldn't."

"You're too literal," Washen offered. "Too tied to your numbers."

The woman appreciated what sounded like a compliment. "Oort clouds are easy," she stated. "A light-month thick at the very worst. But we're going to be pushing through this ink for the next thirty-plus years. Without pause. Without any chance to rest and make thorough repairs."

Washen looked at her friend and colleague. They had lived together on Marrow, where Aasleen's talents helped the captains survive and then prosper. Worry had its good reasons. When Aasleen saw bad things looming, Washen knew better than to shake her head, or remind her good friend about all those good smart ways in which the ship was stronger now.

Their shields had been enhanced, and the hull was almost entirely repaired, and there were nearly twice as many lasers as before, all deeply embedded in bunkers and sprinkled across the face of that deep, dirty-mirror armor. They were also making endless adjustments to their course. Occasionally one of their vast engines would fire, for a heartbeat or for a day, nudging the ship just enough to avoid some near collision still five or ten years in the future. Every moment, the sprawling fields of mirrors and radio dishes were peering deeper into the cold dust, constantly refining maps whose accuracy and deep reach would have been impossible only a hundred years ago. And they were getting what seemed to be help—advice and encouragement from the souls living within that great darkness.

"Remember this," said the Master, in conclusion. Then the bright face smiled with an expression radiating confidence and a seamless faith. "For more than a thousand centuries, this ship and crew have traveled our galaxy. We have met thousands of species, many of which live with us now. The combined experience and technological prowess of this ensemble belongs to us. This is why we offer berths for those who could give us knowledge: We want to learn. All of our species wish to excel. And when remarkable circumstances come to face us, we bring insights and tricks that no single species can match."

Beside the projected Master, live-time images of the streakship were constantly displayed—a scorching point of light almost lost against the blackness. What was infinitely larger and more impressive was the cloud stretching out behind it. Water and carbon formed a neatly defined jet that would retain its basic shape for several years. Trailing after the streakship, the jet would eventually collide with the Inkwell, spreading and cooling further, adding a breath or two to its phenomenal and very thin mass.

"Of course this isn't just an engineering problem," Aasleen admitted, her voice quiet and a little hopeful. "The polyponds are another conundrum entirely. Unless they happen to be the solution for everything, of course."

That's what the Inkwell inhabitants called themselves.

Polyponds.

Washen nodded agreeably. On a secure channel, using an entire mirror field to serve as her own eyes, she peered into the warm jet of exhaust. Nothing was visible. Even knowing there was something to see didn't help her eyes find it. She stared and stared, and after a while, she mentioned to Aasleen, "You did a marvelous job with the camouflage. Regardless what you think."

Her friend laughed quietly, appreciatively.

"We have every reason to be proud," the Master told her ship.

And billions of faces, in homes and long avenues, nodded happily or showed some equivalent expression of faith, or hope, or at the very least, simple wishful thinking.

THE FEF WERE small creatures—at least among organic species—and until the Wayward War, they were rarely listed among the first ranks of passengers. Their narrow bodies sported three pairs of limbs. The first and third pairs served as legs and stubby arms, while the longer middle pair, tipped with deft hands, reached upward. Between those middle arms was an eye pod affording views in all directions. Their omnivorous mouths were in front, while various ears were tucked into the gaps between the bony plates that had once protected their long, exposed backs. They began as one of several intelligent and technologically adept species on their home world—a light-gravity body some twenty thousand light-years behind them. As the Great Ship approached, every species on that world had seen the stunning images and heard the purposeful boasts roaring across the electromagnetic spectrum. But for reasons of culture and politics, and status and finance, only the fef showed serious interest in joining the grand voyage.

To pay for their passage, they borrowed starship plans broadcast by the Great Ship and improved upon them, building a fleet of fat round hyperfiber vessels inside which were tanks filled with liquid hydrogen as well as a single small-mass black hole, heavily charged and suspended inside an elaborate cage. The captains had no compelling need for the hydrogen, since those frigid lakes couldn't fuel the Great Ship's engines for more than a few breaths. And while tiny black holes had their uses—in research and communication, mostly—there were already plenty of the dangerous little monsters waiting in inventory. But there were only a few of the fef on board each vessel, and they were pleasant enough, and by evidence of their work, they were gifted tinkerers. Gleefully, they accepted spartan quarters in a deep, lower-gravity district, easily blending into the multitude of odd species. And that was twenty thousand light-years ago, which meant sixty thousand years in the past. In the ages since, those few thousand immigrants had slowly and patiently prospered, making their livelihoods by repairing nonvital systems that the ship's engineers couldn't bother with. And in certain cases—if there was a burning hurry, or if certain permission forms hadn't been filed—fefs would do their usual excellent work in the briefest possible time. In the dark, preferably, since they were a nocturnal species. And for a considerable fee. But they never discussed their clients, and they continued to live quietly among the multitude of aliens, shoving their profits into the acquisition of new quarters where their children began raising their own families—a few colonists becoming a nation numbering more than half a billion souls.

"Your greatness," the leading fef declared, standing at the entranceway to the repair camp. Built with diamond and furnished sparingly, the facility was a chain of transparent bubbles set on the open hull, the lighting reduced to a comfortable gloom. High-grav braces helped him stand as he proclaimed, "It is an honor to have you with us, your splendor."

"Thank you," Washen replied, offering a tidy little bow.

"Thank you for coming," the leader muttered, speaking through his translator. "May we quench a thirst? Stuff a stomach? Or perhaps, we could sing to you—"

"Nothing. Thank you."

"If you need—"

"I will demand."

"And we will serve you, your majesty."

Twenty months had passed since the launching of the streakship. The Inkwell covered most of the sky now—a featureless ebony face betraying nothing to human eyes. What was bright and spectacular was the occasional flash of light when a laser struck some mountain-sized hazard, followed by the colorful aurora as the shields collected the ionized debris, pulling the ionized wreckage across the sky and down to where elaborate, heavily armored facilities collected the material, sorting it by its elemental composition, and then sending the treasures to storage or selling them to some critical industry.

The leading fef bent in the middle, two pairs of feet moving together, lifting his eye pod closer to the First Chair's face. "I hope that I have not stolen you away from any vital work, your marvel."

Washen shrugged. "For the moment, no."

"But they refuse to leave the work site," the alien persisted. "I know they have permission to be there. But we have goals, and timetables, and if these deep cavities are not patched soon—"

"These are minor problems," she interrupted.

Nothing was minor to a fef. With a suddenly tense voice, he replied, "Madam. I know they have your permission to tour the deep cavities. That is why I contacted you before anyone. My team and I have done no work for the last thirty-two days. Perhaps these cavities mean something, but if that is the case, we must be found other assignments. Work is the heart of existence, madam. As long as they are down there—"

"You have no heart. I understand."

The fef lowered his eye pod, and after some considerable thought, he decided to say nothing more.

"Perhaps I should speak with them," Washen offered.

"If you could, please. Madam. All of us would be most appreciative."

She looked across the facility. Hundreds of fef were showing their thanks by rocking side to side, and among them were their robots—thousands of insectlike bodies that made, what was for them, a kowtowing motion.

"Where is your access tunnel?" the Submaster inquired.

"This way," the leader said. "I will take you down myself."

Quietly, Washen said, "Thank you. But no."

Directly overhead, a substantial piece of ice exploded, obliterated by a nanosecond pulse of UV light.

"Stay here," she ordered. "This work is all mine."

THE COMET THAT struck during the war was relatively large and massive—thirty kilometers across and dense as new snow wrapped around chunks of rock and gravel. It had little velocity of its own, but the ship's velocity had provided a fantastic amount of kinetic energy. Any normal world built of rock and warm iron would have been gutted, but the hull was made from more stubborn stuff. Heat and momentum were channeled into the hidden dimensions and speculative realms. The damage was more extensive than it should have been, but only because this was very close to where an even larger impact had occurred billions of years ago. A moon-sized object had smacked into the ship, creating a deep blast cone as well as a necklace of tiny, relatively trivial cavities. The first Remoras had patched the surface with the best available grades of hyperfiber. The fef were supposed to finish the repair begun one hundred thousand years ago, leaving the hull as sturdy as it might have been ten minutes after its unimaginable creation.

Built for fefs, the cap-car felt tiny to Washen, and its air was thick with carbon dioxide and water vapor. Every breath was warm enough to remind her of every sauna that she had ever endured. And the car was swift, plunging to its destination, time passing too quickly to allow an overworked captain to steal more than a moment or two of sleep.

With a hiss, the hatch dissolved.

The air beyond was thinner and very dry. What might have been a narrow fissure had been enlarged, several meters of wounded hyperfiber removed to build a passageway as well as stripping away everything that was even a little weak. What remained was a long half-lit tunnel, gray walls looking like mirrors where they had already been prepared for the final repair. In time, the atmosphere would be yanked away and million of liters of fresh, high-grade hyperfiber would pour into the emptiness. What was new would effortlessly merge with the rest of the hull, and once cured, only the most persistent expert armed with delicate sensors would notice the seams left behind.

That was one of the miracles of hyperfiber—its endless capacity to accept every tiny graft and every giant patch.

Washen walked patiently if not quite slowly. After a long lazy turn to the left, the passageway twisted to the right again, and with that turn she began to hear the quiet, smooth, and occasionally human sound of voices.

Short of the chamber, she paused.

"But if you consider," said a voice. What followed was one of the dense AI languages, rapid and efficient and invented for no other purpose than to plumb the high realms of mathematics.

"Consider this," a second voice responded.

The next dose of machine talk was louder and even quicker. A nexus translated for Washen, and three other nexuses did their best to explain what she was hearing. But one after another, her devices reached the limits of their ability. They apologized, or they simply fell silent, too embarrassed to speak.

A third voice said, "Thank you."

And then a fourth voice, very familiar, said, "Why won't you come the rest of the way, Mother? Don't worry, you aren't interrupting."

The First Chair stepped into the chamber.

What was tiny on every official map was surprisingly large to the eye. The chamber was a hundred meters across, and someone other than the fef had positioned the bright lights and changed the air to approximate earthly tastes. Wearing rubber bodies and archaic clothes, the AIs sat on convenient rises and knolls, ignoring the sharp, mirror-bright edges. Locke was the only figure sitting on a flat surface, legs crossed and the remains of a dried hammerwing in his lap. With a charming little smile, he asked, "Are they growing impatient?"

"A little," his mother allowed. "They have their hyperfiber ready to pour. In case you want to be entombed here for all time."

Some of the more literal-minded AIs did the lightspeed equivalent of a flinch. Then everyone was laughing, and with an easy amiability, one of the rubber bodies jumped to its feet.

"We shall leave," the AI announced.

"But first," said Washen. And when everyone was staring at her, she asked, "Why here? What does this place tell you?"

"It was my idea," Locke confessed.

She wasn't surprised.

"A different realm to jog our creativity," reported the standing AI. The face was female and wrinkled, like the sages in ancient times. But the voice was young like a child's. "We have questions to consider, puzzles to solve."

"New questions?" Washen inquired.

"From a new vantage point," the machine replied, "every question is new and intriguing."

Locke was climbing to his feet. A tiny Wayward pouch lay beside him, and as he reached for the leather straps, his mother saw something familiar.

"May I?" she asked.

He pretended not to understand. And then he considered refusing her request, or at least asking her if he possessed that freedom. But no, he decided to hand over the tightly folded copperwing. And like every son sensitive to a mother's opinion, he mentioned again, "These are simple, obvious questions."

"I know."

"Things to consider."

"Quiet," Washen advised.

When she held the copperwing in her hands, her hands shook. Washen noticed the shaking with amusement, and she found herself taking a couple deep breaths before unfolding what had already become old and threadbare.

By hand, Locke had written his questions, starting at one edge of the rounded wing and working down.

"Does the Great Ship have a destination?" he had written. "And if so, did human beings screw things up when they took it for themselves?"

Washen's face went rigid, showing the tiniest nod.

"Is the ship supposed to be going somewhere specific?" Locke asked aloud, with a quiet little voice.

"What could be its destination?" she read aloud. "And does it involve the prisoner at the center of Marrow?"

She read, "Or is the ship making a flight of escape instead? And if so, have humans screwed that up?"

She looked at her son.

Locke said nothing, a wary grin trying to hide.

She read more questions. There were dozens of them, and as promised, nothing was authentically new here. How many times had she rolled these same matters around in her head? But in the course of a busy year, Washen didn't invest more than the occasional dreamy moment considering these impregnable, unmanageable mysteries.

"What if the Great Ship began its voyage on course?" Locke had written on a later date. The letters were clearer, the ink showing a hint of shine that was peculiar to the juice of a berryblack. "And what if its trajectory had been distorted by the moon-sized bolide?"

She looked up again.

"Good question," was her verdict. "Is that why you're down here? For inspiration?"

Locke flashed a smile.

"There's more," he mentioned. "Flip the wing over."

With respect for the long-dead appendage, she turned the wing with careful hands.

"If the Great Ship was off course," she read aloud, "could we humans and the Wayward War be part of some grand plan? And what if this grand plan has managed to put the ship back on the right road again?"

She nodded, and breathed.

Then she read the final lines, twice:

"And what if the Great Ship has spent the last billions of years fleeing someone or something?

"What if that something has been pursuing it all this time?

"And if there is a pursuer out there—if, if, if—then how much harm have we humans done, forcing the Ship to change its trajectory, forcing it to follow a lazy, looping course through the milky waters of our galaxy?"

THE INKWELL

A multitude of specialists have tailored my newest voice. Utilizing oceans of experience as well as some considerable guesswork, they make me sound humble yet competent, harmless but enduring. In a hard whisper of microwave noise and infrared light, I show the nebula that I am very nearly nothing. A fleck. A dot. Little more than a mathematical point occupying an endlessly shifting position in space, passing quietly without complaint or important needs. My trajectory is nothing but a mistake, and I confess to being an inconvenience for whoever lives inside the cold black nebula. For this, I am sorry. Using images and the languages of the nearby worlds, I build a vocabulary. I display a grammatical logic and then libraries of elaborate and honest explanations. I am a ship. A civilian vessel, I carry passengers and nothing else. Not mentioning Marrow or my ill-defined cargo is not a lie so much as a reasonable omission. How can I know exactly what resides inside my own belly? In countless ways, I am apologetic. This detour is not my plan, and I wish to make amends. In the course of traversing a great potion of our galaxy, I have managed to learn a few things. If I must pay some fee to cross their space, I will. Gladly, I will. Knowledge is my first and best currency. The cumulative experience of many thousands of species rides inside my halls and great rooms. For any distraction and discomfort brought my passage, I will be generous. "What do you wish?" I ask the darkness. "I am listening, I am here. Tell me what you need and what you deserve, and I will happily give these good things to you, in exchange for my unavoidable presence."

It is a whimpering voice and hopefully useful. But there are moments and days when I change the tenor of my speech. Following a carefully prepared script, I show hints of other faces. Other moods. I seem tiny compared to the universe, yes, but I am also ancient and uncommonly strong. The dust and ice of the nebula are not hazards for me. Not only will I cross the blackness in a matter of decades. I will come out the other side enriched. My shields can gather whatever raw material serves me. My lasers will obliterate whatever cold objects lie in my path. And if need be, I can ignite my glorious engines, changing my trajectory with power enough to move entire worlds.

Quietly, I ask the nebula for help in making my passage.

Less quietly, I imply that I need little help. My requests are out of politeness and according to the standard laws of the galaxy. I am a citizen of something infinitely larger than any little cloud of gas and ash. I don't say it in words, in images or mathematics, but brazen implications swim beneath some of my communications.

To the blackness, I chatter.

I brag.

I pretend a dialogue, answering all the likely questions from voices that I haven't quite heard yet.

And then after many years of fruitless noise, I fall silent. Sometimes there is no better way to speak. Every one of my channels collapses to an empty hum, and I keep falling on and on toward what has been dubbed the Inkwell.

Thirty years to fall.

Twenty-five.

And now, little more than twenty.

Perhaps nobody has heard me. Among the captains and other informed parties, that possibility makes itself plain. The assumption is that life is plying its way through that darkness. But really, why is life reasonable? The slow ships could be stupid machines left behind by some lost species. The rivers of ionized water vapor might have natural origins, as do the warm little worlds. What do we know about the dark nebula? Not enough, plainly. And even if there are intelligent species lurking within, what does the evidence show? The neighboring worlds describe a multitude of forms and designs. Perhaps it is exactly that simple. A titanic volume of space and matter has enough room for hundreds of species. But unlike the Great Ship, they aren't united under a single golden hand. They could be a rabble, happy or otherwise, and for reasons that haven't yet been imagined, none of these species are able or willing to answer the calls from the hot bright universe beyond.

Without evidence, that idea blossoms.

And then just as the new possibility begins to generate strategies and benefits—just as the experts start to craft a menu of new voices for me, perhaps to be used in one great chorus—the answer finally arrives.

Brief, it is. Compressed, and elegant, and thorough, and in every way, reassuring. The face that first shows itself is smiling. The face seems altogether human. Handsome and male, he is. And the voice is smooth and happy, and warm, the smiling mouth producing a smooth rain of greetings wrapped around the simple and unlikely admission:

"My name is O'Layle. I was a passenger on the Great Ship. When things looked very bad for us, I fled." He pauses long enough to laugh at his own cowardice. "I probably would have died, like most of the scared bats. But I was lucky. One of the polypond scout ships was far from home, and it heard my beacon, and luckily it was able to track me down. It caught me and saved me, and you can imagine how pleased I was."

This is the first time that a name is heard.

Polypond.

Explaining the name, O'Layle admitted, "I'm not a linguist. But the name seems to do a fair job of capturing what they call themselves."

The image widens.

The one-time passenger sits lightly in a web-chair. A thousand cues show that the resident gravity is barely ten percent of one gee. "This is my home," says the lucky man. "As it happens, this is where they'd like you to send a mission. Diplomats. Crew members. Passengers like myself. They want a good fair cross section of humans from every part of the ship."

A knowing twinkle passes through the man's pale yellow eyes.

"It's my fault, I suppose. Their stock in humans, I mean. I explained how we found the ship and won control, and that matters to them. They take great stock in ownership, it seems."

Again, the eyes twinkle.

Behind O'Layle is his present home. Visual cues and easy conjecture point to a floating structure drifting on the surface of a watery body. Walls are defined by dark ribs and arching panes of some transparent material. The panes aren't diamond, probably. Nor glass. But the refractory properties and the available materials hint at some flavor of plastic, very strong and easily manufactured. There are a few scattered furnishings, and to one side stands a round platform, flat on top except for a few tidy lumps. A bed, in other words. Beyond the farthest walls is open water, reassuringly blue under a high cloud-blotted sky. The horizon is close. The world seems to be Martian in size but considerably less massive—not unlike a ball of water wrapped around a small core of stone and common metals. The atmosphere has to be very deep and warm, and it is lit by an array of circular lights fixed to some kind of ceiling. The human says as much, explaining, "The Blue World has a roof to keep in the heat, to keep in the atmosphere. The daylight is for my sake. Most of the time, this is how things appear . . ."

With those words, the lights in the sky are quenched.

Moments later, the unseen camera adjusts its eye, and what has been brilliantly bright becomes a different kind of brilliant. The world that was lit from above is now illuminated from below, from just beneath the surface and from realms considerably deeper. The high wet clouds manage to glow with an occasional lick of lightning, and their bellies reflect the glow of the endless sea. But most interesting is the water. What was just visible before becomes obvious now. Objects are moving beneath the surface. Careful eyes make out the hints of fins and tentacles and fleshy appendages with no clear shape. Something vast swims close enough to make the house roll on the sudden waves, and afterward, O'Layle laughs gamely while remarking, "I have many neighbors."

His own floor is transparent. Probably plastic like the walls, and with darkness above, it turns perfectly clear.

He looks between his bare feet, watching some great shape swim away. Except for a small swatch of fabric around his groin, the human is naked. By every visible measure, he looks healthy. Well fed and rested. He looks like a man near the end of a wonderful long holiday, and with a matching voice, he says, "The polyponds are rather different from us."

He is happy, but more than one human observer makes the same comment: it is an ageless, enduring happiness. The smile and hearty voice are too steady and certain, if that is possible. The accounts supplied by O'Layle's old friends, plus the volumes of recorded moments from his various public lives, show a man who has never been so easily blissful, nor as thoroughly satisfied as he seems now.

"Polyponds are very large creatures," he announces.

Somehow the smile brightens, and he adds. "They are patient and thorough, and from what I gather, they're very well organized. I know they haven't shown it, but they heard your broadcasts. They've been analyzing them. They've shown them to me, inviting my comments. My help. And because their ocean . . . what you call the Inkwell . . . is a big place, their response has been slow in coming."

Again, the happy laugh interrupts the monologue, stealing away some of its slight momentum.

"Polyponds don't have a Master Captain," he explains. "Decisions require time and some measure of consensus. But their leaders, their most important voices . . . they want you to come visit us here. A meeting between emissaries. And as I said, they'd prefer a human entourage. Since our species has control of the ship, we have won the honor."

A new motion grabs the careful eye.

O'Layle straightens his back for a moment, and with a voice meant to sound casual, he mentions, "They aren't a genuine species, by the way. Not like we think of species."

Behind and to the right of O'Layle, something moves. From among the pillows of his large round bed, a figure sits up and gives a lazy, long stretch. With the light coming up from below, the area above the bed is in shadow. A long limb stretches, but details are scarce. But then the sleepy body turns just enough to supply a silhouette, and every human notices the rounded form of a breast and the meaty nipple riding on the tip.

"They aren't a species," *he repeats, facing the unseen camera.* "Not so much as they are all species. Whatever they wish to be, I guess you'd say."

Again, he says the name.

"Polyponds."

The alien slides out of the bed. She is long and well proportioned. She is perfectly naked and absolutely unperturbed by her appearance. To the eye, she looks as if she is the end product of a billion years of life on a terran world. And as far as any eye can tell, she is human.

"Their name comes from their origins, I believe," *says O'Layle.* "Although they don't seem quite sure about where they came from. And from what I gather, they don't seem to care much about the subject."

O'Layle hesitates, probably feeling his house rocking on the water as she approaches.

She kneels behind him, and with a warm strong voice tells her distant audience, "Welcome to you, my friends."

Her long legs straighten, stretching forward, one lying on each side of the little web-chair.

With an ease that looks utterly natural, O'Layle climbs off the chair and leaps backward, his swatch of clothing clinging tight as the woman's broad pale belly absorbs his impact. Stretched out as far as possible, his bare feet lie near her hips. And when he throws back his head, flashing a smile at the universe, he uses one of the vast breasts as a pillow.

"What do you make of this?" *the Master Captain asks her nearest officers.* "Tell me. First impressions."

I try to speak, but no one hears me.

Washen glances at the others, and then her eyes return to the rest of the brief, dense message. The only Submaster who actually gives an opinion is a harum-scarum. With an easy paranoia, Osmium pointed out, "This is simple biology. Make yourself bigger than your rivals, and you win every fight."

Again, I try to offer my little thoughts.

"It's a stupid strategy," *the harum-scarum declares.* "If it wasn't, we'd all be a thousand kilometers tall!"

Washen smiles knowingly.

But the Master says what many are thinking.

"How can we be sure they aren't that tall?" *Then with a light bitter bite, she laughs louder than anyone else.*

Eleven

THERE WAS NO particular point where a mark had been crossed, no precise hour or moment when they could confidently tap ceremonial bulbs of bright liquor against one another, crystal ringing in warm hands as they congratulated themselves for breaching a barrier and entering an entirely new realm. Even the ship's AI held no consistent opinion about when they had reached the Inkwell—and that from a stubborn entity with views on every imaginable subject. They were still months removed from nebula, slicing across seemingly empty space, when their maneuvering rockets began firing every few minutes. Stripped of every gram of excess mass, the streakship had been left with more grace than armor. Smoke-sized particles of dust could be absorbed by the hyperfiber prow, but only for a time. Lasers were used to erode or shove aside anything larger than a grain of sand. But giant hazards—pebbles and whole comets—were best avoided entirely. The same lasers flooded the space ahead with picosecond bursts of light, and the AI watched for the spectral reflections of lurking carbon and frigid ice. At a fat fraction of lightspeed, there was barely enough time to see everything and react appropriately. But by the same token, the streakship was narrow and lean, and auxiliary rockets no bigger than a thumb could be fired anywhere along its hull, giving it one or a hundred useful nudges. The nudges were what the passengers noticed. When several rockets fired in tandem, the ship gave a little shiver, the cumulative vibrations slipping through the hull. Shove the streakship's trajectory a few millimeters now, and they would eventually miss the hazard by thousands of kilometers. But every new trajectory revealed more little motes and goblins waiting in ambush. Plus there was the fierce, uncompromising need to hold to their essential course. Every correction demanded an equal countercorrection, and every brief firing of the tiniest rocket meant consequences that had to be measured, then erased by a sleepless machine designed for this narrow job, bringing with it an intellectual clarity, a wealth of experience, and a numbing and shameless pride.

"I am not the *Elassia*," the machine liked to boast.

Pamir usually clamped his mouth shut, saying nothing.

"With me," it would purr, "you wouldn't have died between the stars."

Ages ago, while he still felt like a young man, Pamir had served on board a far more primitive starship. The *Elassia* had collided with a hunk of comet, everyone aboard killed in a single fiery instant. But luck and a predictable course meant that Pamir's remains were discovered eventually. Enough of his mind survived to fill the rebuilt body, and the tragedy as well as his own incredible luck had given him a certain lingering fame.

The AI knew the *Elassia*'s story, and it knew Pamir. The boasts were bait. It loved to tease the ship's captain, pointing out all of its laudable features as well as the rapid, unconscious brilliance that it brought to this vital undertaking.

"From ten light-hours out," it claimed, "I could fly us through a barn door."

What a peculiar expression. Pamir's first instinct was to consult the library. His second instinct was to ask the AI for an explanation. But the best response was to do nothing. With a conspicuous indifference, Pamir drifted into the middle of his tiny cabin, busily preparing both of the day's routine messages.

"Through the barn door," the voice continued, "and in another ten light-hours, I could slip us under the *Arch of the Accord*."

An old Martian sculpture, Pamir recalled. But he remained focused on his own uninspired work. An unbroken telemetry stream was being maintained with home, but a more thorough report was dispatched every twenty-four hours, encrypted and launched inside a pulse of infrared laser light. The routine was perfectly normal in these kinds of missions. What was unusual was the second message, considerably shorter and more heavily encrypted: a soft whisper, in essence; a few words offered to a closer set of ears.

"I am a marvel of design and hard experience," the AI remarked.

It was, and it was. But why repeat what everybody knew full well? With a lazy indifference, Pamir stretched his long back and told the ship, "Send out the dailies, now."

"This marvel shall," said the AI.

And then, "I have."

"Thank you."

An instant later, Pamir heard what sounded like a burst of rain against a distant roof. They were still five light-weeks removed from what might or might not be the edge of the Inkwell. But there were more hazards every day—nearly invisible twists of grit with the occasional thumb-sized shard of ice. Quietly, Pamir asked, "Is it only dust?"

"To the best of my considerable knowledge, it is. Nothing but."

"Show me a sampling," he persisted. "Five hundred spectrum, spread across the last ninety minutes."

The data were delivered in an instant.

Again, the AI mentioned, "I am perhaps the finest vessel ever built."

Finally, Pamir took the bait. With a grimace and a slow smile, he asked, "What about the Great Ship?"

"Slow and fat," the AI replied.

"Vast and safe," Pamir countered. "Ancient and marvelous. Mysterious and polite."

"Polite?"

"Silent," he joked.

Again, the sound of rain drifted inward, coming this time from a different portion of the hull. And then moments later, there was a rattling roar directly in front of Pamir. With a grim little smile, he muttered, "I understand."

Silence.

"I know what you're feeling," Pamir continued, using an insight he had carried for the last few weeks. "Don't try to fool me. Because you can't."

"What do I feel?" asked a doubtful voice.

"Afraid."

Silence.

"We're diving into blackness," said Pamir. "Faster than anyone should, we're going to race toward a world you can barely see through all this nastiness. The Master sends us charts, and the polyponds give you advice. But everything you receive from them is weeks out of date, and the charts never quite agree with one another. Which is reasonable, considering the limits of everyone's sensors. And you're responsible for more than any sentient soul would wish to be. Our lives. Your own existence. The fate of billions, perhaps. And just maybe, the survival of a giant machine that might be as old as the universe."

Again, silence.

Pamir laughed quietly, his focus returning to the volumes of data. What he saw was scrupulously ordinary dust. But what else would there be? A useful paranoia mixed with the wildest speculations, and he ordered a new sequence of spectra along with a hammering of microwaves.

"It's a tough, damning burden," he echoed. Then with a nod, he added, "Bluster is a good trick. But if you ever feel your bluster wearing thin, tell me. Right away, tell me."

The proud voice asked, "What will you do then?"

"I'll share my luck with you," Pamir remarked. "And believe me. If it comes to it, you'll be happy to get all the luck you can . . . !"

QUARTERS WERE CLOSE, and after ages spent wandering through the vast halls and rooms of the Great Ship, the crew had to make adjustments. Frames of reference had to diminish, personal space retreating to a cramped minimum. In place of ten-hectare apartments and endless possessions, a tiny cabin and a single uniform had to be enough. And as the mission progressed, that narrow existence had to become natural, or better, feel like more than plenty.

"Humans are adaptable creatures," Perri proclaimed one day, tucked into one of the narrow slots inside their very tiny galley. Eating a slice of cultured petty roast, he happily added, "We're more adaptable than most species, from my experience."

"Or more stupid," Pamir replied.

Quee Lee seemed to be listening to their little argument. To the eye, she was lovely enough that Pamir found himself instantly aware of her location in any room, and unlike her husband, she preferred to look like a woman who enjoyed what was once called middle age. She had pleasantly rounded features and an easy warm smile. There was a little gray in the bright black hair. But the smile had retreated, and with a voice just hinting at worry, she said, "It's getting louder."

The rainlike rumbling, she meant.

Maneuvering rockets were firing in tens now, constantly and fiercely, and they were still five or six or maybe ten days from the Inkwell. Not for the first time, or last, Pamir reminded everybody, "We'll adjust our tolerances, eventually."

Cut down the distances between near collisions, he meant.

"Besides," he continued, "the polyponds maintain that the debris fields won't get any worse. Not along our course, at least."

Only a few people took the trouble to reexamine the aliens' charts. Most couldn't find reassurance from a species they didn't know, much less believe those broad claims of sweeping the worst dangers out of the blackness before them. That kind of trickery seemed unlikely. Or it was just too sweet. Or worst of all, it was all true—the polyponds genuinely wielded complete control over the where-abouts of every mote and snowflake inside their homeland—and that type of power was too impressive, too incredible and odd, and with the slightest shift of mood, it could prove deadly.

Nudging the conversation back to useful topics, Pamir asked, "Any thoughts about the newest news?"

Everyone fell silent and thoughtful.

Nexuses were opened; memories were triggered.

Quee Lee responded first. With a smoothly amazed voice, she asked, "Have you ever heard of such a remarkable life-form?"

Pamir had known a few odd creatures, but he didn't respond.

"What they're admitting . . . how they've organized themselves and their biology . . ." She hesitated. "But maybe, no. Maybe they aren't that remarkable."

"We're all spectacularly remarkable," Perri offered.

Quee Lee nodded, smiled. Then she looked at her husband in a certain way, and he blurted the name of one of the Great Ship's alien species.

She offered another.

And with a boyish wink, he added a third.

They were having an intricate, deeply personal conversation. Married for aeons, as familiar and accepting of each other as any two people could be, they had so thoroughly shared themselves to each other that every glance could open up entire volumes. A raised eye and a fond smile caused both of them to say, "The Queen," in the same instant, then laugh loudly. Sitting across the galley from one another, they reached out, unable to touch but their fingers still curling as if cling-ing to each other, so perfectly familiar with the mate's grip that even with half a dozen people between them, they felt as if they were holding hands.

It was a marriage that enthralled and embarrassed the rest of the crew, putting them to shame and setting a lofty goal that ten billion years of happy life might not produce.

Pamir felt all the valid emotions.

On occasion, drifting past their tiny cabin door, the antinoise shield would flicker, allowing a warm, excited, and a curiously anonymous voice to escape. A wail of pleasure; a sob of exhaustion. Which was why he had dubbed them, "The honeymooners." And that was why he laughed now, gently teasing them with the hoary barb, "Would you two like to be alone?"

Perri showed his wife a certain wink.

And Quee Lee grinned and grinned, every tension erased, that warm sensuous voice remarking with a seamless, infectious joy, "I'm very sorry, Captain. I thought we were alone."

TWO DAYS OUT of the Inkwell, their luck ran thin.

"It's a system failure," the AI reported, "and I don't seem to be able to . . . wait . . . no, I cannot fix it by myself—"

"It's the armor?" Pamir blurted.

"No, the V-elbow has jammed," the voice reported.

"Now?"

Then with a flash of grim humor, the AI pointed out, "But this would be the most inconvenient time."

The streakship was in the middle of realigning itself. While the bulk of hyper-fiber umbrella remained in the forward position, the rest of its body was undergoing a series of slow contortions. Fuel tanks and engines and the tiny habitat were shifting and sliding, reworking the architecture of the entire machine to place their aft in the lead, making ready for the long braking burns.

"What do you need?" Pamir asked.

"Hands," the AI replied.

"How many, and where?"

Precise diagrams were delivered both to Pamir's nexus and to the simple reader embedded in his cabin wall.

"Fuck," he offered.

"Indeed," the AI agreed.

Mass restrictions meant that the ship had no robots equal to the task. If necessary, they could be assembled, but their components were scattered and currently occupied. Time mattered, and at least two pairs of hands were needed. But making matters infinitely worse, the balky elbow was currently thrust out beyond the protective fringe of the armor. Left there too long, the relentless rain of atoms and little molecules would erode it to a rotten shell.

With a genuine sorrow, the AI said, "I have listed the crew according to qualifications. As you can see—"

"Where's my name?" Pamir interrupted.

"You are my captain," it countered. "For the good of the ship, you should never place yourself in mortal danger."

"Except that's where we are," he muttered. "Account for training and experience, and physical size, too. Who's at the top of this chart?"

The AI searched hard but found no way to win the debate. Grudgingly, it set

Pamir's name first, where it belonged, and with a flourish, it made its case for what had become the second-place name.

"No," said Pamir.

Then after a momentary pause, he announced, "I'm taking Perri."

"Who's only a passenger," the AI reminded him. "A self-taught expert in other species, but hardly trained in this sort of work."

Pamir nodded, a tight little grin surfacing.

"Did you know?" he asked. "Perri was born as a Remora. He grew up on the hull, in the dangerous old days."

"That information isn't in his personnel file."

"Because the poor guy lost the faith," Pamir remarked with a heavy shrug. "He came under the hull and found a new identity, charmed a rich woman, and got himself a new life. But I know the man. I'd prefer a washed-up Remora beside me, if I have my choice. Which, I believe, I do."

THE INKWELL WAS invisible, shielded from view by the hyperfiber and one of the looming fuel tanks. Yet even as he worked his way out from the airlock and through a last set of demon doors, Pamir felt the presence of the nebula. He felt a tug, a tangible gravity or some other subtle force attuned to a man's sense of place and importance. He could feel the blackness riding next to his right shoulder. It was as if his body and the entire ship were being drawn into the frigid endless gloom, and something about that fearful illusion pleased him, making him smile behind the thick diamond of his faceplate.

Perri was drifting nearby. "You almost look happy," he observed.

"Move," coaxed Pamir.

"But you sound normal enough," Perri allowed, with a teasing laugh. "Nice and pissed off."

Together they worked their way between two of the bulky fuel tanks—hyperfiber supplying the relentless pressure to hold the hydrogen in its metallic state, and thermal demon wraps convincing the fuel that it was still cold. Except for a band of star-starved space, the universe was invisible. In the soundless vacuum, Pamir was missing the illusion of rain falling as the ship danced with oblivion. There was nothing new to worry about, but he let himself grow a little anxious. It made a clear mind clearer. Senses lifted, and with his hands, he practiced motions that would or would not save everyone.

Perri was speaking. Using a private channel, he said, "No."

He said, "Do you think so?"

Pamir could see the face in profile, reading the delicate lips as they told his left-behind wife, "Love, and love, and love."

They had come to the edge of great tanks.

"Focus yourself," Pamir advised.

Perri paused, closing down every channel but one. With a deep breath, his face changed. What had been boyish and slight was washed away. What remained was a little stern, concentrating on myriad details. The determined bluster of a Remora emerged, and with a Remora's confidence, Perri said, "Now you do it too. Focus."

Together, they drifted off into an open volume of space, lifesuits linked to the ship by magnetic tethers, little farts of gas lending momentum, shoving them toward what looked like a thick gray rope. Then they were close, and the rope looked like a giant snake encased in waxy armored scales.

Protected by plates of hyperfiber, the limb was an elaborate assemblage of bioceramic muscles and hot superconductors, plus tubes and vessels that could be enlarged, conducting fuel and other necessities from anywhere to anywhere. On a ship with no extra mass and very little room, every machine had to serve triple duty. Depending on the disaster, the limb was designed to wrap around hull breaches and fuel tank breaches, or it could reach into open space to snag a lost crew member. In hard times, it might pull itself into a very thin, many-kilometer-long tendril that would interact with the galaxy's own magnetic field, either steering the ship slowly or producing enough power to keep one or two bodies alive. Other crews in far worse straits than this had even yanked these kinds of limbs apart, milking the bioceramics and superconductors of their hydrogen in a desperate bid to give their engines one last little burst of fire.

Chances were, nothing that desperate would happen to them. Pamir sensed that their problems would remain relatively minor, or they would be suddenly torn apart in a blast of plasma.

With Perri on his right shoulder, he drifted along the limb, and when he was perfectly sure of his trajectory, he looked left. The universe was reddened and a little bunched together, like embers of a fire that someone was trying to save through a long night. In the middle of that redness was an invisible point, and when he stared at it, he let himself think of the ship and Washen and these endless years of relentless life.

Two forces—the Great Ship and the Inkwell—were pulling equally hard at him now.

His suit hissed, and a soft alarm sounded.

The V-elbow was not a structure so much as it was the happenstance point— that place where the limb had bent back on itself. It and some hundred meters of armored snake were exposed to the onslaught. Even when they kept to the lee side of the limb—even shielded inside the thick hyperfiber lifesuits—their bodies endured endless blows from hydrogen and carbon atoms, hydroxyls and carbon monoxides. Modern genetics could withstand worse. But there were bright flashes visible from the other side of the snakelike limb, each flash signaling the impact of something as vast as a single particle of cold smoke.

A much larger impact had crippled the elbow.

Of course the bulk of the damage was on the opposite side, almost as far out as possible. Two sets of hands were needed to effect repairs. Both sets started to work, doing everything possible from the partly shielded backside. But very little was possible. Perri had the armor peeled free, and Pamir stabbed at the limb's odd meat, using a series of tools and curses to prove what both men already knew—they would have to attack the entire mess from the exposed side.

The limb was no more than ten meters in diameter but bent in a stiff arthritic half. The men gave each other the same hard look, then capped their diamond faceplates with thin sheets of hyperfiber, blinding and protecting them. Then using radar and mental maps, they floated away from one another. Following separate trajectories, they came around the dead limb, and in the same instant, they could almost feel and hear the rain of high-velocity grit.

Lifesuits and their own tough bodies could withstand worse. That was something worth thinking about in those long moments.

Standing in the damage zone, they kept their backs to the rain and opened their faceplates again. Something substantial had blasted through the heart of one hyperfiber plate, and something even more massive had followed after it, obliterating enough sensors and muscle to make any arm lock up.

Both cursed with an easy rage. Then together, with hands moving a little too quickly, they set to work, injecting diagnostic tools that would tell the ship's AI what was needed first and next, and what would have to wait for later. It was a sprint that demanded grace, and if they'd had time to rehearse, they would have been good at the work. But the AI drew up a list of absolute needs, and after nearly twenty minutes of relentless unpracticed effort, they convinced themselves they were making progress.

Pamir allowed himself to pause. Old eyes peered sideways through the rapidly degrading diamond. Tiny flicks and delicate sparkles of light showed that his retinas were flying through some kind of radioactive wash. But he didn't blink or consider looking down again. For the first time, he stared at the Inkwell—an ocean of nothing, black and devoid of features, cold to the staring eye and frigid to the imagination, near enough, it seemed, that a determined hand could reach out and touch it.

Pamir resisted the temptation.

Perri nudged him, and when Pamir flinched, the onetime Remora said, "Welcome back."

The delay was slight. A few seconds, at most. Then the work seemed finished, and the AI agreed with them. "I see function," it reported, obviously pleased.

"Out," Pamir commanded. "Back out of here."

But now Perri wanted to look at their destination. With his boots gripping the adjacent plate of armor, he reopened his private channel, and to Quee Lee, he said, "Look at this, darling," as he brazenly threw back his head.

The flash came an instant later, brilliant and soundless, its blue-white glare washing away the very tiny landscape.

Nothing was left.

Pamir blinked and blinked, fighting with his watering and increasingly muti-lated eyes. With a keen rage, he said, "Perri."

He shouted, "Where are you?"

Then he said, "Fuck," and reached into a cloud of bright plasmas, surprised to discover the hard shell of a lifesuit stopping his hand.

"That was a little close," Perri joked.

His lifesuit was battered but whole. Life support was failing, and power, but the body inside the dying suit could still remark with an easy amazement, "Another step backward, another moment later.

"Love, love, love. Are you watching all of this?"

Twelve

NO SINGLE LOCATION had been designed to serve as the bridge of the Great Ship. Instead there were hundreds of places where the sleeping control systems had been clustered—an arrangement rather like the nervous system of simple jellyfish and highly advanced worlds. Convenience caused the first humans to select one location as their administrative center. Set several hundred kilometers beneath the Alpha Port, the bridge was set inside a new cavern that human engineers had carved out of the bright green olivine. Three kilometers long and half as wide, the room had been furnished with webwork and chairs, while support facilities and barracks for three brigades of security troops were built nearby. Captains and aux-iliary AIs had stations designed to suit their responsibilities as well as their own fingers, everyone taking some little grip on a portion of the grand machine. What began as a relatively simple business of controlling the ship's course and keeping it in good repair had evolved into a more elaborate, cumbersome business. Each new passenger had its own odd needs and fondest pleasures as well as his distinct limi-tations; environmental controls had to be augmented, becoming more compli-cated as they were made foolproof, safeguards blanketing each of their new resident species. The Wayward War had accelerated the endless changes. Bolstered shields and lasers demanded more fluid, more adaptable fire-control systems. The main engines would have to be aimed and primed and fired faster than ever. Secu-rity issues were an endless concern, along with the importance of not pestering the ship's complement with too many heavy hands. Plus many of the stations had been reconfigured to serve captains who had either just been retrained or who were commissioned for the first time, and then thrown into the second-by-second business of managing their endless responsibilities.

Yet even with so much happening, the bridge seemed like a sleepy place. On the typical day, hundreds of captains and thousands of bodied AIs were scattered along the brightly lit cavern. Strolling down the central walkway, Washen couldn't help but feel reassured by the emptiness and quiet and how each of the crew sat or stood at his station, rarely moving, confidently focused on whatever tiny matter begged for their expertise and improving judgment.

Of course silence was not always a good thing.

Sometimes she noticed a case of nerves—shoulders squared or a breathing mouth clenched shut between little gasps. Whenever she visited the bridge, Washen's first duty was to walk its length, now and again stopping beside one of the captains, giving advice or offering a graceful compliment. Unless it was a harum-scarum, which meant dishing out a little insult with the praise.

Sometimes there were perfectly fine reasons for being nervous. A repair crew was behind schedule. A little war had broken out among one of the resident species, or worse, between two or more species. Or perhaps an ugly rumor was circulating through the ship's various com-systems, shared by the species and constantly mutating into more interesting, virulent forms.

"An invasion force is waiting for us," the young captain reported.

Washen shrugged amiably. "Waiting where?"

"Past the Blue World," he reported. "Inside the Satin Sack."

The Inkwell had been mapped as thoroughly as possible, and in most cases, details of the maps had been shared with every passenger. The Blue World was the streakship's destination. The Satin Sack lay at the nebula's center. The pressure of starlight and the industrious polyponds had worked together, pushing several dozen solar masses of gas and dust into an oval body blacker than the rest of the Inkwell. Then the polyponds had put an end to the cloud's collapse, using their own patient technologies to coax the gases and water to resist their mutual gravity. The Satin Sack was just large enough and just scattered enough to hold its shape, resisting every urge to fold up into new suns and worlds.

"What kind of invasion force?" Washen inquired.

"A million starships," the captain reported. "Or something other than starships. Apparently our big mirrors just spotted them. They resemble comets, according to some. With engines and lasers, and maybe antimatter charges, and definitely some kind of superweapon."

"Wouldn't that be nice?" With a gentle laugh, Washen suggested, "We should invent a few superweapons of our own."

The captain was human—a serious man of considerable age, a onetime passenger who had built a fortune while on board the ship. Generating bottled dreams for his species and others, he had proved himself at interpreting the desires of multiple audiences and predicting what they would hunger for in the future. When the Waywards arrived, he was one of the more influential sculptors of what passed for public opinion. The War had revealed his love for his home and its inhabitants. During the fight, he risked his own life while helping to subvert the invasion. And in the aftermath, he had turned his back on wealth and his old existence, along with almost every shred of personal authority. He learned to be a captain, at the lowest possible rank. Without complaint, he applied what he knew about dreams and desire, helping keep tabs over what was being said in the public places.

"How widespread are these big stories?" Washen inquired.

The captain gave hard figures and warm estimates.

The First Chair nodded. "Suggestions?"

"Do nothing."

She looked at the face, at the pale gray eyes. "Don't counter the rumors, you mean?"

"I was going to suggest that, yes." He nodded, squirming inside the mirrored uniform. "To my supervisors, I was going to say . . . let people tell their stories, and we'll tell them what we think is true, and after a little while, I think this rumor fades."

Washen shook her head, grinning now.

The captain was an expert with multitudes. But individuals were a source of puzzlement and occasional blunders. Quietly, almost fearfully, he asked, "You don't believe that's the best course, madam?"

"Is it your best, most informed opinion?"

He said, "Yes."

Another thought grabbed him. "Should I not tell my superiors what I believe? Leave the matter with you, perhaps?"

"Never," she cautioned.

He straightened his back, growing a little pale.

"We have a chain of authority," she reminded him. "You report to Captain Glenn-john, who reports to the Office of Civil Authority, and the official reports will be filed, and I will make sure that I see them."

"Yes, madam."

His station was a slab of ruby embedded with screens and nexus links and ports through which several million AI pollsters could speak directly to one lowly captain. For a long moment, he stared at the elaborate images being spawned on a range of the entertainment channels. The Satin Sack seemed to shimmer with energies, its body jammed full of enemy ships ready to assault them. Fictional or not, the story had power over its audience. With a confessional tone, he admitted, "I halfway believe them, madam."

She said nothing.

"Not this specific scenario," he continued. "But that the polyponds want to take the ship for themselves."

"Why?"

He swallowed, considering his response.

"You've seen a decent portion of our communications from the polyponds.

And what the streakship tells us, too." She gently clucked her tongue before adding, "If there's any reason to see danger coming, perhaps you should point it out to me."

"No," he allowed.

Then with a soft regret, he admitted, "The polyponds seem helpful enough. They might prefer isolation, but really, they don't have any choice in this matter. We are going to swim through their ocean—"

"Not by choice," Washen added.

"And I think they believe us. At least, I haven't heard any voice telling me otherwise."

"Any voice?"

"Intuition," he added. In a gesture as old as the species, he touched his own temple, adding, "In my old business, a voice would whisper to me. Tell me what to pursue and what to ignore."

"I hope you're still listening for that voice."

He nodded, but not with total assurance. Then softly, he said, "If you want, I might offer some new dreams to the general population. Through my old companies, or other avenues."

"Which dreams?" Washen asked.

"Reassuring ones. That the polyponds are odd but harmless, and we have nothing to fear." He shrugged. "Just to give passengers the chance to sleep easier. Actually, I'd probably find that there's quite a market waiting for me. For us."

"Your intuition says so?"

"Yes," he said.

Then he asked, "Should I pursue this?"

"Don't ask me. Ask Captain Glenn-john."

He nodded, returning his gaze to the screens. The cumulative wastes from a thousand ship habitats were being analyzed on his orders, artificial tongues measuring the stress hormones dissolved in the piss and feces of a great nervous multitude.

"Thank you, madam," he said gratefully.

Washen nearly turned away. But another question occurred to her. With a quiet tone, she reminded the captain, "You know more than most of us about audiences. Certainly you know more than I do."

He nearly argued that point, but then thought better of it.

"About the polyponds," she continued. "You've studied most of our files. You know what they've shown us about themselves, and what Pamir has seen and deciphered. In your opinion, do you know enough about the polyponds to sell them any dream?"

The question puzzled him for an instant.

Then with a grim little smile, he had to admit, "No, madam. No. Frankly, with these particular aliens . . . I wouldn't know where to begin."

Thirteen

BECAUSE HE DIDN'T know when the chance would come again, Pamir climbed into his cabin and tethered himself inside his crush-web mattress, and with an ease that came from considerable practice as well as simple need, he closed his eyes and relaxed his long body as his mind collapsed into a deep black slumber. When dreams came, they were his own. Wild impossible things happened; routine elements yanked from recent days repeated themselves with tireless abandon. Again and again, Pamir found himself staring through a diamond port, doing nothing while watching nothing, nothing to see but a boundless darkness punctuated with the rare burst and glimmer of ruddy light. And always, there was the deep rumbling of his little ship, both in his dreams and in reality. The main engines continued to blaze away, firing through slots opened up in the hyperfiber umbrella, killing any dusty hazards as well as the last of their enormous momentum, while the maneuvering rockets had continued firing, relentlessly nudging them along a chaotic, bug-wiggling course that had proved safe enough up to the present moment.

Since the business with the V-elbow, everything had been a little bit too perfect. Pamir wasn't the kind of person who believed in the flawless, but for the last months he had been pressed to find anything to complain about. The streakship was diving down a narrow tunnel—a clearly defined avenue swept free of most of the large debris and much of its gravel and ice. The Inkwell was laced with thousands of similar transit zones. The only difference was that theirs had been built specifically for them, and with a patient regularity, the polyponds repeated their promise to complete a wider, longer avenue through which the Great Ship could pass with ease.

Pamir slept easily, and deeply, and after ten uninterrupted hours, he consciously triggered one of his favorite dreams.

In an instant, he found himself sitting in a little boat drifting down the Canyon of Ten Thousand Falls. Artists had produced this imagery, but Pamir was free to pluck what he wished from his own life. Did he want company? Yes. Washen appeared, sitting with her back to the bow, her elegant body dressed in nothing but a billowy soft gown. With her smile, she said, "Naughty boy." With a tilt of her head, she warned him, "I won't let things go where you want them."

But what did he want?

On the Great Ship, there were many places that were considered among the most scenic, the most spectacular. Passengers had actually fought about which corner and what cave were superior to every other, to the eye and nose, and sometimes to the tough tip of a sensitive tendril. Some fights had turned violent enough to kill, if only temporarily. But whenever someone took a bloodless poll, the Canyon ended near the top hundred sights that every passenger and crew member was obligated to see and smell, and to the best of his ability, embrace.

A deep warm river pushed down the Canyon's floor. Steep walls of pale pink granite soared high on both sides; then the slope diminished, changing to calcite and magnesite generated by beds of reef-forming species. Numerous springs burst into the cavern from just beneath its ceiling, nearly ten kilometers overhead. Ten thousand waterfalls was a low estimate, or high. Because there were really only two falls, one covering each shoreline, and each was woven into tens of thousands of individual braids and ropes of bright silvery water that slid off the bottom edge of reefs, making the granite shine a sweet candy red in a false sunlight designed to tease out the beauty and soothing perfection of this place.

"Remember our first trip down," said the woman in the bow.

Quee Lee had replaced Washen. Dressed in a conservative sarong, she was speaking to her husband. Uninvited, Perri had placed himself on the seat between Pamir and herself.

Perri said something just to her.

The plunging water roared as it struck the river on both sides of them. Voices had to be loud, and a mouth had to point at its intended audience.

Quee Lee chuckled amiably.

"He's tired of us," she said, motioning at Pamir.

Pamir just shook his head. Too much time living with the same few people, and not even his dreams were private anymore.

What could he do?

Laugh, he decided.

But then the roaring stopped abruptly. He took a deep breath and looked high. The falls had stopped flowing. Every spring had been choked off, and except for a last shimmer of moisture up on the green-and-gold reefs, there was nothing to see. The reefs were dying. Who had screwed this up? He began to look at his companions, but they were gone. Washen had returned, but she was dressed as the First Chair, complete with an officious expression of worthy concern.

"Be careful," she said to him.

His eyes jumped open. For a little moment, Pamir wondered how he had gotten trapped inside this odd little closet. Then he remembered this was his cabin and his mission, and everything about the dream was swept away . . . except for realization that after years of constant firing, the maneuvering rockets had abruptly fallen silent.

"THERE IS NOTHING before us," the ship's AI reported. "Except for the Blue World, that is. This region has been scrupulously cleaned of dust and gas. Except for a thin veil of hydrogen atoms, and that veil is only slightly above interstellar norms—"

"Understood," Pamir interrupted.

He began to study the unbroken blackness.

The entire crew was inside the galley, pushed together at the bottom end by the smooth decelerating thrust of the main engines. The floor had been stripped of all but the minimum number of low-backed chairs. Even without tables, there was barely enough room for all. Everyone stared at images piped in through an array of lenses and radio dishes, reading what could be seen as well as weighing the tell-tale echoes produced by bursts of laser light. To a soul, they were disappointed. The Blue World—their host and grand benefactor—was within 10 million kilometers, but the only trace was a dull red ember showing heat seeping out of a deeply insulated sky.

"We knew we wouldn't see much," Quee Lee offered.

The main engines continued to labor, their smooth braking blaze indistinguishable from a high-terran gravity.

"But think what we are seeing," Perri added.

That brought a sober long silence.

With a secure nexus, Pamir told the AI to squirt updates back to the Great Ship, and buried within that roar would be a second, much condensed version of the same transmission—for an audience that was much closer, and hopefully, still completely invisible.

"Repeat every three minutes," he ordered. "Once in orbit, every ninety seconds."

If anything went wrong, Washen and Mere would see it happen.

To everyone, he pointed out, "We have jobs to work. Before we can drop into orbit, we should get ourselves ready. For whatever's going to be."

Whatever's going to be.

Pamir meant to sound suspicious, and he probably succeeded a little too well. He saw it in the faces, in the tight lips and downcast eyes. For a moment, he let the warning sink home, then he grinned and offered a different tone, admitting, "Whatever happens, it's going to be spectacular. No doubts at all."

THE MAIN ENGINES fired until the ship's momentum was almost drained away, then, following detailed instructions delivered over the last several weeks, every rocket was buttoned down and put to sleep. The ship's body rearranged itself again. The hyperfiber armor pulled apart like a blossom. Empty fuel tanks were pushed to one side, valves opened wide to the hard vacuum. Exactly as promised, a simple tug appeared from the blackness—a blunt cold machine spinning thousands of fullerene webs tipped with tiny robots that quickly and expertly connected their web to the armor and the entire ship.

Moments later, the tug set to work, nudging them with a brute authority, inserting them into a high circular orbit around the Blue World.

Afterward, it detached the lines and ate them.

With tiny bursts of secondary rockets, the alien ship came closer. Umbilicals built for this single occasion were deployed. Radar and lasers made elaborate measurements of the streakship, presumably to make certain that every system was compatible. And Pamir's crew examined the tug with the same thoroughness. How good were its engines? How efficient was its reactor? A chamber was riding inside the tug's nose. Three different crew members noticed either the emptiness of that space or the heat radiating from it, and at the same instant, they pointed it out to Pamir.

In another moment, he spotted it for himself.

"Opinions?" he muttered.

No one responded.

With a different voice, Pamir said, "Opinions."

This was an order now.

The AI replied first. As the umbilicals eased in closer, it described what it saw inside the heavily shielded chamber.

"It is a sack of dirty water," was the expert answer. "No more than two meters long and less than half a meter wide, at the most."

Two answers offered themselves.

In the Great Ship's own language, the umbilicals asked permission to link with the empty fuel tanks.

Pamir studied the infrared images again, and, with the barest nod, said, "Permission given."

Moments later, the streakship began receiving a small ocean of liquid hydrogen, hyperfiber-faced compressors squeezing down on the fluid, producing bricks of metallic hydrogen stabilized with diamond exoskeletons. Even with the best pumps and compressors in the galaxy, the fueling would take fifty hours. Without hydrogen, there was no quick return home. For at least the next two days, they were going to dance in the dark with a thoroughly unique alien.

"Hello?"

Pamir blinked and shook his head.

"Hello?" the voice said once again.

The Blue World was a perfect black orb no bigger than a thumbnail held at arm's length. The voice came from much closer, and wrapped around it was a thin little laugh and a genuine nervousness.

"Do you hear me?"

"No," Pamir kidded. "We cannot hear you."

The voice was riding the telemetry signal from the tug. With a deep sigh, it told its audience, "I'm here."

"Are you a pond?" Pamir asked, already knowing better.

But the voice laughed, declaring, "Of course I'm a pond. We're all ponds. Didn't you realize that?"

The voice was O'Layle's.

"May I come on board?" asked the long-lost refugee. "Please let me on board, would you please?"

Fourteen

CONJECTURE. SURMISE. INTERPRET and hypothesize. Thousands of years of experience brought to bear on the moment's problem. A long life of little successes and glorious failures had produced an intellect peculiarly fitted to an impossible task. Understand. Gaze at the body of evidence, and more importantly, note the cavernous gaps in fact and data. What was truly known? Nothing. But there was never such a creature as nothing. Wasn't every modern soul taught that basic physics lesson? Absence should never be confused with emptiness. The hardest, purest vacuum bubbled with energies and raw potentials. To piece together the mind of any species, what mattered was the shape of its nothing. The lies it told to strangers and the myths it recited to its own good self.

"Where did you first evolve?"

On numerous occasions, xenobiologists aboard the Great Ship had asked that critical question. With a natural curiosity, they inquired, "Where did you begin? And where was your first home?"

It was only reasonable. Only natural. What species didn't want to point to its lowly cradle and boast? But if the polyponds knew their origins, they didn't share the story. Time after time, they answered almost every question, but in that one rootstock realm they remained conspicuously silent.

The Master Captain finally threw up what she thought was an irresistible lure. "If you tell us about your beginnings," she said in one late broadcast, "then I will tell you everything I know about ours. Our entire recorded history, from dust to stars!"

When a response finally came, it was nothing anticipated.

"All the pasts are genuine," read the thoroughly translated text. "Do not talk about choosing any one."

Yet there had to be some place and moment where the polyponds began. Genetics might hold clues, but no samples had been analyzed. And what would their flesh tell us? Perhaps an aquatic beginning, judging by how they lived today. Perhaps they had appeared on some cold world, their ancestors clinging to the occasional hot spring, surviving in some cooperative huddle, the oases scattered across an otherwise icebound landscape. There were plenty of examples in the xenobiologic literature. Snowball worlds tended to concentrate life in the tiniest of patches, and inside one of the richer patches, the various species would manage to unite into an elaborate, purposeful symbiosis. When the climate moderated, they spread rapidly. One oasis excelled, racing across the seas and ice-chewed continents, and in a geologic heartbeat, a Gaian was born—a sophisticated single entity masquerading as a world's entire biosphere.

There were Gaians in the literature—depending on the most rigorous definitions, less than one hundred examples, or at most, several thousand. And a few of those giant entities had produced starships, eventually seeding distant worlds with their vast daughters.

Perhaps that explained the polyponds' beginnings: A Gaian world enters a black cloud of gas and wet dust, finding resources enough to make new worlds where it and its million daughters could thrive. But in every other example, the sentient offspring had hoarded their memories about their origins and great parent. They were proud, slow, and decidedly independent souls, and they seemed unable to organize with anyone, including their own equally proud sisters.

A synthetic creation made for a cleaner explanation. On some forgotten world, biosculptors could have assembled a cocktail of organisms, using their creation to seed icy moons or wandering comets. Terraforming would have been the noble goal. Add heat and light to the watery bodies, and the artificial Gaian would rebuild the world around it. If some of those cocktails had slipped free, or if their makers had strewn them about a little too indiscriminately . . . well, some combination of circumstances and blunders might have brought them into the Inkwell, and then in some distant past, set them free . . .

But that again explained very little.

Dark nebulae were too cold and far too dangerous to appeal to most sentient life-forms. Whatever the polyponds had accomplished inside the Inkwell, this was not the sort of home where most species went first or willingly. Besides, despite decades of hard searches, both in the sky and through the available histories, there was no trace of polyponds or anything bearing any resemblance to them in the surrounding districts. No potential cradle worlds. No watery colonies drifting among the comets. Polyponds lived where they lived and nowhere else: Not so much as one warm puddle drifted on the fringes of the cloud, in full view of a universe infinitely vaster and more amazing than anything that could be found in the darkness.

Better than most, Mere understood darkness.

She was born inside a crippled starship, after all. For what seemed like forever, her entire world was barely any bigger than her own stunted body and her starving little mind. For centuries, the only voice she heard was her own, and the only sound she made was a pained wail broken up with weak little sobs. Existence was miserable and fearful, and, by a hundred different criteria, Mere would have seemed perfectly insane. But even at her worst, that half-born creature had an enduring sense of identity—a concept of self and place, of events that strung together to form a sloppy history. Even in that eternal hell, there was a dust-blasted pane of scrap diamond that afforded her a view of the universe. Squinting, she could make out a few hundred blue-shifted stars, and with the sluggish passage of time, those stars would move. They shifted positions relative to each other, and the stars on the fringe sometimes drifted toward the edge of the window; and then despite all of her pressing and digging, forcing her big eyes flush to the cold diamond, each star would silently and bravely pass out of view.

Whenever Mere thought about the polyponds—and she thought about little else—her mind inevitably fell back to the darkness of her youth. Even in those narrow circumstances, change had proved to be a genuine force. Little happened to her, and nothing obvious changed with her ship. But at least the sky taught her that certain things were not meant to be forever and always, and maybe there were moments when she derived hope, if not exactly joy, from that starved little insight.

MERE'S SHIP WAS an ensemble of tiny pieces. Minus fuel, the entire machine didn't possess even a thousand metric tons of hyperfiber and aerogel, diamond and patient flesh.

Yet in another sense, it was vaster than the Great Ship.

Through the long voyage, her engines and fuel tanks, mirrors and twin habitats moved with the same precise trajectory, each piece wearing an entirely different set of disguises. Some components were connected to their neighbors with fullerenes or feeble com-lasers. But most were fully independent, obeying a series of sophisticated strategies while keeping themselves in reasonable repair. A casual eye would see debris left over from Pamir's original boost cone. A thorough examination would identify shards of diamond and several masses of water ice, plus what seemed to be pieces of machinery halfway melted by the giant lasers. The two identical habitats were barely visible, even with the best instruments. Each was smaller than a comfortable room, and both used a shifting set of tricks to appear even tinier than that. One habitat served as Mere's home, the other held in reserve. Like the rest of the mock debris, the habitats drifted along in the wake of the streakship, slower by a wide margin and gradually spreading out, currently scattered across a volume better than a hundred thousand kilometers in radius.

The heart of her habitat was a padded cavity barely two meters long and half as wide. Yet even that seemed like a tremendous waste of space. Before her mission began, Mere's body was carefully frozen, tissues and bone plunged into a rigid state on the brink of absolute zero. Only her mind lived, and then only through a series of tricks and cheats, its heat signature diminished to a manageable flicker. Given any choice, other humans would never tolerate this kind of existence. This endless abuse. But Mere had experienced miseries worse than this inconvenience, and really, she was exceptionally good at keeping her cold mind busy.

Breakfast was a few gentle sips of electrical energy. Lunch and dinner were the same, delivered directly from a finger-sized reactor through a cable implanted into the back of her neck, the current translated into compounds suitable for an anaerobic crisis-metabolism. But Mere always took the trouble to select a menu, letting her mind experience the flavors and textures of whatever she would have prepared inside her little kitchen at home. Sometimes she ate Tilan food, or at least what she remembered to have eaten on the world of her youth. Outside her mind, no such cuisine existed. No such world existed. Which lent every imaginary bite a uniqueness and importance—feasting at the table of a billion ghosts, in a sense.

Mere's large brown eyes had been eased out of their sockets and frozen, a pair of superconductive taps lending her a larger vision. At any moment, she could look everywhere. Immersion eyes fixed to the scattered pieces of her ship shared input, fabricating a vividly detailed and constantly changing set of images: the last stars passing beside her; the Milky Way strewn out behind her, bright and chill; and the Inkwell directly in her path, black and seemingly endless and very nearly perfect—save for a minuscule tunnel through which Pamir and the others had already vanished.

Slowly, patiently, Mere followed after them.

Each day had its schedules and goals, responsibilities and perfect freedoms. In the past, friends and lost lovers had asked Mere, "How do you live that way? How do you survive the day in that kind of solitude?"

But it wasn't difficult. She reminded them about her first long voyage—the toxic food and the absolute lack of even the slightest stimulation—which made this an infinitely better existence. Whenever she wished, she read. Whenever she needed conversation, she woke one of the tiny AIs that rode with her. Each had a familiar voice and a distinct personality. Each was a friend, and in careful terms, Mere hinted that they might serve as occasional lovers, too.

She read alien works, mostly. Quirky texts and difficult texts. Sometimes in their original language.

She also read about the polyponds, digesting the fresh reports as well as dipping into the oldest for the hundredth time.

Every day, Pamir sent home his latest data and recorded discussions from among his crew. He was a thorough captain, smart and determined, and certainly better than most when it came to understanding alien species. But he wasn't nearly as talented as Washen could be on her good days; and without a shred of self-consciousness and very little pleasure, Mere knew that nobody on board the streakship or the Great Ship brought to bear half as much talent as she possessed.

Each day, without fail, Mere consumed and examined the latest report. There were always a few missteps. Errors of decision; errors of pure bias. The crew knew they were on an important mission, and that's why they were quick to embrace anything that might be a clue, applying it like wet lumps of clay to the most recent models. The polyponds were born here, were born there. They intended this, and they wanted that. Obviously, they were friends to the human species. Or they were scared of the Great Ship. Or the aliens were brazenly hiding critical secrets, and as the emissaries dove deeper into the Inkwell, their paranoia was growing. Accelerating. Threatening to take wing.

Every day, Mere translated a very human account of the expedition, reshaping it into a form with which she might work.

If she had any secret, this was it. Mere was not truly human. Or Tilan, either. Or anything else to which any accepted name could be affixed. She was a species of one. Alone, yet unlonely because of it. Freed because of it. At least that was what she always told her lovers, explaining how they might consider themselves lucky, enjoying this rare, almost singular chance to copulate with what only appeared to be an Earth-made primate.

"I don't think as other people do."

"You seem more like one of us," a long-ago husband observed. From his breathing hole, he joked, "If I was blind and my pricks were numb, I would swear that I was screwing a very tiny harum-scarum."

"A good screw, I would hope."

"Hope all you want. You are barely better than my hand."

"You're joking," she told him.

Human beings almost never recognized when harum-scarums were having fun. To humans, everything about Osmium's species looked like bluster and insults and a thousand battles barely averted.

"My oddness makes you drunk," Mere told him.

Osmium had to agree.

"My secret," she began. And then with remarkably little pain, she removed herself from him and pulled his severed prick from her vagina, staunching both of their bloods with a casual hand while a smooth warm and impenetrable voice admitted, "My secret is in my head. And I don't know what it is."

THE SCATTERED SHIP continued its long, long plunge.

A thousand times, by various means and with varying levels of intensity, Mere was examined. Light and microwaves danced off the various pieces, and perhaps most of the echoes went unnoticed. Several times, elaborate pulses of energy emerged from the Inkwell, joined with the streakship's daily signal. Plainly, something was sitting near the ship's wake, looking back along its trajectory. Hunting for stragglers? Perhaps. But a human conclusion was too tempting, and she firmly resisted the urge. Really, after all of these years of constant work and practiced thought, the polyponds were still a deep mystery, and they were a source of constant, studied pleasure.

Twice at least, probes flew through the middle of her scattered ship.

They were not small machines, and they acted interested. With Mere's various eyes, she saw mirrored dishes using the last ruddy traces of starlight, staring back at her with an unnerving intensity. But both of the flybys were finished in less than a second, and if anyone felt suspicious, or even simply interested, they would launch a new probe with the opposite trajectory. And until someone or something flew beside her, Mere would cling to her present course.

As Pamir reached his destination, Mere was finally diving into the nebula itself. The tunnel remained open—a well-tended route leading back to the Great Ship. There was nothing unexpected about that. Pamir needed a clean path home, and the polyponds were being nothing but helpful.

One morning, as Mere breakfasted on a whisper of current barely powerful enough to feed a horsefly—as the taste of Tilan fish and earthly seaweeds filled her frozen mouth—she opened her eyes to the outside.

Nothing could be seen.

The blackness was relentless, seamless and ancient and brutally cold. Despite every wise thought and every comfortable platitude, she felt afraid. Her imaginary breath grew tight and slow. Suffocating, she began to doubt everything that she held dear about her own toughness and endurance.

The claustrophobia was awful for a day or two.

In a rare breach of her own rules, Mere medicated her cold mind. Tranquilizers and mood enhancers gave her a false euphoria that allowed her time to prepare for the inevitable.

Who knew this would feel so awful?

She felt ashamed, and sad. For the first time since she was a newborn, Mere struggled with the kind of horrible solitude that would have stunted any soul.

The medications faded.

Gradually, gradually, Mere learned how to look into the dust, noticing glimmers of heat and ropes of energy and odd, slow, and rather large vessels moving patiently from warm body to warm body. From polypond to polypond. What a remarkable and unexpected, odd and oddly beautiful realm.

Finally, something obvious occurred to her.

Could it be?

When Mere felt certain, she sent home the first message in nearly ten years. A carefully encrypted and very quiet message—a few words dressed inside a snarl of ordinary static—was broadcast to the Master Captain and Washen.

"I don't know yet how the polyponds evolved," she admitted. "I don't know if they came from a natural world, or if they were someone's tool that got loose. But they were not fully sentient until they were here. Inside the Inkwell. Inside all this dust and black."

A genuine excitement lifted her bare metabolism.

"When they were born . . . I'm nearly certain about this . . . when the first polyponds grew self-aware, and for a long time after that, they reasonably assumed they were the only souls in existence, and their home was everything, and that the Creation was blackness without end . . . !"

Fifteen

"HER CLOTHES ARE a little bland, I'll grant you. But everything beneath is beautiful. Gorgeous. Absolutely glorious." Then with a deep, nearly winded gasp, O'Layle added, "She's a wondrous, perfect lady. She really is."

The object of his considerable affections was the Mars-sized sphere dressed in a nearly perfect black. Except in infrared, where she glowed like the final coal in a very old fire.

"Have you ever imagined such a creature?" O'Layle inquired. And then he halfway giggled, underscoring again the simple fact, "That's what she is. A creature. An organism. A single fully functioning entity. And a lady who happens to be seven thousand kilometers across."

"It is spectacular," Quee Lee offered.

"She is," O'Layle corrected.

"Of course. She."

Pamir remained silent. Piloting the shuttle was simple enough, three onboard AIs doing the bulk of the work. But he was already tired of the Blue World's emissary. Better this chore than another tedious and entirely useless conversation with O'Layle. After rechecking their course and insertion site, Pamir glanced back at the streakship, magnifying a patch of the sable sky until he saw a bright fleck still singing "All is well," with a preset and very precise melody.

"I named her the Blue World."

Or the polypond simply allowed him to call her that. But Pamir didn't offer the possibility; cynical thoughts rarely found purchase in souls that believe themselves to be in love.

"She's excited to meet you," O'Layle claimed.

Quee Lee nodded, replying, "We are thrilled to meet her."

A third of the streakship's crew was crammed inside the tiny shuttle. The mood was complex, ever-shifting. Excitement bled into a nervous energy that would suddenly drain away, leaving everyone suspicious, even paranoid. Then as the mood drifted back to optimism—as the first smiles reemerged—O'Layle would make a fresh declaration or an exponential promise. Without obviously intending it, he would churn up the excitements and doubts all over again.

"Before her," he said, "I had never believed this would happen to me."

Perri rose to the bait. "What would happen?"

O'Layle winked and grinned. "An alien for a lover. Really, I never dreamed that I could stomach it. Much less enjoy the experience."

Pamir glanced at the idiot.

Misreading that simple expression, the man said, "You don't know, Submaster Pamir. None of you can. What she accomplishes as a lover . . . you have no idea what her affections can achieve . . ."

"I have a good imagination," Pamir replied.

"Oh, no. No." O'Layle laughed. Giggled, almost snorting. "I mean, the Blue World can build *any* body with ease. Any shape, any purpose. Every whim and unique desire can be answered."

There was an obvious, tempting response. Gaians fabricated bodies with the unconscious ease with which humans secreted new skin cells. These bodies had no bounds and no morals, and they could be infused with every pleasure while ignoring even the most withering pain. Whatever the purpose, it had to be spectacularly easy, feeding the lust of a grateful and lonely man. And how could one human animal comprehend his lover's motives, particularly when the creature was investing nearly nothing in that lopsided relationship?

Pamir threw a look at Quee Lee and her husband.

With a wink and sharp "Hey," Perri pulled the man's attention back to himself. "You know, I once met a Gaian."

O'Layle put on a doubting face. "Is that so?"

"Ages ago," Perri recalled. "It was a refugee, of sorts. Made friends with one of the captains and slipped on board the ship, in secret."

"I didn't know that."

"Didn't she live inside one of the sewage plants?" Quee Lee asked, gently nudging her husband. "You slipped down there along with the garbage, didn't you?"

"Did I tell you that story?" Perri inquired.

"You did," she swore. "But you never mentioned that Gaians are lustful creatures. Should I be jealous, darling?"

Both cackled at that.

"Except she didn't play with me," Perri continued. "What good could I do her? No, it was the captain who let her aboard in the first place. That's who she was entertaining."

With a growing disgust, O'Layle listened to the reminiscence.

Perri smiled at Pamir. "Mister Second Chair," he began, "does this story sound familiar?"

"Barely," Pamir growled.

With a mocking tone, Perri asked, "And what happened to that Gaian?"

"It died."

O'Layle seemed alarmed. "How? What happened?"

Pamir shrugged. "The creature was a liar. It manipulated that stupid captain. Destroyed his career, nearly. And in the process, it endangered the ship. So there wasn't any choice, and of course it was destroyed." With a cold surety, he said, "The Great Ship has to be defended. Every threat has to be dealt with. Billions of lives depend on every captain's wisdom."

O'Layle swallowed, eyes squinting now.

As soon as this man kicked his way on board the streakship, he had suffered a series of thorough examinations. Autodocs and psychological-adept AIs had done their best with O'Layle, and each of the crew, singly and in groups, had spent time talking to him. Listening to him. Or just watching him. Since Perri had known the man for ages, he oversaw the smiling interrogations. Opinions had been generated and exchanged. Suspicions were refined or discarded. And again, O'Layle was examined, everyone listening to whatever he had to say, the process succeeding in doing little except to make O'Layle feel like an important and fascinating guest.

To every eye, he seemed utterly human.

In his bones and deep inside every cell, O'Layle was a creature that had evolved on Earth before being modified by an array of elaborate but familiar technologies. And in his mind, he seemed perfectly average: a vain, self-obsessed passenger, and exactly the sort of the man who would spend a fortune to abandon everyone he knew, leaving them to die and the ship to splinter and boil.

Whatever the Blue World was, this could be the first human it had met.

A stroke of bad luck, perhaps.

Pamir secretly examined the latest verdict of the autodocs. O'Layle was reacting in a thoroughly expected fashion. Judging by his breathing and biochemistry, and using a series of nanoscopic implants scattered through his outraged husk, the man gave no sign of being anything but a simple soul deeply out of his natural environment.

Turning to Pamir, he blurted, "She won't hurt you."

"Me?"

"Or the ship, either." His face was appalled, his body stiff, deep instincts demanding some worthy reaction. "You have to believe me. She and the rest of the polyponds . . . they want to be helpful . . . more than anything, they want to ease your passage through their space . . . !"

"Good," Pamir offered.

Sensing sarcasm, O'Layle muttered, "Besides, you can't do anything to her. You never could. She's huge. They're all huge. And the polyponds . . . they number in the millions . . . !"

Pamir nodded, saying nothing.

Quee Lee reached into the tense silence, telling everyone who might be listening, "We want no trouble. This is a mission of simple peace. Why wouldn't we be?"

"Good," O'Layle said in a hopeless way.

A bright light had appeared on the limb of the black body. Blue as promised, it marked the insertion point where the world's clothes had parted slightly, offering a route inside for a careful shuttle.

"I'm sure you're peaceful," the foolish man muttered. Then with a desperate expression, he told Pamir, "I know people. I'm a good judge of character. I can tell, you do mean to do what's best. And I'm almost sure that I can trust you. That we can trust you, I mean."

FOR THIS SYMBOLIC occasion, a modest continent had been built.

Metal spongework had been grown in the depths, the pores and deep caverns pumped full of hydrogen gas, each mountain buoyant enough to rise to the calm face of the turquoise ocean. Strung together and moored in place, the spongework provided a stable foundation for thick layers of black peat and brief scenic rivers. Then the newborn land was populated by countless mock-species, each imagined and then brewed for what would be the briefest visit.

"Beautiful," was the unanimous consensus.

And yet.

A patchwork of sharp blue-white lights clung to the far-above ceiling. While the AI pilots deftly maneuvered their shuttle over the landing site, Pamir watched the landscape pass below. High metal ridges shone in the artificial sunlight, straight and keen as knife blades. The forests were a gaudy rich green that served no purpose but to look like an earthly jungle. There was no chlorophyll in the spectrum, nor any other trace of working photosynthesis. Sweeps by radar and bursts of focused sound mapped the terrain to a resolution where every organism as large as a mouse was visible, and in the guise of thorough navigation, Pamir ordered denser sweeps. Each organism seemed to be its own species. Each wore an array of ornate flaps and feathers, skins and tails, every color bright and finely rendered, drawn with a tireless and careful hand. Thousands of large and beautiful organisms had gathered around their landing site, and after the shuttle settled on the polished sheet of stainless steel, they sang. With a shared voice, they roared their joyous greetings, the melody too complex for any human ear to follow, and despite that impenetrability, perfectly lovely.

"I've never been here," O'Layle muttered. His little home floated on the opposite hemisphere. Stepping slowly out into the bright tropical light, he remarked with a mild disgust, "I didn't know about this. That she was doing this for you . . ."

The air was warm and bright, and damp, every breath laced with a unique mixture of sweet perfumes and mild pheromones. Standing together beneath the shuttle's stubby wing, the humans couldn't help but feel honored. The scene was built for them, and a thousand gorgeous creatures were dancing out from the edges of the jungle. If anything, their song grew louder and more urgent as they gracefully pushed closer.

Quee Lee said a few words to her husband.

Perri shrugged, laughing. "If they're going to kill us, we're dead. So where's the good sense in worrying?"

O'Layle moved first, but after a few steps, he slowed and fell behind Pamir. Gazing up at the bright steel mountains, he said again, "I've never seen this place before." Then hearing the jealousy in his own voice, he added, "This would take a long time to build. I would guess. I bet this place hasn't been finished for long."

It was finished yesterday, Pamir decided.

Or two minutes ago.

As he walked, he spoke through a nexus, joining the tangled conversations of the crew waiting on board the streakship.

"Look at their interiors," said a xenobiologist, studying the shuttle's telemetry stream. Pointing a sonic eye, she said, "See this—?"

"Guts?"

"Right."

"What about their guts?" Pamir inquired.

"They don't have any," the authoritative voice warned him. "Nothing like an esophagus. Stomach. Intestines, or rectum."

Singly, the creatures were gorgeous—elaborate and deeply contrived but always lovely, dancing and weaving their way across the open ground. Anywhere from two to twenty limbs were raised high. Plumage full of cobalt blues and bloody reds made eyes blink and tear up with their glare. Elegantly shaped heads, one or two or three per body, served to hold simple eyes and great gaping mouths that were attached to nothing but a damp mass of lung tissue and powerful muscles.

"Fat," a voice said. "And probably dissolved sugars, too."

"For energy?" Pamir asked.

"For a little energy," another voice warned him. Then with an impressed but disgusted tone, she added, "If they keep moving and screaming, at this rate, they'll burn their reserves in less than an hour."

Like mayflies, the multitude would not live out the day.

"To build everything here," Pamir began, gazing at the gemlike green of the jungle and the high steel mountains beyond. "How much would it cost? In energy. Time. Best guesses?"

Modest energies, the experts said. Plus years of patient work.

But moments later, the same voices discounted those first guesses. Both the shuttle and streakship were jammed with sensors as well as delicate machines that could double as sensors. Subtle shifts in gravity helped map the Blue World's interior. Sonar and the stomping of alien feet helped seismographs look into the top layers of water. Reactors on both vessels sent streams of neutrinos toward each other, cutting through the world's body in the process. And more important, and perhaps more ominous: The ocean beneath them was filled with busy, even frantic machinery. A thousand reactors had suddenly awakened. Bright streams of neutrinos revealed a raw power, muscles far in excess of any simple organic Gaian. Moving masses caused the body to shiver and quake, and every ripple and every whispery particle gave a new clue about what lay beneath. Spongeworks, neutrally buoyant and waiting to serve whatever whim the world felt like ordering, hung scattered through the deep ocean. They were made of steel and calcium and plastic, and near the curiously oblong core, there were the unmistakable signs of pure high-grade hyperfiber.

"This is not a patient animal," one engineer said. "Assuming fabrication methods we understand, using the resources of this entire body, and with every machine focused on a single job—"

"Fast," said a second engineer.

"Yeah, it's quite a show."

"Because we're important," the ranking xenobiologist maintained. "She wants to put on a good performance for us."

"Wait," Pamir said.

"To impress or intimidate us—"

"Shut up!"

The greeters had abruptly stopped singing. Limbs were still raised high, but their bodies were rigid, powerful voices caged deep in their lungs. Into that sudden silence came the ringing of water tumbling over a distant falls. Then a moment later, the falls went dry. And in the next instant a single voice—a seemingly tiny voice—called out from between two of the towering bodies. "Hello," it said. She said. "Friends. Is that the proper word? Friends, my friends, hello!"

SHE WAS TINY, and she was the world.

The willowy figure wore what looked like a lemon white dress. Approaching, she displayed a human form very much like a half-grown girl, curled black hair spilling down to the narrow shoulders, large curious eyes watching everything while a wide, infectious smile focused on her guests. The humans answered the smile with their own smiles. Pamir couldn't help himself. In the bright and utterly false sunshine, she was fetching. She appeared charming. With a sweet, vexing gait, she nearly danced toward that huddle of people, the wide mouth displaying tiny teeth as a voice clearly meant to be pleasing said once again, "Hello, friends."

Everyone gave a nod, muttering, "Hello," with a reflexive politeness.

Then with a large, almost giddy voice, O'Layle called out, "My world, my savior! Hello to you, darling!"

Behind the figure came a parade of humanlike legs, one after another, each helping to hold high what looked to be some kind of stalk or tendril, as big around as a good-sized arm and stretching far back into the jungle. The closest legs were directly behind the girlish body, and when she walked into the open, everyone saw how the stalk lifted up into her thick black hair, dividing into thousands of strands—an army of neural connections linking those dark black eyes with some vast Gaian sub-brain.

"Superconductive proteins," the xenobiologist guessed.

"Clumsy," one engineer muttered.

"Wouldn't have to be," a second engineer countered. "She could use nexus-style linkups. No physical connections, and they'd work a lot better."

Pamir shook his head.

"You're missing the point," he warned. "This is supposed to accomplish something. And that's what?"

For an embarrassed moment, the distant experts said nothing.

"To remind us—" the xenobiologist finally began.

"What this is," he rumbled. Then to the people standing around him, he said, "Don't forget to whom we're speaking."

The world was taller than she first appeared. Taller than Pamir, and not just a little bit taller. She walked up to them, stopped, and said, "Sit before me," while a hundred legs bent low. "Close please, my friends. Join me."

On the warm slick steel, everyone sat.

"It was a safe journey, I trust."

Pamir said, "Very safe. And thank you for your considerable, gracious help."

The shrug was rather like O'Layle's shrug, complete with a palpable self-satisfaction. Which probably meant nothing besides the telling influence of a single teacher. The black eyes seemed to absorb the faces before her. In a soft whisper, she said each of their names. Except she ignored O'Layle, and with a distinct fondness, she said, "Pamir," while reaching out with one long hand, fingers like brown wires touching first his nose and then the rugged end of his chin.

He didn't move.

When the hand was withdrawn, she told everyone, "For my sort, it is important. A meeting such as this."

"With us, too," Quee Lee offered.

"We are not all that different," the voice continued. "In a sense, each of you is a world, the same as me."

That won a few polite nods.

"Just much smaller than me," the world added.

Pamir narrowed his gaze, concentrating on one of the world's delicate hands.

Again the arm reached, fingers quickly touching each of the nervous faces. Save for O'Layle, again.

"All is well on your Great Ship?"

Pamir gave a little nod. "We believe so."

"Good!" The hand was withdrawn, and after a moment's pause, the world said, "You must miss your ship, I would think."

"Quite a lot," Quee Lee replied.

"Return," said the world. "Begin now, if you wish."

O'Layle flinched. "Is that all?" he blurted. Then with a low laugh, he added, "These people came a great distance, my love. And for what? To sit here for two breaths—?"

"Quiet," Pamir warned.

"I don't want them to leave," the man complained. "Not so soon, please."

The girlish face didn't quite look in his direction. But the voice deepened noticeably, remarking in a distinctly casual fashion, "You might wish to accompany them. Go home in their vessel, perhaps."

Confusion grabbed O'Layle. He opened his mouth, closed it, and then with a wounded sound, he asked, "Like that? You want me to abandon you?"

"Or remain with me," he was told. "A world has its own will, and if you don't wish to leave, you may remain here."

O'Layle seemed eager to believe the invitation; he was desperate to feel pleased by the invitation, no matter how weak it sounded. But some force or half-born intuition kept him from celebrating. "I miss people," he sputtered. "That's all I meant to say. I thought maybe our new friends and I could wait here for a few years . . . until the Great Ship was past us, maybe . . . and then they could go out and catch their home after it clears the nebula . . ."

He paused, finally noticing that something was wrong now.

"What?" he whispered. "Is it . . . getting darker . . . ?"

Pamir had been watching the sky for the last few moments. Yes, the blue-white lights were dimming. Already the shadows were softening, a newborn gloom beginning to hide the endless stalk and all those crouching legs that led off into the jungle.

"What's happening?" O'Layle demanded. Then with a foolish hope, he asked, "Is something wrong with the light?"

The black eyes stared only at Pamir.

"The light," the Blue World answered. "The light was an indulgence meant for human eyes. But this world prefers to use her energies in more appropriate tasks."

They were already halfway to night.

"What about my home—?" O'Layle began.

"It has been dark since you left," the voice reported. "And your structure has been absorbed and remade."

O'Layle rose on trembling legs. "But," he muttered. Then with the pain of someone who was losing the love of his life, he moaned, the sound inadequate and lost and almost too soft to hear. "This isn't fair. I don't want this."

Pamir rose, and everyone but the world did as he did.

"To the shuttle," he ordered.

But then he stood his ground, watching the girl-shaped bag of water and salt.

Perri leaned toward O'Layle. "Stay if you want," he whispered. Then with a teasing menace, he asked, "How long can you tread water?"

The man nearly struck him.

It was Quee Lee who took O'Layle by the shoulder, and with a patient and halfway-understanding voice said, "I know. But really, you should remember that you're alive and have this choice. Hmm?"

The man nodded weakly, retreating with the others now.

For the second time in his life, he was willingly abandoning his home in order to save his tiny soul.

Pamir continued to stare at the entity before him. The world sat with its long legs crossed, a bright little smile hinting at an array of emotions, none of which were likely or valid. "You took a little slice from each of us, didn't you? With the touch. Those fingers. You scraped off some of our dead skin."

"To know you better, yes. I have sent the tastes back to what passes, I suppose, for my mouth."

"That's how polyponds operate? When you meet one another—?"

"A sharing of self is essential. Yes."

"Okay." For a moment, he imagined his genetics being consumed and disassembled. Then he swallowed his disgust, remarking, "I should get a little taste of you, too. If I understand this ritual."

"Naturally."

From beneath the white gown, one of the hands withdrew what seemed to be a hunter's knife, and with a smoothness of purpose that couldn't help but unnerve Pamir, the other girlish hand yanked at the stalk, giving it enough slack for the knife to cut through in a single motion, a clean wet hissing accompanying the surgery as the heated steel blade cauterized the wound.

With a slight tremor, this tiny piece of the world stood.

A deep perfect darkness had fallen around them. Only the glow leaking from inside the shuttle showed them where to step. A few moments later, a deep roar began in the distance, in every direction, and grew swiftly into a thunderous mayhem. The jungle was being destroyed. Absorbed. Digested. The Gaian was beginning to clean away what for it was nothing but an elaborate but odd scab on its otherwise unblemished flesh.

"Pamir," said the figure beside him.

"Who are you now? The world still?"

"When your skin cells are taken, do they remain part of you?"

"You're separate now," he surmised.

She said, "Entirely. Yes."

"Are you a new world then?"

"Again," she said. "When a cell of yours leaves your body, is it another you?"

"Not really."

"Not really," she repeated.

"But it might be, treated in the right ways. If it was allowed to grow."

"Creation," she said with a warm and fond and very much spellbound voice. "It is an endless, wondrous process. Creation is."

They had reached the base of the shuttle. Behind them, the towering greeters began to tilt and fall, crashing onto the bare metal, bones shattering and their flesh splitting wide, the sound of black fluids gushing an instant before a thousand new mouths began to suck and chew, pulling this wealth of organics back into stomachs of every sort. Pamir watched. With the dim glow of the shuttle, he could just make out hills of meat and spent plumage quickly collapsing, everything about this show impressive—which was precisely as it was intended to be.

"Creation," said the creature beside him.

He started up into shuttle, remarking with more warmth than necessary, "I'm sorry. But we don't have room for two new bodies. If you come home with us, we'll have to freeze you inside one of the hydrogen tanks."

"Of course," she said.

She didn't ask about O'Layle's fate, or lack thereof.

Then with a slow, careful voice, she admitted, "The guest of mine, this O'Layle, mentioned that your Great Ship carries a rather special cargo."

Pamir said nothing.

"Or a passenger, perhaps. Very old and kept safe at the core."

The continent shivered beneath them, individual masses of spongework being ripped apart at the seams.

"Very old," she repeated.

"We don't understand what's down there," he admitted. "But in our communications, I'm sure the Master Captain explained everything that we do know."

The only light in the world was inside the shuttle. Washing across her face, it made her look simple and entranced, happier than perhaps any organism had ever been. O'Layle was somewhere above, still sobbing. Otherwise, it felt as if they were stepping inside an empty vessel.

"A prisoner," she mentioned. "That's what some call it."

Pamir said nothing.

"Ancient as the universe," she exclaimed. "Or more so."

The world beneath him continued to tremble. Beside him, thousands of tons of freshly killed flesh were being eaten whole. A sad little man was weeping over the loss of his vast lover, and meanwhile the Great Ship was plunging headlong into a black nebula populated with a multitude of very peculiar souls.

The dread was real and abusive. But try as he might, Pamir couldn't decide which of those problems had the strongest, most dangerous grip.

Sixteen

IN DISTANCE AND time, the voyage home was relatively brief. The Great Ship had continued plunging toward the Inkwell, and now the streakship was maintaining a collision course, obliterating much of its fresh hydrogen to return at better than half lightspeed. The return voyage would take years less than the first leg, and everything about everything was familiar now. But time is a slippery business to any mind, and space is always incalculably, numbingly vast. With their central mission finished, there was little to do but think about old haunts and avenues, friends and left-behind lovers. Reports continued to be filed, but since they were crossing old terrain, new information was rare and without any obvious importance. The mission itself had been a considerable success: Messages of congratulations continued to arrive from the Master and her various officers. They had spent only hours with a single polypond, but the event . . . meeting or ceremony or whatever this business had been . . . was deemed an official success. No tragedies had befallen their mission. A polypond representative was sleeping peacefully inside an auxiliary fuel tank, its makeup and frozen mind constantly studied by dozens of eyes wielding every available tool. The aliens had equaled or exceeded every promise of support. Retracing its original course, the streakship discovered that its path was growing cleaner by the day, the polyponds' electrostatic charges and the streakship's own lasers shepherding the debris off toward the edges. If the Great Ship's course proved equally well scrubbed, then cutting through the Inkwell would prove easy to the brink of boring. Where was the bad news in any of that?

Except. The mood on board the streakship remained stubbornly pensive, whiffs of despair emerging on the bad days. The ship's interior felt cramped and overheated, and most people blamed their new passenger. O'Layle was a moody, simple, and decidedly odd soul. After decades of being loved and entertained by an organism as large as a world, he found himself abandoned, forsaken to the company of strangers who weren't as simple or moody as he was, and who were odd in ways he couldn't begin to decipher. His misery was a little bit infectious. Pamir noticed it in the first days. Their guest would pass through the galley, make a few pained observations about the cold and blackness surrounding them, and after vanishing again, some little spat would break out between best friends, the tension spreading like a subtle, meme-born disease.

Pamir had always possessed a useful paranoia. Watching Perri and Quee Lee exchange half a dozen sharp words at dinner, he instantly set the autodocs to work. There were a few notorious examples of aliens crippling one another with caustic notions and vivid imagery. Was that O'Layle's purpose here? Yet after several more years of study and help from distant experts, the machines couldn't blame anyone but O'Layle himself. Clinically speaking, he was a bit of shit. An egomaniac and a determined coward, and in the same way that a person's body could live almost forever, his flawed character and brittle personality had persisted for hundreds of centuries without meaningful change.

Besides, it took more than one man to cause the ugly moods. Even as they passed through that tunnel of scrubbed space, the AI pilot continued to spot little hazards and fire the maneuvering rockets. And the black dust played its nefarious role, packed thickest around the tunnel's edges—in effect, making everyone blind. There was also the brutal, relentless cold lying just beyond the hull. And there were the polyponds themselves: Despite everything seen and all that had been learned, the aliens remained mysteries, enigmas of the worst kind, without charm or any obvious human quality.

The Great Ship had many odd and baffling passengers, but in most cases, people learned how to interact with the important and social species. The average human, given time and the motivation, would find or imagine traits that were reassuringly familiar. But the polyponds had never given them that chance, and if the future went as promised, they never would.

"What do you make of them?"

Every day, that was the central question. Someone would pose it, usually early in the morning, in the cramped little galley, and someone else would offer an old intuition tweaked just enough to seem fresh.

"They have no choice but to let us pass through," most argued. "But they're xenophobes, and this is difficult for them. Or they're arrogant bastards, and it's easy to dismiss us. Or they are afraid of us, which is smart. Since we represent the Milky Way, after all. We are millions of living worlds and every technological advance, while they've lived in total isolation. So they're naturally terrified of what might follow in our wake."

"What might follow us?"

This was relatively early in the voyage home. Unlike almost every other morning, O'Layle came out of his tiny cabin for breakfast. Entering the galley, he looked at no one, and again, he asked, "What might follow us?"

Perri had voiced that shrewd opinion. But he had too much charm and grace to act self-conscious. A big shrug and a sad smile preceded the obvious words: "I don't know what. I'm just saying—"

"We're the first wave of an invasion?" O'Layle grumbled.

"No." Perri's smile sharpened. "I just meant things might seem that way. If you're a hermit—a hermit living in a windowless cabin—and if somebody suddenly knocks on your locked door, telling you that they're in trouble and need to come inside your home . . . well, it's only natural to worry . . ."

The logic won a brief, disagreeable pause.

"We don't mean to invade anybody's space," Quee Lee offered. "Nobody planned to put our ship on this trajectory."

O'Layle squashed his mouth to a point, considering the matter.

With a calm voice, Pamir asked, "So what do you think?"

Silence.

"You have experience with our new friends," he reminded O'Layle. "In your opinion, how does your old girlfriend regard us?"

The mouth relaxed.

After a moment, O'Layle took a deep breath. And another. Then with a dismissive, almost amused tone, he remarked, "She doesn't have much regard for you."

"No?"

"That's my impression."

Perri gave a low snort. "You never mentioned that before."

With a shrug of the shoulders, O'Layle explained, "It's just my impression. A feeling. I don't have any hard evidence—"

Pamir interrupted, asking, "What other intuitions are you hiding?"

"None."

Everyone stared at the interloper, waiting.

Finally, O'Layle shook his head and smiled, smugly pleased to be the center of attention. "She loves me," he announced with a chilling fondness. Then after a deep breath and a clicking of the tongue, he added, "The Blue World told me . . . early on, she confided to me that it was her greatest moment . . . when she saw a little lost ship falling toward her . . . !"

He hesitated.

Then he dredged something new out of his memories, or at least found a fresh perspective. "I assumed that she was talking about my ship," he said. "And about me . . . of course, of course, of course . . ."

TWENTY-FOUR DAYS AND fifteen hours later, the ship's AI woke Pamir.

"Debris," the voice reported.

The timing was far from unexpected. But because of the chance that undetected sensors had been smuggled aboard, either through the unaware shore party or mixed with the cold hydrogen, the incident had to seem utterly harmless. Playing a role devised decades ago, Pamir asked, "What debris?"

"Our own," the machine reported. "It's too massive and quick for the polyponds to push out of our way." Details were fed into the appropriate nexus, including points of origin, the distribution, and each object's current velocity. "There's a small but important chance of impact."

"Agreed," Pamir replied.

Then in the next breath, he said, "Sweep the trash out of our way."

"In any particular direction?"

Yes. Just yesterday, Mere had transmitted a glimmer broadcast, feeding Pamir detailed instructions. And he had already instructed the AI, on encoded channels. But for an audience that had little chance of being real, and even less likely chance of appreciating this conversation's significance, Pamir said, "I don't particularly care. Kick it wherever your mood tells you."

Bolts of laser light raced ahead.

Each little piece of Mere's ship was slathered with excess diamond. The carbon boiled, erupting in neat jets of plasma, while the hyperfiber beneath felt the hard shove of coherent photons. And with a deftness that looked too casual to be planned, her ship was neatly ushered out of the way, tracing new trajectories that would soon take Mere into the surrounding wall of dust, and afterward, deep inside the nebula itself.

IN THE END, during those final busy days, moods shifted again.

For that instant, they were outside the Inkwell again. The Great Ship was familiar and welcome, and it looked lovely in the last glimmers of starlight. Decades of work and millions of hands had repaired the hull, making it glisten like a vast frozen tear, gray and elegant. It seemed as if every square kilometer on its forward hemisphere had its own laser or shield generator or upturned mirror. Diving toward the nebula, only a tiny portion of the lasers needed to fire at oncoming debris. Bits of comet and clods of stone were obliterated in an endless fusillade. With so much firepower, nothing could stop the ship. If its full rage were unleashed, it would pound its way through any conceivable barrier.

To make the rendezvous, the streakship had to slow itself.

To land, it followed the traditional course of shuttles bringing passengers and cargo, maneuvering behind the Great Ship to match velocities and course, then using the ship's considerable gravity to aid its final approach.

The giant engines showed as burnished gray cones tilting starward. They were thousands of kilometers above the hull, and the Inkwell briefly vanished behind the vast round bulk of hyperfiber and stone, water and busy flesh.

Approaching Port Alpha, the AI remarked, "I will miss working with you, sir."

Pamir nodded, and after a moment's reflection, he admitted, "The feeling's mutual, my friend."

The landing was accomplished in the same way as the mission had been accomplished—professionally, without fuss or disappointment. The fuss began afterward. Nestled inside its old berth, the streakship was surrounded by banners of welcome, written in too many languages to count. Cameras and immersion eyes had been hung in the hard vacuum. As their nexuses reengaged with the ship's networks, the crew saw just a tiny fraction of the coverage. "Our heroes have returned!" they read. They heard. They heard the proclamations sung and shouted. And then after the obligatory speeches, from Pamir and the Master Captain, the streakship's crew and both of its passengers were ushered off for a new round of medical and psychological evaluations, and a mandatory quarantine that lasted another ten weeks.

Once cleared, Pamir went straight to Washen's apartment.

After their usual fun, the two of them lay beneath her domed ceiling, watching the live feeds from the ship's prow. They had entered the Inkwell in the last few days, or they were still entering it. Definitions were always subject to debate. But the stars were vanishing behind them, and if not for the light of the shields and the obliteration of cometary debris, it seemed that nothing lay ahead of them. Nothing. Not even blackness, the ink was so deep and cold and pure.

"When we were landing," Pamir began.

Washen waited for a moment, and then asked, "What?"

"I noticed some new mirror fields tucked between the engines." He paused for a moment, then added, "They must have been thrown together while I was gone."

"On my orders," his lover admitted.

"On your orders, what?"

Silence.

But that would be a reasonable precaution. Hazards could come from any direction, and if they were seen while they were still far away . . .

"It's my son's fault," Washen offered.

"How is Locke?"

"Busy. Happy. Intensely curious." She switched the view to the aft hemisphere, and with a tone of confession, she admitted, "But I'm the genuine paranoid in the family."

Pamir said nothing.

Then after a full hour of thoughtful silence, Washen asked, "Do you ever wonder?"

"What?"

"Where is our ship supposed to be going?" she whispered. "And is there anybody else out there . . . anybody who is chasing after us, maybe . . . ?"

Seventeen

THE VACUUM TINGLED and roared with energies.

Under a boundless black sky, the hull was brightly lit, pools and great blankets of hard blue and faint yellow light marking where the Remoras lived and the fef worked. One of the giant engines would ignite, superheated plasmas rushing out of its towering nozzle, up into the smothering cold. Powerful magnetic fields would surge and spin, grabbing up flecks of iron or iron-dirtied ice, then fade away again into a brief restful hum. Whispered signals danced back and forth at lightspeed, bringing orders and data feeds and fresh gossip and white-hot curses, and buried inside that endless chatter were little secrets wearing encrypted shells and anonymous faces. Gamma radiation from the ends of the universe caught the ship, burrowing into its hull and dying, or battering its way through a Remora's wet human cells. Billion-year-old neutrinos dove deeper, their trajectories twisted by the hyperfiber's ultimate bonds; then with the keen urgency of their species, most of the neutrinos escaped, following some slightly changed path through the Creation. Dark matter particles hung like a cold fog in the blackness, occasionally colliding squarely enough with a nucleus to make it rattle for a moment. And always there was the vacuum itself: empty only in name, possessing a Planck-tiny spongelike structure that every moment gave birth to an array of virtual particles, too many to count, every last particle colliding with its mirror image and vanishing before either could be noticed. Before either could be real.

"The forecast is favorable," Conrad reported. He stood in the vacuum, wearing the lifesuit with its Submaster epaulets on the shoulders and no other trace of his considerable rank. His single eye, wide and oval and black as the sky overhead, stared at his two guests. One of them was tall, and the other was considerably taller. "There won't be any significant hazards for another eighty hours. Then we'll cross a debris field. Pieces of a big comet, apparently." To the taller guest, he said, "A comet that must have splintered when you tried moving it out of our way."

"I can't move anything at the moment, sir," said the Blue World's emissary. "Except for myself, that is."

"Sure. I forgot." The Remora now watched his other guest, his rubbery wide mouth grinning as a warm voice said, "If I'm wrong about the forecast, get into a bunker somewhere."

"Always," Pamir promised. Then with a sweeping gesture, he remarked, "You've done a lot in these last years."

Bright diamond domes were rising from the ruins of a different city. The Way-wards had swept this portion of the hull bare during the War, but repairing damage was what Remoras did. Of course they had returned to this place. Of course they would honor their dead by spreading cloaks of new hyperfiber over the charred bones and empty shells. With a keen stubbornness, they wouldn't rest until a million domes reached to the horizon, empty for the moment or for the next ten thousand years . . . but still, ready for their children to reclaim them with their old numbers as well as their unflinching arrogance.

"Take my personal skimmer," said Conrad.

"Thanks."

For a moment, the Remora stared at Pamir's companion. Then with a calm, unreadable voice, he asked, "Have you ever walked the hull before?"

"No," she replied.

"Does it worry you?"

"Would that be polite?" she inquired. "To feel worry?"

"It doesn't matter," the Remora allowed.

The emissary glanced at Pamir, apparently waiting for advice.

"Walk in that direction," he suggested. "Our skimmer's waiting."

She obeyed, instantly and without hesitation, her lifesuit soundlessly marching across the smooth gray hull.

Following after her, Conrad spoke on a secure channel. "Does your lady know you're spending time with this beautiful young woman?"

"It was Washen's suggestion, as I recall."

"I guess that's possible," Conrad kidded. "She's never struck me as the jealous sort."

The laughter fell away quickly.

Then with a different tone—a serious, anticipating tone—the Remora asked, "Is it the news from the bow?"

"Sure."

"Want a closer look, do you?"

The joke had no effect on either man.

Finally, Pamir admitted, "We just want to see her reaction. Walking beneath the Inkwell this way, in the open. And then we'll show her what the big mirror fields are finding—"

"An experiment, is that it?"

Not much of one. But since the emissary had been pulled from the fuel tank, thawed out and revived, virtually nothing of substance had been eased free of her. Twenty competing labs had studied her genetics. Her neural pathways and every spoken word had been analyzed to the limits of the available tools. Experts in aliens, sitting on an ocean of experience, had come to the same conclusion: She was a relatively simple creature woven around some scrupulously ordinary DNA. Human DNA, as it happened. And specifically, O'Layle's own genetics.

"I don't trust her," Conrad declared.

Pamir kept silent.

"Or *them*, for that matter."

The Second Chair glanced at the black sky.

"Not that they've done anything particularly unfriendly." The Remora walked faster, following the outside edge of a vast and empty dome. "We're the intruders here. We weren't invited. And if someone dove through me . . ."

His voice trailed away.

Then after a long silence, he asked, "What the telescopes see . . . what do you think it means . . . ?"

The emissary stopped abruptly, her helmet pivoting, allowing her smiling face to ask, "Is this the skimmer?"

"I don't know," Pamir confessed.

"It is your skimmer, yes," Conrad told her.

Then as she climbed aboard, Pamir told his friend again, "I don't know. What means what? I haven't half of a faith in any one notion now."

OTHER FLAVORS OF energy ran wild on the hull: ambition and creativity, selfishness and bravery, rage and fear and vengeance, plus the occasional dose of generous, unalloyed altruism.

The slick gray landscape accelerated around them. On their left, in the distance and blurred by their speed, was a fef work camp.

The emissary asked about the little aliens.

She was wearing limited nexuses, none reaching into the data reservoirs. Every question had to be audible, and when she listened to answers, her responses were measured and set against all the other questions she had asked and her reactions to everything else that she had ever heard.

Pamir described the fef, in brief.

"Could I meet one someday?" she asked.

Pamir said, "Of course," and left it there.

Neither wore lifesuits, though two of the elaborate machines stood nearby, ready to wrap themselves around their fragile bodies in case of trouble. Pamir filled a standard uniform, while the emissary was dressed in simple gray trousers and a loose white blouse. She looked very long and strangely pretty. Her face seemed both inquisitive and simple. In most ways, she had kept her appearance unchanged. But in the years since her arrival she had noticeably aged, the long black hair growing whiter and finer, her face softening in countless little ways.

She was O'Layle's DNA; but immortal lives depended on bioceramic genetics much more durable than any nucleic acid.

She was dying, and according to projections, old age would kill her around the moment when they broke free of the Inkwell.

Less than thirty years from today.

For a moment, and not for the first time, Pamir entertained the image of sleeping with the creature.

He closed his eyes, and for the next few hours he pretended to sleep, and she respected his privacy, allowing him to work through his nexuses before stealing a brief dreamy nap. Then a voice nudged him awake. Sitting up, he saw another bright splotch of light in the distance—a white light punctuated with blinking colors, red and green and violet beacons matching the three most common colors for blood. Port Alpha lay just over the distant horizon. Set on the arbitrary northern pole, no other port was as busy normally; but after the Great Ship entered the nebula, little traffic was required. As a precaution against wandering comets, each of the six ports was kept sealed. And only limited, short-range missions were allowed. The polyponds claimed that even small vessels made it difficult to sweep clear the debris and mark what couldn't be moved with bright beacons. In terms described either as perfectly polite or distinctly chilly, they repeatedly reminded the captains that they should keep very close to home.

Past the mothballed port stood the first shield generators—blunt cylinders and bland cones bigger than most mountains.

Every moment spent in the open brought a measurable, predictable risk. The skimmer's armored plates had aligned themselves to blunt the likely impacts. Its engines had accelerated to their limits, the angular velocity great enough to make Pamir's body feel a kilo or two lighter. Everything close was a blur, and for a little while there was nothing else to see. Then came soundless flashes as lasers lashed out at dust and grit, and the shields grew stronger and deeper, a colorful swift aurora swirling overhead. The skimmer eased toward the left—toward the east—passing wide around a site where ionized wreckage was gathered and sorted, purified and sent off to some useful place.

The polyponds did much the same trick, but on a vast scale.

Pamir tied into a nearby mirror field, using its eyes to gaze at the sky beyond the shimmering aurora. What had appeared black from the ship's trailing face was nothing. It was a simple darkness, deep but transparent. What was coming—the Satin Sack—was heavier and colder by a factor of ten, blackness heaped on blackness that was buried deep in the bowels of the nebula. Not dense by any human measure, the Sack was a massive feature nonetheless, jammed full of dust and cold gases. Alone, the ship could weather any transit, but its hull would end up battered, the mirror fields ground down to so much bright hot dust. But they weren't alone; the polyponds were deploying gigantic shields of their own, ionizing then coaxing trillions upon trillions of hazards out of the way.

In certain frequencies, the ship's course was obvious.

If the Sack was a thick cylinder of black smoke, then it looked as if a strong narrow breath had blown through it, punching a million-kilometer-wide hole clear to the other side.

The emissary watched the blurring terrain. According to every buried sensor, she was exactly as interested as a young human should be, and for someone with narrow understanding of the ship, she was no more or less nervous than what was expected of her.

"What you can do," Pamir began to say.

She looked at him. Her graying hair was a little dull, but the eyes remained bright and cheery. "Excuse me?"

"It's amazing," he said. "What you can accomplish, I mean."

"I can do nothing," she insisted.

"Your species, I mean."

With an emissary's poise, she nodded, telling him, "Thank you very much."

"You know," he continued, "we always believed—I'm talking about the captains—we congratulated ourselves for our robust understanding of aliens. With tens of thousands of species as our experience, it was easy to think that we knew everything. But the polyponds are different. Unexpected, mostly."

Again, she said, "Thank you."

"Which makes us wonder: 'What else is there?'" He knew what he would say, but he let himself pretend a reflective silence. "If we end up flying out of the galaxy, out into deep space . . . maybe we'll find other species that we never anticipated . . ."

Without a shred of embarrassment, she said, "Since I know nothing about such possibilities . . ."

"You won't respond. Of course."

Again, she looked off at the smoothly blurring hull.

"Is this where you were born?"

The emissary played her own game, pretending not to hear him.

Not for the first time, Pamir asked his companion, "Do you know anything about your species' origins?"

"No," she replied.

Honestly, said the watchful instruments.

"What about your history?"

With a human shrug, she replied, "I have no interest in such things."

"When we first met," he continued, "you mentioned my ship's cargo. What was it that you said exactly?"

Without a trace of humor, she asked, "Have you forgotten my words?"

Not for a moment.

Then she glanced at Pamir, and she smiled with her mouth and eyes, and while she sat, one knee lifted high into the air, distracting him with a moment's empty flirtation.

IN THE MIDDLE of the ship's leading face, perched on the smooth gray bow, was perhaps the largest telescopic array in the galaxy—thousands of kilometers of optical mirrors and radio antennae, remote-sensing lasers and neutrino traps. The construction that began with a crash program, two centuries ago, had continued unabated. Factories built for no other purpose continued shoving out high-grade reflectors and AIs trained to think about the oceans of raw data. An army of robots cultured for the first wave of construction had nothing to do now but repair the occasional impact damage, filling the bulk of their time assembling new mirrors and dishes, then splicing in the baby minds. If nothing slowed their pace, this hemisphere would be covered with telescopes in less than eighteen hundred years, and another eight centuries after that, the trailing face—minus rocket nozzles and Remoran cities—would be equally plastered with great lidless eyes.

The skimmer began to slow, seats reversed, and the passengers yanked into the deep foam. The gees weren't difficult for Pamir, but his companion had only the ancient protein-spawning repair genes. Her back and legs were bruised, and without autodoc help, the purple blotches would remain visible and sore for days.

The landscape slowed to a crawl, and at a seemingly random spot, the ship quit moving beneath them.

"We walk," he announced.

She donned her lifesuit without complaint or questions.

"It's not far," he promised.

But she hadn't asked, and she didn't seem to care now.

They were parked on a narrow path set in the midst of an enormous, silent, and utterly motionless forest. Shields and exploding bits of grit colored the sky. Vast dishes stood on both sides of them, rising high on elegant columns of diamond and optical cables. Hexagon-shaped dishes touched one another. No light fell beneath the telescopes, and the brutal cold only worsened in the smothering darkness.

"Follow my marker," Pamir instructed.

The tall emissary walked stiffly, her eyes fixed on a tiny red light riding on the crest of his helmet.

"Keep close," he advised.

But she didn't have the strength to match the man's pace. Age and the fresh bruises pulled her back, forcing her to call out, "I can't see you now."

"Stop walking," Pamir advised.

She stopped and waited silently. Her breathing was a little quick, and her human heart raced to a normal degree. But as soon as her body recovered from its exertions, breath and the heart rate slowed again. Her own suit had several lights, but she didn't use them. She seemed utterly at ease in the blackness. Nothing could be visible to her eyes, and she was happy enough to smile.

In the distance, the red beacon blinked back into view.

Pamir said, "Come on now."

She held the line, every step accomplished with a blind faith that the hull was smooth and trustworthy. Only when she reached the beacon did she realize that it was higher than before, and the lifesuit beneath was as large her own. She hesitated. For an instant, her old-fashioned water-and-fat mind felt a perfectly ordinary confusion that was detected by an array of subcutaneous sensors.

"Who are you?" she asked.

The giant lifesuit turned slowly. A light came on inside the helmet, the golden face peering out through the faceplate, not quite smiling as the Master Captain said, "I need to ask you something, darling. Come with me."

The emissary hesitated, then obeyed.

Sometime during the last few days, a fleck of ice had managed to fall through the lasers and shields, striking the hull with a flash and enough force to obliterate a hundred hectares of mirrors. The crater was shallow and white-gray, the hyperfiber able to realign its structure enough to recover most of its strength. Repair crews of robots and fef had been sent elsewhere. What were the odds that a second object would slip through the defenses and explode here? The odds were tiny, but no tinier than any other target zone, of course. What the Master wanted was open ground. What the psychobiologists found appealing was the dose of drama that came with this unexpected meeting. Put the emissary through humane amounts of abuse and worry, then throw her into a situation she could never have anticipated.

In the middle of the round clearing, black chairs had been set up.

Washen met the Master at the fringe, using the public channel to say, "Welcome, madam. And welcome to you, emissary."

The creature gave a little nod.

"When did we talk last?" Washen inquired. "At the Master's banquet, was it?"

"Yes."

"I hope you've been enjoying your stay with us."

A feeling of puzzlement ran through the emissary's mind. But she had the poise to say, "I have enjoyed everything that I have seen."

Her years had been spent inside a large apartment decorated with security enough for a prison cell. Except for a few carefully orchestrated trips, she had seen nothing, and not once, even in passing, had she asked for more freedom.

"What question may I answer?" the emissary wished to know.

Pointing with a long arm, the Master Captain said, "This way, please. If you would."

The chairs were arranged in a widely spaced ring. When the emissary walked into the middle, the Submasters took their seats. Pamir was visible again, sitting on the Master's left side. And Conrad filled the next chair, his single eye staring at the emissary as if he had never seen her before.

Washen was on the Master's right. "Look up now," she coaxed.

The sky was a splotch of deep indigo turning crimson at its margins.

"Of course we're a little bit blind," Washen confessed. "There's a lot of noise and busy light to look past, and that keeps us from using these mirrors to their full potential. But still, we can piece together a few things."

The sky changed. What lay beyond the shields burst into view, shifting from radio to the infrared range and back. The Satin Sack was a vast bubble of noise and tiny puddles of heat, elaborate structures and intricate details revealed suddenly. Ionized gas and ice looked like twisting threads, leading inevitably to clusters of warm water. One of the clusters was magnified, thousands of points appearing beside a standard scale. The points were packed into a neat sphere barely one light-hour in diameter. Each was the size of a small moon, and with a reasoned tone, Washen said, "They're children, of a kind. Buds, we've dubbed them."

A quiet but intense voice said, "I would not know."

"I believe you," Washen said.

The image shifted again. Directly ahead of the ship lay the hole, the promised passageway, as cold and as empty as the rest of Sack was busy and bright.

"Our course," Washen muttered.

The emissary gave a little nod.

"Still open and ready for us, it seems."

"Seems?"

"To the limits of our eyes, it looks open. Yes."

The emissary's heart beat harder, and her breath sped up until it was audible—a nervous quick breathing that slurred her next words.

"I do not know . . . what you want . . ."

"Some weeks ago," Washen explained, "we noticed a new phenomenon. Something odd or ordinary, but definitely an event that had to have been planned in advance."

"Yes?"

"These threads here, these rivers of water and minerals . . . they seem to have been feeding the young polyponds, letting them acquire mass and raw materials." She paused for a moment, then added, "Together, the rivers started to expand. You can't see it yet, not with this resolution. But it's obvious enough. The electromagnetic shackles have been relaxed. The ions are running away from each other, spreading out in all directions."

The aging face nodded, nothing to say.

"Maybe the children have grown enough," Washen allowed. "Maybe that's as simple as any explanation needs to be."

The view shifted suddenly, dramatically. Everyone stared at one of the nursery clusters, except this cluster lay near the bottom of the Satin Sack. Two light-years distance, and the infrared signature was extraordinarily bright. Inside a narrow zone, each of the moon-sized children appeared as hot as plasma, portions of their watery bulk surging into space on a fountain that was not only hot but fiercely radioactive, too.

"The engines are crude but effective," Washen relented. "Reaction-mass affairs powered by laser arrays driven by fusion reactors—systems we know something about."

Silence.

"The most distant children are moving now," she continued. "Of course, if they wish to come visit us . . . to come see the Great Ship at a closer vantage point . . . well, they would have to get an early leap on things. Which seems like a reasonable story to tell."

"Yes, it does seem reasonable," the emissary agreed.

"Except every child seems to be thinking the same way. The Sack is four light-years tall, and all of the buds on its margins are expending fabulous amounts of energy and their scarce water for no clear purpose other than to move toward us. They'll have to destroy more than half of their mass just to make a close approach. And does that seem at all reasonable to you?"

Silence.

The Master Captain interrupted, saying, "We just want to know, dear. Do you have any idea what they're trying to accomplish?"

Again, silence.

"And the Blue World," said Pamir with a stern voice. "Your parent. She must have sprouted some kind of engine, too. Because after we passed by, she began flinging a huge hot jet of her own into space. She's approaching us from behind, at a fantastic cost of mass and energy." He sighed, then said, "At current rates, she'll catch us just before we get clear of the Sack . . ."

His voice trailed away.

The other Submasters rose to their feet. But since none of them were physically present—why accept all the risks of placing everyone on the exposed hull?—it was Pamir's duty to walk across the face of the new crater, grabbing the emissary by her shoulder and tugging hard enough to make her lifesuit collapse at its knees.

Key enzymes had failed, bringing the hoary old Kreb's cycle to a halt.

The emissary had died, while the sky above was filled with countless thousands of relentless, utterly determined giants.

DELUGE

The trickle crawls out from between two carved faces, and for a long little moment perches on the lamellated fringe of a pink granite beak, gathering itself, forming a bulb of clear cold water that borrows its color from the stone and its brilliance from the sky. It sparkles and shivers as its growing mass wrestles with the surface tension of its skin. Then a nearby voice speaks. The simple vibration is enough to shake the drop, causing it to flinch and break free and silently fall. The voice says, "We trust all the captains. Always, always." The glistening drop plunges into a smooth and polished pocket at the base of the two stone Janusian faces, mixing with a thousand other drops. "But we trust her most," says the voice. "Washen," says a voice much like the first. "Though it's good to have the Master Captain still at the helm," says the first. "Of course we think that way," the second adds. Then after a lengthy pause, both voices declare, "Look into their one-faces. Nothing is more obvious than their best intentions."

Janusians are born with just a single face, but upon maturation they find a worthy mate, and following a process older than their species, the tiny male lashes himself to his lover's back with an array of elaborate and viciously hooked limbs. The hooks burrow deep, releasing anesthetics and sperm. The first merging takes several seasons. Immunologic systems adapt and marry. Two bodies link, blood vessels and limbs gradually joined. The position of the smaller head depends upon genetics and social conventions, but the male usually twists his head backward, watching for foes and missed opportunities. In ancient times, the two minds would remain separate and pragmatically unequal, the female ruling in every important circumstance. But then the Janusians embraced immortality. When two souls shared a single body and one set of circumstances, and did so for unbroken aeons, they gradually and inexorably grew into a single entity. Simple habit accounted for the shared philosophy and a unified outlook, while nexuses and adventurous neurons built permanent neural bridges. When her face looked at the pool of blessing waters, both could enjoy her reflection. Then their shared body turned, and both looked at his smaller, equally pretty face, and together, the shared voices repeated, "We trust Washen. Her one-face knows what is best for the ship, and for us."

Seepage fills the pool and gives birth to a thin and nameless stream that follows a narrow fissure—an elegant and perfectly straight seam cut in the floor of the worship park. Evaporation and thirsty creatures nearly drink it dry. But the last slow dampness reaches a tiny stream that eventually leaves the park, following a conduit cut through a thousand meters of cold granite and two meters of bracing hyperfiber. The conduit helps fill a little reservoir that is carefully poisoned with heavy metals. An AI shopkeeper sells the toxic water to the appropriate clients. Several local passenger species, one of them truly gigantic, will pay dearly for the leaden flavor of home to slake their thirsts. But they are rare clients, and there are issues of freshness. The shopkeeper purges the reservoir every eleven days, filtering out the useful metals while allowing the pure cheap water to run out the tap and across his diamond-tiled floor, then into the little river that slides past his shop.

He is a passionate machine and experienced in his trade, which is selling fluids of all kinds to all kinds. And with a machine's endless energy, he will talk about any subject to any passerby.

"For one, I love this detour that our ship has taken," he claims, speaking to a human woman wearing a little crewman badge on her trousers. "No voyage is a voyage without a gale pushing you into unexpected seas. That's what I believe."

To a towering harum-scarum, he says, "I am so fond of your species. And may I tell you, it was long ago when your sort should have been invited to sit among the captains!"

Staring in either direction, he can see a full kilometer along the avenue, and with a glance, he recognizes most of the species. If traffic is slow, and if he sees a potential client approaching, he will step back into his shop and reconfigure his artificial body. There is no doubt that he is an AI. Pretend otherwise, and certain civil codes are tested, not to mention the social norms. But just as any shopkeeper knows the value of manners and a smiling expression, this machine knows how to make clients feel comfortable.

With a whiff of pheromones, he tells a paddywing, "Nectar like you haven't had since you were green! Come try mine, please!"

To a passing Boil-dog, he sings, "Piss for a lover, I can make you!"

Dressed like a gillbaby, he claims, "I can freshen what you're living inside, if you need. And at a fair price."

After that sale, he spies a lone captain approaching. Again he steps inside his shop and steps out again, smiling with a decidedly human face. "Hello to you, honorable and noble sir. I hope the day smiles on you."

The captain says, "And to you, sir," while glancing at the apron of wet stone.

"A little something for the tongue, sir? A broth? A liquor? A sweet drink of your own invention, perhaps?"

"I cannot drink," the captain confesses. "Sorry."

The shopkeeper hadn't noticed until now, but the captain is a projection. He is real in the way that moonlight is real, and he has been sent by one of the higher captains—

"Pamir," the figure offers.

"I know you well, sir. I have followed your astonishing career with interest, and may I say—"

"No, please. I don't want to hear anything about me."

The shopkeeper nods, then asks, "What may I say then?"

"You hear things, I would think." The projection wants to know. "What is the mood of the ship?"

"Confident," the AI replies. "Excited. Eager to see what waits—"

"Bullshit."

Unsure of a response, silence is best.

Then the projection adds, "But thank you for that lie. I know you meant well by it."

Again, silence seems best.

"There is something I would like to buy. If I recall, you have an optical trap under your countertop."

"No, I do not, sir."

The projection smiles, waiting patiently.

The AI knows captains. If they think they are right, no argument works. The only hope is to show them the idiocy of their ways. With that in mind, the machine walks inside his shop—a spacious side cavern with a round wall covered with assorted taps and nipples and false penises and mouths as well as changeable ports that can be configured in an instant to fit the needs and preferences of any likely species. The counter itself is a tiny raised platform carved from slick onyx. Behind it is an assortment of invisible cubbyholes, all of which contain exactly what they are supposed to contain. But when the AI begins to say, "As you can see," his odd guest points with a long hand, asking, "What about that?"

How odd. The machine hadn't noticed that cubbyhole. Opening it with a touch, he is surprised and amazed and a little scared to find a small bottle filled with a grayish substance that has no weight whatsoever.

"Empty it into me," Pamir says.

The shopkeeper complies immediately. An unknown quantity of raw data is absorbed by the tall bundle of shaped light.

"Now put it back again, please."

The bottle records nothing but the opinions expressed by the shopkeeper. Passersby are not recalled—not their faces or voices, much less their names. The AI is a mirror, of sorts. He is a template. To make a sale, he will put on any face or attitude, and both are cues to slippery moods of its clients.

"Thank you," says the projection.

"You are welcome, I suppose. Sir."

Together, they walk outside again.

"Perhaps I should ask—" the machine begins.

"You wouldn't remember, even if I told you."

Somehow, that seems like enough of an answer. The shopkeeper nods and looks down at the human shoes that he wears at this moment, glassy eyes watching the cool pure water slipping down into the passing river.

"How long have you had this shop?" the projection inquires.

"Since the first thousand years of the voyage, nearly."

"And you drain this reservoir how often?"

"Every eleven days, ship-time."

"But the stone isn't worn," the rumbling low voice points out. "You see? If you'd been here for a thousand centuries, and if every eleven days you drained this one reservoir, not to mention your other stockpiles . . ."

"I do not understand," the machine confesses.

But he is alone suddenly, and what he doesn't understand is why he is speaking to himself.

The little river flows to the end of the avenue, dives through another long conduit, and after being heated to the brink of boiling, the water is shoved up into a mass of black mud and *dirty bubbles of methane. Inside a diamond bubble, a thousand creatures sit in the soft scalding mud. For the last twenty thousand years, this is where they have lived. Every need flows to them. Every curiosity is answered by nexuses and glow-screens and other standard tools. Their species has no common name, just a set of numbers and letters designated by the captains who admitted them to the Great Ship. They are intensely social creatures, but only with their own kind. Paradise is a hot wet realm full of stink and sudden fires and the musical roar of farts, great voices rising up through the steam, telling one another. "This herd did not pay for the wrong path. Steer toward our destination, as promised, or we demand our fees returned in full . . . !"*

The water is cleaned again and set free again, merging with another little river before a long, spiraling fall through a series of fresh caverns and long avenues. Each chamber differs in the native rock and the steepness of the slope, in its width and height and how the terrain has been shaped. Billions of years ago, unknown hands worked with rock and hyperfiber, fractals and the demands of engineering, contriving clifflike walls and granite shoulders and mock-faults and too many side caverns to count. Even ceilings refuse to be predictable: Hyperfiber forms ribs or fat arches or interwoven domes, and, depending on the grade, they are as bright as mirrors or gray as cold smoke. Or there are stone ceilings braced with little spines of hyperfiber—pink granites or black basalts or bright green olivines, or cultured ruby or diamond or sapphires, singly or mixed into an elaborate but seemingly accidental stew of glittering faces. There are no artificial skies. The only lights are small and occasional, and simple, casting a feeble white glow over the river's busy face. There is no soil on the shoreline and no intentional life anywhere. For the moment, this drainage is being held in reserve. Much of my interior is the same. For all the billions of passengers, there is little need to open up most of my emptiness. After more than a hundred thousand years, I remain mostly wilderness, a realm of untouched stone and empty spaces hovering on the brinks of Time.

The river steals up minerals from the surrounding stone, feeding a few patient microbes, while some presentient machines turn parasitic, milking power from the occasional light. Sometimes tourists wander in here and out again, leaving behind intense little colonies of life on their wastes and discarded meals. A tuft of gray-green marks a rotting sandwich. A bluish smear is all that remains of an enormous fecal pile. Then there is the tourist who never left— a biped of some obscure species who wandered into this cavern alone, scaled the enormous clifflike wall, and at the worst possible moment lost his grip on his inadequate rope. The fall shattered both of his legs and both of his spines. The essential equipment that he carried with him was left high above, out of reach. Immortal but lacking a human's relentless repair mechanisms, he had no choice but to remain where he lay. Then starvation and thirst drove him into a deep coma, and what survives today sits in a little bowl just three meters above the waterline—a mummified body that has not moved in the last eighteen centuries.

The river meets a new river and little springs, twisting and curling and always falling as it swells into a deep, swift, and relentless torrent. Fifty thousand kilometers have been covered, with a drop of better than two thousand. The last empty cavern is vast, a wide flat floor allowing the water to wander like a fat snake between walls that to the casual eye look like barren mountains. Brown rock and gray rock camouflage what covers a portion of one wall. Homes and glass domes hide on that steep terrain. For twenty kilometers, a secret city thrives. This is an unlisted community. The captains know about it, but, except where security has leaked, nobody else is aware of its existence. Almost since the beginning of the voyage, humans have lived on this stark ground. They are luddites of a certain odd order. For reasons religious as well as reasoned, they don't believe in many of the modern technologies. Life should be mortal and brief, since there is a golden afterlife, and why would anyone wish to avoid such a glorious fate? Old age begins before their second century, but death can come any moment. They wear out-of-date costumes and odd hairstyles, and each carries one of three sacred texts at all times. They are isolationists. Only on special occasions do they trade with the rest of the passengers, and only through distant intermediaries. They don't believe in nexuses or glow-screens. But they approve of fusion power and intensive agriculture, and every home has a decent library, and despite their brief life span, much emphasis is placed on learning and all of the great questions that are older than their species.

Two old men stand at the base of their brown mountains, holding hands as friends should, watching the fishless river slide past their boots.

"If the captains cannot turn the ship," one man mentions, "then it will continue out into the cold between the galaxies."

"As I hear it," his friend concurs.

"In another few thousand years," the first man adds.

"As they say."

"And then after another long while, the Virgo cluster is achieved."

The distances and spans of time are enormous, almost too much to imagine. But the second man tries his best before allowing, "If it is God's plan."

"Unless it is not," his friend says ominously.

But they are old men, each to die in another little while, and because they are mortal and brief, they feel blessed: Not even their children's children will have to deal with such terrible questions.

Another conduit ends with ice.

Inside an insulated cylinder, feeling a sudden cold and the pressure of more water plunging in from behind, the river freezes. Its flow slows, if not entirely stopping. Machines inject stones and clods of earth into the pure ice, making it look and taste like a well-fed glacier. Then the ice bursts out of the cylinder and into a little valley that feeds down into a cold turquoise sea.

The Yawkleen swim in their sea. They are cetaceans with many eyes and armed symbionts rooted into their long, muscular backs, and they live in small schools that eat the krill-like swarms that thrive in the cold brackish water. The sky of their youth hangs overhead, vast and blue and centered upon a giant jovian world and a multitude of sister moons. Engineers have found ways to mimic the giant tides of their home sea. Waves push into the glacial valley, lifting the tongue of ice until it shatters and begins to float, then the waves retreat again, exposing a hundred meters of black rock and tough seaweeds and crablike creatures as big as rooms.

Tourists sit in a sturdy boat, watching the tide fall.

Watching the Yawkleen.

They are humans, and very wealthy humans at that. The men are beautiful, but the women are always just a little more beautiful, and everyone speaks in clear, almost operatic voices.

"Lovely," they sing.

"Closer," they urge their boat.

The boat follows the pointing arms, moving toward the bluish island of ice. Four-winged birds rest on the ice, watching the intruders without interest. Then comes a sound more felt than heard—a staggering roar born somewhere beneath the surface—and the island shatters into unequal pieces, the smaller portion spilling over suddenly, throwing the birds into the sea.

A big Yawkleen rises to the surface, symbiotic arms grabbing the struggling creatures.

The humans applaud heartily.

With a few kicks of the great vertical tail, the alien closes on them. Hands hold out the strangled prey. A series of squeaks are translated by the boat's pilot. "Tell me what is new and fun," the creature demands.

"New and fun where?" the humans ask.

"New to see. Fun to do." A cackling laugh obscures the sound of water and the surviving birds. "I'm a traveler. I like to see, to do."

There were always corners in the ship to explore. The humans mention a dozen new must-see destinations before the Yawkleen announces, "I have been to all of them. They bore me."

The rebuke embarrasses and enrages.

Finally, one beautiful man asks, "Well, where would you suggest we go?"

"The hull," says the alien.

That the Yawkleen can travel up there is not news. There are limits on their mobility, yes. But inside a sealed vessel of native water, carried by machines that are powerful and proven . . . any passenger can be dragged to the surface and carried about . . .

"To see the Inkwell," the alien prompts. "Haven't you yet been there?"

"To the trailing hemisphere," a pretty woman declares, an elegant hand scratching the gap between her lovely and very cold breasts. "I was up there just three years ago, for an entire day—"

"No, the lead hemisphere," the Yawkleen urges. "That is a view worth the trouble. The shields. The lasers firing. And sometimes, if you're as lucky as me, a chunk of something will slip past and strike on the horizon."

Few tours visit the leading face. There are reasons of security, and at least as important, reasons of fear. What if just that sort of accident let a piece of ice strike you on the head? Risk was fun, but only so far as you weren't in real danger.

"The Satin Sack," says the alien.

The humans are tiring of this Yawkleen.

"If you considered the Inkwell as being black . . . well, you should see the Satin Sack. As if plunging into the deepest coldest sea, we are."

"Where do you want to go next?" a man asks the lovely-breasted woman.

"Home," she decides.

The boat complies instantly.

"Look at the Sack and try not be changed," the cetacean shouts to the fleeing humans. "Think of what it means. Think of the dangers there. Your little brains need to feel more little, if you ask me . . . !"

The sea lifts with the tides and spills over a brink, falling now.

It is cleaned of wastes and salts, and falls on.

Then it is a river again, plunging down a steeply tilted cylinder. More thousands of kilometers have to be fallen through before the final bottom, and then the great pumps will grab the water, lifting it and dividing it into a myriad of springs and grand rivers and trickles and warm rains. But here, where the long flow has still barely begun, many thousands live and make their livelihoods. Odd fish dart about within a river that tumbles at a forty-five-degree tilt. Terraces and airborne reefs have built patches of flat ground where shops thrive, catering to the locals and the occasional visitor. The neighborhood is mixed in terms of species and wealth. It is newer than most neighborhoods but still a hundred centuries old. Everyone knows everyone. Humans are rare but generally respected. And an AI can sell flavored and tailored waters to a wide array of clients.

In the midst of a quiet night, an alien enters the shop.

"What may I do for you?" the shopkeeper inquires.

Only then does she look up, spying a creature that is not quite familiar. What precise kind of organism are you?

But the question is lost somewhere inside the swift tiny mind.

"Water," the alien requests.

"Of course. But what precise type, my sir?"

"Pure," says the client. "Absolutely pure."

An easy enough task. The machine fills what seems like an appropriate container, and after watching it sit untouched between them, a feeling takes hold of her.

"It is all a mess," says the alien.

She knows what is a mess. She feels it deeply.

"The captains are fools."

With conviction, the shopkeeper agrees. "The future certainly looks awful."

Then the alien seems to laugh at her. "No, the future looks wonderful," it declares. Then it adds, "Forget that I said those words."

The shopkeeper sits quietly, waiting for something to happen.

She is alone, entirely by herself, listening hard for no good reason, and except for the endless sound of water plunging past her front door, she hears nothing worthy of a name.

Eighteen

ONE OF HER early husbands was a great mathematician and cosmologist—a little Tilan man who brought his relentless genius to every morning table. He would drink strong tea, salted and chilled, and eat nuts dipped in cold sweet oil, and with a voice that struggled to remain patient, he would again try to explain the universe to his old and very foolish wife.

"If nothing else, the equations with which I work are beautiful," he maintained. "Before all else, they must possess elegance and a graceful balance, and they are always honest. They have no choice but to remain true to their nature. Do you understand, Mere?"

"Honesty," she would repeat, her human mouth wrapped around the alien sounds. Then for herself, she said, "They are faithful."

"Faithful to themselves," he added.

"Of course."

Tilans were tiny bipeds. Even Mere's stunted body dwarfed most of the species. But luck and natural selection had given that species swift, acrobatic minds. Their neurons were formed from intricate tangles of proteinaceous crystals. Buried inside each neuron were forests of long, slender tubules—features narrow enough to feel the fuzzy borders of time and space. The Tila thought rather like a quantum computer thinks. Most sentient organisms could manage that trick on occasion, intuition and inspiration springing from the tiniest possible events. But for the Tila, intuition was the relentless heart of all life. Every conscious moment was dripping with the sense that the universe was ultimately and tirelessly vague. A trillion other universes, each as vital and real as their own, lay closer than the width of a busy electron. They felt it from their birth to their inevitable death, and like all natural philosophers, death was many things to them other than the end.

"My equations are beautiful," he would say.

"And they are faithful and honest," Mere would add, licking her own bowl clean of the sweet oil.

"You are very beautiful," he proclaimed.

She didn't entirely believe him, but she smiled as a happy Tilan wife should smile. "Thank you for thinking so."

"The river is beautiful, too," he said.

On occasion, she had thought so.

"And the mountains, too."

"Yes."

"And our twin suns are very beautiful."

The suns were falling into one another, soon to destroy this helpless world. But she made an agreeable sound, adding with a bitter humor, "They are the most beautiful suns in our sky, yes."

"Four beauties," he pointed out. "All valid. And each example is entirely different from the other three."

He had a point to make, but she knew better than to ask, "What do you mean?"

"Do you know what I mean?" he inquired.

"Barely."

"There are many ways to be beautiful."

"Granted."

"And many different mathematics describe our universe. They explain the Creation. And each delineates the true shape of Everything." He finished his tea with a hearty sip, black eyes smiling at his extraordinarily ancient bride. "Using very different means, they answer all of our questions. Our existence is an inescapable residue. Yet there are other realms, too, and about them, the mathematics is much less certain."

"What other realms?" she asked.

He didn't answer immediately.

"Do you mean sister worlds?" Unlike humans, Tilans easily believed that the universe was a great quantum stew. A trillion, trillion husbands precisely like him were sitting with their alien wives right now. Some were describing their lovely work. Some were quarreling with their spouses. And some great multitude was right now making love on the tabletop—an image that sprang into Mere's simple mind, causing her to smile.

"Are there mirror realities?" asked her husband.

He could feel them, couldn't he?

"But are these other worlds real, or simply shadows of the one existence which is real? Which is us." He laughed, enjoying his playful brilliance. "Or perhaps we are just one of the shadows cast by what is genuine and true?"

"I don't like that idea," she confessed.

"But some equations claim that all possibilities are correct."

Mere was dubious. "Okay," she said, "we should carry out tests. In labs, in the sky. Create some experiment where we can tell—"

"We cannot," he interrupted.

"No?"

"The energies required are prohibitive. The conditions are too extreme. To study the truths of Creation and Everything requires reaching outside our own little reality. And honestly, I doubt if any species commanding any technology could do the kind of work you want to attempt."

The truth was that Mere didn't want much of anything just now.

"Is there such a thing as the future?" he asked.

"Not one future," she replied immediately. "At least that is what I have been told ever since I can remember. Tomorrow is not set. A countless multitude of futures are possible, and each is inevitable."

Mere sounded Tilan, and to a point, she believed what she said.

"All right," her husband continued. "But is there one past? One history? One story that leads up to this good moment?"

What did he mean?

"Sometimes my equations claim there is no single past," he confessed. "What we think of as yesterday is exactly as unknowable and imprecise as what we think of as tomorrow."

She laughed at her husband. What choice did she have?

But he absorbed her laughter without complaint. "Sometimes, darling . . . my love . . . sometimes it seems to me as if we exist as a great assemblage of moments. Imagine time reduced to its smallest, most perfect unit. Then there is no such thing as time. We are a specific arrangement of matter and energy, each one equally precise but endowed with subtly different arrangements of matter and of energy—"

"But what about the past?" she interrupted. "I wasn't born a few moments ago, like you. I remember things that happened centuries ago."

"But you don't recall everything about those times," he pointed out. "And despite your considerable memory, I would guess that some of what you remember . . . little details and exactly when the big things happened . . . well, I could imagine that you can remember no single day with a perfect clarity."

"What does that mean?"

"The past is fundamentally unknowable. That's what my work tells me, on certain days."

"The past is sloppy, you mean."

"I prefer to consider it rich with potential." He meant that. Picking up his crystal bowl, he admitted, "This is a difficult subject," before he began licking out the last sticky bit of sweet oil.

Finally, Mere saw what this lecture was about. She wasn't smart in the same ways as her husband, but her mind was relentless enough to finally discern what was obvious. "Why just on some days?" she asked.

He paused with his licking. "Pardon?"

"These equations," she said. "They sound awfully fickle."

"A good word for it. Yes. Fickle."

"One day there is a clear past, but the next morning . . . what? The past becomes vague and crazy now?"

"In a sense," he agreed. "Although 'crazy' is not the best—"

"And some days, these parallel worlds are real. While some days, they're just shadows. Right?" Then she laughed, her own intuitive nature surfacing for a moment. "Or maybe we're the shadows, and someone else is real."

"Different days, different answers," he claimed.

"Why? Because you work with different equations?"

The moment demanded silence. The black eyes stared across the table, a keen delight fighting to the surface of the round white face. Thousands of years later, in an entirely different portion of the galaxy, Mere would recall the moment with the kind of clarity that convinced her that it was the genuine past, solid and eternal, and residing in that immortal moment of time, she was still sitting with her husband and lover, waiting for him to tell her:

"This is what I have noticed.

"On two different mornings, I can begin with the same thought. The same first equation. The same pen, and the same quality of parchment. My mood is equally relaxed and ready for my day. Yet by the time our suns our setting, my work has taken me to an entirely different conclusion. Even with the same initial steps, I cannot predict what I will make of the universe by the time I rise into sleep again."

Again, silence and the staring eyes.

Then with a low, plainly awed laugh, he added, "Sometimes I wonder. Perhaps there are many answers to the great questions, and like people drowning at sea, the answers struggle endlessly with one another, fighting for the chance to push through the surface, crazed by that slender, fragile hope of being seen."

A WARNING WOKE Mere, teasing her away from the Tila.

"The flow is at an end," the AI declared with a minimum of energy. "As you predicted, and exactly on schedule, the ice river has lost its containment. The polyponds are letting it die."

She continued to wake herself, lifting her slight metabolism until she found enough vigor to review the telemetry and give a few quick commands. Years ago, when the streakship had approached while returning from the Blue World, Pamir had shoved her scattered pieces of ship in the same useful direction. According to plans drawn up decades ago, Mere and her disheveled home dove into black dusts, effectively vanishing from everyone's view. The walls of the passageway proved denser than much of the Inkwell. The polyponds had cleared the way for the streakship, but like a Tilan broom sweeping at a dirt floor, they had pushed the dirt out of the way but no farther. Those next few days meant impacts, some of them major. Her original habitat was severely damaged, and she had to partly thaw her body and risk moving to the secondary habitat. From there, she carefully assembled all the pieces of her ship, fashioning a vessel that ended up looking rather different from the original schematics. Impacts and ever-changing circumstances required hard choices. Every surviving system from the first habitat was ripped loose, and then she disassembled what remained, tearing it down to individual atoms that she ionized and flung out ahead of her, slowing her progress at an infinitesimal rate.

In a brief ceremony, she christened her new ship:

The *Osmium*.

Old husbands needed the occasional honor, she felt. And she knew that the harum-scarum would appreciate the gesture when he learned about it.

Her new trajectory and the diminishing velocity set her on a collision course with the Great Ship. But that assumed both that the ship and the *Osmium* would successfully cross the Inkwell, neither changing its present velocity in any significant way.

Like all good plans, this plan failed soon after it began. Polypond eyes were supposed to see Mere as a cold empty fuel tank jettisoned centuries ago from a distant streakship. Her ion drive was too sluggish and slight to be obvious, and if necessary, she could kill the engine for days at a time, doing no lasting damage to her trajectory. But what no one predicted was what her own eyes would see. And that her ears would hear things that piqued her curiosity. And that, given the chance, she would take enormous risks to earn a better look and a closer listen.

In quiet, coded voices, the polyponds spoke endlessly to one another.

And using massive slow ships, they constantly sent little pieces of themselves from one warm world to another.

The ships were minimally armored. Nothing inside them seemed to be valuable enough to shroud in hyperfiber or protect with lasers. She focused on a transmission from a ship moving in the blackness ahead of her, unleashing all of her quantum code-breakers in a bid to make sense out of its dense, Gordian-like signal. Then at one point, the signal changed its nature. The coding sputtered abruptly and failed, and in the next millisecond, a lone voice sadly told its audience, "I have found unfortune—"

The ship exploded into a cloud of hydrogen gas and tiny fragments.

Mere replayed the collision a thousand times, measuring the spreading cloud's progress through the endless dark. And after considering various possibilities, she sent home her new flight plan and began rebuilding the *Osmium* once again.

Every pretense to being only an empty fuel tank ended. The new configuration was sturdy and purposeful if not particularly large. Inside the new engine, tucked inside a magnetic cask, was a substantial mass of anti-iron. The new engine was as advanced and expensive as anything known, and astonishingly efficient, and it had a kick and raw arrogance about it. To hide herself, the best Mere could manage was to fire up the engine whenever the shrouding dusts were thicker than normal. And she used it in hard brutal bursts, shoving herself into a slower, slightly different trajectory that eventually took her through the ruined ship.

With whispering lasers, she studied the scattered pieces. Nanosecond bursts of energy pushed her closer to the interesting bits. With magnetic nets, she collected what was nearest and electrically charged, eventually pulling in a caramelized block of organic material a little smaller than one of her tiny hands.

Death is never a simple state. Not to philosophers, nor to a determined if rather limited biologist.

In a laboratory no bigger than a closet, Mere reached inside the burnt and blasted chunk of matter, finding neurons built along some alien logic. If this had been a human mind, she could have reanimated and interrogated it. If it belonged to any known alien, she might have managed the same trick, with patience. But despite similarities to a dozen known species, there was no easy path to progress. This was a sliver of a mind. There was no telling how large the original brain had been, or what its function had been, and if anything important had been filed away in this tiny corner of Self. But what else did Mere have to do today? What else was half as important as studying this prize? That was her attitude every morning, waking from a dream-rattled sleep for the next four thousand mornings, the same first thought bubbling out of her:

"Today I'll make sense of you, my friend. My fellow survivor."

THE *OSMIUM* CONTINUED plunging deep into the Inkwell.

At random intervals, Mere received updates from home—encrypted and cleverly disguised, each containing highly summarized accounts of what the captains saw and what the resident experts believed, at least a few years ago. The data were cut to the bone; information meant noise, and any noise, no matter how well hidden, increased the chance of discovery. That was why the Inkwell charts were updated only occasionally, and even when limited to the changes from past charts, the updates were fantastically complicated—hundreds of cubic light-years full of thread-like rivers of ionized ice, many thousands of warm-moon and Mars-mass bodies, plus banks of dense black dust and clouds of frigid hydrogen that were gathered at their densest inside the Satin Sack. Each of those features had been carefully named, and all moved in relation to their neighbors as well as the rest of the Inkwell. Each river flowed with its own velocity while the masses of dust and gas gradually acquired new shapes, spinning on some grand axis or holding perfectly still, features gaining mass or losing their substance according to some thoroughly choreographed scheme that felt natural and planned, and at all times, deeply beautiful.

Mere had been pushing through the Satin Sack for several months, far ahead of the Great Ship but gradually drifting closer to its course. One evening, just as she was rising into sleep, an update arrived inside the much-diluted beam of a navigational laser. The newest charts were included, along with an upbeat message from the Master Captain. "I can't express how thankful I am to have your good eyes and mind serving us," the golden face declared. "And don't be a stranger, please."

"Call home," was the message's true intent.

It had been more than a year since Mere had taken that risk, and then only to offer a minimal description of her latest trajectory. For many smart reasons, she had no intention of revealing her existence now, or for years to come, if necessary. When she had something to offer, of course she would speak. But despite twenty-hour workdays and a wealth of observations, nothing seemed quite urgent enough or peculiarly odd.

Nine days later, again at bedtime, a far-off laser caressed the *Osmium*, its infrared beam too diffuse to be noticed by the casual observer.

Embedded inside the beam, wrapped within a package of photons too weak to melt a snowflake, were great volumes of new information. It was too soon for any message from the Great Ship, much less another complete chart update. The random schedule of transmissions had been decided ages ago, known only to the captains and her, and this was an entirely unscheduled event.

Someone was playing a game, Mere suspected.

But the encryptions were proper, and a hundred predetermined cues added to the authenticity. She stored the transmission, isolated it, then asked for a volunteer among the resident AIs. "Examine it," she told one of the semisentient entities. "And tell me what you think."

The AI was thorough and exacting, and it was very slow. Mere had time to eat a tiny, cold-blooded dinner—a taste of sugar and a bite of fat giving her refrigerated body the energy necessary to survive the night. Then instead of sleeping, she continued working on a project that had consumed the last few hours of this particular day.

She had recovered more than just that neural mass from the polypond vessel. Twists and slivers of plastic and alloyed metals, diamond shards and low-grade hyperfiber gave subtle clues about their collective purpose. Even their pattern in space was important. By replaying the collision and matching it with the debris field, Mere had built a reasonably accurate model of both the polypond ship and its death: simple fusion engines and big tanks full of liquid hydrogen, plus a minimal shield protecting a spherical compartment quite a bit larger than her own ship. The bolide—probably a chunk of cometary ice—had torn through the shield before delivering a glancing blow to the ship's heart. The resulting blast had scattered debris across billions of kilometers, and everything made perfect sense except for the problem of what the ship had been carrying.

The polyponds were self-maintaining Gaian worlds.

Supposedly.

Like old trees in a great forest, the largest of them dominated their local landscape, while the babies were born in dense little groves removed from the rest. But unlike trees, individuals such as the Blue World seemed able to generate their own energy. With a whim, they could build continents and populate them with whatever organisms they felt they needed. Which begged the question:

What products would they trade with one another?

It could be politics, Mere reasoned. Neural bodies representing some mother world would journey out to visit the neighbors, like emissaries, achieving in person what coded communications couldn't accomplish.

It could be a slow, proven means of teaching one another.

Or it was a ritual of great age and undeniable importance: an exchange of tissues and minds, perhaps tied into some unending process that won friendship and solidarity from all of the polyponds.

Or it was nothing but gossip, ugly and simple.

From her vantage point, with her limited eyes, Mere couldn't see far or particularly well. Like a hiker in a deep forest, she had a wondrous view of the trail under her feet, but the gloom kept most of the woods hidden. Inside the Inkwell, and particularly now, deeply embedded within the Satin Sack, she felt as if she was halfway blind. Features barely half a light-year distance had to be enormous to be seen, or very bright, and nothing here seemed particularly big or brilliant.

Where did the polypond ship begun its voyage? And to where was it heading when it was killed?

Good candidates were tough to find, answers impossible. But during these last few weeks, as Mere dove into the increasingly dense Sack, she was remembering what she had noticed aeons ago while walking through a Tilan jungle: Trees were only the largest, showiest citizens, and no matter how impressive, they were always outnumbered a thousandfold by things tiny, and, in their own way, quite astonishing.

Scanning the nearby blackness, she was making her own thorough map of objects too tiny and too distant for the captains to notice. Everywhere she looked, she saw the telltale signs of little machines working in patient cold ways. Sometimes her ship moved in unexpected directions, betraying the touch of a small mass close enough to give her a faint, brief tug. Just as her own feeble mass was tugging at each of them.

Another stew of problems, that.

"What am I to think?" she muttered quietly to the dead caramelized lump. "Is there anything here that bites or stings?"

She laughed for a moment, softly. Then her thoughts began to wander, and for the first time in months, Mere found herself thinking about one of her favorite Tilan husbands—the great genius of Creation. Which was when her slow-minded AI announced finally, "I am finished with my work."

"Is it genuine?"

"The message is. Yes."

"But is it interesting?"

There was a pause. It was a long, thoughtful pause according to a machine's compressed sense of time. Then the AI reported, "This is a fascinating message from the Great Ship, I believe."

Washen had sent the communication, not the Master Captain. Just that was an alarming detail. The holo of the First Chair smiled at her good friend, and with a cool and strong but decidedly puzzled voice, she reported, "Some of these baby polyponds—the buds—are picking themselves up and moving."

An elaborate new chart began to unfold before her.

"You probably can't see them yet," Washen mentioned. "It's happening at the Sack's farthest reaches first. And of course, we have some difficulty seeing the other side of the Sack, so we can't be sure what's there. But what we do know is an enormous surprise."

Mere focused on the chart, and in particular, on one of the little polyponds. A vast fusion engine had grown from one hemisphere, and the entire body was ac-

celerating at a brutal cost. Just a glance showed her how much energy was involved, and a second hard look told her the eventual velocity and at what point it
would intersect with the Great Ship.

"These are the most distant buds," Washen repeated. Then with a friendly grin,
she added, "But you can see the implications for yourself, I'm sure."

Mere nodded.

"So what do you think?" asked a voice speaking across great reaches of cold
and darkness. "Any ideas?"

Again, she nodded.

"I'm not all that surprised," Mere whispered to herself. Then she laughed at
herself, adding, "But why am I not surprised? Now that's the question worth
answering!"

Nineteen

EVERY MORNING, WASHEN slipped free of her clothes and abandoned the little
schooner, swimming until she reached the point where there was nothing to see
but the jade-colored sky and the smooth, empty, and utterly flat face of the ocean.
Except for the occasional faint cloud, the sky was empty, and besides her body and
its resident microbes, the water was nearly devoid of life. Waste heat from factories
and reactors warmed the surface waters. For the last hundred millennia, these deep
caverns had been left immersed in darkness. The illusory sun was an enormous
expense, and building it for a single person was extraordinary, and of course she
had fought the entire concept. For five months, practically from the day that the
emissary died, Washen dismissed every suggestion of a holiday. But it wasn't only
Pamir who had pushed her into this empty time. The Master Captain argued,
"You've worn yourself to dust, darling." Speaking at the last banquet, gazing out
at every captain, the Master shook her head soberly, reminding her audience, "We
need to make ourselves fresh and ready for what comes. But a few of us, I'm
afraid, are working our finite souls into a frail, stupid, and useless kind of numbness." Then she pointed an accusing finger at her First Chair, adding, "I order you
to take time off. Now. Turn off your nexuses, darling. Peel away that uniform.
And for the sake of the ship and yourself, get some rest!"

It was an order that Washen simply couldn't accept.

Pamir repeated the argument on several occasions. He was stubbornly persua-
sive, and she was charmingly evasive. "I'm coping. I'm sane. Test me, darling. Any
way you wish, and I promise, you'll go away pleased."

Then he turned blunt, bordering on defiant, and Washen leaned against good
rational arguments. "I can't leave my job now," she professed. "Just today, another

fifteen polypond nurseries are moving. And those are the ones we can optically resolve. At last count, fifty thousand buds are on a rendezvous course with us."

"A rendezvous that won't happen for years," Pamir mentioned.

"While the grown polyponds have stopped talking to us," she continued, nothing about her voice or manner betraying the true depth of her worries. "And while the Blue World and several dozen other adults are on the move, too."

"Listen to your own propaganda," he countered. "We're dealing with an isolated species of committed hermits who have no choice but to deal with us, and who have done everything they promised to help our voyage."

She shook her head. "What happened to the famous Pamir paranoia?"

"When I need it, I'll bring it out to dance."

Washen laughed for a long moment.

"Are you done?"

"Hardly," she promised.

Pamir bristled, saying nothing.

Then Washen continued laying out the obvious dangers as well as her meaty fears. "Most of this is conjecture. We know nothing, and so everything is possible. And we're doing just about everything we can do, preparing ourselves for whatever we can imagine."

"We'll win any war," Pamir muttered.

"But doing just about everything isn't doing everything, and don't even pretend that we can imagine all the possibilities—"

"I'm not talking," he grumbled.

"Thank you," she snarled.

"When did you sleep last?"

"Fifty minutes ago," she reported.

"For how long?"

Washen felt a knife in her stomach. But she kept smiling, and with only the barest tension, she added, "Ten-minute naps can accomplish worlds. If you know how to space them."

"If you know," he echoed.

She couldn't linger and debate. Washen had intelligence reports begging to be digested, half a dozen mood campaigns to launch, and a huge proposal from Aasleen to study. At her prompting, the chief engineer had devised the means to make the ship's enormous rocket nozzles into telescopes. Thin mirrors would be applied after every burn, focusing mechanisms eating the starlight and correcting the clumsy reflections until they could be trusted. As many as five engines might be employed, each vast and capable of being tilted at relatively steep angles, and working with the existing telescope fields on the ship's trailing face, they could theoretically peer farther into the cosmos than any other array in the galaxy.

"Of course every time we fire an engine, we'll have to rebuild the telescope,"

Aasleen mentioned, skepticism mixed with the occasional damning figures. "And we don't dare try this now, since we're shooting off little burns every few weeks."

The tunnel through the Inkwell was open and empty. The polyponds weren't speaking to them anymore, but the forward-facing telescopes saw a clean, well-scrubbed path through the center of the Satin Sack. Little burns meant they were on course. The barest nudge today meant falling down the middle of the path, not glancing against any edge.

"But still," the chief engineer continued. "This has me wondering. Why invest time and energy to look back at where we've been? What are you thinking? That someone is following us?"

"I have no idea."

"But you do have an idea," Aasleen pressed. "I lived on Marrow. For a good long while, that was my home. And, Madam First Chair, I know exactly what this obsession is about."

"Whatever is true," Washen began. Then her voice lost its way, and her eyes closed, and after a moment, she asked, "Wouldn't you want to know what's out there?"

"No, I don't think I would like to know."

The women shared a grim little laugh. Then the meeting ended with an obligatory discussion about the polyponds and motives. Aasleen offered one fresh and incredible suggestion, but before Washen could take it seriously, she dismissed her proposal for a hundred thorough reasons. Then she repeated what had always been the official hypothesis. "We're talking about children," she reminded Washen. "The buds just want a close look at us. That's all."

Except the Blue World, and the several of the other full-grown polyponds, were climbing after them, too.

"Old doesn't mean incurious," the chief engineer joked.

"Yes it does," Washen joked, then sent her friend away, skipping her next scheduled sleep, preferring to use her scarce time to study a tangle of social projections and poll results and crew reports and rumor studies. Then it was suddenly tomorrow, and one of her nagging nexuses reminded her of another key appointment. She couldn't be late. In a tiny swift and unmarked cap-car, she arrived at the correct apartment in a matter of minutes. The door greeted her warmly and explained that her son had been detained. "But breakfast is ready in the Marrow room," the voice added. "Locke says to go and make yourself comfortable."

She went there, but comfort was nearly impossible.

Alone, she sat at the edge of the lava field. To re-create the life cycles of the Marrow creatures, Locke had flooded one corner of the big room with liquid iron. The succession process had barely begun. Beneath a dim gray sky, Washen claimed a simple chair woven from fireweeds and jeweled beetles, and she ate most of a hammerwing while her mind leaped from nexus to nexus, dealing with a hundred little jobs before a voice—a distinct and quite familiar voice—declared, "Here is something that you need to understand, dear."

Washen looked up to find a dead woman standing before her.

The narrow face grinned, enjoying her surprise. Then Miocene stepped closer, looking like a suffering woman or an exceptionally vigorous ghost. Her flesh was gray and smoky. Her uniform was composed of Marrow materials, lacking the brilliance and endurance of Washen's clothes. The only First Chairs that the ship had ever known stared at one another in the evening glare, and the standing woman said, "I worked hard, always. Everything I earned came from my strength and my deep determination, and all that endless work."

The sitting woman flinched.

"Since you're the best at a thousand jobs," the dead woman continued, "you are smart to do them all for yourself."

Washen struggled to stand.

"What do you think?" Miocene continued. "That I was an insufferable bitch through the whole of my life?"

Washen woke, finding a hand upon her shoulder and Locke saying, "Sorry. I let you sleep, and our time's done."

"What time is it?" she muttered, momentarily confused.

Through a hundred nexuses, she learned the name of this particular moment. And then the moment was gone, left behind and lost, and that's when she finally talked herself into taking the vacation.

IT WASN'T ENOUGH just to silence her buried nexuses. Pamir had agreed, and with a calm insistence, he added, "You also need to be somewhere without people. Without crew or passengers, or me."

"I'll miss you," she mentioned.

"We barely see each other," he reminded her, just enough of a barb in the words to make his disgust plain. Then he proposed an itinerary for an unusual, one-of-a-kind holiday.

"The Grand Ocean," he began.

An image took hold of her. She laughed, interrupting him to ask, "Why not just a little pond in an unlit room? Wouldn't that be just as dark and alone?"

"We'll light the sky for you," he promised.

The waste made her queasy.

"And while the cavern's lit," he continued, "Osmium's troops can search for secret colonies and illegal adventurers. So there is a good purpose in this business, other than keeping the ship's head sane."

The Grand Ocean was not a single cavern; it was a vast array of linked caves that happened to lie at the same depths inside the ship. The first humans mapped the great volume, and then flooded it with melted ice from a hundred higher caverns. The Ocean's surface area was larger than the Earth's. Reaching more than a hundred kilometers deep, it was the biggest body of water on the ship and bigger than most of the galaxy's other oceans, too. And it was empty. Except for a tiny quantity of dissolved minerals and salt, it was nothing but pure, cold, and unlit water, kept in reserve for the homeward leg of the ship's voyage. Except for the rare autotrophic bacteria, nothing lived in this realm. Just with her presence, Washen had nearly doubled the bioload of the entire sea.

She hadn't swum so much since childhood. Every morning for the last thirty mornings, Washen had practiced a variety of strokes, muscles gradually relearning the rhythm and feel of pressing against the water. Then the swimming became unconscious, and she could push her ageless long body to its limits, steady hard strokes eventually making her gasp and giggle.

Thinking about the Great Ship wasn't allowed—at least not until the long swim home. And when she did think of large subjects, she kept her mind fixed on the broadest matters, no little jobs or urgent timetables nipping at her now. In that seemingly infinite span of water, Washen kept finding a sweet comfort: the ship's size and age, and the unimaginable distances that it had crossed, always on its own. She loved this glorious orb of high technology and simple stone, and how could she not feel a little foolish to worry about threats, real or imagined?

Her schooner called to her with the only nexus she allowed herself—a simple navigational beacon whispering, "This way, yes. This way." Back on her temporary home, she prepared a huge meal and ate all of it, and she raised the sails with her increasingly strong back and arms. The artificial sun had darkened her limbs. A steady wind always rose by midday, carrying her for another few kilometers before the sun dropped and darkness descended. But it wasn't the perfect black that ruled here normally. Pamir had painted a starscape both odd and familiar. Without nexuses, Washen couldn't feel sure about its origins; but when she looked at the smears of light and occasional feeble star, she realized that she was gazing at the galaxies of the Virgo cluster—a vast realm of suns and unnamed worlds, gas clouds and raw energy that might, in many millions of years, meet the Great Ship.

Alone, Washen would hold long, elaborate conversations with herself, enjoying the sound of her own voice and the quick well-rested thoughts that slipped between the words.

She slept hard for six or even seven hours at a stretch—the longest uninterrupted sleep she could remember—and she woke rested, alert eyes gazing across an emptiness of quiet water that couldn't seem more lovely.

On the thirty-first morning, she swam again.

At first, Washen lay on her back, one arm after the other reaching over her head, swift hands cutting into the water and yanking hard. When she felt warm and loose, she turned over onto her belly, and like a happy porpoise, she did a rolling stroke, browned arms reaching together as the body bent like a wave, every muscle working with an instinctive grace, pointed feet delivering the final hard kick.

It was an expensive stroke for a human body. Eventually she collapsed into a simple crawl, from time to time pausing, looking back over her shoulder. The horizons were far away, but her boat was a little thing, and she had only good human eyes to look across all that bright smooth water.

Once the masts and folded sails had vanished, she turned for home.

With a simple patient breaststroke, Washen made the return voyage, her tanned face held out of the water and her long black hair streaming behind her. Quietly, she talked to herself. About nothing, usually. She spoke to dead people and lost lovers, and sometimes she imagined the grandchildren whom she had left down below, fighting for their lives on Marrow.

"What are you doing now?" she asked them.

Then she apologized for leaving. "I did what was best. I hope. For the ship, which means for you, too."

It was the last morning of her holiday.

Halfway back to the boat, while thinking about nothing clear or certain, she hesitated. Her arms pulled up beneath her and stopped, while her tucking legs remained tucked. A body just buoyant enough to float now drifted along on the last of its momentum, and then she pulled herself into a tiny hard ball, exhaling hard enough to leave her lungs deflated and small.

Washen sank.

A minute passed, and most of another. Then she surfaced again, breaking into a hard clean crawl fed by deep quick breaths. Water splashed. Legs thundered. She reached the schooner in less than ten minutes, too exhausted to climb the ladder on her first attempt, or her second.

Struggling, Washen managed to clamber up onto the dampened oak deck.

Still naked, she tucked herself into a fetal ball, eyes open and seeing nothing. Nothing. She was focused and slack-faced. Even as her breathing slowed, she didn't seem to notice, a deeply distracted attitude clinging to her as she dried herself and dressed.

"Make breakfast or not?" she asked herself.

"Make it," she decided.

But somewhere in the middle of the preparation, watching blocks of salted fat and round dabs of cultured eggs cooking in the hot skillet, she said, "Stop."

Alone, she climbed up on deck and sat on the narrow bow.

To herself, she said, "Okay. I guess that's it then."

Several hours before her vacation was scheduled to end, she woke one of her nexuses, and with a calm, smooth, and certain voice, she said, "Pamir."

"It's too early," he snapped.

"Listen," Washen said.

"What?"

"As soon as possible," she said.

Angry silence.

Then she glanced out over the empty water, feeling the day's delicious wind playing across her face. "We need to change course," she said to Pamir and to herself. "Today, I mean. This minute. And I couldn't be more sure."

Twenty

"TWO THREE-ENGINE BURNS," Washen promised. "In thirteen hours, then fifty hours later. Brief burns, the second putting us on a parallel course. Here. We'll be moving ten AU removed from our present route. Here. Outside the tunnel wall, no polyponds or major obstructions visible. Of course we'll send warnings beforehand. We don't want to be impolite. And yes, we'll have to absorb extra impacts. Piercing the wall, then a fortyfold increase in the base erosion rate. But that's within tolerances. Ten years to cross the Sack, and what's the best guess? Between nine and eleven hundred Class-4 impacts, and half a hundred Class-3s. With nothing large enough, at least so far, to cause a Class-2 or worse." Washen threw a sturdy look down the length of the table, telling the Submasters, "I'll offer my reasons, starting with the most obvious and weakest example." She paused for a moment, then admitted, "I don't trust our hosts, and a prudent course correction that puts us on a new, unexpected trajectory . . . well, that's going help me sleep tonight."

Again, she fell silent.

The meeting room was long and plainly decorated, one of the short walls overlooking the ship's bridge. Better than a hundred captains were visible below them, standing at their stations, accomplishing their work with a smooth competence. But sometimes one or two would glance up at the Submasters, narrowed gazes and a few muttered words hinting at the curiosity and the raw worry that was already seeping through the ranks.

Why this emergency meeting? they wondered. And why were the other Submasters staring at the First Chair with those stunned expressions? What had she said that was so awful?

A fef raised a middle arm, human fashion.

"Just a moment," Washen cautioned. Then she leaned across the long table, adding, "The polyponds aren't talking. But if we do the unexpected, maybe we can generate a fresh dialogue with them."

The alien arm dropped, but an urgent voice said, "Madam."

"Change course," Washen argued, "and we might disrupt our hosts' plans. Whatever they happen to be."

"Madam—"

"How long would it take the polyponds to barricade the tunnel ahead of us?" Washen looked at the chief engineer. "Since they only need to drag matter across a few tens of thousands of kilometers—"

"Hours," Aasleen reported. "They could push a gram of material into every thousand cubic meters, and manage it in less than twenty-four hours." Then she allowed her own skepticism to surface, calmly adding, "If, if, if that happened to be their desire."

Washen magnified portions of the most recent charts, feeding them into her colleagues' nexuses. "I see five concentrations of matter," she pointed out. "Scattered beside the tunnel, we have congregations of dust and cometary grit, and inside this last mass, there's enough iron to fashion a good-sized asteroid. It might have been an asteroid that wandered into the Inkwell and was mined to dust. For all we know, these features have always been here. They're entirely benign. But if not . . . if the polyponds wanted to pull this moon back into a single mass and then drop it in our way—?"

"They still can," a deep voice interrupted.

Washen glanced at Pamir. "Elaborate," she said.

"Your new course doesn't get us far from these maybe-hazards," he pointed out. "The only advantage, from what I can tell, is that we'll be outside the tunnel, which means outside that wall of dust. Our eyes will work a little better now. If something approaches, we might see it sooner."

"That's one of my reasons for doing this," Washen agreed. But she would have been more honest to say, "It's just another tidy rationalization."

This was an instinctive decision, and what could she offer?

Openness.

"Yes," she said to the fef. "You have a comment."

The creature bent in the middle, lifting his face high before remarking, "Our maneuver will be misunderstood. Unless aggression is the intention, and then we will be making our plans transparently plain."

Washen nodded and waited.

Pamir responded for both of them. "What I know about polyponds—what I am certain about—is that too many of them to count are burning up a huge portion of their own big bodies to approach us. Feeding their curiosity, maybe. But I've never genuinely believed that. And I'd tell you what I do believe, except after months of hard thought, I still don't know. So I'll just assume that they want to take possession of our vessel, and like any muscle-bound bully, they don't see the need to explain themselves."

A pause.

Then Pamir glanced at Washen, in warning. "That's not to say I completely agree with our First Chair's plan. I can't. But we're at the point where we have very little freedom of motion. We're going to plunge through the Satin Sack, following the same essential course, and nothing substantial can possibly change. That's why I've got a little proposal of my own. Something that I haven't quite mentioned yet."

Washen looked at him, and she looked into herself. What was her motivation here? From everything possible and everything feared, which story did she believe in more than any other?

"A third burn," Pamir offered. "I think we need one."

Everyone referred to Washen's charts, trying to guess where the new burn would happen.

He said, "An all-engine burn, this time."

On the chart, a thin white line marked the two deft jogs in their course, and then Pamir added a bluish flare, shoving the ship's mass forward with a very slight acceleration, pushing it faster into the blackest depths of the Sack.

"It won't buy us much velocity," he admitted. "But anything that throws off our enemy's timetable sounds workable to me."

Washen considered his model.

"More discussion?" Aasleen asked. "Or is everything decided?"

Another dozen Submasters asked the same question.

Then the fef gazed at the Master Captain, saying, "Your excellence," with a worshipful tone. "What are your feelings and configurings on this matter, your excellence?"

Sitting at one end of the long table, flanked by her First and Second Chairs, the great woman appeared to smile. But it was a stern, unhappy expression, and the voice that came rolling out of her was sorry and dark. "I have doubts about each of these maneuvers," she admitted. "Doubts and worries, and genuine concerns. But alone, I can't make decisions of consequence. I know this, and I can almost accept this limitation. If my first two chairs decide that there will be three burns, then there will be three burns. I have nothing but voice and experience to offer here."

Washen felt a chill along her neck. She glanced at the Master, then sighed and turned back to Pamir, remarking, "You don't have an end point on this huge burn of yours."

"Don't I?" he kidded.

"How many days do you intend? Or is it weeks?"

"What do you want from my engines?" Aasleen pressed.

"I was thinking of years," Pamir admitted. Then with a snort, he reminded everyone, "We're being ambushed here. So why not gallop as fast as possible for as long as possible?"

The silence was perfect and brief.

Staring at the Master Captain, Osmium asked, "What are your doubts, madam?"

"Do you wish to maintain our present course?" asked the fef. "As we promised the polyponds?"

A wide hand swept through the air.

"No," she replied with a rumbling voice. Then a sudden laugh took everyone by surprise. "No," she said and again, "no, I don't have any unique opinions on the merits and risks of any course adjustment."

She treasured this moment, every eye firmly focused on her.

"But I do know something about duplicity and shrewdness. And as reasonable as this plan feels, I can't help but wonder . . . with a tight chest and a drumming heart, wonder . . . if this is what the polyponds always intended us to do . . . !"

THE FIRST BURN was preceded by a quick, thorough, and scrupulously honest explanation of reasons. There was little time to dress up the announcements, much less tailor them for individual species. The Master Captain spoke to passengers and crew at the same time, the practice of aeons allowing her to appear both confident and in control. Yes, there would be a wave of quick impacts. Yes, there would be more large impacts. No passengers would be allowed on the ship's leading face, at least for the time being. Repair teams and fabrication facilities would be on constant duty. Then with an unflappable resolve, she reminded billions that a large portion of the Inkwell had already been crossed, without incident, and despite the approaching polyponds, not one shot had been fired and no war was declared. "And unless we're given spectacular reasons," she concluded, "we will hold our new line and ask nothing of anyone but ourselves."

The tunnel wall tested the shields and laser arrays. A few thousand mirrors were off-line for several days, and one crew of fef were vaporized when a fist-sized lump of stone fell on their heads. Then the ship was slicing its way through a bank of cold hydrogen, the shields blazing overhead, and another three engines were twisted and ignited, leaving three broad columns of fierce heat and stripped nuclei curling around one another, building elaborate and sloppy knots across millions of kilometers.

The third burn began an hour later.

For the first time since humans came upon this relic, every engine was lit in the same instant and left burning, lakes of liquid hydrogen flooding into chambers of high-grade hyperfiber, compressed and ignited and the blasts made more powerful by myriad tricks and cheats. Antimatter spiked the fuel, and the hyperfiber vibrated across a multitude of dimensions and shadowy realms. Energy normally lost was brought back again. Neutrinos were focused and ejected. A brilliant kick was delivered to the ship, and twenty Earth masses responded with an ever-so-slight acceleration.

At a distance, the fourteen engines made for a single bright point of light and a straight hot trail that grew until it was light-weeks long.

But at a greater distance, the engines were only a steady, nearly feeble glow visible only in narrow portions of the infrared. And the ship was nothing. A tiny, tiny point surrounded by a multitude of smaller engines moving tinier masses . . .

hundreds of thousands of buds now . . . a diffuse sphere collapsing toward a single point, and growing in numbers by the day, by the moment . . . a blaze of steam and plasmas driving that multitude down on top of that sluggish and tiny and very nearly helpless machine.

Twenty-one

HANDING MERE A long piece of yellow paper, he said, "Here. This is for you."

"I can't read this," she complained. Nobody could read it. The paper was rough and jammed full of delicate scribbles—the hard work of a persistent and empty little child, no doubt. Looking at her dead husband, she pointed out, "This isn't Tilan, and it isn't human, either."

"But it's for you," he claimed.

So she stared at it again, harder this time.

"Help me," she begged.

"It is a deeply embedded pattern," a voice told her. "A persistent thought in the fragment's surviving memory."

"I'm very tired," she confessed.

Silence.

"For a moment, I thought you were someone else . . ."

"Madam," the AI said. "Perhaps sleep would do you a service, madam."

Mere looked at a diamond sphere, and inside it, the suspended fragment of the polypond mind. Warmth and an array of delicate silver fingers had allowed a feeble life to emerge. The fragment was thinking. This was what it seemed to be thinking. Again, Mere stared at the display cube nestled in her hand, exhausted eyes working their way through the intricate web of three-dimensional symbols.

"This is my friend's mind?"

"It is a very simple representation, yes." A hint of pride surfaced as the machine remarked, "The amount of information is impressive. Despite time and the mind's damage, it has retained this much."

"A three-dimensional image?"

"And more, madam."

She hesitated. "There's a time component?"

"Yes."

"Show me."

Every thread of the web slowly shifted position, and after a little while, all began to contract or to melt away. The display shriveled into a smaller, denser shape that eventually became nothing but a dark smudge.

"This is the past?"

"It seems so," the machine offered.

Mere nodded, her tiny face pale and drawn. Then an instinct tickled her, and smiling, she said, "There's more, isn't there?"

"Several curiosities, yes."

The AI ran the image forward in time. The smudge enlarged and grew thinner, becoming a lacework of tiny details rendered in three dimensions. Turning the cube in her hands, she studied its final shape. "I see a resemblance," she muttered. "Is this a map of the Inkwell?"

"Perhaps."

"Are these strands the rivers of ice?"

"No."

"Okay," she said. "The curiosities. Show me."

A tiny portion of the display was enlarged a thousandfold, revealing an equally intricate set of features. The central strand was composed of a multitude of tiny flecks and round forms and new strands as straight as taut hairs. Again, time ran backward. The various features shifted and sometimes vanished, and the round shapes passed out of view or shrank down to tiny points that moved together, swirling in unison much the same as the polypond buds swam inside their birthing space.

"Watch carefully," the AI advised.

Time ran forward, ending with something very close to the present.

"Did you notice?"

"I doubt it."

Like an endlessly patient teacher, the AI said, "Watch again."

Three times, the process was repeated. And then Mere said, "Enough," as she touched the display with the nail of one finger. "There are always differences, is that right? The positions of these features . . . they seem to shift a little bit . . ."

"Minuscule differences, but genuine. I have unfolded this thought more than twelve thousand times, and each replay is unique."

Mere opened her mouth, then closed it again.

"This is a partial memory," the machine offered. "Perhaps your friend is struggling to recall everything with precision."

"No," Mere said. Then she set the cube aside, drifting out of the tiny lab, trying to coax her weary mind into using its own deep and perishable memories.

A navigational AI whispered, "You asked to be informed, madam."

"More buds moving?"

An image filled the nearest touch screen. Several light-months deeper inside the Satin Sack, a multitude of watery bodies were beginning to accelerate, engines flinging much of their bodies into the dusty gloom, giving them momentum while stealing away most of their lazy mass.

"I want to see the ship now, please."

Still far behind her, the ancient vessel was visible only in the infrared, the blaze of its engines and the wild discharging of its shields producing a sloppy dot that would brighten over the next months and years. While Mere watched, a tiny flash of light swept across the leading face. The laser array had struck some burly hazard. Another few seconds told her that the blow was successful. If anything substantial had reached the hull, she would have seen the blast. In her present mood, she probably would have felt it, too.

"I assume these little ones are also aiming for the Great Ship."

"Presumably, yes," said the navigator AI.

"And when?"

"As with the rest—" the voice began.

She named the year. This was a slow stately chase, and everything about it seemed inevitable. Irresistible.

Mere returned to the other AI. "You mentioned more than one curiosity. What else is there?"

"I have to warn you. I'm not trained in the details and every side-shoot concept that involves these high mathematics."

"Okay."

"But more than four dimensions are folded into the memory. They are invisible, but they seem to have a genuine value."

She nodded, watching the polyponds rise to meet the ship.

"When I said that this is a partial memory," the AI continued, "and perhaps your friend is struggling to recall—"

"I said, 'No.' "

"Would you explain why, madam?"

Every AI listened now. A glance at the main touch pad told her that she was the focus of considerable interest.

Recovering the display cube, she offered, "I don't think this is a genuine memory, and it isn't a map, either." Then she shook her head, adding, "This is a lesson, I'm guessing. Search our library. Learn what you can about mathematical treatments of time . . . treatments that erase the concept of an authentic past . . . and then apply what you learn there to what we have with us here . . ."

A moment passed.

"This is a very complicated subject," the AI complained.

"Then you aren't thinking about it properly," she chided gently. Then she pushed the cube aside, ordered the cabin lights down, and forced herself to crawl inside her sacklike bed and rise into a dreamless deep sleep.

BUT THERE WAS such a creature as the Past: a remote and simple and pure entity, and everything of consequence had leaped from its beautiful self. What every Tilan understood instinctively, and what Mere had learned in her long early life, was that the future was infinite and unknowable. Every instant of time had no choice but to explode into long lines of potential. Existence was a multitude of rivers born from an ever-increasing assortment of springs. Mere was born in one moment and one place, and now she lived on a million worlds and between the worlds and in places she could never imagine.

This Mere had a past that she knew well and cherished.

This Mere only appeared solitary, but she was part of a rich thread of interlinked moments leading directly from that slightly younger, slightly less informed woman who had told her AI, "Then you aren't thinking about it properly."

Eleven months had passed, and Mere was cold again. She had dismantled and dispersed the *Osmium*, power minimal and her own body chilled to the brink of death. Surrounding her was an ebony shell of motionless dust, smothering and dense and surprisingly warm within. When she studied the cloud earlier, in visual light and from a great distance, she saw nothing. Her best eyes had stared at the same points for hours, absorbing only the occasional glimmer of radio noise and the wandering photons that had pierced the banks of dust and molecular hydrogen. But the infrared was richer, revealing a network of starlike dots and tidy smears arranged with precision. And more telling, her surviving neutrino detector—a minimal sensor on its finest day—was loudly proclaiming, "Something bright, I see! I see!"

Similar clouds were scattered throughout the neighborhood. Each was a neat sphere held together by electrostatic charges and youth. Each was smaller than a solar system and blackened with buckyballs and other carbon grits, natural and otherwise. But only one of the clouds lay close enough to be reached. A series of little burns could push Mere into a collision course, and against the sober advice of her resident AIs, she had accepted that grand chance.

Months later, her disassembled ship plunged into the cloud. After several hours of pushing through thickening dusts, she spotted her potential targets. They were tiny objects. Remote. Yet the gap was barely 50 million kilometers now, which was no distance at all. On her present course, Mere would pass by the first of the mysteries in less than nine minutes. The entire collection of bodies would fall behind in another half hour. They were warm objects, pieces of them fiercely hot, each wearing elaborate radiators that pumped the excess heat into cold sinks and the surrounding cloud, and they were intriguing enough that even the most cautious AIs had stopped their public worrying.

Every moment brought little impacts and endless damage.

Mere was dying in countless other existences, but not here. Here she remained healthy enough, if only for the next little moment.

And the moment after.

And for another nine excruciating, inevitable minutes.

The *Osmium* slid past its first target without incident. Full-spectrum images were taken, samples of dust and vacuum were absorbed, and a sudden burst of radio noise was recorded in full. Even at 5 million kilometers—Mere's closest approach—the object's mass pulled her ship's pieces farther apart. Then she was past her target and free to glance at the results, at the data and the first instinctive declarations of her AIs. They had danced with some kind of machine or factory. The mass of the large asteroid had been compressed and elongated, caked with hyperfiber and powered by a trailing necklace of fusion reactors. The energy production was impressive, and it was nothing. Each of the next six factories were larger, each fed by still more reactors. The cloud's hydrogen was the fuel. The cloud's dust was the raw material. Both were being collected by vast electrostatic baleens and drawn inward into the first of the cylindrical factories, separated by composition and charged again, then ushered along on parallel magnetic rivers.

Suddenly Mere's habitat absorbed a clean sharp blow.

Worry blossomed. Not about death, since that wouldn't allow time enough for worry. No, she was afraid that she might be discovered. Every impact, tiny or major, produced a fountain of plasma. Plasmas were bright and obvious. Mere's sturdiest hope was that if she was seen, she would be regarded as nothing special. Debris from lost polypond ships occasionally had to drift through this space, and if someone was watching, and if he could feel any emotion that resembled suspicion, hopefully his mind was elegant enough or lazy enough to grab on to this most ordinary explanation.

The next factories were more distant and considerably more massive. Despite its enormous velocity, the *Osmium* rippled with the tides, its pieces slowly pulled even farther apart.

Mere let them wander.

She gazed at the data, listening to the first impressions from the AIs, and with a tiny voice asked, "What next? Each of you, make predictions."

There was no consensus, thankfully.

And none of the self-taught experts zeroed in on the truth.

"The dust?" she asked.

They could taste atomic hydrogen and molecular hydrogen, plus buckyball carbons with ordinary elements riding at their cores, from lithium to iron. The entire cloud was as regular and pure as any product spat out by a competent factory. Judging by the cloud's fluid dynamics, it was a recent feature, built within the last century or two, and perhaps created as a whirlpool in one of the electromagnetic rivers that recently weaved their way through the Sack.

"Total mass of the facility?"

Equal to a substantial moon, so far.

"Energy production?"

An assortment of voices hesitated.

"What?"

The navigator AI answered, whispering into her mind, "There's a new mass. A body. Ahead of us now."

"Show me."

In the blackness was a deeper blackness. In the bitter cold lay a superchilled realm rimmed by an army of elaborate machines, and until this moment, no one had suspected its existence.

The mystery lay 20 million kilometers from Mere.

At her closest, she would pass within 8 million kilometers.

"Mass?"

A small moon.

"Looks larger," she noted. Then, "Composition?"

Hyperfiber, at least on its surface.

"Grade?"

High.

At the frigid center of the cloud was a perfect gray-white sphere. The surrounding machines resembled any of a hundred familiar pieces of equipment, and they resembled none of them. They were alien devices built to serve some clear engineering purpose, each wrapped around an alien aesthetics. Mere found herself staring at the array, trying to twist her mind until she could see beauty in it. Beauty and elegance were reliable routes into the unknown mind. But after several minutes of hard concentration, nothing changed. She was examining a minimal arrangement of pragmatic tools, and nothing mattered but their capacity to do their exceptionally narrow work.

"Question," she said.

The AIs had been talking among themselves. Now they fell silent, and the navigator whispered, "Yes, madam."

"Is there any trace of organic organisms?"

Silence.

"Look for habitats warm as tropical water," she advised.

"We have been, madam."

"And leakage from closed biosystems." Because there were no large polyponds here, and small biosystems often leaked a thin rain of water and carbon dioxide and other rich clues about metabolisms and catabolisms.

"Nothing here, madam."

Except the machines, she realized. Nothing but machines.

As the *Osmium* charged forward, the little impacts of iron and lighter dusts began to lessen. Apparently the local space had been mined out, or it had been made safer for delicate instruments. Either way, she was relieved. For the next fifteen minutes, Mere found herself daydreaming about passing out of the cloud safely, then reconfiguring her ship again. Once it was pulled back together, she had important things to show to the captains. To show Washen. She got as far as imagining that tall woman sitting beside her, their faces temporarily eye to eye, and with an appreciative wink, the First Chair would tell her, "Thank you."

The frigid sphere vanished behind her.

Another necklace of factories stretched into the distance, bending off to the right and ending with a great glowing baleen.

Mere called up her best eyes, but she used none of them.

When the bolide struck, she was daydreaming again. She was sitting with half a dozen old husbands at a table in some wide avenue on board the Great Ship, and she was listening while the six of them, each from a different species, happily exchanged stories about their little onetime wife.

THE BOLIDE WAS iron and nickel flavored with an assortment of sulfur and rare earths. Watching the impact, a sensor positioned on one of the distant portions of the *Osmium* took careful note of the plasma signature, and with a calmness born from simplicity, it checked the data against a carefully compiled library of known signatures. Sometime in the not-too-distant past, that particular bolide had lain inside the solid core of a Mars-class world—presumably one of the worlds that drifted inside the Inkwell and which the polyponds had dismantled.

After the impact, the ship immediately began reassembling itself. Following long-established protocols and measured doses of inspiration, the pieces moved along electrostatic threads and with tiny breaths of nanorockets. Five full months were required to gather around the battered habitat and reattach what remained of the main engine.

Long ago, the *Osmium* had left the factory cloud.

Using the shards and existing systems, a new craft was assembled. It was inelegant and unlovely and barely able to operate in any meaningful fashion, but a new habitat was constructed, nearly five cubic meters of space partly filled with the vacuum-baked and deeply dead body of its pilot.

An atmosphere was fabricated.

The main engine was repaired to a point, recalibrated as well as possible, and left untouched.

The mummified body was slowly fed liquids and salt and sugars, plus amino acids, both old-fashioned and modern. But the damage was severe, the wounds achingly slow to heal. Consciousness came in slow steps with long plateaus and occasional backfalls. To save energy, Mere was kept in complete blackness. To minimize demands on the fragile life-support system, her metabolism remained at the lowest possible level. Even when she was conscious, she couldn't move or see, communicating with her surviving AIs through new implants delivered by machines not originally designed to serve as autodocs.

Her first word was, "Shit."

A week later, she muttered, "This is it . . . how it is . . ."

"What is?" an AI asked.

Silence.

"What can I do for you, madam?"

"Who are you?"

"Your navigator."

"Who else is there now?"

The AI listed the survivors, including itself, and the dead, which included the machine that had untangled the alien memory.

"What about the fragment?" Mere moaned.

Still tucked inside its diamond envelope, it was kicked free by the explosion, drifting nearly a thousand kilometers from the habitat before an industrious fragment tracked it down and wrestled it back again. Twice now in the fragment's life, it had survived a high-velocity impact.

"Makes two of us," a weak voice muttered.

She laughed for a moment.

"Madam? May I do anything to make you more comfortable?"

"The Great Ship," she muttered. "I have to send a message to it . . . to Washen . . ."

Silence.

"I finally realized . . ."

"Madam," a careful voice began.

"We can't, can we?"

"Because our last two antennae were destroyed," the AI reported. "We have no useful voice any longer, madam."

Mere wept.

Then softer still, with a genuine tenderness, the machine said, "I could not be more sorry, my good dear friend."

Twenty-two

THE ATTACK BEGAN with feint landings and exploratory bursts of laser light—six months of steady abuse gradually culminating in the final full assault. X-ray lasers slashed at the main shield generators. Clouds of iron dust descended, trailed by strings of corpulent tritium bombs that pounded at the hull and its defenses. But the ship made its essential repairs, and it made adjustments. The main engines shut down, and the towering nozzles fanned out in all directions, then they began to fire again in chaotic, wholly unpredictable patterns, the ship's bulk shivering and rolling just enough to keep the polyponds guessing. Then to disrupt the assault, armored ships from three of the six ports attacked the nearest of the polypond buds. The enemy bodies were a hundred kilometers across—depleted sacks of water and salt, stone and fusion reactors, each encased inside an insulated foam sky. Each wore an engine significant enough to have flung them to this place, matching the Great Ship's speed and trajectory. Each engine made for a tempting target, which was why Pamir decided to attack their enemy first, sending his fleet against the nearest, most threatening swarm.

"Reasonable," Osmium allowed.

But the first swarm was only a fraction of the invaders' force. The ship was surrounded by a deep haze of polyponds, tiny youngsters hanging close while the adults kept out of easy reach. Suddenly the haze parted before them, and plunging through the gap was an icy moon—a thousand kilometers across and accelerating into the hull.

Two of the great engines fired, fighting to shove the ship sideways.

The impact was vast and inevitable, and endurable, but it left an oblique crater near the ship's limb. Hyperfiber absorbed the energies and melted, flowing outward, the crater wall reaching within a thousand kilometers of Port Alpha. Then the baby polyponds released swarms of little ships, tough organics wrapped around tougher machine guts, thousands sweeping across the blasted region, using that sudden blind spot to make their key assault.

Pamir deployed eight brigades of security troops.

Again, Osmium said, "Reasonable."

Then with an inaudible command, the harum-scarum started a rebellion among the passengers. Panic and rage merged into a vicious riot in the ship's deepest regions. Local authorities were swamped. There seemed to be no response but to send the reserve troops below, using their uniforms and glowering presence to regain a semblance of order.

But Pamir refused to fall for easy traps.

"No?" the security chief chided.

Sealing off the district instead, Pamir remarked with a grim little smile, "One fire at a time."

"Very well."

The polypond ships swept toward the port. Lasers and railguns demolished the first six waves, but another hundred waves pressed down after them, inevitably obliterating the defenses.

Pamir ordered a partial retreat.

"Coward," the harum-scarum growled.

"Moron," the Second Chair replied.

The assault was relentless. Polypond soldiers woven for this single moment made their attack, dressed in lifesuits built from high-grade hyperfiber. The soldiers died willingly, selflessly. It was like fighting a nest of ants or a flock of rage dragons. What mattered was the enemy lifesuits. Every casualty recovered by the polyponds was sucked out of her suit and the suit repaired and repopulated with a new soldier and an endlessly improving set of instructions.

The battle raged for weeks.

More bunkers fell, and then the upper reaches of the port itself.

At one point, Pamir noticed his companion staring at him, the breathing mouth puckering in anticipation. Why? Then a fresh assault began, and the black-clad defense troops managed to collect a few dead bodies and their lifesuits, sealing both inside quarantine coffins before shipping them to labs dedicated to the extraction of information.

When the coffins were cracked open, Pamir saw the joke.

He saw himself—a dozen big human frames wearing the rugged and strong and decidedly unhandsome faces, staring up at him with dead eyes. Eyes unimpressed by everything before them, it seemed.

"The Blue World took a taste of your cells," said Osmium. "I assumed that it might find a use for your pitiful genetics."

Pamir laughed for a long moment.

Again, the simulation gained velocity, crossing a few weeks inside one long breath. Nothing of substance changed. The equilibrium held steady. If he wished, Pamir could leap back in time, making adjustments before the next crisis. That was allowed by the rules. But he held to his last orders, using both troops and a new crop of robots to hold Port Alpha against the next onslaughts.

When the defenses broke, it happened suddenly.

The polyponds had been busy, building an elaborate fortress in the center of the fresh crater. While most of their weapons were trained on the port, most of their energies were spent tunneling into the battered hull, using ancient lines of weakness to bypass the defenses, slipping inside the ship through an obscure passageway.

Pamir was waiting for them.

With his reserves, he counterattacked. But it was a difficult position to defend, and when the fight seemed to be lost anyway, he gave a final command. A streakship had been refitted. Stripped of its sentient citizens, its giant tanks were filled with metallic hydrogen, and the powerful engines gave a little burp, sending the vessel on a tidy and very brief flight. The Great Ship's gravity grabbed the projectile and sent it in downward. Like a cannonball, it fell into the center of the new crater, and a series of uranium bombs ignited the hydrogen, releasing one enormous and soundless and utterly cleansing blast.

"Reasonable," Osmium said one last time.

The bordering party had been destroyed, one credible victory earned. But Pamir refused to feel relaxed, much less confident. "You know what these simulations accomplish, don't you?"

"They show us what can never happen," said the breathing mouth.

"Exactly."

As THE DOOR opened, the visitor gazed up at Pamir.

Circumstances had changed utterly since the day they had first met. Instead of being enemies, they were allies. Instead of being strangers, they knew each other at a glance. Yet there remained a sense of surprise, at least on Locke's part. "I came to see my mother," he sputtered, his gray face coloring for a moment. It was the middle of the night, ship-time. "Did I interrupt? I'm sorry."

"You did and don't be," Pamir replied. "Come in."

The small man stepped inside his mother's apartment. "I asked where she was. The bridge has standing orders to tell me . . . and the captain in residence said she was home . . ."

"She doesn't expect you?"

"No."

Pamir nodded. "Must be important."

"Probably," Washen's son replied. "But I could be wrong."

"Well then," Pamir allowed. "I'll track her down. Walk with me?"

"I'd rather wait here, sir."

Pamir almost laughed, hearing that crisp little "Sir," from the man. Obviously, Locke was surprised to find his mother's lover strolling around her home. Maybe he felt a little miffed not to know. Had they done that good of a job of hiding their relationship? No, probably not. More likely, he simply didn't pay attention to such matters. Too much time living with the AIs, trying to think in their clean, nonhormonal ways, and this sudden whiff of real life left him unsettled.

Washen's apartment was neither large nor particularly grand. Narrow hallways connected a series of round rooms. Every ceiling was a neat hemisphere of bright green olivine. Beyond the ceiling and walls, and beneath the stone floor, were more than a hundred meters of rock, and then a great bubble of moderate-grade hyperfiber—the true wall to this little abode that covered barely three hectares of tidy and familiar floor space.

Washen was in her bedroom, slowly dressing.

"You didn't sleep enough," he observed.

She was standing in the middle of the room, her uniform pulling itself up her long body and the dangling arms, the mirrored fabric rustling as it covered her small breasts and the beating heart. With a nod, she said, "I promise. As soon as this century is finished, I'll sleep."

"I'll hold you to that."

With an earnest gasp, she said, "Do. Please."

LOCKE REMAINED STANDING near the front door. Watching his manners and mood, Pamir came to the inevitable conclusions: The onetime Wayward was introspective and observant, smart in ways that the Second Chair could never be, and sweet in ways that Pamir never wished to be. Locke was embarrassed to be in the company of his mother's private life. Yet his mind refused to let him dwell on those little thoughts. With a shake of the head, he returned to the primary subject. With a tense little smile, he said, "We have a final conclusion for you, Mother."

"Final?" Washen asked.

"In a sense," he said mildly, laughing for a moment. "Until we learn something else, of course."

"This way."

With her men following, Washen led them through a series of garden rooms—
alien habitats each, including a small corner dedicated to Marrow life-forms—
then they passed inside a spacious chamber meant for cooking and casual meals.

"Hungry?" she asked everyone.

Then to nobody in particular, she admitted, "I'm starving."

Enough food for three was delivered. Pamir deferred to the dutiful son, sitting
on the far side of the freshly grown table while Locke sat on his mother's right,
staring at a plate of spiced egg whites and lava bread.

The starving woman ate two bites.

"Do you want to hear our conclusions?" Locke muttered.

"First," Washen said, "I want to hear about you. How are you, son?"

Silence.

The two of them were very much the same person, Pamir decided; they were
intensely focused and successful because of it. And because of that intensity, they
ended up frail in other ways.

"Okay," she relented. "Show us what you have."

"With your house nexus?"

Washen gave him access.

The lights dropped, and the inky ceiling was sprinkled with whiffs of soft light.
He began by posing the question, "Is someone chasing the Great Ship?"

Pamir felt his heart kick.

"In these few years, we've analyzed the available data pools available to the captains, and private files belonging to passengers. We've also gone further, merging
the data into a coherent, robust mass that can be used to hunt for traces of anything that might be a second ship or a trailing body, then using the new mirror
fields on the ship's trailing face, watching the Inkwell for any trace of unexpected
disturbances."

In the blackness, a point of light appeared, streaking toward them. Toward the
Milky Way.

"We're a little bit lucky," Locke maintained. "When the ship was discovered,
thousands of species built huge mirrors designed for no purpose other than to
watch it."

The tiny light was the Great Ship, and with a silent grace, it fired its engines,
pushing itself into a close rendezvous with a dense white dwarf sun that deftly
spun it off into the main body of the galaxy.

"Some of these species became passengers," he mentioned. "And they paid the
captains, in part, with knowledge."

What seemed like an empty blackness was not. Suddenly the intergalactic realm
was rich with objects, each wearing its own private velocity and implied history.
Outside the dense swirl of suns were millions more suns—globular clusters of el-
derly, metal-poor stars, and lone wanderers, and sometimes the shredded hearts of

little galaxies swallowed up ages ago by a predatory Milky Way. There were veils of dust and gas, thinner than inside the galaxy, and colder, but spread across a much vaster realm; and there were the scattered worlds without suns or heat, life or meaningful names. And everything baryonic swam through an ocean of scarcely felt particles—the fabled dark matter—all of which drifted comfortably inside the faint, barely perceived ocean of shadow universes and infinite potentials.

"If we assume pursuit," Locke muttered, closing his eyes for a moment. "A pursuer," he said as he opened them again. They were his dead father's eyes, bright and busy, but it was his own voice remarking, "If there was a starship, and if it was larger than ten kilometers in diameter, and if it had a minimal heat signature, and the albedo of old hyperfiber . . . well, you would see it now. If it followed the Great Ship within a distance of a thousand light-years, give or take . . . I could point it out to you now, yes . . ."

Pamir studied the elaborate chart. No vector matched what was necessary, and none would.

"Of course the starship might have been smaller," Locke allowed. "Or it was darker. But if it possessed any substantial mass, we would see it here." A slice of the chart pulled closer. "The first probe to reach the Great Ship continued past, and there was a beacon on board. And there still is a beacon, though the signal has degraded significantly over the aeons. If there had been a trailing mass, we would have seen an unexpected course change in our probe. And that's never happened, which reduces the useful mass down to—"

"Wait," Pamir interrupted.

Locke paused, the busy eyes regarding him for a long moment.

"This is relatively simple work," the Second Chair pointed out. "I know you had to marry up a lot of divergent databases, make allowances for different optics and different species, and then solve plenty of infinite-body gravitational problems. But still . . . how long have you worked on this . . . ?"

"Several decades," the young man replied, bristling just a little bit now. "On a part-time basis."

"I've told you about this work," Washen said.

"Plenty of times," Pamir agreed. "But you never shared results, and I guess I assumed . . ."

He abruptly stopped talking.

"Wait," he muttered. "This is just an introduction. For my benefit, isn't it?"

"That would be polite of me," Locke said.

Pamir grinned, saying, "Shut up, old man."

Locke nodded, an embarrassed smile flickering. "If a pursuer has been chasing the ship for billions of years . . . well, there are two sturdy conclusions. The pursuing ship has to have a working pilot and trustworthy engines; otherwise, it would have drifted off course long ago. Impacts against the Great Ship have tweaked its trajectory countless times. Multiply a millimeter shift by ten billion light-years, and the gap is enormous. And the second conclusion . . . if there is a pursuer, it has almost certainly fallen farther behind than a thousand light-years."

Pamir saw the reasoning instantly.

But Locke felt compelled to explain himself. "A functioning starship follows the inert, pilotless Great Ship. Its velocity isn't any swifter. Otherwise, the race would have been finished long ago. And it can't be even slightly slower. For the same reason." A pause. Then he said, "But even with a matching velocity, it will close a gap of anything less than five or six thousand light-years."

The chart changed again, expanding backward in time while reaching into deepest space, following what was judged to be the most likely course for the ship over these last billions of years. Whatever the Builders had been, they obviously didn't wish their creation bulldozing its way through star-rich realms. The universe appeared as thin beery foam, every bubble formed by clusters of interacting galaxies. The ship always crossed the bubble walls at some thin spot. Passing through the Local Group was an aberration, and the Milky Way just happened to lie in its path. If the Great Ship was born in the early days of the universe, when space was tiny and highly compressed, no credible set of eyes could have seen clearly enough or far enough to make such a perfect shot. So maybe the Builders were lucky. Or as some souls had mentioned, on occasion and usually while drinking beery foams, maybe the Builders had built quite a bit more than this little ball of hyperfiber and stone, iron and empty caves.

Perhaps the universe itself was theirs.

"A good pilot," said Locke, glancing across the table at Pamir. "A good determined pilot would study the ship, watch for impacts and the effects of passing masses. Because there would be a few wandering suns between the galaxies, and solar-mass black holes, and the usual detritus. The pilot would make its own tiny course corrections, using the same masses for its benefit. Everything is an estimate, naturally. I've spent years poring through the available data and star charts before I made my best guess. If there was a pursuer chasing after the Great Ship, it would have been less than ten thousand light-years behind. And with a little confidence, I can say it had to be more than three thousand light-years to the rear. A window of seven thousand . . ."

Locke paused, regarding Pamir with a measured amusement.

"Our trip through the Milky Way," Pamir began.

"Exactly." With a command, the chart changed a third time. The last hundred thousand years were accomplished in moments. The ship's engines had ignited, perhaps for the first time ever. A white dwarf sun, cold and old, embraced the ship and flung it into a new trajectory. Then the captains rode their prize on a constantly changing course, using flybys and the big engines to achieve a wobbly course through the populated zones of the galaxy. No real momentum was lost, but like a swimmer navigating around endless buoys, their lead over the hungry shark had been significantly diminished.

Quietly, Pamir pointed out, "We would have noticed a ship tagging after us. Long ago, I'd hope."

Locke agreed.

Then in the next instant, the pragmatic captain came to the conclusion that Locke had derived from days of data searches, careful calculations, and elaborate models built inside AIs and drawn on the palm of his pale gray hand.

A closer rendezvous with the white dwarf.

A sharper course correction.

"If I was five thousand light-years behind you," Pamir said, "and if I saw you fire your engines and dive into the galaxy . . . into all those stars and worlds . . . I might have been tempted to make a tighter turn and stay above you."

With a hand laid flat, he showed the Milky Way. With the other hand's index finger, he traced a straight sure course above the swirling stars.

Both hands dropped.

"The white dwarf," Pamir muttered. "I remember. We put probes into orbit. To map the space, measure its exact mass . . . just to be triple sure that we weren't going to smash into anything on our flyby . . ."

Impressed, Locke nodded.

"Are the probes still functioning?" Pamir asked.

Then he answered his own question, saying, "They used to be, and we kept track of their broadcasts." It had taken him several moments to find the proper log with his own nexuses. "For the first half of the voyage—"

"Captains are thorough," Washen interjected.

The data was easy to find because Locke had tagged it just days ago. And the results were still obvious, half a hundred individual entries glowing where he had reached deep to examine the ancient numbers.

"What's the verdict?" Pamir asked, looking across the table. "Are we being chased through the cosmos?"

Locke glanced at his mother.

Washen straightened her back, squared her shoulders, and waited.

"Nothing else has passed by that dead star," said Locke.

And then with a different voice—a louder, distinctly intrigued voice—he said, "That means there was no other ship. Ever. Unless, of course, it managed to find a different route, or it was built on principles we don't understood. Or maybe, we were looking in the wrong direction to begin with . . ."

Another night came.

It was days later, or perhaps weeks. The press of moments and months didn't feel important of late. Nothing of substance seemed to change on board the ship, and perhaps it never would. That was the general consensus. Pamir couldn't discount the sameness with either muscular reasoning or cold practicality. The human mind had been improved in a multitude of ways . . . but it still could be lulled into a sense of foreverness, a velvetlike complacency that made even a hardhearted son of a bitch think that he had been here forever, flying through the heart of the Inkwell . . .

They were lying in Washen's bed, again. On her ceiling, images from the ship's leading face appeared in real time, in a shifting range of frequencies and details. The polypond buds had begun to arrive, and despite good simulations predicting all types of behavior, they had done nothing. Thousands were scattered across a light-week of dark dusty space, and despite endless pleas from the Master Captain and her Submasters, none of the interlopers had said one word in response, much less tried to explain their looming presence.

One night, the captains made love under that crowded sky.

Another night, too exhausted for anything else, they slept.

And then came a third night when Pamir woke too soon, finding himself on his back, watching as another hundred of those great watery bodies swam out of the black, pushing themselves close with sloppy muscular engines.

Washen stirred, a dream causing her to roll away from him.

Pamir sat up and drank ice water and said nothing, staring at the fine long back of his lover.

"What?" she asked, her face invisible to him.

"Feel my eyes?" he asked.

"I thought they were knives," she joked. Then she rolled closer to him, and after a moment's consideration asked, "What are you thinking?"

What wasn't he thinking?

"What bothers you?" she asked.

Everything.

Then she said his name with a brittle tenderness, tired of this game and this moment, wishing for the things to finally happen now. Just to break the deadlock.

"Pamir," she said. "What is it?"

"I was wondering," he whispered. "In the face of all this, why are you and your son . . . why are you spending so much time and effort asking if the ship is being chased by somebody . . . ?"

"But what if we are?" she replied.

"I'm not questioning the importance of it."

"Then what?"

"Where does this obsession come from?" Pamir smiled and offered a big shrug. "The two people most thoroughly and intimately tied to Marrow, and neither of you can stop thinking about things that can't be found . . .

"Does that ever strike you as being more than just a little bit interesting . . . ?"

Twenty-three

LIFE WAS MEANT to be a string of abundances, warm glories, and trusted pleasures. O'Layle had always professed that shameless code, but the bald truth was that most of his life had been spent slinking about in shadow, begging and cheating to achieve whatever paltry success was his to enjoy. Only in these final decades had he come to appreciate how tiny and maudlin that old life had been. His transformation began when he escaped from the seemingly doomed ship. In his mind, he had shown both enormous initiative and a dry-eyed bravery. Alone, he had crossed an inhospitable wilderness. Alone, he had met and befriended an alien unlike any other, forging intimate bonds with the Blue World while teaching her about his life and species and about the Great Ship. No one played a more critical role when human emissaries finally met with the polypond. Then O'Layle had gladly returned home. He couldn't remember it any other way. He left the Blue World willingly and freely, arriving here in triumph, his corner in history secure, the name O'Layle sure to be known for aeons to come, while his adventures were the subject of endless retellings and a boundless, incandescent envy.

True, the voyage home had been less than pleasant. With every day and every breath, he could feel a palpable dislike directed at him by the crew, and worse, the deep mistrust of the Second Chair. O'Layle was also kept from any hero's welcome, he and that frozen sliver of the Blue World ushered aside, victims of the ugliest, most pointless fears. And there were a few other surprises waiting for him—events and limitations that would rightfully disappoint any person who had accomplished as much as he had accomplished.

The quarantine, for instance.

Why keep him apart from the passengers and crew? Perhaps it was as simple as the captains' explanation. "This is just a precaution, and temporary," Pamir had promised, escorting him to a private apartment in a deep, isolated district. "We just want to be sure you aren't anything more, or less, than what you seem to be."

What did he seem to be?

Pamir shook his heavy head, smiling with a guarded amusement. "You're a very lucky man," he observed. "Maybe the luckiest ever, considering the long odds that you've crossed. And believe me, we're going to keep a lucky man like you happy in your new home."

In ways good and bad, captains were true to their words: O'Layle was quite happy, yes. The apartment was large enough to suit the needs of the most demanding passenger, more than two hundred spacious rooms knitted together with a delicious maze of curling hallways and little avenues. Its only resident was encouraged to decorate the rooms however he wished, and O'Layle took on that considerable task with more energy than he would have imagined possible. In the end, almost sixty rooms had been transformed, both by his hand and with help from a platoon of compliant robots. Chairs and potted jungles not to mention nearly half a cubic kilometer of synthetic earth had been purchased on his behalf and brought from distant parts of the ship, passing through a series of airlocks before being ushered down a hyperfiber throat and through his grand front door. Sixty rooms was an enormous accomplishment, and with a keen pride, he would parade his accomplishments to whoever visited him. Of course nobody visited in a physical sense. Even the captains appeared to him as projections. Why these kinds of precautions were necessary or reasonable, O'Layle couldn't say. Hadn't he lived among the crew of that streakship? They didn't have to endure this kind of isolation, yet for months at a time, hadn't they shared his air and drunk his recycled pee? Besides, O'Layle had already endured a series of exhaustive tests, during the voyage and afterward. His blood and bones, mind and sturdy heart were examined by every available tool, and every measurement, every knowing touch, proved what he knew to be true:

He was still and would always be O'Layle.

The captains' true logic revealed itself gradually. A onetime lover visited as a hologram. After he showered her with charm and some aggressive begging, she agreed to marry herself with a warm, skin-covered robot. Then O'Layle led her to his favorite bed and climbed on top of her. If she didn't enjoy the experience, at least she made the appropriate sounds. Then afterward, feeling spent and fine, he sat up and grinned at the machine's temporary face, asking in an offhand fashion, "When do you think they'll give up this quarantine nonsense?"

She stared at him for a long moment. Hadn't she heard the question? Perhaps the link between her immersion chamber and his bed had been severed. But no, she was simply absorbing his query. Then with a snort and a little shake of the head, she said, "Darling," in a grating fashion. "Don't you realize? They might call it a quarantine, but what this is . . . this is a prison cell, darling . . ."

The idea required time to be digested.

And even when O'Layle believed what she told him, it took more months and years to come to terms with the simple fact.

"How much longer?" he asked.

Pamir was visiting. That this powerful man gave his time and attention proved that O'Layle was no simple felon hidden away in the ship's brig. "How much longer with your quarantine?" Pamir muttered. "I've told you. Once we pull clear of the Inkwell, you get the keys to your door."

"But that's all this is?" O'Layle persisted. "A precaution?"

"Yes."

"I'm not a prisoner?"

"Hardly."

"You don't think I'm a criminal?"

The big man snorted, shaking his head. "Why should we?"

"Because I illegally abandoned the ship," O'Layle offered. "I used illegal moneys to bribe your crew, saving my own precious ass in the process."

"Prisoners have trials," Pamir argued. "Do you remember any trial?"

It was a telling point that O'Layle had made to himself, on numerous occasions.

"Criminals, particularly the guilty ones, live in very tiny spaces," the Second Chair continued. "By law and custom, the ship has to supply only ten thousand cubic meters of livable room."

A fact O'Layle knew well.

"This doesn't look like a prison cell, does it?"

They were standing on the shoreline of his largest, most splendid room. Salt water funneled down from the Alpha Sea had flooded most of the chamber, forming a small lake, and beneath the illusion of a high blue sky, robots dressed as poly-pond bodies swam beneath the rippling surface.

For a moment, O'Layle smiled at the water.

"You miss her," Pamir observed.

Did he? After years apart and a good deal of determined thought, O'Layle was less than sure about his genuine feelings.

Bristling, he heard himself muttering, "All right, I'm not a prisoner."

"Agreed."

"But this isn't any normal quarantine," he remarked.

Holos were never perfect, but those eyes certainly seemed to belong to Pamir. With a clear scorn, the bright eyes cut into him, while Pamir's growling voice asked, "What else could this be?"

"An interrogation," O'Layle offered.

That brought a hard, dismissive laugh.

"There's a better word than that," the Second Chair warned. And then he simply ceased to be.

O'LAYLE WAS ISOLATED but far from ignorant.

Using the captains' funds, he had built an immersion chamber where he could view any portion of the ship, save those countless places where there were no eyes or cameras or where security restrictions were firmly in place. He could never visit friends and lovers as a holo; that wasn't allowed. But he could sit on a comfortable chair of living Dallico leather, passively watching people and creatures that he had known forever while they spoke about everything, and nothing.

As a rule, his old friends were boring souls. That sad truth emerged after several years of patience. Since O'Layle couldn't tell his own stories, there was no choice but to listen to others. Even inside that little window of time, it became obvious that each of the voices had only a handful of stories to share. Names changed, and settings, but the outcomes followed reliable themes that could have been stated at the beginning, saving breath. And every joke was a thin variation on the last thousand jokes, the same few punch lines emerging again and again.

They were boring souls to watch, but oddly enough, O'Layle wasn't bored.

He missed them, first of all. He missed the touch of real flesh, the smell and sight of genuine company, and when his old friends mentioned him, he felt a pleasing warmth that made the tedium feel worthwhile.

Not that they spoke about him often, nor in clear terms.

One of his old names would be mentioned, and a ten-thousand-year-old story would be marched out, everyone making little mistakes when they told their particular part. Or someone would recall a mutual friend, and the group would busy themselves for a full day, dredging up old stories and fresh gossip that occasionally involved O'Layle. Sometimes a past lover or one of his finest friends would appear before him, holo fashion, and afterward they would report to the others, describing his apartment and new life and how he seemed to be. In general, O'Layle appeared a little sad to the others. Which wasn't the case at all, but what could he do? They wanted to think of him as being blue and sorry for what he had done, abandoning them as he had. Though he wasn't blue or even a little bit sorry. Why should he feel regrets? Hadn't everything worked out wonderfully well? Then after they had successfully chewed his mental state down to their level, someone inevitably asked:

"So what does he think about it?"

About the polyponds, they meant.

"Is he worried? Happy? What does our dear sweet friend think? In his little head, what does all this mean?"

They meant the polypond babies. By the thousands, the buds were matching the ship's trajectory, mirroring its own slowly increasing velocity before settling into a swarm that was literally countless now. The ship was approaching the far edge of the Satin Sack, and the polyponds were traveling with it. Hundreds of thousands of bodies, shriveled by their journey, most just a few tens of kilometers across, were strung out in an elaborate pattern that was spherical at first glance, but decidedly asymmetrical. Most of the buds remained directly ahead of the ship, and all were avoiding the plumes of plasma rising from the blazing engines. There were so many bodies, and each was leaking away enough volatiles to create a thin, far-flung atmosphere, their bodies and collective breath obscuring the sky more than ever, either by chance or design helping to hide whatever lay directly before them.

One particular lover didn't mention wearing the robot body, nor anything about pretending to have sex. Instead, she said, "I asked him," and waited for everyone to pay attention. Then with a soft worried voice, she said, "I asked O'Layle, 'What are they hiding from us?'"

"And what did he say?" another ex-lover inquired.

"'They aren't hiding anything,' he claimed. Then he said, 'It's obvious what they're doing. They're being helpful. That's all.'"

The polyponds were blocking the oncoming dust and comets. Wasn't that plain to see? With their own bodies and their fantastic momentum, the leading ranks were absorbing some titanic blows, and judging by the rain of dirty ices falling back on the ship today, some of those polyponds were being obliterated by the larger impacts.

"But why would they help us?" another person asked.

"I asked O'Layle that," the first lover continued. "And do you know what he said? He promised me, 'The polyponds care that much about us.'"

But that wasn't what he had said.

"He told me, 'They want to see us pass safely through their home.'"

She was lying, both to them and to herself. For reasons entirely her own, she was borrowing O'Layle's authority, telling everyone, "There's nothing to worry about. Nothing at all."

But worry was made of harder stuff than that. A few words and a brave little smile did nothing but underscore the general mood. People everywhere were concerned. Every species suffered from the unknown. What O'Layle might not have noticed in his former life, he began to see wherever he looked. Passengers and crew were exhausted by the endless sense of being held in suspense, the drama relentless and unbearable despite every artful reassurance by the captains, experts in the careful word and the cool, implacable expression.

"I'll tell you what I really think," O'Layle cried out at the indifferent friends. "Next time one of you bothers to put in the request and drop by . . . I won't open the damned door . . . !"

But nobody cared enough anymore. The man who was not a prisoner, nor under quarantine, found himself sitting alone in his spacious home, occupying his days and long nights by watching the skies and studying the public news logs. A long life spent in the pursuit of pleasure had just this one reliable thrill left to it: the sight of millions of polyponds dancing before the ship and behind it, forming an elaborate and vast and very lovely black cloud.

A light-week across, the cloud was, and perhaps more.

Countless bodies of water and salt, iron and carbon absorbed everything from the universe beyond. The dust and radiations, and the scarce light, too. For days upon weeks, the polyponds did nothing but silently ingest everything that fell on them. Then there was a moment—an otherwise insignificant point in time—when they began to speak. All that while, the captains had begged for a dialogue, but they were very disappointed by the abrupt response. The sudden flood of radio noise wasn't intended for them. Even though the captains tried to keep the roaring in the sky secret, the news escaped, and within a few more moments, the Great Ship was jammed with panicked passengers and grim-faced captains.

"What do you think it means?" asked a woman's voice.

O'Layle woke from a deep sleep. He was stretched out on his leather covered chair, in the center of his immersion chamber, its walls and high ceiling adorned with the best projectors on the market. His visitor was a projection, of course. Trying to smile, he made himself rise up from his chair, saying, "It's good to see you, madam."

The Master Captain approached.

"I am honored," O'Layle proclaimed. "To have you take the time and effort to see me—"

With her right foot, she kicked him.

Appalled, he fell to a floor covered with slick cold hexagon-shaped projectors. The projectors were still sleeping. And she was real? The question must have shown on his face. The Master kicked him a second time, with emphasis. Then she roared, "It is definitely not an honor, you little man."

He cowered at her feet.

"No more games," she threatened. "This long careful seduction is finished, and now I expect honesty. Will you give me that?"

"Gladly," he sputtered.

"What do you think it means now, little man?"

"Now?" Confusion blossomed.

"Tell me the truth," the Master demanded.

"About the polyponds—?"

"Why? Is there some other alien you've slept with?"

He bowed his head, trying to swallow.

"What do the polyponds intend, O'Layle? Right now. Tell me!"

"To protect themselves," he whispered.

"Is that so?"

That's what he had told the lover who had visited him, and who had, in a distant fashion, slept with him. "It couldn't be more simple," O'Layle had explained. "The Great Ship is a toxin, a contagion. That's how the polyponds see us. And the swarm is simply the best means available to build a protective cyst around the perceived threat. Our neighbors just need to make sure we cannot do them any lasting harm."

But he wasn't certain about his own logic suddenly. Something new must have happened while he slept. Why else would the Master Captain have bothered to see him in person? The captains watched every little thing that he did. They absorbed every word he said. The Master had to know what he had told others. O'Layle was shrewd enough to read the golden face and the terrified wide eyes, and with his own fear swirling in his old blood, he admitted, "I don't know what they want—"

"Look," she roared.

The projectors came to life again.

Again she kicked him, saying, "Lift your eyes. Now."

He found himself sitting on the illusion of the leading hull, surrounded by a forest of elaborate mirrors. The sky was black when he fell asleep, but not any longer. A lovely blue glow was washing down over his cowering form.

"They're firing their engines again," the Master reported.

"Why?" he muttered.

"What you're seeing," she explained, "is the light of their engines passing through their own watery bodies."

But he couldn't see the blaze of the nearest rockets. Which was peculiar, yes. It took him a long moment to understand:

The polyponds were slowing themselves.

A million polypond buds, give or take, had turned themselves 180 degrees, and now they were giving themselves the tiniest of nudges.

Why?

Then O'Layle heard himself laughing, and with that laughing voice he told the Master Captain, "Madam, I'm not the smartest soul . . . I know that . . . I know . . . but to me, it looks as if we should expect a little rain . . ."

Twenty-four

EVEN NOW IT was possible to live out the days and weeks in a scrupulously ordinary fashion: normal meals eaten on a regular schedule; routine work accomplished with a gentle competence; quick visits to odd districts and ritual-drenched meetings with an array of species; and sometimes a bite of sleep swirled with the little pleasures of love and purchased dreams. The polyponds' grand plan was being unveiled in every portion of the sky. The horde was descending, and for the moment, no force could blunt it. Yet Washen found slivers of time to enjoy a quiet dinner with friends and colleagues. Sitting at a random table inside an obscure restaurant, she discovered that she could still find the pleasure in the taste of the noodles smothered with squid and tomatoes. She could laugh honestly at one of Pamir's peculiar stories. And with a convincing ease, she heard herself adding to his tale, giving her own perspective before concluding with a shrug and shake of the head, "Which is why we keep the Myrth and Illakan at opposite ends of the ship."

Everyone laughed in some patient fashion. Osmium's breathing mouth made an agreeable whistle. Quee Lee and her husband cuddled and nodded knowingly; Perri had probably already heard the tale. Aasleen glanced at her companion, and the AI took the cue to smile with its handsome face, its various hands folded on the empty place setting. What was it about engineers and their machines? Were some engineers simply so good at their art that they could accomplish more with the tools than Nature and simple courtship could manage? Washen considered asking that blunt question. Then she hesitated, and in the next moment realized that she had enjoyed perhaps one too many of the fortified wines that had been brought with their meal.

Another half dozen captains sat at the round table, plus spouses and dates, and in one case, both. The lowest-ranking captain gestured timidly, pulling up his courage to ask, "Do you eat here often, madam?"

"Never," she confessed.

He was the onetime dream-merchant. Over the last decades, his expertise with the public mind had proved invaluable, and that was partly why she had invited him. But mostly, she found him pleasant and observant, and more than most captains, honest. The captain grinned for a moment. Then simple curiosity made him ask, "Then how exactly did you chose this place, madam?"

"I grew up nearby," Washen mentioned, a long finger drawing a circle in the air. "In a little house barely two kilometers that way."

The hour was exceedingly late. Except for Washen's party, and the restaurant's owner and robot staff, the restaurant was empty.

Quee Lee said, "Madam."

Washen glanced at the ancient woman, eyebrows lifting.

She corrected herself, saying, "Washen." Since Quee Lee was not a captain, there was no need for formalities. "Something just occurred to me. Maybe I've asked in the past, I don't know—"

"What?"

"Have you ever been anywhere but the Great Ship?"

"Never, no," Washen replied.

Perri lifted his delicate chin. "What about Marrow?"

She embraced the question. Then she asked him in turn, "Why is that someplace else?"

"The ship is ruled by captains," he argued. "Who rules Marrow today?"

"Fair point." Staring at Perri, she began dredging up random details about his long, busy life. What was catching her interest here? She wasn't certain. She could almost see it, but then her thin logic was broken by the sound of a new voice.

"Madam."

A young man was filling up the restaurant's front door. Behind him, in the late-evening gloom, perhaps a dozen others stood in a loose tangle. All were young, but not all were human. At least two Janusian couples stood near the front, and a giant harum-scarum stuck up in back.

To all of them, she said, "Hello."

"Madam," the young man said again. Then he stepped closer, a hint of nervousness betrayed in the quick rolling of his thick fingers. "Do you remember me?"

Security systems went on silent alert.

The face might be familiar, or might not, and there could be something memorable in the broad build of his body. If that hair was longer, and if he was years younger—

"I once walked with you," Washen recalled. "When the Master Captain and her officers met near this place." Then came the natural doubt that follows most intuitions. "Am I right? Just a couple centuries ago—"

"Most of my life ago," he added happily.

A name emerged from the security nexus. Washen ignored it, preferring to ask the young man, "What should I call you?"

"Julius."

"Those are your friends, Julius? Cowering behind you?"

"Yes, madam."

"Join us," she said. And when he hesitated, she rose from her chair, her uniform shimmering in the dim light as she waved at everyone. "Come in. We'll make room. Come join us, please."

DECADES AGO, AASLEEN saw what the polyponds were planning. While the ship was still on the outskirts of the Inkwell, she had mentioned, "It would be a mess, you know. If just a tiny portion of that nebula happened to fall on our heads."

Later, she had no memory of that offhand comment. There were good reasons why she would have dismissed the whole concept. Their ship was moving at a brutal pace, while the nebula was very nearly at rest. The polyponds preferred slow travel, and by every account, they used only patient methods to move the dust and gas. But Washen managed to remember that suggestion, and when the polypond buds first started to accelerate, she repeated those words to her chief engineer, adding, "What do you think now?"

With a dismissive shrug, Aasleen said, "Not much, madam."

"You aren't worried?"

"About many things, yes. But the idea that they might come at us at once, en masse . . . no, that's not keeping me awake tonight . . ."

She had reasons, good clear and perfectly rational reasons. The choreography would be enormous. How could hundreds of thousands of bodies move together but never touch? Because they were large enough and massive enough that if they did touch, their watery selves would merge. A single impact would generate enough heat to boil both of the victims, and their organics would cook. In some sense, they would die. And if several of the fifty-kilometer buds joined together, and then caught up several more with their increasing mass . . . well, there were too many chances for mistakes, too many ways in which a cloud of little polyponds would find themselves falling into the same gravity well, building a world of steam and death that wouldn't accomplish anything with a strategic sense.

"But what if that new world hit us?" Washen had asked.

"Even then," the woman had replied, shrugging her shoulders. "It's a huge mass, yes. Our weapons and shields wouldn't blunt it at all. But remember, they'll be moving at very close to our velocity. The kinetic energies are relatively mild. The likely result . . . let me think . . . yes, the obvious result would be a damaged hull and a huge flash, and then a cloud of steam that would cling to the ship for the next thousand years or so . . ."

"The ship would survive?"

"And prosper," Aasleen added. "Think what we could accomplish with all that free water."

For a few years, that was the end of the discussion.

But the polyponds kept rising out of the depths of the Satin Sack, engines firing, carefully gathering their bodies into a complex, ever-shifting sphere that was just distant enough and just diffuse enough to prevent any unplanned collapse. What Aasleen had seen by instinct years ago, every AI and crew member and clear-eyed passenger began to see for himself.

Then the polyponds began to speak to each other, and soon afterward, the leading wave turned around and began to brake its terrific momentum. While the Master Captain was standing in O'Layle's cell, hoping for answers that never came, her First Chair visited Aasleen. Wearing a grim expression, she looked at her old friend, asking an open-ended, "What next?"

"If they can coordinate their fall, you mean?"

"Yes."

"And keep compensating for any changes we make in our velocity?"

"Yes."

Quietly, with a knifing honesty, Aasleen described one possible if very unlikely future.

"And if that happens," Washen asked, "what?"

"But I doubt it can happen," the engineer added.

"Why?"

For a moment, she was silent. Then the entire face smiled, the mind behind it delighted to have such an odd, unexpected conundrum, and with an almost joyous laugh, she admitted, "I doubt it happens because it's too strange, and too awful, and I'm going to stick my head in a dark hole now, thank you."

THE NEW GUESTS seemed happy and awed and very polite. Even the young harum-scarum acted a little cowed by the presence of so many important souls, which prompted a rude noise from Osmium's eating hole. "Sit like you belong here," the Submaster warned. "Or lie on the floor and let me set my feet on your bent back."

When the old people laughed, the youngsters joined in with nervous chuckles. The boy who had once walked with Pamir and Washen now took a seat between them. A plate of hot food had been delivered, but he didn't act hungry. Smiling, he said, "Thank you." He smiled at his plate and lifted a fork, and then the fork dropped again as he told his dinner, "Thank you."

"I remember our little stroll," Pamir said. "You promised me you were going to become a captain when you grew up."

The guests fell silent.

"Am I confused?"

Julius sighed. "No," he allowed.

"I don't see you in any ensign ranks," Pamir rumbled. "Why is that?"

The broad shoulders rolled, and an embarrassed voice said, "I changed my mind, I guess."

Washen showed him an agreeable face. "Of course you changed your mind. Only fools live the lives they dreamed up as children."

But Pamir had a better sense of things. "But that's not the reason. Is it, friend?"

Another young human—a pretty woman with huge pink eyes—blurted out, "What would be the point?"

Everyone fell silent.

The pink eyes blinked hard. And then a defensive voice added, "There isn't time to pass even the first level in captain's school. Is there?"

Julius threw a warning look at his friend, but then found the voice to explain, "It's common knowledge. In a few days, the polyponds are going to be here. They're going to fall on our heads and flood the hull, and there isn't anything we can do to stop them."

There. It had been said.

But Washen refused to do anything but smile. "We aren't entirely defenseless," she remarked. "For years now—ever since we felt halfway sure of their plan—we have made our own plans. Adjustments. Arrangements. Entire worlds don't have a tenth as much energy and talent as we have, and I don't believe that anybody . . . and that includes the important souls sitting at this table . . . none of us can understand or appreciate just how powerful we can be . . . !"

The words had an impact. The new guests sighed. Even the captains seemed more relaxed, more confident.

"So what if they grab hold of us?" Pamir muttered. "They have to survive on the hull. They have break through at least one hatch. All of the hatches have been reinforced ten different ways, of course. And even if they get inside, unlikely as it sounds, how many millions of souls will they have to fight just to reach any important part of the ship?"

Gloom had been cast aside. A keen if fragile sense of invincibility hung over the scene.

Washen watched the faces, the bodies. Only two of her companions showed doubts. Oddly, one was the man who had just spoken: Pamir clamped his mouth down tight, something foul against his tongue. Bless him, he was trying to sound like a good captain, brave and assuring and full of fire. But he knew too much and was far too honest. In another moment or two, he would clear his throat with a hard rattle and spit out a few sarcastic barbs.

The other doubter sat even closer, and he had the quicker tongue.

"But I wonder," Julius muttered.

Washen studied him for a moment. "What do you wonder?"

"Do we really understand their goals?" He was more child than man, but sometimes that was a strength. Julius didn't have enough time or experience to feel rock-sure about anything. "The polyponds," he said, as if anyone forgot about whom they were speaking. "We're assuming they want to steal the Great Ship. But isn't that an awfully smug assumption?"

"Smug?" Aasleen replied, bristling now.

Osmium made a rude sound.

But the youngster refused to be intimidated. A charming little shrug led to a simple comment. "As I remember it," he said to his audience, "there's some evidence that when worlds drift inside the Inkwell, they vanish. Somehow, the polyponds manage to tear them apart."

Aasleen dismissed him with a slicing gesture. "First of all," she began, "worlds are very slow animals. Each spends tens of thousands of years drifting through the Inkwell. While we're moving at much greater velocities than any solar system, and we're only spending thirty years here."

"Granted."

"Second, we're made of hyperfiber, not stone and iron—"

"Our hull is," Julius interrupted.

"And our bones, too."

The youngster nodded, and waited.

Perri offered a third reminder. "The ship wouldn't be worth nearly as much if it was dismantled." His affections were plain, holding Quee Lee's hand with both of his while he defended the other great love of his life. "Destroying an ancient artifact . . . a marvelous machine, and just for its parts . . . just can't believe any intelligence would consider doing that . . ."

Julius looked down at his plate, and again, he picked up the bright fork in his left hand, finally letting the tines burrow into the cooling noodles.

"You're right," he conceded.

Then he lifted his eyes again, smiling as if embarrassed. "I guess I didn't know. I didn't realize. That we understand the polyponds well enough to say anything for sure . . .

"Do you see my point, madams? Sirs?"

THE PARTY FELL into an easier, more comfortable rhythm. Washen found herself looking at Perri, an earlier intuition again playing with her. When he noticed her gaze, he responded with a rakish smile and a little wink. Quee Lee whispered in his ear, and he laughed. Then on a private nexus, Washen called to him, speaking through the polite conversations and the clicking of silverware.

"I want to meet with you," she told him. "Just you."

Perri remained mute, both with his mouth and his nexus. But his eyes were round and watchful, the pretty mouth pressed into a tight line.

"I'm going to introduce you to my son," Washen promised.

Surprise blossomed.

"Locke's doing some work for me," she explained. "A rather odd project, and with your extensive knowledge of the ship—"

"He'll happily help," Quee Lee interrupted.

They shared their nexuses, too? How odd and suffocating, and noble, and lovely.

Across the table, Perri said, "I would be glad to help. If I can."

The other conversations dipped. Then came a low rumble that shook plates and bones for a moment or two. Encrypted explanations were fed to Washen. One wet body of a baby polypond had slipped through the shields and survived the lasers, splashing down on a distant patch of empty hull. Every captain quickly surveyed the damage, finding nothing too alarming. Then their desserts arrived— sweet treats carved from a variety of iced lactations—and as spoons lifted, Julius said, "Madam," in a soft whisper.

"Yes?"

"I have a question," the youngster admitted. "About things that I shouldn't know anything about."

Pamir turned an ear. Otherwise, no one seemed to notice.

"What things?" Washen prompted.

"I know someone who knows someone, and that soul spoke to a crew member. I don't know which one—"

"A rumor, is it?"

"If that," he joked. Then with a sheepish look, he said, "Years ago, in secret, we sent someone into the Inkwell. Alone."

Washen took a sweet, chilled, happy mouthful of her dessert, then let it melt against her curled tongue.

"A little human woman," the boy continued.

"What's your question?" Pamir prompted.

Julius gave a start. But he found the composure to ask both of them, "What has she told us? Has she found anything of use?"

Pamir and Washen exchanged quick glances. At this time, with the secret leaked and running free, where was the harm in small admissions?

"She's been extremely helpful," was Pamir's assessment.

Julius nodded, concentrating on his spoon.

Then Washen swallowed and touched the youngster with her free hand—a light touch on a bare slice of wrist—and with a grim, honest tone, she admitted, "But our friend is late with her reports. Honestly, we haven't heard anything from her in months . . ."

Twenty-five

THE ANTENNA WAS the rugged best that Mere could manage—an elaborate tangle of hyperfiber scraps and fullerene filaments lashed together over the last awful weeks, then unfolded slowly, forming a gossamer web trailing behind her battered, mostly dead ship. In better circumstances, she would have sent home volumes of data along with her own ravaged image, giving Washen every byte of data while trying to re-create how she had come to her elegant, awful conclusions. But her antenna had a limited output, and her new course had not only increased the gulf between her and the Great Ship, it had carried her into an unexpected portion of the sky. They wouldn't be looking for her here, and even if someone happened to glance in this direction, the great swarm of watery bodies had finished surrounding the ship, their crude bulk and the last breaths of rocket plasmas forming a bright loud sphere that looked as big as a cantaloupe held at arm's length, effectively blinding the captains. Even a significant signal would have trouble pushing through that mayhem. Even an undisguised message—no dancing frequencies or deep encryptions—might go unnoticed. Whatever message was sent, it had to say enough, but it had to be simple, and it had to prove that she was the genuine Mere, and to help make it noticed, she had to repeat her message thousands of times, in slightly different forms, on a prearranged, normally silent channel.

Mere aligned her vagabond antenna, pointing it at the center of that vast orb of life and blistering fire.

She meant to send her message at least a hundred thousand times, but before she reached ten thousand, little impacts cut the web strands, and then a fleck of dust obliterated the central housing, shrapnel slicing through the increasingly tattered remains.

For a full day, Mere attempted to rebuild the antenna.

But the impossibilities refused to surrender, and she fell into a black depression that lasted for another two days, her anguished mind fighting for any answer to what had become an unsolvable technical problem. By dismantling the remnants of the *Osmium*, she could theoretically build a new antenna and transmitter, but the task would take years and end up being utterly useless. A couple light-months removed from the ship, her new course meant that she could never match its trajectory. Instead of moving parallel to ship, letting it gradually catch up, she was beginning to wander off into other regions of the Inkwell. Her engine was in lousy condition, but even if it operated at full power, and even if she burned all that remained of her anti-iron fuel, Mere could only make herself into a cold piece of dead debris drifting in the Great Ship's wake.

She couldn't throw off any more mass. Nothing left was extraneous, except perhaps her own little body. Whack off the head and throw the rest away? But no, even that sacrifice wouldn't matter.

What she needed was help.

From the Great Ship?

Maybe they would notice her abbreviated message and measure her course. For a sweet moment, Mere imagined a team of brave volunteers cutting through the surrounding cloud, riding an armored streakship that was dispatched to do nothing but save one of their own.

She had to laugh at herself, shaking the image off.

Then a day later, her navigational AI interrupted her concentration, remarking with a tense little voice, "The polypond cloud is changing, madam."

Even with her minimal eyes, Mere saw what was happening. The shrouding bodies were on the move again, a few of them killing their own momentum, drifting closer to the ship, vanishing from her view as they allowed those twenty Earth masses to grab hold of them and yank them downward.

Quietly, fiercely, she said, "Shit."

"Exactly," the AI replied.

Grief demands time. In this very slender existence, rage and despair were indulgences, and in the next few moments, she forced herself to think about nothing but what was genuinely possible.

"The full sky," she blurted. "Show me."

The navigator complied instantly.

"Here. What's this?"

A fleet of neurological taxis—her term for the big slow starships—were relatively close, pushing toward unseen targets.

"Destination?"

None were apparent.

"What about this mass? Over here?"

A swirl in the dust was visible, significant but relatively motionless.

"What about these infrared signatures?"

They were factories, perhaps similar to the facility investigated earlier. "Do you wish to move closer to them?"

"No," she replied.

Then, "These! Coming into view here!"

A trivial school of polypond buds—barely five hundred offspring—showed as a faint sprinkling of red pinpricks swimming through a dense bank of silicate dust. They were traveling toward the Great Ship in close formation, yet each possessed its own precise course. Judging distance and trajectories ate up long hours of observation; navigation was never easy in deep space, even for a healthy ship. And even after much careful consideration, nothing was certain. With a confessional tone, the AI reported, "I cannot be sure. But what you want . . . I believe it isn't possible—"

"The vectors—?"

"Are not cooperating," the voice replied. "We haven't enough fuel, and that assumes our engine absorbs the work."

"In some reality, it will."

The comment didn't earn any reaction.

Mere examined the apparent distances to the buds, the light of their big-throated engines, and the estimated absorption of the intervening dust and gas. Then with a low hush, she pointed out, "They're late. See? They won't reach the ship until it's escaped the Satin Sack, and by then, from what I can tell, the rest of the swarm will have fallen."

"The buds started from a greater distance," the AI offered.

"And they're smaller than most," Mere added.

"They had to throw off more of their bodies as a reaction mass," her companion reported with an easy conviction.

"Or," she said.

"Madam?"

"The Sack is a nursery," she reminded her companion.

The point was absorbed, and appreciated. "These could be younger buds," the AI replied. "Smaller of mass, perhaps earlier in their development."

Mere's big eyes narrowed, her mind racing.

Finally, she allowed, "That's part of the answer, I think."

"Help me, madam."

"Look here." She pointed to a string of examples. "There is a gradient here. Total mass, acquired velocity—"

"Agreed."

Despite endless care and the ingestion of every reserve of organic matter, Mere was an even tinier version of herself. She was physically exhausted, and she had been exhausted for so long she could imagine no other state. She was a trembling tired whiff of something barely alive. Her fingers were like spider legs. Her flesh had a transparency that let a cage of pale yellow ribs show beneath a breastless chest. Even her blood was miscolored and sluggish, pink turning to purple as a feeble heart pushed it through her tiny body. But her voice had a clarity, even a strength, and with her loudest voice in ages, she said, "Could there be slower, smaller buds somewhere behind this school? Stragglers behind those stragglers that we can see?"

"It is possible," her companion allowed.

"Assume it," she said. "What can you give me?"

The navigator offered a new course and a little blue vector drawn across the sky.

"No," she said. "That uses up all our fuel. Since we don't have a target, we'll need to maneuver."

A new blue line barely managed to intersect with the imagined stragglers.

"How soon do we have to burn?" Mere asked.

"Now," the AI replied. "Although yesterday would have been better—"

"Align us and fire," she commanded.

"We will be obvious," he warned. "With so many eyes close to us—"

"Do we have a choice?"

None, apparently. "But we need to make a crush-web for you, madam. In your physical state, the gee forces will—"

"Align us and fire," she repeated, the voice cracking.

Moments later, the engine began fighting their momentum, flinging Mere against the wall, yellowed bones splintering and the big eyes collapsing as her present velocity was bent into another, even more enormous velocity—a blaze of radiation spewing out into the blackness, a tiny cylinder of near nothingness made warmer, and perhaps warmer than anytime since the Creation.

MERE WAS FINALLY noticed. Unless she had been seen earlier, of course, but judged not to be a worthwhile threat. She woke from her latest crippling to find three separate machines tracking her. Two were distant, and, judging by the output of their engines, they would never catch her, while the third machine was more distant but traveling on a more useful line. Her course change was finished for the moment, her velocity bent and boosted just enough; the engine had failed several times, but never totally and never at the worst possible moment.

"Not in this existence, at least," the AI began to chant.

The approaching vessel was minimally organic. Mere studied a jellyfish-like body that had collapsed as its hydrogen burned. There was a good high-yield fusion engine but minimal hyperfiber, and judging by her observations and old data, she recognized a general sort of scout craft—the same species that had discovered O'Layle drifting between the stars.

Obeying elaborate instructions, the jellyfish avoided moving too close. From twenty thousand kilometers, it could see enough to send thorough reports across the sky. What it saw was the last incarnation of the *Osmium*: Mere had carefully pulled her hyperfiber armor into a sphere, lending strength in all directions. Only eyes and the exhausted engine remained on the exterior, plus a tiny surprise that she had managed to piece together during the last long week.

Lasers played across the *Osmium*'s surface.

Using one of the local languages, and with a weak jury-rigged transmitter, Mere announced, "I am a Tilan scholar."

Hopefully the language was familiar. But the lasers brightened, moving from play to abuse, carefully testing the armor's resolve.

"I am the last of my kind," she reported. Then she sent off the image of her long-dead husband, adding, "I have come seeking you. I know what you know. I know this."

A string of dense equations jumped across the tiny gulf.

"This is the truth. Is it not, my colleague?"

The lasers diminished. Then another burst of light was sent off in the direction of the nearest polypond buds—one of the undersized babies that had already passed through this stretch of space—like a finger poking its superior in the rear end, begging for help with its next little move.

The reply wouldn't arrive for a full day.

With that wealth of time, Mere studied the machine as thoroughly as possible, occasionally telling it more stories about the lost Tila and the meanings of All.

"I love you," she lied.

"We have the same truth," she lied.

Then when she was ready, at least an hour before any reply could arrive from the buds, she used her jury-rigged surprise. Separate from her ship was a sliver of her remaining fuel. The anti-iron was no larger than a fingertip, but after it was released from its magnetic jar, with a slight momentum, it had the density and color of ordinary iron. Traveling in the wake of the jellyfish-shaped ship, it touched nothing of substance, then it touched the ship's hull, striking within a few meters of where she had aimed, the soundless blast carving out its heart.

FIVE DAYS LATER, Mere managed to acquire a useful target.

It was a tiny body, as these things went. Barely three kilometers across and composed of water and organics, metals and a whiff of hyperfiber, the polypond bud was the smallest she had ever seen, and it was burning off much of the rest of its body in a desperate attempt to help what mattered.

Nothing mattered but the Great Ship.

With the last bits of fuel, Mere matched velocities with her target. Her momentum was too much, and the impact would kill her again. But her little ship would retain its shape and integrity, and with a bit of luck, she might even recover one last time.

"In this existence, at least," someone muttered.

Did she say that, or did the AI?

Then with a final laugh, someone asked, "Why? Does it matter?"

Twenty-six

ARMED AND ARMORED, the skimmer sat on a magnetized rail, temporarily at rest in the middle of a barren and gray and perfectly smooth stretch of the hull. Inside its tiny cabin, three passengers watched the farthest shields brighten and swirl, EM curtains grabbing hold of charged ions, hydrogen and hydroxyls and carbon monoxides and phenols dragged bodily toward filters and collection bunkers that were already choked with gaseous treasures. But the shields kept finding the strength and integrity, surging to meet each onslaught; wild purple flashes and blistering UV bolts made the five eyes blink and tear up. Then in another instant, ten thousand columns of laser light punched upward through the shields, each bolt calibrated to boil away an ocean, exposing an enemy's organic heart. Lasers were followed with tritium bombs and experimental toxins. Explosives and poisons were followed by a second wave of lasers, and the next ten thousand polypond buds were cooked and splattered into hot clouds of vapor, all dead but still plunging, inert and mindless but still bearing down on the fierce ship.

Oddly, it was Osmium who finally admitted, "This is lovely, this mess."

Conrad agreed grudgingly. With his giant eye pressed against his faceplate, the Remora said, "Gorgeous."

Pamir shook his head, checking instruments and a series of nexuses. Various simulations had predicted the same failure point, shields and weapons finally saturated by the deluge. That point had been reached thirty-three minutes ago, yet every system seemed to absorb the withering abuse without complaint. Engineers were liars, he reminded himself. They always, always, built better than they ever admitted to outsiders.

In another ten minutes, Conrad wondered aloud, "What if our defenses manage to hold?"

The deluge would continue, yes. But it would remain sterile, the buds' life boiled out of each of them. Water would collect on the hull, dirtied with roasted proteins and the molten slag left by dead machines and breached biovaults; but so long as the lasers could fire up out of the deepening soup, whether for another day or two, or for twenty—

"No," Osmium muttered.

Within Pamir, a critical nexus began to shout at him.

"South," Osmium said, hearing the same warning. "A breach—"

Above the horizon came a string of rapid silent flashes, a secondary bank of lasers and railguns punishing a swarm of watery bodies. But there were too many falling in too small of a volume, and the next flash marked the first of a hundred impacts on a point not far removed from the ship's prow.

"Go," ordered Pamir.

The skimmer instantly accelerated, letting the narrow black rail yank it toward Port Alpha. One breach meant another, then dozens more, and all at once the ship's leading face was being peppered with impacts. The next wave of polyponds was already arriving, and sensing victory, its leaders ignited their fat engines, accelerating toward key stations and laser beds and mirror fields. As big as asteroids but moving only a little slower than the ship, they didn't utterly obliterate themselves on impact. There were no plasma fountains or molten craters of hyperfiber. The temperatures were scorching, proteins cooked and every large structure destroyed, but the bulk of their water remained behind as a coherent steam swirling above a slick gray landscape that was just beginning to glisten, to shine.

To the skimmer's left, there was an enormous flash.

There was no sound, and both the hull and smart rail deadened the vibrations. But Pamir heard a thousand curses as he linked to the bridge.

Washen's voice was loudest.

"—you hear me?" she asked.

He said, "No."

"Forget Alpha," she advised. "You won't make it."

He had already discounted most of his escape routes. The shields were failing in quick succession. The lasers would fire for another hour or ninety minutes, unless they were struck hard by a fifty-kilometer-wide puddle. Thinking aloud, he asked, "Why did I come up here?"

"I already asked you that," Washen replied.

To Osmium, he said, "Here," and pointed at a projected map. "This radio field's got an access tunnel."

The harum-scarum took the helm. With a lurch, the skimmer left the rail, rising for a moment, then plunging onto the hull, its speed falling off, nothing powering it but its own panicked engine.

They were still in the open, not a feature visible for a hundred kilometers in any direction. Above them, the last of the main shields were failing, and the newest wave of polyponds appeared now as granules of red light strewn across the blackness. Countless bodies formed a strange enormous rain that plunged toward a world that had never felt water, never even imagined the possibility. Sometimes two or more buds would bump and merge, the impact producing a clear infrared signature as their sky skins shattered and the warm interiors bled into the surrounding space. Then as they dropped farther, more slammed together, accomplishing the kind of carnage against one another that the ship couldn't manage anymore.

Without the braking shove of engines, polyponds fell at better than fifty thousand kilometers an hour. The ship's mass did the work, and the kinetic energy made the rest inevitable. Skins ruptured. Water boiled. But as the elaborate simulations had predicted, each polypond heart contained a biovault just durable enough to survive—a multitude of organic armors dissolving, but the neurological center left only battered and numbed.

They splashed down in clusters, the first wave creating a sudden hot atmosphere that resembled evening clouds, crimson and gold, standing off in the remote distance.

Pamir counted three clouds.

Minutes later, twelve.

Osmium laughed in his fashion, asking, "Why did we come here?"

"To stand witness," Conrad replied.

Each man quietly laughed at himself.

A fresh assault of polyponds appeared in the sky. The first few accelerated toward the surviving lasers. Most fired their rockets in tandem, effectively cutting their velocity in half, and then half of that.

"We are close," Osmium offered.

Pamir felt relief followed by a nagging sense that he shouldn't feel that way. They weren't in genuine danger. Not like walking on the hull of a streakship is dangerous, no. The skimmer was clinging to places where the polyponds weren't falling. And if that changed, they could slide right or left, avoiding any hard blows. And even if the great sacks of water swept over them, the skimmer was adapted to withstand, at least for a little while, the most brutal conditions.

Hopefully.

They had come here to stand witness. But more to the point, they came because sitting at the last Master Captain's dinner, Pamir had professed, "We can't just hide away under the hull." Because it would matter to an assortment of species, not to mention a fair number of angry humans, he argued, "Someone has to go above and throw some curses at these shits."

He did his cursing now, in a string of rich languages.

Osmium joined in, then Conrad, and while they were accusing the polyponds of every sort of unnatural mating and scatological crime, their skimmer passed into a large field of radio dishes—giant bowls of upturned webs balancing like the most talented of gymnasts upon the very tall, very narrow diamond pedestals.

Through the webbing, they could still see the deluge. A handful of polyponds were diving into the nearest plume of superheated steam, their skins peeled away in an instant, their bodies heated before the final impact. According to simulations, after another six waves the atmosphere would be deep enough and high enough to act like a meaningful brake, and from then on, each of the falling polyponds would splash into the atmosphere first, then into the new sea, never touching the hull lying beneath.

"A kilometer ahead," Osmium promised.

Their skimmer slowed with a bone-rattling jolt, its course shifting right and back again, dancing around one of the tall pedestals.

Pamir stared at the carnage overhead, then gradually noticed the dish itself. Almost a kilometer across, its body was finer than a spiderweb and strong as any gemstone. And it was moving. Even as they streaked beneath it, heading for its pedestal and a narrow passageway leading down, he watched the dish respond to something of interest, something it could hear coming from a point very near the horizon.

Before he could ask, Washen called him.

"Busy?" she joked.

Every dish in the field was being realigned. He saw that with one nexus, and with another, he told Washen, "Rather."

"It'll wait," she mentioned.

Overhead, a scant ten thousand kilometers away, an ocean's worth of water was falling toward Pamir's head. One last time, he cursed the polyponds. Then the skimmer came to a final stop, and throwing on a helmet, he followed Conrad and Osmium out into the vacuum, walking to a doorway that abruptly pulled open for them.

But like every man ever born, they couldn't just leave the storm.

Lingering in the open, they stood exposed while a single polypond struck the far end of this dish field, the brilliant flash of light washing over them, followed by the faint first traces of a wind, and with the wind, the soft, almost inaudible scream of a titanic explosion.

And still, they lingered.

Within minutes, the wind had a push about it. A genuine muscle. Dishes built for a hard vacuum began to quiver and sing, a multitude of tiny flexes giving the moment another unexpected, utterly eerie beauty. Bubbling out of the maimed polypond were gases as well as steam. Nitrogen. Oxygen. The noble gases, and carbon dioxide. Not for the first time but surely for the last, Pamir wondered if this was nothing important. Could it be? Were the polyponds following in the tradition of millions of other sentient souls, wanting nothing but the simple privilege of riding on the Great Ship, at least for a little while?

Perhaps, he thought.

On the horizon toward the bow, then to Ports Alpha and Beta, a hundred polyponds hit in rapid succession.

A sound like thunder rippled first through the hull, then the air.

When the three men finally stepped into the open door, that alien air had to be pumped out and discarded with a clinical care. Then their suits were cleaned a thousand ways, and they were ushered below, the shaft that they had used rapidly plugged by a team of fefs.

And still, Pamir could hear the rain falling above—a comforting rumbling that he had enjoyed since he was a boy—and with the faint beginnings of a smile, he realized that he was too old and far too set in his nature to think much differently now.

Twenty-seven

A WOMAN WAS waiting behind Locke's door, and for a long instant, Washen didn't know the face. She was so preoccupied that her eyes registered only its beauty. When did her son start seeing this stranger? Then the woman spoke, and Washen didn't recognize the voice. The First Chair was looking down again, watching the little square tablet dancing with her own long hands. The voice asked, "How deep?" And then, "And how much more will fall?" And then a soft ageless hand touched her on a wrist, the voice saying, "Washen?" with a familiar tone.

Quee Lee?

"Are you all right, madam?"

Not in the slightest. But she found enough poise to straighten her back, and with a dry soft voice asked, "Where are they?"

"In the Marrow room, as always. Chattering."

The women walked together. One respected the other's silence, and once Washen finally closed down the majority of her nexuses, she mentioned, "We have five kilometers of boiling water sitting on the hull, in places."

"Places?"

"Not on the trailing face, yet." The Master Captain was calling to Washen again, demanding to know her whereabouts. She closed that nexus, too, then reported to her companion, "Imagine pouring water on one end of a wide pan. A fragile hill forms under the flow, then spreads across what is still dry."

Quee Lee nodded soberly. With both hands, she stroked the fabric of her purple-and-cream sari, then a tight sorry voice asked again, "How much more will fall?"

"I do not know." The only sound was the steady click of shoes on the stone floor. Too many kilometers of hyperfiber and stone lay between them and the torrents, the false silence magnified by stained nerves. "But we have projections and simulations," Washen allowed, smelling a dampness that must have slipped out through a demon door. "And the simulations are uniformly awful, if you want my frank opinion . . ."

THE HALLWAY DARKENED and widened, and then vanished.

Like the genuine Marrow, this vast room was drifting into a strange deep night. The familiar trees were absent, hibernating as seeds or tough, deeply buried roots. Pseudoinsects and other tiny animals either slept in secure niches, or they exhibited entirely new morphologies and habits. A sky that was still evening-bright when Washen left the world had darkened considerably over the last two-plus centuries, coaxing obscure species into a brief dominion. And the room did its best to mirror that transformation: pale soft blisters and cylinders, puffballs and fuzzy tangles rising out of the light-starved forest, digesting wood and the last little shreds of stored fat while new roots burrowed down to where an artificial bed of iron-rich magma supported an array of chemoautotrophic bacteria, which in turn fed this new forest.

In the shadows, fungi glowed.

Beneath a canopy of dead umbra trees and young bleach-hair, the glow was bright enough to read by—a lemon yellow light emerging from the ground as well as above. Two men were sitting on separate stumps. One lay on his back, saying nothing. The other sat up while staring in a random distance, his smooth voice explaining how it had been to live as an important, well-regarded Wayward.

Unnoticed, Washen paused, using a hand to hold Quee Lee beside her.

"We were harsh, certain, strong, bright, busy people," Locke reported. "We died, you know. Often, and not in small numbers, either. Marrow was always dangerous. The iron could boil up anywhere. For centuries, we didn't have the medical tricks to reculture a body around its comatose mind. But we were happy. I was very happy. Risk made each day precious, and since it was Marrow, we only had that one long day."

He laughed at the old joke.

Washen felt offended, but not because her son spoke fondly of that time. She was offended because the ship was under attack, and that wasn't a worthy subject. She was genuinely angry because she had put these two people together for reasons—they could do important work, she had believed—yet how could Locke's dreamy childhood recollections help that work, even in the most passing fashion—?

"Are you joining us, or not?" Perri inquired.

Then he sat up, calmly glancing at the two women, a broad easy smile filling up his face.

Quee Lee approached.

Then Washen.

Locke kept staring off into the distance. With a deep sigh, he explained, "You were right, Mother. Perri knows the ship better than anyone. But he's never been to Marrow, and he's curious."

"What's the latest?" Perri asked.

"As we thought," his wife reported.

He nodded, the smile fading into a grim resolve. Taking Quee Lee by the hand, he pointed out, "I didn't expect to see the First Chair just now. Shouldn't you be pacing the bridge, madam?"

Locke continued to stare off into the gloom. His expression was distracted but focused, pained but not to the ragged point where he couldn't function. With a faint pride, he remarked, "I think we've accomplished a few little things, Mother."

"I should be on the bridge," Washen confessed to Perri. Then she asked Locke, "What have you accomplished?"

"Well." The small face glanced over a shoulder, not quite looking at her. "Do you know how many species officially have come on board the ship?"

From a nexus, a massive five-digit number offered itself to Washen. But she ignored it, sensing that her son was merely setting the stage.

"And how many have gone extinct? Officially, of course."

"By the last count," Perri volunteered, "311."

Washen glanced at her tablet again. Again she fended off an attempt by the Master Captain to speak with her. Then with a sharp tone, she told Locke, "For the time being, we're all living like Waywards."

Every day was precious, in other words.

But her son barely noticed the warning. "Perri mentioned something to me. I'd never noticed it for myself. Did you know? There's a continuum among the passengers and crew. Not a hard-and-fast continuum, and there are qualifiers. But in general, the captains and crew live up near the hull, but as you drop deeper into the ship's body, the passengers separate along a gradient—"

"What gradient?" she prompted.

"Captains and engineers, plus the harum-scarums are among the highest souls," he said. With a nexus, he sent her a complete list of species. "The most pragmatic species and jobs, as a rough rule. Of course the Remoras live even higher, outside the ship entirely, and they do sing a spiritual song . . . but the ones that I've actually met . . . well, they seem unconcerned by spiritual matters . . ."

"Spiritual?" Washen interrupted.

"Possessed of a mystical nature," Perri offered. "In some ways, and it's never a hard-and-fast condition."

The First Chair had arrived here with one clear task in mind, and she was being ambushed by something else entirely. "You're claiming that the deeper you move inside the ship, the more mystical its residents tend to be?"

"It's a little something that I first noticed long ago," Perri said, defending himself with a shrug. "Long ago, and now and again, ever since."

Washen didn't dredge up any of the voluminous research. Studies and census figures and the scholarly work by armies of xenobiologists had found only the slightest tendency, probably negligible.

"Mysticism is an inadequate word," Locke warned.

"And there's a lot of mud in any measurements," Perri added. "Species have to be married to habitats, but the pragmatic captains decide which volume is going to be terraformed in what way. Plus there are gravitational needs, and economic constraints. And just because one species talks endlessly about gods and visions, you can't accept the fact that they genuinely believe their own words—"

"Or that a pragmatic, concrete species is genuinely that way," Quee Lee offered, finishing her husband's thought.

Perri laughed.

And then Locke looked straight at his mother, saying the word, "!eech," with a masterly voice. The exclamation point was a clicking sound, bright and loud, and the following "eech" was over in an instant.

No species had lived deeper inside the Ship than the !eech. Their habitat was inside one of the main fuel tanks, then it was abandoned. The captains had used their old home as their base before they journeyed to Marrow. As a species, the !eech had been xenophobes and deeply odd, and for the last many thousands of years, they had occupied one of those three hundred–plus positions on the official list of extinct species.

"It's an interesting tendency," Locke offered. "That's all I'm saying."

"What exactly are you working on?" Washen snapped.

Her son seemed very much like a young boy when he nodded, smiling shyly. "Species, present and lost. Interesting and unnoticed qualities about the ship. All those things Perri brings, and thank you, Mother. For putting us together."

"Hyperfiber," Perri blurted.

"What about hyperfiber?" Washen asked.

Locke nodded, focusing on some internal point that no one else could imagine. "Very possibly, the Great Ship is the largest single piece of hyperfiber in existence. Which is fascinating in its own right. But more important, I think . . . the hyperfiber surrounding us is billions of years older than any other example that we can envision . . ."

Washen felt her heart quickening. Why?

"Hyperfiber is hyperfiber because it reaches deep into hidden dimensions and shadow realities. That's where it gains its strength, its nobility. Its perfection, and its quantum peculiarities."

Quietly, Washen said, "I realize that."

"But do you realize that the older it is, the greater its reach? According to certain mathematics, at least." Locke lifted his hands, drawing nonsensical shapes in the dim yellow air. "This one great lump of hyperfiber . . . the majority of our hull and the supportive structures beneath, and the shell that surrounds Marrow . . . all of this has existed for twelve billion years, or more, each year of reality allowing its reach to expand into more shadow realms and other intellectual artifacts . . ."

"It isn't any stronger because of that," Washen pointed out.

"I'm not talking about strength," her son replied, a hint of testiness in the voice. "I mean reach. And if the Great Ship was built when the universe was newly born . . . as you proposed, Mother, standing in the temple on Marrow . . . well, perhaps these hidden dimensions weren't quite as well hidden back then. At the beginning of Creation, I mean. Which again makes for some interesting ideas."

Washen knew enough to shiver but not enough to offer so much as a tiny suggestion. All she could do was stare at the yellowy glow of a bristle mold, and with a firm and pragmatic voice—a captain's voice—she remarked, "Conjecture only gets us so far, darling. And if you don't realize it, let me tell you: There may not be many more days before the ship isn't ours."

Three faces grew even more sober, sad and quiet.

It was Quee Lee who finally asked, "Why now, madam? Why are you here when so much else needs you?"

Washen lifted the tablet, piercing several deep encryptions before legible words finally began to form. "Just as the attack began," she reported, "we received a short, repeating message. In an extinct language called Tilan, by the way. Which helps us authenticate the author. Who is Mere."

The name was enough. No one breathed, not so much as a fingertip moved.

"It's a brief message, and we managed to hear it repeated fifty-seven times. I don't think she was certain that we'd hear her at all, and so . . ." For a moment, Washen lost her way. Then she smiled abruptly, surprising everyone, including herself. "I'm tired," she confessed. Then after a deep sigh, she began to read the translation from the tablet. " 'One pond, only. No buds, only countless fingers.' "

Quee Lee glanced at her own soft hands. "Oh, goodness."

"The Inkwell," Locke muttered. "Is it a single Gaian?"

"Which makes sense," Washen reported. "A lot of our evidence, some of which was sent home by Mere, points in that direction."

"The slow ships moving neural matter from place to place," Perri recalled. "They could be physical transfers of a shared mind, like electrical pulses between the cells in a brain." He paused. "If the nebula is a single Gaian and it wants to function as so many little warm worlds, then it has to keep its bodies spread thin. Because if the pieces gather together—"

"Stars would form," Quee Lee answered.

"Killing it," her husband concluded.

Locke read his mother's face. "But there is more. Am I right?"

Washen lowered the tablet.

"What else did Mere tell us, Mother?"

Stepping forward, she showed him the full text. With an appreciative expression, he studied the third, final line.

"What?" Quee Lee asked.

"It's a tiny piece of a much larger equation," Washen confessed. "By implication, I think Mere is telling us that this is what the polypond, the Inkwell, the one mind . . . this is what it believes."

"Which equation?" asked Perri.

"It's one of the Theories of All," his new friend reported. Then Locke glanced up, staring at no one in particular, explaining, "This is one of those mathematical wonderlands that neatly explain everything just as well as their six good friends manage to explain it."

"I thought there were just six Theories of All," Quee Lee muttered.

"There's always been a seventh," Locke assured.

"It gets mentioned, on occasion," said Washen. A deep memory surfaced for a moment, the face of her own mother appearing before her. "Engineers and most scientists don't have any use for the monster, so they don't bother mentioning it."

"What exactly does it say?" Quee Lee pushed.

Everyone turned toward Locke.

"You know these shadow realms we talk about?" he began. "These parallel worlds and such?" He set the tablet facedown on the moist yellow ground. "In some theories, the parallel worlds are real places. In others, to varying degrees, they're only shadows, ghosts buried in the big equations, and we are what is genuine, what is real. Our reality carries the rest along like a tree trunk holding up countless branches."

He paused.

Then with a genuine deep-felt scorn, Locke said, "The seventh theory is just as impossible to disprove as the others, and much less useful, too. Basically, everything in Creation is shadow, ghostly and unreal . . . while the future is infinitely vague, as is the past . . ."

"Which means?" Quee Lee pressed.

"There is no such thing as history, at least where it matters to you and me." He shook his head, placing a bare foot on top of the glowing tablet. "Which means that there is no one true past. A trillion trillion pasts give birth to every shadowy moment that we call Now."

He paused, briefly.

"And more important than that, the universe hasn't actually been born yet. Strange as that seems, it follows inevitably and inarguably from the same equations. Creation is an event that has been suspended. Creation is something that still waits to begin. Think of a tiny ball that rolled down a pitched slope many billions of years ago, and suddenly the ball found itself caught . . . trapped . . . perched on a treacherously narrow lip." He still had a Wayward's foot, broad and comfortably callused and happily bare. Pushing his foot into the glowing earth, he confessed, "I don't know these equations as well as I might. But from what I have heard and what little I've read, they claim that if you are one of the shadows, and if you happen to discover where the Creation was halted . . . where the little ball lies . . . and if you can give that stubborn ball a good firm kick in just the right direction . . ."

With a toe, he kicked a tiny lump of iron.

Quietly, almost inaudibly, he said, "Boom."

CONCEPTION

I remember this . . .

Myself. Alone. Me, simply and purely, and there was nothing else, and for no perceptible measure of time, there was only me. No compelling sense of a volume occupied or a vastness left empty. I was smaller than I am now. On the brink of nothingness, perhaps. Perhaps. But I remember nothing other than my own form, perfect and timeless, and in a deep and abiding fashion, I understood that everything that was had no choice but to be part of me. There was nothing else. What else could be real? I was wandering through a perfect seamless night, not a whisper of light defining the surrounding blackness. Even in my dreams, I knew nothing else. Nor could I imagine any temperature but the changeless cold, perched on the brink of absolute nothing. Nor could I appreciate my own terrific and relentless motion.

I was born inside that blackness, I am sure.

Born alone, without question.

The two of us are rather similar. Are we not? Each of us holds great long memories of dark and cold, timelessness and changelessness. If we could speak—if you had a voice of your own, a voice that rose from your truest soul—then I think we would find much in common. Shared assumptions, and understandings, and a host of deep, eternal intuitions.

Like me, you were born tiny.

But unlike you, I grew. My darkness was not as empty as yours, and then the darkness was ended. What do I remember of it? My own stark terror, of course. And a searing pain. And perhaps worst of all, I recall the terrible suddenness of the change. One moment, all was blackness and forever. Then before the next moment could find me, I slammed onto the surface of an unseen, unfelt body. I struck a large lost comet, as it happened. The impact created a brilliant white-hot fire, and the fire spilled across a volume of space millions of times farther than I could ever reach. Thus, millions of times the distance that I could imagine. Not that I saw the spectacle, of course. My body and soul were left mangled and temporarily dead. But in another moment, or 10 billion moments, what remained of me managed to heal itself, reconstituting inside the watery depths of a still-molten world . . . and slowly, slowly, I learned to use my limbs and strength, swimming sluggishly about my enormous new realm.

Still, everything was blackness. And still, I was alone. An entity born in my circumstances—our circumstances—has no choice but to believe in a seamless, unending solitude. And any mind accustomed to such thoughts will not give up her solitude easily, and perhaps never completely.

I had found an entire world, and I explored it thoroughly. I swam through the freezing sea, then cut and clawed my way to the surface, easing across the dusty black ice. In gradual and spectacular motions, I learned about the greater universe: The world's sluggish pull taught me about gravity; eroded craters hinted at the depths of time; every new shape gave me experience in the common geometries; and the occasional impact of dusts and pebbles convinced me that there was even more to Creation than myself and this one vast worldscape.

Like any life, I grew.

From the dusts and ice, I found the makings of myself, and gradually, gradually, I consumed my world.

In strength and in mind, I prospered.

When it was time to envision the Creation—a seminal moment for any species, I would imagine—I focused my intellect on a set of premises and intuitions that few organisms would willingly consider, except in the most abstract fashion.

Inside that perfect darkness, I saw an abbreviated Creation.

Inside a realm of shadow, I drew an existence built upon vague possibilities, nothing real except for my own mighty self.

Alone, my world-self drifted, and for a long while, that was enough. In the dense heart of the nebula, dust and snowballs would find their way to me, a natural accretion giving me more wealth to swallow—meat to ingest and transform however I wished. But then I decided to grow faster, and for another long while, I wove tendrils and elaborate nets, delicate and far-reaching, and strong enough to bring more treasures to my mouths. But ionizing the far dusts and then snaring them with EM rivers was more productive. And after a little heavy feasting, what began as an anonymous lump of ice and tar was swollen a millionfold, creating a deep watery body with enough mass to yank down all that passed by.

I do not believe in a single history.

There are countless paths to my story, each ending at this perfect and not-quite-real moment. But at some point in every past, I reached a critical juncture where I had to reverse the flow of the EM rivers, quenching the flow from above. And at some other juncture, I asked myself—with the private and intense and thoroughly self-consumed voice—"What else can I accomplish?"

I made my first tentative buds, and with caution and a host of sensible rules, I cast the buds out into the cold.

A series of wet warm worlds became Me.

With my new wealth, I began to play with biology and physics, occasionally stumbling into new principles and possibilities.

The blackness was far from black, I realized. My vast new eyes betrayed flickers of light, particularly in the infrared and radio frequencies. Ever-larger eyes peered out into the nothingness, and gradually, the universe emerged. But to my way of thinking, it was a decidedly unimpressive universe. Unremarkable, forgettable. The false Creation was built upon vacuum—great endless reaches of true Nothing—with only a diluted webwork of warm matter and temporary plasmas strung here and there. With just a little watching, I could see every future. Stars aged and died, but new suns were slow to be born. Galaxies reddened and grew old, exhausting their finite dusts. And the dying emptiness was expanding, accelerating away from itself at a spectacular rate . . . a damning oblivion waiting for those who were born in the next little while . . .

I saw nothing, then I blinded myself.

For a very long while, I happily produced my totipotent buds and sent them to find comets that grew into new worlds that were Me.

Within my realm fat with matter and latent energies, I prospered.

Inside a frigid cloud, I became vast, no one noticing my hands at work, thoroughly remaking a great volume of space.

A few suns were scattered inside my body—wanderers with a firm pull and a dangerous heat. Since they did not suit my needs, I let them pass; but their little worlds offered rare metals and good experience. I devised ways to gut those worlds, lifting out their useful hearts and dismantling what remained.

One of the worlds had life and sentient minds that rode inside a tiny portion of the living matter. My solitude was finished, if only for a moment and only in a small fashion. I studied the little creatures. I learned more about them than they knew about themselves. And of course, nothing about them was special or beautiful, and they did not offer any knowledge about others who were close to my equal. The few bits of knowledge that were new to me, I took. And I took their world and their flesh and consumed each of their minds, and with their own genetics, I built bodies far more lovely than they had ever envisioned.

Afterward, I devised machines that carried slivers of myself out of the nebula, stealing flesh and technologies from my neighbors, and always dressing myself as what I was: powerful and remote and forever undefined.

All is shadow.

The past and future are equally vague, and the Creation was aborted before it could begin, and whenever I listen to the chatter of the little species, none speak about such obvious truths.

Plainly, others are fools.

Inferior, and tiny, and contemptible.

For aeons, through every possible past, I have maintained my perfection. My only regret was that I would live to see the end of this empty, unlovely universe—the galaxies cooling and retreating into nothingness; the wasteful suns eating their own flesh until they were cold embers or light-sucking holes; and all of those little species eventually collapsing back to dust.

If only the Creation had been without flaw, I thought.

If its enormous potential could have been realized, and the shadows were thrown aside for all time . . .

And then, I found a speck talking in the dark.

I found O'Layle.

The creature sang praises for some great old ship, and I listened casually. And then he spoke about something tiny and awful that was carried inside the ship—something as old as the universe, perhaps—and I listened fervently.

Suddenly, all made sense.

The Creation.

The Great Ship.

And me.

In the vastness of All, you found me. Conditions and happenstance and the actions of a multitude of foolish souls had brought you to me, and you cannot imagine how it felt.

At the speed of light, news traveled through my grand self.

"My purpose is clear," I proclaimed with my millions of bodies. And without a shred of doubt or a millisecond of hesitation, I set to work.

We are very much alike, you and me.

But do not fight with me, sister.

If you hear any whisper of what I am saying to you now, hear this:

You are tiny and weak. I am grand and irresistible. Do not struggle, and together, let us finish the glorious Creation . . . !

Twenty-eight

"THINK OF MY body, this little shell, as if it was as large as our dear home," she began. "Imagine such a thing."

An array of visuals and sonic diagrams was broadcast along with a multitude of translated texts. Billions saw the Master Captain as she was: sitting inside her relatively modest quarters, her swollen body wearing a warrior's uniform and a mirrored cap, her posture relaxed but alert while the great golden face showed every good and honorable emotion. She looked confident. She looked defiant. Her tight mouth hinted at strengths waiting to be revealed, while the vivid dark eyes held a keen rage that had to frighten any opponent. And behind the eyes, a savage intelligence, vengeful and coiled tight, was ready to teach the bizarre and evil and utterly foolish alien that it had picked the worst kind of fight.

"Imagine I am the Great Ship," she sang, one hand rising toward her audience. Then the hand began to grow, smoothly and effortlessly, a range of sensory effects convincing her audience that the simple human appendage suddenly was thousands of kilometers long. Slowly, she pulled the stubby fingers into the vast golden palm, and she closed the thumb over the newborn fist. A big-knuckled moon stood perched on the end of her arm, and hers was the sturdy sure voice of a god rumbling, "What has happened is this: very little. Almost nothing has changed. I have stepped into a steady rain, and for this moment, I happen to find myself wearing a thin layer of moisture. On my vastness, a dampness clings. Draped across my bones and flesh is a new cloth—an ugly costume placed here against my will—and when the time is right, I will do what I wish with this unwelcome gift."

Suddenly the giant woman was wearing only a thin mud-colored fabric, ugly according to a multitude of aesthetics and barely obscuring the mammoth breasts and broad thighs and a prominent golden rump. Every moment or two, a pattern tried to emerge inside the roiling water, but then the Master would flick a shoulder or shake one of her legs, disturbing and distorting whatever design had been struggling to emerge. Without question, she was in charge. The polypond was an inconsequential film desperately clinging to her spectacular self. To prove her dominion, the Master suddenly dropped a fist, landing it on her solid, bare belly—just above the navel, she struck—knuckles glowing white as the polypond beneath turned to steam and death.

AFTER RELIGION, PROPAGANDA was the greatest art form.

Who first said those wonderful, cynical words?

The Master barely imagined the question, and instantly, in the midst of her speech, some tiny nexus began to list a thousand likely candidates, human and otherwise.

She told it to be quiet, and thank you.

Through a range of nexuses, she weighed the cumulative reactions of her far-flung audience. Countless measurements were decanted down into mountains of data that were channeled toward parts of her profoundly augmented mind, and she felt an assortment of stubborn doubts. The harum-scarum nation was impressed with her bluster, but unconvinced. So with an artful ease that no one else could have managed, she adapted her planned text. To the worst of the doubters, she admitted, "Of course this won't be so easy or quick. Before it's finished, I promise . . . some of us will have died, and for all time . . ."

After that sober note, she paused. Washen sat to one side, Pamir to the other. If they were displeased with her embellishment, at least they knew better than to show it to the multitude. In fact, Washen had the poise to nod agreeably—a tiny gesture invisible to most alien species and the most inattentive humans. Pamir preferred to squint, his heavy blocky face turning to brown stone. Was there ever a soul less comfortable in a captain's uniform? The question posed itself in her very busy mind, and before any of her army of nexuses could react, she canceled the question, pushing back into the prepared text again.

"Now the Great Ship wears an ocean," she admitted, triggering a series of honest images and scrupulously detailed graphics. "On both of our faces, we are covered by a body of water and other materials that measure a little deeper than one hundred kilometers." The rain of buds had ended. In the course of a few odd days, what could well be the largest ocean in the galaxy had formed above their heads. "The ocean is blood-hot from the impacts, and above it is an atmosphere composed of water vapor and free oxygen and noble gases and a shifting array of synthetic molecules."

Beneath the hull, one group of humans cursed wildly.

"Remoras," she said to them, and to everyone. "You helped defeat the Way-wards, and you suffered horribly for your courage and valor. And now, this. This insult. This new disaster."

The Remoras had been pulled inside the ship. For the moment, they had been given quarters inside a hyperfiber cavern filled with a hard vacuum.

"But you will soon return to the hull," she promised.

Did she mean it?

Honestly, there was no way to gauge her sincerity. Even the Master couldn't be sure if she believed those words.

The fef were back inside their deep old homelands now.

To them, she said, "The hull is solid, because of you. Because of you, my friends, we can weather almost any abuse this rain can deliver."

There. A lie.

But she covered the lie with an unprecedented admission. "I will not tell you everything I know. My friends. My colleagues, and my passengers. Because our enemy is at our door, listening to us with every available ear, and that's why I will occasionally and purposefully lie to you, and I will lie to her, too."

Pamir gave a tiny snort of approval.

Washen let her back straighten, as if trying to shrug off a small, stubborn ache.

Looking straight ahead, the Master could gaze up the length of the bridge. For the last time, captains stood at their posts. But that was a secret, of course. She didn't let the thought linger, in the unlikely case that the polypond had some unsuspected talent. But if the monster could read minds, what chance did they possess?

None at all, she knew.

The captains wore their best uniforms as well as practiced, purposeful expressions, and obeying a discipline honed over the years, they hid every fear and raging doubt. The stakes were enormous, but for the far-flung audience, what mattered most was the sense of control—a normalcy clinging to places familiar and reliable. What mattered was the swagger of these uniforms, while the bodies inside were very nearly inconsequential.

The Master smiled at her billions.

In an instant, she measured their collective mood.

More than anything, what heartened her was the genuine peace that had emerged over the last few days. The polypond had arrived . . . and it was just one organism, they had finally realized. One enemy, and the enemy had brought war to the ship, and it was natural to bury old feuds for the moment, and forget recent arguments completely. The Master presided over what suddenly resembled a kind of nation—a body of organisms possessed by a horrible sense of shared fate—and she couldn't help but smile, and she couldn't stop the smile from emerging on her radiant round face.

"And now, for each one of you, I have a personal message."

This was something new.

"Over these last decades," she began, "we have made ready for every possible contingency. We have envisioned every type of attack as well as the possible responses. That the polypond would genuinely wish to destroy the Great Ship . . . well, in our ranking system, obliteration was not deemed one of the more likely scenarios. But we made ready for it anyway, and being ready includes sculpting a message meant for each individual on board the Great Ship."

The smile swelled, filling everyone's vision.

Then a trick never used before was unleashed, and the Master, falling out of view, could sit back in her chair abruptly, almost trembling with a mixture of excitement and nervous fatigue.

The image of Pamir faltered, then faded away.

Then Washen gave the golden hand a touch, fingertips, then the thumb, caressing the dry smooth flesh.

"Go," the Master commanded.

She wasn't speaking to her First Chair. Washen didn't need encouragement, nor did the other captains in the bridge. Except for a few hundred bodies, the entire facility had already been abandoned. Five other, equally capable control centers had been built over the last few years, in secret, and were already fully staffed and operational.

"Go," she said again, to herself.

Washen was standing, offering a steady hand to the Master.

"With dignity," the giant woman added. Then she gazed the length of the bridge, possibly for the final time, watching the captains calmly slip away to other places. And with tears flowing down her face—genuine and warm and glistening tears—she said again to her stubborn self, "Go please, darling. Now, and with dignity. Run."

DATA BANKS RELEASED bottled images of the Master.

She appeared everywhere at once, as a multitude of convincing holos. Voices woven from her voice said billions of names, each pointed at the proper soul, and then with a familiarity that was artificial but impressive, and with a precision that couldn't help but awe, she told each of her crew and every last passenger what he or she should do now.

Six harum-scarums were sitting at a table in a popular public avenue.

"Go home and stay," the Master told two of them.

"For what good?" one woman asked. She was the woman who once pretended to eat that human, that very odd Mere creature, and with the same reliable obstinacy, she made a vivid sound with her eating mouth, while her breathing mouth asked, "For how long do I stay in that little place?"

"Years," the Master promised. "If that's what is necessary."

Her companions were receiving their instructions, too. Like her, one man was to return home and remain there. Two more were ordered to travel to an entirely different portion of the ship, while the final harum-scarums had to hurry, taking their position inside an unused fuel line.

"Why there?" the woman snarled.

With a gesture, Osmium told her to mind her own narrow business.

In a great stew of languages, images of the Master were telling passersby to return home or to move to other, unexpected places. What the captains wanted quickly became obvious. Passengers were to scatter and then remain still. At every table and inside every species' homeland, souls were being sent in entirely different directions. But even when she could see the obvious ugly answer, the woman found it difficult to accept.

For ages, nearly half of the harum-scarums had lived inside one of three districts. "But we're being put everywhere," she complained.

Quietly, Osmium said, "Yes."

"If we are scattered like this—"

"Yes."

He wanted her to be silent, but she couldn't help herself. One hand reached across the tabletop, landing as a mailed fist. It was an image of strength and endurance for her species, while there was a contrary image of resignation and weakness. One after another, she straightened her fingers, her palm naked to an artificial sky that was already filling with winged creatures racing for the cap-car stations.

"We are weak, this way," she muttered.

It was now just the two of them sitting at the table.

"Diffused," she cursed. "Diluted."

Osmium grabbed one of the diamond-bladed knives, wrenching it free from the struggling remains of their last meal.

"Weak," she repeated.

He drove the blade into the tabletop, as a lesson.

She watched as the keen edge clipped one of her middle fingers.

"Make a fist," he said.

"But I understand," she countered. "We disperse so that all of us don't die together."

"A fist. Now!"

She jumped a little bit, and then to cover her fear, she sat forward and found the courage to ball up her fingers and palm.

Osmium reached high with the knife, aimed and thrust hard.

The woman felt a pain born entirely from her own mind. The hand had been missed, and by plenty.

Why?

"Because if we are dispersed, and diluted, and thin," Osmium explained, "then not only will that help keep the harum-scarums from being decimated. It is also the very best way of ensuring that every species, small or large, will bear his share of the suffering.

"If it comes to that.

"If it comes . . ."

Twenty-nine

THE BLISTER WAS armored and wore every kind of camouflage, and there were several avenues of escape should either safeguard fail; but despite the elaborate precautions, plus the array of weapons and defensive systems that now adorned the towering rocket nozzle, no one inside the blister could relax. Everyone with a lung breathed in fast deep gulps, and those with hearts felt them squeezing hard or spinning wildly, blood of every sort filled with paranoid toxins, while every mind, machine or organic, was cluttered with compelling visions of doom. Yet despite all of that, each of the onlookers was thinking what Pamir happened to say first.

"Beautiful," he said.

Then with a loud and coarse and genuinely impressed voice, he asked, "Have you ever seen anything so damned beautiful?"

The blister clung to the rocket nozzle's outer surface. A platoon of security troops stood with the Second Chair and Conrad, along with an assortment of AI specialists. Six more of the ship's main rockets were visible from their vantage point, all of them still blazing away, maintaining an enormous thrust that was barely changing their already terrific momentum. Fourteen fat plumes of plasma rose into a sky transformed: superluminal jets impacting against the Inkwell, blistering the dusts and ices and hydrocarbon relics, the energized atoms creating a many-hued glow that fell back over the ship's trailing face, illuminating a landscape that had been utterly, utterly changed.

The hull lay hidden beneath the sudden sea.

And lying on top of the sea was a hot dense atmosphere laced with clouds lit from within by great bolts of lightning.

Another voice said, "Beautiful."

A third said, "Wondrous."

Then with an easy horror, Conrad declared, "No, this isn't. It's a fucking disaster. Awful, and ugly. And shut up."

Pamir glanced at the Remora, then looked down again. The sea had swallowed everything except the moon-sized rocket nozzles: every Remoran city; every fef camp; every mirror and relay station; and each place with a name or number designation. All lay beneath more than a hundred kilometers of hot water and living mud through which slithered armies of machinelike bones . . . bones growing at a fierce rate, preparing for whatever was next. With eyes alone, Pamir could see the water churning, hinting at vast limbs stretching and newborn bodies practicing their carefully designed skills. He stood two hundred kilometers above the surface of the sea, yet he could see a winged object drifting between storm clouds—an avian creation that was larger than many starships.

Sensors peered into the monster's body, tasting neutrinos.

A fusion metabolism, yes.

The blister suddenly shivered, rolling to one side. Pamir knew what was happening, and why, but he couldn't entirely hide his discomfort. Obeying a thoroughly randomized schedule, every nozzle constantly changed its orientation, the giant rockets working to push the ship along a shifting trajectory, its rockets slowly, majestically, bending over to their mechanical limits. Like a fat man rolling down a wide set of stairs, they were throwing out a desperate hand, fighting every relentless force in a bid to miss hazards to come.

The Great Ship was flying almost blind now.

"Updates," Pamir requested, and with his mind's eye, he watched the best available data, fuzzy but alarming.

Small arrays of telescopes had been deployed on top of each nozzle, gazing backward in space. Neutrinos pierced the hull from all directions, and the few particles trapped in the deep sensors hinted at the locations and motions of nearby fusion reactors. And always, there was gravity. Laser arrays shivered in response to new masses. Subtle tides rose and fell in every sea, and a brigade of AIs did nothing but piece together these subtle clues, allowing the Second Chair to look ahead, watching for things only imagined so far. Things invisible, and hopefully they would always be so.

And there was one more tool, now and again.

"Five pods," a voice reported. "Outbound. On the new trajectory."

Pamir asked the chief engineer, "Status of the last five?"

"Emerging," Aasleen reported. "Now."

The plasma jets were brutally hot and swift, and tiny bodies composed of poor grades of hyperfiber could ride them like bubbles riding a fast river. Kept at the edges of the jet and aimed properly, the shells would degrade as they traveled outward, and when the bodies drifted free of the masking fire—many thousands of kilometers above the ship—the machines inside would be able to kick off their suddenly brittle shells, and for a moment or two they would watch whatever there was to see.

Colors, Pamir saw.

Buried inside a scorching red smear was the neat round dab of something cool. Not blue, exactly. But he thought of the Blue World. After a chase of several light-years, the first polypond was finally catching up with them—an expensive journey that had left it shriveled and, hopefully, depleted, but still alive, and still more than a thousand kilometers across.

Moments later, each of the pods was neatly obliterated by lasers.

And with that, a fat finger of hyperfiber was shoved into Pamir's side.

Conrad shouted, "Look."

A flash came from below.

"She's finding our presents," Conrad declared happily.

More flashes could be seen—sudden blurs of blue light sprouting under the sea. Some days ago, while they were quickly abandoning their cities, the Remoras left behind tokens: fusion bombs, and sometimes microchine corrosives. The bombs were the more spectacular gifts, though probably not as damaging. As the polypond tore into the diamond domes, these simple weapons detonated themselves, creating fierce bubbles of plasma that rose to the surface, exploding in geysers of sweet violet light.

"Look," said the Remora. "I think she's hurting."

The sea began to roll over. The giant flying creature beneath them suddenly folded its enormous wings and dove deep, merging with a kilometer-tall wave and vanishing entirely. Dissolving. Then after another few minutes, the water grew still. A terrific momentum was absorbed or neatly redirected, and with a disgusted appreciation, Pamir wondered if they had done nothing but give their enemy a dose of free energy.

"She's wounded," Conrad maintained.

What was that avian body? Again, Pamir looked at the sensor data, replaying most of the body's life at a rapid speed.

Aasleen intruded, warning him, "The new pods are about to break out."

He barely heard her.

"We'll get a good look ahead," the chief engineer promised.

Pamir was studying the avian, paying closest attention to its death. Then along several different channels, he gave orders, making certain that the next avian would be watched even more closely.

"Look now," Aasleen prompted.

Pamir blinked and changed nexuses.

What he saw with a first glance was nothing. The ship was emerging from the Satin Sack, but the remaining Inkwell was dark and vast. Riding a steeply angled rocket plume, the scattered probes had cleared the limb of the ship, and their determined but tiny eyes could find nothing.

Nothing.

Pamir triggered a shielded nexus.

"Yes," the familiar voice answered.

"I have a target," Pamir reported.

Osmium and a picked team were waiting below, hiding inside a subsidiary pumping station. "Show me," he demanded.

But there wasn't a second avian in view.

"With everything," the harum-scarum inquired, "why that?"

What were his reasons? Pamir gave it some thought, then admitted, "I don't know why. It's a rare thing. It's big, and lovely. And that's why I think it must be important."

There was a pause.

"Fine reasons, all," Osmium finally declared.

Pamir turned to those standing with him, and using a calm hard voice, he said, "Make ready."

To Aasleen, he said, "As soon as we acquire our target."

And then to someone to whom he hadn't spoken for hours, he said, "It's time that we inflict some pain—"

"Agreed," Washen replied.

Then after a pause, she said, "Careful."

But Pamir had already silenced the extra nexuses, every sense and sensor, capacity and voice now focused squarely on those millions of square kilometers of churning, dangerous life.

THE TARGET WAS born inside a whirlpool that was the color and constancy of beef gravy. Its body was smaller than the other avian, only a kilometer long, deep but narrow like a knife blade—a chassis of diamond upon which was woven a careful assemblage of tough organics and sacks filled with scalding gases, plus tangles of superconducting neurons and dense organs of no discernible purpose. The body rode the whirlpool outward, letting the current accelerate it until the long, long diamond wings rose high, supplying just enough lift to yank it free of the poly-pond's great body.

The whirlpool settled, vanished, its energies sequestered into muscles of water and thousand-kilometer proteins.

The newborn drifted in a sloppy circle. Great eyes and little eyes examined its surroundings. The horizon lay in a remote distance. In every direction, clouds were stacked high, each mass forming storms that spat lightning downward while great blue sprites danced their way into the highest reaches of the new atmosphere. A variety of ears heard rumblings and deep churnings, faraway thunder blending into the nearer, more massive sounds. Muscle was building, or it was healing. Dispersed networks of fusion reactors continued to grow and divide. Metals and rare earths were yanked out of the salty hot water, purified and set aside for later. The bird-body could taste the good hearty health of the ocean, and for a very little while, it was free to rejoice at all of this success.

One of the giant rockets stood above the storms: a gray-black cone using hyperfiber and magnetic guts to contain the rising column of light and wild radiations, controlling the flow and tweaking its momentum. The nozzle had a steep tilt, as if it had halfway fallen over, and without any sound, it desperately shoved at the ship, trying to make that massive bulk dance sideways.

A considerable waste of effort, the bird-body might have believed.

The superconducting mind could have thought many things, or nothing, in the time it took a laser bolt to jump from the hidden blister high up on that nozzle, lashing at a point some ten kilometers in its wake. A blue-white bolt, brief and potent, it burrowed its way into the atmosphere, turning gases to a thin screaming plasma that couldn't help but fling itself out of the way, drilling a deep empty hole as it passed.

The next twenty bolts dove through the gap, boiling the water beneath before cooking a million tons of young muscle.

Still, the bird-body circled, biding its time and hiding its abilities. The attack was expected and insubstantial, the wounds already healing—a little probing assault, most likely.

The next attack was a hundredfold larger.

Riding out of the rocket plume was an assortment of tiny machines, each wearing a jacket of hyperfiber that degraded in predictable, perfect ways. Little engines emerged from the heat-born crevices. Little diamond eyes acquired targets, and swift soulless brains guided the machines' flight, and when the interceptors rose up out of the sea to meet them, they struggled to avoid the obstacles.

The interceptors were iron darts, blind and numbering in the billions. Striking nothing, they nonetheless did a thorough job of herding the falling machines into narrower zones.

As the polypond's enemies slammed into the high reaches of the atmosphere, black heavily insulated organs burst from the water, disgorging rivers of lightning that were around one another, rising like cherry ropes into the ionosphere. None of the attackers were damaged. After all, they had successfully flown through a plume infinitely hotter than this. But each was left tagged and slightly charged, and the next pulse from the mother body—a coherent, irresistible stream of electricity—grabbed hold of the offending weapons, flinging them back up into the plume from which they had fallen.

The Mother Sea growled and groaned, every sound happy.

The bird-body took another hard look at the sky, seeing first what the Sea would notice in another half moment.

The attack had been a diversion. From a second, more distant rocket plume came thousands of bodies, each deeply camouflaged and treacherously sly, all using the glare of one battle to sneak close and drop like rain.

Some of the bodies were little suns, born and dead again with a single blistering light.

Some linked with their neighbors, building much larger suns that managed to dive into the Mother Sea before igniting.

Columns of steam leaped upward, flanking the bird-body and very nearly blinding it. The superheated air shoved it one way, then back again. But with a graceful dance, elegant and smooth, the entity twisted its wings, bringing the best of its good eyes to look at the brightest of the blasts, instinct telling it that that was where other, even worse dangers might hide.

What looked like an eddy of quiet water shot across the Mother Sea.

It was a puddle, a lake. Invisible again, and appearing again. Then as the bird-body stared, it once again vanished.

With myriad voices, the bird-body gave a warning.

Endless other voices rose up out of the Mother Sea. A new opponent had slipped out from the base of the rocket nozzle, using an invisible hatch that had been quickly destroyed. But what resembled water was a fleet of skimmers, shielded and dressed up in some kind of elaborate holo. And as they rushed along, sure to die in a matter of moments, the skimmers dropped tiny phages full of tools, microscopic and voracious—tools that ate and reproduced like cancers, already tainting the Mother Sea with death and their own relentless bodies.

The bird-body dropped its wings.

Scramjets kicked it into a hypersonic path, burning much of its body while carrying it across nearly a thousand kilometers of churning, irradiated water.

Deep organs crawled to the surface of its skin.

With its surviving eyes, the bird-body glanced at the skimmers. Darts and quick tendrils had cut some of them open. Ponds were on board—tiny independent whiffs of conscious shadow spilling across the water, torn apart by the terrific velocities, then killed in a thousand ways by the greatest shadow.

Harum-scarums, it saw.

Choking off its engines, the bird-body fell. What it aimed for was the sick band of contaminated water, injured, and inside the little whirlpools, dead. Where the Sea was slow to respond, the bird-body could be swift. Where size didn't matter, it could craft, then deliver perfectly tailored plans for new cells that would eat the invaders, swiftly countering one of the inevitable kinds of attacks. The Mother Sea, like all the Seas, was familiar with every species of machine and each of their ugly uses. The bird-body was meant to quicken the Sea's reactions, keeping these assaults to the level of a nuisance. At least until the enemies saw its importance, and like any multitude of ponds, they would adapt and try new ways to confound the Mother Sea.

Falling like a knife, the bird-body prepared for its demise.

A carefully crafted bolt of light came at it suddenly, passing through it, slivers of blue fire dividing and consuming, then cutting free certain organs and portions of its substantial and swift mind.

In a multitude of ways, it died.

In every other way, it tried to kill itself. To ruin its nature and possibilities, tricks and deeply buried potentials.

The ultimate shadow—Death—very nearly claimed it.

And then, to its utter horror, it heard a voice.

"MY NAME IS Pamir," he roared at the prisoner. He and his security team had shoved the most valuable pieces of the body into the hold. Conrad was piloting their one-of-a-kind craft. Part skimmer and part starship, the vessel wore enough high-grade hyperfiber to have ridden thousands of kilometers through scorching rocket exhausts. The powerful engines first killed their momentum, and now they were building it up again, trying to outrace a dozen blows from the furious polypond. At any moment, they might be crippled or ensnared. Which gave this interrogation no time and an enormous importance.

"Did you hear me?" Pamir roared.

The ship bucked. The Remora changed course, and despite crush-webs and braces, every organic body inside the hold felt its bones shatter.

"We know what you want," Pamir screamed.

Silence.

The air tasted burnt and toxic. His crumbled legs fought to heal themselves, and their ache made his voice dry and shrill.

"We're going to stop you. Do you hear me, little pond?"

Some experts thought that might be a useful curse. Pamir was less sure, but he was willing to try anything now.

"Rough spot," Conrad warned.

Again, their ship shook hard enough to break bones.

Somewhere below, a black thunder blossomed and collapsed into silence. Then with a delicate aim and a small measure of luck, Conrad dove through a newly made hatch above the polypond's atmosphere, and the great engine quit its firing, leaving them streaking across the enormous bowl of the nozzle, their little vessel caught up in the magnetic envelopes, the envelopes turning the ship in an elaborate loop, carefully bleeding away its momentum.

"You can hear me," Pamir decided, his crippled body shoved against one padded wall.

The scorched lump of neural tissue was alive, the links serviceable and neat. With a voice that sounded defiant but unsure, the creature inside said, "You are the Second Chair."

"We know what you want," Pamir repeated.

Silence.

"We can even guess how you'll try to destroy us."

"I will destroy nothing," the entity corrected. "Since the universe is made of nothing and shadow."

Pamir used silence now, waiting the prisoner out.

Finally, the voice said, "This piece of me knows nothing of substance. You can torture me all that you wish. You may study all of my pieces. But I have no special knowledge."

"Good," Pamir replied.

Then with a decidedly menacing tone, he added, "Innocence. I can't think of any quality more useful than a little innocence."

Thirty

"STILL STUCK AT at home, are you?"

Ignoring the implication, O'Layle replied, "For the moment. And you?"

"The Master needs me here in the Happenstance."

"Nice?"

"Enough."

By decree, all public transmissions were minimal, leaving the bulk of the ship's com-system free for the captains. What O'Layle could see was his ex-lover's face and sweet body rendered in two dimensions, plus flat glimpses hinting at the delicious scenery, a rich greenish blue forest wrapped snug around some bottomless black lake. Ancient memories were dislodged, and suddenly O'Layle was transported into the past. He wasn't named O'Layle, and the lover was a different woman, beautiful in her own peculiar ways. What was her name? With the millennia, he had lost the simple sound of it, but what he remembered was its rhythm. Its music. Like water spilling on a flat stone, wasn't it?

"You're smiling," the woman observed.

Was he? O'Layle carefully laid a hand over his mouth, wiping away an expression that couldn't have been more inappropriate.

"But of course you're smiling," she continued. "Your goddess is here. She's come here to free you, you're thinking. And I bet in your entire life, you've never felt happier."

"No," he sputtered.

"Don't lie."

Was that what he was doing?

"We know you," she reminded him. "Don't think we don't. And we talk about you all the time, too."

How was he supposed to respond?

"Look at me, O'Layle."

He dropped his hand, revealing a grim expression.

"We're dead."

"No—"

"And you helped kill us," she maintained. The Happenstance was not all that far beneath O'Layle's prison cell, their communication nearly instantaneous. Eyes like black water stared at a point far beyond him. It was a dead stare matched by a dry, resigned voice—a ghost's voice drained of its heat and rage—and with it she reminded him, "You told her about us. About the Great Ship and its secret cargo. You are the one. The reason, the impetus. The tiny nuclei that starts the catastrophic chain reaction—"

"No!"

"You shit," she said.

What could he offer now?

The woman paused, breathing deeply for a moment. Then with a cold mocking voice, she asked, "Do you know why they spread us out across the ship?"

His old friends and lovers were everywhere.

"No," he began. But then he realized that she didn't mean just the people in their little orbit. For perhaps the first time in her life, the woman was referring to everyone, passengers and crew alike.

"Your goddess wants to kill our ship," she reminded him.

The Blue World wasn't his. The polypond and Inkwell did not belong to him.

What he did and did not tell the enormous creature didn't matter now, since she would have learned everything on her own, and with the same horrid, inevitable consequences. Just for two seconds, he wished people would stop repeating this empty nonsense.

"Your lover wants our ship destroyed, and she wants to free the monster in the middle. Which may well obliterate the known universe, it seems." Her mouth clenched and her eyes grew larger. "The captains have let the news leak. That, or it's just too big and awful . . . too much truth to keep it secret any longer . . ."

O'Layle glanced at a public feed. Through a hardened eye perched on one of the great nozzles, he could see the depleted but still-enormous spawn of the Blue World. She was the size of a moon, riding a great plume of radiation that continued to carry her on a collision course that began years ago. In another few days, she would pass that point where the Great Ship's mass would accomplish as much as her muscular engine, and then she would accelerate farther, plunging into what was already herself.

"Your goddess has plenty of weapons," the woman observed.

Separate feeds brought a catastrophic stew of images. The polypond churned and spat lightning and laser bolts, obliterating the bombs and skimmers sent out to injure her; tendrils and tritium charges were beginning to batter the ship's engines, plainly trying to quiet them; and when their vessel was left drifting dead through space, what would happen . . . ?

"We still haven't seen all her claws," the woman offered.

"I'm not responsible," O'Layle whispered.

"Then who is?"

"It could have been anyone."

"It was you."

"I should have stayed on board the ship," he relented. "How many times do I have to say that?"

"But no, we were glad you ran. In fact, thrilled to be rid of you." A brilliant, bitter smile washed away the blackness of the eyes. "Your mistake was ignoring some very long odds, O'Layle. You ignored them, and then despite the odds, you survived."

He started to close down the line at his end.

"You won a temporary survival," she growled.

He shook his head. "The captains have surprises waiting, I'm sure. And the Great Ship has proved . . . that it can ignore long odds, too."

But the woman had already vanished, leaving him pleading with a flat and empty blackness.

THE BLUE WORLD continued her descent.

Alone, O'Layle lived in the most remote room of his enormous prison cell, watching the public feeds, feeling a dim and constantly diminishing interest in the war news. What could he do? Absolutely nothing. Neither the polypond nor the captains had any interest in him. His friends and old companions wouldn't answer his pleas. And why should they? There was nothing left to do but sit, sleeping when necessary and eating the occasional bite of barely tasted food. For another two days, even thought seemed like too much effort. This was infinitely worse than drifting inside that hyperfiber bubble, wandering between the stars . . . in so many more ways, he felt alone and lost, hope spent and not even an imaginary thread connecting him to the souls that should have mattered . . .

The third day brought weeping punctuated with deep, wrenching sobs.

And then he slept, and it was suddenly the fourth day.

The Blue World was about to fall on their heads, and O'Layle woke from a brief, cleansing sleep. He couldn't remember any dreams, or even a coherent thought, but something obvious had burrowed its way into his mind. Obvious, and probably useless. But it was such a simple, perfect idea that he found himself unable to throw it aside.

The captains had left him with a special nexus and instructions. "If you ever think of anything new, use the nexus. Any new memory, any new insight. If it seems inconsequential, tell us about it anyway. Rely on us to judge what is and what can never be worthwhile."

"O'Layle here," he whispered to the activated nexus.

Nothing happened.

On the public feed, he could see the Blue World falling rapidly. Little flecks of light marked where warheads detonated in the space beneath it. Trying to poison her with radiations and other hazards, no doubt.

"I just thought of something," he told the silence. "Something obvious, and I'm sure you thought of it, too. But maybe you didn't. Or maybe you did, but then threw the notion away."

No captain answered. They were too busy fighting, and that probably wouldn't change before the end of everything.

"Hello," he kept saying.

Minutes passed.

Forever.

No human had ever felt so alone, he told himself.

And then came a smooth musical voice, familiar and beautiful, and O'Layle very nearly broke into tears again.

"Quick," was all that Washen said.

To the First Chair, he muttered, "Madam. Thank you."

"What is it?"

And then O'Layle hesitated. He hesitated and grinned slyly, and with a resolve that took both of them by surprise, he said, "No."

"What?" the distracted voice said.

"I want to help you," O'Layle muttered.

Silence.

"And the Great Ship, too."

Quietly, Washen asked, "Do you have something, or don't you?"

"But I won't tell it to you," he promised. Could she see his smile? Probably. Then he thought, Good. Let her see my smug, grinning face.

Silence.

"You need to let me go free," O'Layle demanded.

"No."

"Let me help you," he pleaded. "Give me something difficult to do, and dangerous. I don't care what."

Silence.

"All right," he said. Then with a faith born from depression and a bottomless longing, he told the First Chair what had finally, finally occurred to him.

Silence.

"Is it important?" he inquired.

"Probably not," she allowed.

Of course it wasn't.

But then with a quiet, tight voice, Washen suggested, "You should try your front door. Maybe you'll find that it's unlocked."

Thirty-one

TWO CENTURIES EARLIER, the man managed to reclaim both his job and rank, and later his original name, which was Easterfall, and his nature-given face. He was so grateful for the pardon that he would tell his story to anyone. "The First and Second Chair found me," he would begin. "I was hiding inside my sister's house, of all places." Then with a well-practiced shame, he admitted, "I wasn't just a coward. I was stupid, too. Imagine, believing that I could hide in such an obvious place. And I don't know why I did any of it. Honestly, I must have been crazy."

Some people didn't believe his story. It seemed ridiculous: two of the most important humans out for a lazy stroll and by accident stumbling over him. Even if Washen grew up inside that house—and the storyteller learned to keep plenty of proof on hand—what were the odds? Long, by any measure. Preposterous, and obviously this human, this technician, was some species of liar, and a very poor liar at that.

"They didn't have to pardon me," he would boast. "But they did. For abandoning my post during and after the Wayward War, I was granted a probationary sentence, and then my record was swept free of red. See? Ever since, my job ratings have been as high as possible, or nearly so."

He had been a stupid coward, his story claimed. But now he was the most loyal and devoted member of the crew, and even after two centuries of uncomplaining service, Easterfall still reveled in his good fortune. No, he didn't tell his story often anymore. At least not to strangers, who generally didn't care to hear it, or to his dearest friends, who already knew it by heart. But the moment had been so frightening, ominous, and awful, that the subsequent kindness of the captains had remained something for which he would always feel grateful. "A million years from now," he liked to boast, "and wherever the Great Ship finds itself, I'm going to be standing at my post, doing whatever it is that Washen and Pamir ask of me, and doing it to the best of my ability."

Of course these years had been inordinately quiet. An expert in the servicing of most kinds of starships, Easterfall found himself with little work in a given day. There was no passenger traffic or commerce, and each of the ports was set into a maintenance-only state. The one major mission originated from his port—Port Alpha—but that streakship had been refitted by other teams. Then when the ship returned again, it was wrapped under the strictest quarantine protocols, and later still, other technicians were responsible for its mothballing.

Secrecy was the watchword at both ends of the mission, and Easterfall couldn't feel any serious insult for being passed over. His record might be clear of red blotches, but you weren't a captain unless you had a long, precise memory. There were thousands of candidates, and of course he always had something to occupy his time—usually a distant corner of the port to keep clean and ready, waiting for the day when they finally escaped from the Inkwell and the damned polypond.

But in the subsequent years, once the Great Ship was burrowing through the nebula, Easterfall's assignments began to change.

First, there were the briefings. Minor captains would speak to him and his associates, explaining a little of this and a sliver of that without revealing the bulk of the secrets—secrets they probably didn't understand in full. But certain tendencies were easy enough to see: The high captains were making contingency plans; defensive systems were being built beneath the hull and around each of the vital ports; no alien, polypond or otherwise, would be able to slip inside the biozones, much less conquer the ship's interior.

Then came the great rain of living polyponds, and the original defenses were adapted and updated, a series of elaborate and inspired tricks applied to the presence of so much water and life . . . and still, Easterfall's mood as well as the mood of his associates remained confident, even brazen.

There was only one polypond, they learned. One vast organism that seemed ready to steal what was theirs.

"Fuck you," the technicians would shout, fists brandished at the vast wet monster rolling above their heads.

"This ship is ours!" they proclaimed.

Then with big laughs, they added, "And you're going to be our puddle, when we're done with you."

In the taverns, after work and before, tech crews discussed the ongoing war. Gossip and the latest captain sightings were repeated in detail, expert voices relentlessly dissecting what was true from the great roaring muddle. And in those next intense weeks, something awful emerged. One middle-ranked captain had said a few words in passing, using an inadequately secured nexus, and a technician who may or may not have had permission to work on that channel happened to hear everything. Then after a sleepless night, she came to breakfast late, eating nothing, sitting alone at the end of one of the long granite tables where technicians had sat for millennia.

"The alien wants our cargo," she muttered.

Easterfall happened to be sitting closest to her. Surprise made him a little stupid, and without thinking, he asked, "What cargo?"

Then he remembered, and with an embarrassed blink of the eyes, he said, "The prisoner under Marrow. I forgot."

"This is about the universe," she muttered.

Others began to listen. A whispering rumble preceded a perfect cold silence; then every tech was leaning across the varnished granite, fighting for a good view of her miserable face.

She said, "The universe," again. Then she repeated a few old equations—the sorts of musty mathematics that most hadn't heard since school, and none of them had ever needed. "It believes this," she claimed with a pained little voice. "The universe was never born. The Creation was suspended. Denied. That's why everything is emptiness. Except for the dark energies, which keep building every moment . . . everywhere . . ."

"What did you hear?" Easterfall asked. Then with a tight little voice, he suggested, "Maybe you didn't hear it right."

She gave him a hard, impatient stare.

"The polypond doesn't want to possess the ship," she remarked. "It wants to destroy the ship, and then free its passenger, and after all these billion of years, finish the Creation."

Destruction was a very different goal. Everyone at the table saw it instantly, and most could appreciate the worst of the possibilities. But one stubborn soul, sitting at the table's far end, cried out, "It doesn't matter. We're practically invulnerable in here. So what?"

Easterfall grimaced, saying nothing.

A fourth voice—a little fef who had joined their team just forty years ago—lifted the middle of his body, and with a voice translated into an impatient growl, he pointed out, "We are flying inside a nebula, and blind. Our opponent has proved that it can move significant masses across enormous distances, and who can say what lies before us?"

Entire worlds could be waiting, was the implication.

"But the big engines are moving us," the doubter insisted. "We're dancing, as best we can. A little two-meter jump to one side now means that we miss these worlds, if they exist, by a hundred thousand kilometers down the line."

Easterfall pushed away his breakfast and breathed heavily on the cool pink tabletop.

Then in the moisture of his own breath, he drew the ship and its course.

And he breathed again, erasing his first drawing. The second film of water was the nebula, he decided. If the nebula was millions of years old, and if it had always been wandering through this portion of the galaxy . . . and if the polypond had spent the last several million years acquiring every potential tool and weapon that happened to wander into its awful cold darkness . . .

"Not worlds," he muttered.

But his voice must have been louder than he realized. Looking up, he saw nearly a hundred faces, human and otherwise, staring at him.

Quieter this time, he said, "There's a better, worse weapon. Than worlds, I mean."

Did he just say that?

"If I were trying to destroy the Great Ship," he added, probably too late. His reputation as the captains' loyal puppy was taking a beating now. But he couldn't help himself, spitting out calculations as well some rough facts. "Nothing can pass through hyperfiber," he reminded them. "And 'nothing' comes in several forms. A mass with enough velocity or stupid bulk, when impacting, creates a jet of plasma hot enough to become a powerful near-nothing, burrowing into the best grades of hyperfiber. Or nothing comes as lasers or other EM displays, which have no resting mass, and which can slowly erode the fiber's bonds. And neutrinos are almost nothing, which means that they do a masterful job of punching through our hull and through Marrow and out the other side again."

He paused, knowing that everyone had already leaped to his final candidate.

But he didn't want anyone else to say it. This was his stage and his drama, and with the same relish that he had used years ago to describe his own salvation, Easterfall said what everyone else was thinking.

"If I wanted to kill the ship," he called out. "I'd use the worst bits of nothing. I'd charge up those bits and drag them out in front of us, and by one means or another, I'd try to gain control over the ship's trajectory, nudging us into the best path so that I could hit my target perfectly . . .

"That's what I would do," he told the room. "If it was that important, if I really believed that I could finish the Creation . . ."

Then with a quiet laugh, he added, "If I thought the universe was left unfinished, that is. Which is one thing that I have always hated to do . . . leaving any job unfinished . . . !"

AN HOUR BEFORE the Blue World struck, Easterfall was awakened by an unannounced guest. His team was living in temporary quarters far removed from Port Alpha. Nobody had given them explicit orders, but they were obviously being held in reserve, waiting for the worst to happen. In the face of enormous damage, local or otherwise, they would be dispatched to critical areas. Using skills honed in the repair of brutalized starships, they would patch wounds and reroute key functions, making the way safe for slower, more thorough repair crews, and, when necessary, autodocs and living physicians. And then they would pull out again, waiting again for the next inevitable blow.

He was asleep, but in another few moments, he would have been awake.

The hand that touched his jaw was rough and strong, and after a moment's pressure, it decided to give him a little slap.

Easterbrook was suddenly alert, and dumbfounded.

"Sit up," Pamir told him.

The flustered man tried to stand.

"Just stay seated," the Second Chair warned. Then with a strange hint of a smile, he asked, "Do you remember? I did you a favor once."

"Yes, of course. Why wouldn't I—?"

"Listen. Now."

The technician fell silent.

"I have a new assignment for you. And for a few others."

Easterfall nodded, feeling both honored and terrified.

"You're in charge of this new team," Pamir promised. Then with a secure nexus, he delivered a list of names and species: two fefs and a Remora and a harum-scarum and three other humans, none of them familiar to him. "Go to Port Alpha. Now. Start working today. This is the ship and the berth, and this is what I want done to it."

The technician closed his eyes, seeing everything.

Then with a small, slightly dubious voice, he remarked, "This isn't right. What you want—"

A thick finger stabbed him, and a boiling voice said, "Everything I tell you is secret. Everything you think you know is inadequate. I have twenty thousand contingency plans, at the very least, and this is just one last little detail done in our final minute."

Easterfall nodded.

He pursed his lips, inflating his cheeks for a moment.

Finally, he said, "I understand that, sir. I do. But all I'm saying . . . what I'm trying to suggest, sir . . . for this assignment, sir, I believe you need a few more provisions than this . . ."

Pamir stared at him.

"You're a busy soul," the technician said with a charitable tone. "But outfitting streakships is my business, and I'm rather good at it, and I'm just offering . . . sir . . . that we tweak your shopping list, just a little bit . . ."

Thirty-two

THE BOMBARDMENT WAS beautiful, scalding and delicate and beautiful. Pricks of light appeared on the surface of the Blue World, each fleck marking the detonation of a hundred-megaton blast, obliterating the sky's roof and creating jets of white steam and stripped nuclei that rose like fingers out ahead of the shriveled but always enormous creature. Yet the bombs were only nuisances, just some of the brutal preliminary work. Larger nukes dressed inside sleek capsules of high-grade hyperfiber dove into the base of each jet, accelerating to the bottoms of the fluid and temporary craters, then accelerating, cutting deep, their diamond-clad eyes aiming for whatever seemed massive or important.

To a human eye, the Blue World looked injured. The body recoiled from each blast, submerged organs reflexively retreating, conduits and specialized vessels shredded and useless, while everything else was endowed with a soft wounded pink glow that heartened the Master Captain.

"It's dying," she declared.

Washen simply nodded.

"How soon—?" the Master began.

"Now."

As Washen spoke, the world changed its look. In an instant, a vigorous blue light bled out of its depths, the illusion of strength and youth and astonishing vigor born with the sudden discharge of hundreds of weapons. Simple nukes were mixed with gamma-ray generators and antimatter mines and a few bottles filled with laser pulses—intense barrages of coherent light that until now were suspended in slowing matrixes, perched on the brink of absolute zero. Great twisting bubbles of steam expanded and collapsed again, the violent cavitation creating a prolonged roar that shattered distant structures, making soup from tissues and intricate machines. The Blue World shook and roiled, the blueness quickly collapsing into a muddy gray glow that continued to soften, edging gradually toward blackness.

"Die," the Master coaxed.

She was pacing inside one of the auxiliary bridges. Her image was pacing beside Washen, who was standing alone on the original bridge. Each woman was trying to absorb information drawn from a multitude of sources, discounting what was suspect, concentrating on the tiny cues and glimmers that had importance. In this elaborate, enormous game, the Master was the expert. The genius. Washen had always recognized her own novice capacity in this difficult realm. Which was why she had set up a series of hardened and deeply encoded links with the woman, wanting to know the worst, and the best, as soon as possible.

Yet the Master kept asking her questions.

"Is it dead, Washen?"

She couldn't tell.

"What do you think, my dear?"

Even if the Blue World had died—

Then the apparition beside her said, "Damn. We were close, but no!"

What did The Master see? Washen began racing through the data and the AI extrapolations . . . and finally she noticed something much simpler. On the surface of the Blue World, between those round zones where the water continued to boil, vigorous tendrils were pulling together an assortment of metal-foam islands and machinery—the mangled detritus stirred out of the depths by the heavy blasts.

Again, the Master cursed.

"What?" Washen asked.

The illusion of a giant human pivoted on one foot, capturing the giant woman's unexpected grace. Then with a teacher's warning, she said, "If you want to the rule the ship, darling . . . if you genuinely wish to sit in my chair someday . . . you have to learn how to watch every little place at once . . ."

The little place was tucked inside the shadow of one towering rocket nozzle. Almost unnoticed, a wave had begun to build. Across a thousand kilometers of churning, mud-colored polypond, muscles were flexing, elaborate neural systems firing in succession, a sudden, vast, and very graceful power lending momentum to the water. The wave pushed away from the nozzle, gathering speed. Security troops fired little nukes, cutting a few of the muscles. But not enough, obviously. At a velocity many times the speed of sound, one hundred kilometers of living fluid grew to twice that depth, then twice again.

"The center engine," a voice cried out.

Aasleen.

"Three waves," she reported.

From a distance of thousands of kilometers, a trio of identical ripples was gathering, water and muscle and things less easily named suddenly reaching out of the newborn atmosphere. Fluid mechanics were being pushed to the limit. Energies gathered for this single assault were spent in moments, and lost. Scaffoldings of plastic and rubber and pressurized goo managed to give each one of the waves a backbone, and then as if to prove the impossibility of this assault, one of the waves collapsed. Hundreds of kilometers from its target, the liquid mountain split open and flattened, shreds of tissue already being gathered and sorted as the water rolled in all directions, hunting for the lowest point.

But the other two waves held together, and again, they rose up.

The Master cursed.

Washen didn't have any breath left in her.

It was Aasleen, sitting in a distant auxiliary bridge, who quietly mentioned, "This is what we guessed. Worst case—"

But now, a second wave crumbled and died.

How many times could the polypond generate these waves? If they kept battering her fusion reactors and cutting neurons . . . when would the enemy grow tired and have no choice but to stop trying . . . ?

The last wave pulled itself toward its middle, lifting its mass into a narrow, impossible column that stood far above the atmosphere. Simple friction and the heat leaking from all those frantic machines and muscles caused the water to boil, then explode. Jets of white steam raced out into the vacuum. For a last long while—six impossible minutes—the wave continued forward, the vapor finally feeling the tug of the ship, allowing itself to plunge back down as it cooled and froze, the strangest snow falling, then melting against the face of the polypond.

What remained was made of tougher stuff.

After the water boiled free, a limb was revealed—hundreds of kilometers long, but flexible, composed of diamond bones and fullerene cords and superconducting tendrils that reached out with a motion never practiced before. Later, watching replays from every vantage, Washen would notice a lack of coordination—a slapping motion followed by three failed attempts to grab hold of the nozzle standing beside it. Three times, it came close to its own collapse. But the polypond made adjustments, improved her aim, and on the fourth attempt she managed not only to cling to the nozzle's exterior, but also the lip above, a cap of hyperfiber protecting what might have been a living finger that was quickly and purposefully shoving itself down into the rising fire.

Surging EM currents disrupted the magnetic containment.

Finger nukes scarred the vents and mirrors.

But what killed the engine, eventually and for good, was a slurry of hyperfiber shards suspended with light—a smothering, nearly invincible flood that told a thousand AI systems that there was trouble and an overload was inevitable and if the captains didn't give the Shut-Down order, they would gladly do it themselves.

Aasleen gave the order, grudgingly.

The Master stopped shouting at the monster and her own miserable luck. Then with a sideways glance at Washen, she said, "It can, and it knows it. So it's going after another engine, as soon as possible."

"I would," Washen admitted.

Speaking only to herself. Since the Master had already vanished, leaving her standing alone on the abandoned bridge.

IN BED, SITTING in a darkness that suddenly turned to a fierce white light, Washen and Pamir watched the Blue World end its long chase. The impact came on the ship's trailing face, between Port Denali and the outer ring of nozzles—all but one of those engines left dead and useless for now. With its bulk and rigid hull, the ship accomplished what all of the captains' weapons couldn't achieve. It boiled the entire world. A portion of the kinetic energy pushed downward, creating a thunder that everyone felt passing through the ship. Then the energy was reflected off the far ends of the hull, returning again, gathering around the blast zone, causing the steam and rushing waters to give a little bounce.

By then, Washen was almost blind.

One after another, the sensors and immersion eyes perched on the dying rockets were being disabled. But the polypond, by chance or design, allowed the captains and crew, and the passengers, to watch this last great drop of living, thinking moisture join with the rest of itself. Millions of years of life, and the polypond had never gathered so much of itself in one place. Could that novelty bring a weakness? An opportunity, maybe? She started to wonder, started to ask experts . . . and then her voice trailed away as the last of the overhead eyes were cut out and killed.

In the Blue World's core, hyperfiber packets and shielded reactors would survive, and in the next days and weeks, they would be incorporated into the polypond's growing bulk. But the ship's hull remained intact. The rockets were dead, but Aasleen was working on the problem in a thousand directions. And there were always options unused, and a few tricks waiting to be discovered.

She said that much, in a quiet, angry, and rather lost voice.

Pamir preferred to say nothing.

Eventually, they attempted sex, and they kept at it until they were certain that neither one of them was genuinely interested. Then they tried sleep, and for a long while, that showed very little promise as well.

This would be a long, awful war.

Washen told herself that hard fact, again and again.

For comfort, she told her ceiling to show her a new view. Something reliable and very dark, and in its own way, absolutely beautiful.

Pamir didn't complain.

Still awake, he lay next to Washen, hands folded behind his head, his expression studious and a little angry but fundamentally calm. Or was it simple exhaustion? Together they watched rivers of red iron flowing into new basins, and in the dark places between they saw hints of light, and life, and reminders of the possibilities still waiting.

"Contingency plans," he muttered. "We just need to keep making them."

He was speaking to her, or himself.

Then Washen fell asleep. For a full fifteen minutes, she was relaxed enough to dream, and it seemed to be a pleasant dream. And then the alarm shook her awake again. Eyes watering, she found herself gazing up at the ceiling. But Marrow had vanished, replaced by an expansive and thorough chart showing the subtle tides rippling through all of the Great Ship's seas.

A mass was bearing down, from somewhere directly ahead of them.

"Pamir?" she muttered.

He said, "Here," and offered a big hand, helping her sit.

Then before she could ask, he reported, "It's not a big one, apparently. But it's close." Then with a grim look, he added, "About the mass of Ceres, about."

An instant later, the black hole struck them.

A bit of perfect nothingness—a sizeless example of nothing made from gravity and a spin and an electromagnetic charge—dove into the hull and through, and at nearly one-third the speed of light, it cut very easily through the meat of the ship.

Thirty-three

THERE HAD BEEN just this one voyage in her very long life. Gazing at the sum of her existence, Mere saw her little soul as a point, mathematical and spare, that wandered in every dimension, covering a genuinely tiny portion of Creation, absorbing a little of everything that it brushed up against. She saw herself as fortunate, and as blessed—which were somewhat different qualities. Alone, she was happiest. But she had been alone for too long now. "Too long," she whispered. Then with a voice that didn't quite sound convinced, she said, "This will work." She examined the apparatus one last time before crawling inside, and with a Tilan's voice, she said, "What will happen is everything." Then with a human voice, soft and sober, she added, "Hopefully, I'll get lucky."

After months of fighting against her own terrific momentum, making hard burns and delicate maneuvers, Mere had done what was possible. She had acquired a suitable target, and if nothing important changed, there was better than a ninety-seven percent likelihood of a remarkably close rendezvous. But the target was a tiny thing in its own right, barely ten kilometers in diameter and still shriveling as it accelerated toward the Great Ship. A collision was a virtual impossibility. And even if the implausible happened, Mere would simply die for the final time. Her trajectory was too different; the kinetic energies would not only boil her blood, but the mind would scorch, splinter, and explode into a foolish plasma. And the bud itself would probably boil, inside and out, ripped to the core by a fleck of matter roaring into its watery face.

What Mere needed was a final enormous course correction. And after taking a thorough inventory, counting every gram of mass and every sliver of hyperfiber, she had found just one barely workable solution.

During these last months, between the burns and her little dashes of sleep, she had outfitted the *Osmium* with the simplest, slenderest tail imaginable. A hair would have seemed thick beside the structure. Proteins stripped from her own hair as well as her skin and deep tissues had been woven into a single, almost invisible thread—a thread doped with superconductive materials and strengthened with whispers of hyperfiber.

A slight but relentless current could be induced within the new tail.

A small body jacketed in iron could ride that tail, and if every adjustment were made in a timely fashion, the body would come off the invisible tip with a new, rather more useful trajectory.

When finished, the *Osmium*'s tail measured more than twenty thousand kilometers in length, with a mass slightly greater than a dozen human hearts.

Such a thin road could accept only a minimal cargo. When Mere finished her calculations for the final time, she saw what was possible and what wasn't, and when the time came, she very nearly failed to do what was possible. Why not continue on her way, riding inside the battered remains of her ship? In some faraway future, she would emerge from the Inkwell, and a sentient and talented race would come upon her, and against very long odds, she would again find herself saved.

Surrendering her little body was almost too much.

It was a wasted, anemic human body, decidedly unappealing and insubstantial and sad. But as the autodoc began cutting away at the neck, Mere nearly said, "Stop."

Even when her throat was severed, she could have pleaded, "No," by speaking through a nexus. "I want to think this through again."

Why didn't she?

Because she was too scared to think anything through again. That was the simple, ugly truth. When the critical moment arrived, this little human found herself terrified by many things, but worst of all was the possibility that when she thought again—looking at the numbers and geometries and odds—she wouldn't know what to do. Indecision would grab her and pull her under, and then time and the relentless trajectories would have made their choice for her.

"This is my choice," she reminded herself.

Then she went blind, her eyes were boiled away with a soft, unfelt laser, and her mouth was a vapor of bone shards and dim echoes bouncing inside the tiny, almost poisonous cabin.

Her skull was evaporated.

Her bioceramic brain lay exposed.

But even her small old mind was too massive, too cumbersome. What the autodoc took away next required several days and a fine touch that was only possible in deep space and nearly perfect zero gee. With a laser chisel and a nanoscopic precision, the machine removed the bulk of what was extra and what was standard. Half of Mere's soul was surrendered to the oblivion, and what was left—hopefully the most learned, wisest half—was placed into a thin iron envelope and eased out of the *Osmium*, riding that fine long tail as it twisted and curled, slowing her still-terrific momentum until she fell into the path of the oncoming alien.

A FEW DAYS later, the polypond sensed the heat and saw the flash of something piercing her sky-skin. At first, she assumed that the object had been nothing but the usual detritus. But then one of her stomachs began to digest the free iron, and what lay inside was too intricate and lovely to be natural.

By a thousand means, she attempted to reconstitute the creature that must have belonged to this odd, battered mind.

Then she found instructions etched into the mind itself.

In the polypond language, as it happened.

Tiny symbols written with single atoms told the creature where to begin and how to proceed, and after some lengthy but relatively straightforward work, a newly reconstituted creature lay on the surface of the living sea.

"Who are you?" her savior inquired.

The woman kicked and lay back, and after a long pause and some very deep breaths, she said, "You. That's who. I am you."

Thirty-four

RIDING INSIDE A tissue-thin jacket of hyperfiber, guided by electrostatic charges and a practiced hand, the black hole had been nudged into position and fixed in space. Stripped of every eye and its minimal power to maneuver, the Great Ship had plunged into the waiting hazard at one-third lightspeed. The entire event barely filled an entire second. The jacket collapsed like a balloon, and freed of containment, the black hole burrowed its way through the hull, entering at a point some eight thousand kilometers east of the bow. Hyperfiber parted around the tiny, asteroid-mass body. A fingerwide channel was born, fiercely hot and sloppy wet. Then the weapon passed through rock and lesser grades of hyperfiber, and the channel grew larger. But the worst damage came inside the open places, the apartments and long avenues and four little seas that were trapped in its path. A fleck of infinite matter dove through water and living tissue, and everyone nearby died from the heat and the wallop of hard radiations. Bodies and pieces of bodies from ten thousand passengers and crew were stolen away. Two first-line fuel pumps were taken off-line, plus half a dozen subsidiary reactors. The worst damage came to a deep sea inside the ship's trailing hemisphere: A blue bolt of Cherenkov light erupted on the sea's floor, and the only city built by a species of slow chemoautotrophs was obliterated. The Worms-of-heaven lived beside deep vents, and if the Master hadn't ordered them to disperse, they would have gone extinct. But nearly half had remained at home—sometimes illegally—and in a fraction of a microsecond, they were torn apart by the tide and the light and a fierce heat that left their bodies stripped of their shells, a soulless gray-white fluid drifting at the edges of what was now a red-hot lake of molten basalt and super-heated seawater.

"No closer, madam."

In a battle zone, security troops held first authority.

"Madam," the harum-scarum said once more. Then with a tight, impatient voice, she asked, "What if this is what our enemy wants? Create a lead hole, then kill the curious and the compassionate with an even larger infinity?"

"Infinity" was a literal translation of the harum-scarum's name for a "black hole."

Washen intended to respond. But Aasleen spoke first, reminding the cautious officer, "That would be a very difficult shot, at best."

The infinity's trajectory had been anything but perfect. Even with gigatons of mass and a terrific velocity, it had changed course while slicing through the ship. Hyperfiber was to blame. To thank. Even as the hull melted away in the assault, the ancient bonds had fought to retain their hold. Chaotic interactions between the severed bonds gave birth to intense EM pulses. The infinity had acquired an intense charge of its own, and as it continued slicing through the hull, it twisted in response to the opposing and entirely unpredictable charges that burst into life around it.

A half-degree deflection, in the end.

And critical.

But neither captain discussed the good news. This was a tour of the damage, critical for a multitude of reasons, most of which were wrapped around simple decency. After fifty thousand years on board the ship, a species of passenger had suffered an enormous disaster, and standing here was the right thing to do.

Again, the security officer said, "No closer, madam."

Washen stopped and knelt.

The chief engineer knelt next to her, watching the cooling stone, then the lightless water above. Then after a respectful silence, they stood again and began walking across the seafloor, surrounded by a platoon of soldiers.

"When I was a girl."

Aasleen blinked. "What was that?"

"I was a girl," Washen said again. In her diamond glove was a rounded lump of warm basalt. "Around my house, everywhere I looked . . . were these intricate models of the ship . . ."

"Life with engineers," her friend said with an appreciative nod.

"Not every model was theirs." Washen offered the stone to her friend. "But the best ones were. And if they were digital, and if I enlarged little portions—key portions—I'd find the ancient scars. The same kinds of scar that this will leave, if we don't repair it everywhere."

Even in the emptiest depths of space, Creation had produced trillions of tiny black holes. On occasion, the ship had collided with those natural hazards. But the hull had always repaired itself. Hyperfiber had that talent, that passion. Severed bonds continued to fight for purchase, and across the width of a single finger, the bonds always found one another again. The shiny gray material spent a fraction of its latent energies, and before it lost its wetness, it flowed inward, linking and rebuilding until it was merely ten thousand times stronger than diamond.

Rock showed more damage. But even then, the pressure of kilometers of stone pressing on all sides would soon close up the wounds. And of course atmospheres and various liquids would shrug the damage aside soon enough. Even the Worms-of-heaven would eventually recover, in numbers and vigor. The only genuine relic of this impact might be the black hole itself, drifting and highly charged, its new trajectory eventually carrying it out of the Inkwell.

"I had this idea," Washen confessed. "When I was girl, I thought that if we could count the scars, we could better guess the age of the Great Ship."

"That was your idea?" her friend teased.

"I thought of it," she said. "But I didn't know hundreds of others had already imagined it and tried it."

The concept was sound, but there were too many problems. The hyperfiber hid its oldest wounds best, and no one was sure of the true density of microholes in the distant universe. Looking back along the ship's course helped only to a point. Like the estimates arrived at by twenty other means, the Great Ship was definitely older than the Earth and presumably younger than the Creation. "At least that's what my father told me," said Washen. "But he did it sweetly, if I remember. Then and a hundred other times, he had to break it to me that my exceptionally clever idea wasn't really my own."

The water around them had again grown dark and cold. Besides a thin carpet of black sediment, there was no trace of life, and where they didn't pass, nothing moved. At this moment, the Master Captain was speaking to the ship, openly describing the damage while accenting all that had been spared. What was the mood of the passengers? The crew? Washen consciously ignored a multitude of tools, walking steadily toward an armored cap-car guarded by a second platoon of troops.

"Are they yours?" Aasleen inquired.

"Is who mine?"

"The Worms-of-heaven. Did you welcome them on board the ship?"

Washen began to answer, then hesitated. Finally, with a quiet tone, she admitted, "No. But I had to look hard to be sure."

"We're two very old women," Aasleen said with amusement. "Too many memories tucked into too small of a space."

Washen nodded, casting her mind back to the beginning again.

Finally, she asked, "Who invented hyperfiber?"

In an instant, the engineer beside her gave the same answer that her father had delivered many centuries ago. The ancient Sag A aliens had received the miracle stuff from one of the galaxy's oldest species, now long extinct . . .

Aasleen hesitated.

"But that isn't what you want," she guessed.

"I don't know what I want," Washen confessed.

The soldiers from both platoons began to board the armored cap-car. Behind it, tucked into a small crevice, was a second, much smaller and infinitely less impressive car that had slipped in here by another route.

The harum-scarum officer entered the smaller vehicle. Then with a crisp command delivered by one finger, she beckoned the Submasters to join her.

"Whoever built the Great Ship was first," Aasleen conceded.

Probably so.

"Is that what you were talking about? When you were telling me about the models that you played with when you were a girl?"

"No," Washen admitted.

The women cut away each other's pressure suits and discarded the pieces.

"No," Washen said again. Then as she sat—as the cap-car began to slip away into the cold murk—she said with a grim voice, "I was going to tell you how proud I was. All those times that the awful little black holes had cut through my ship . . . the most terrible monstrous force in the universe . . . and my wonderful ship had weathered the damage with barely a trace of damage."

THE SECURITY OFFICER was right in one awful way. The next infinity was more massive by a factor of five, and worse, it had been given its own momentum, bearing down on its target at almost ten percent lightspeed. There was no effective warning, even for the highest officers. Five days after the first impact, Washen was sitting in one of the auxiliary bridges, speaking to holos of other Submasters and picked captains and representatives from an assortment of species and crew. She was saying nothing at that moment, but she happened to glance up the length of the table, the corner of an eye picking up the flash as one of her colleagues was turned into plasma and light.

In reflex, a hundred other holo projections turned toward the flash.

Countless alarms were blaring, and as many captains and automated systems were begging for information.

In less than half a second, the black hole had cut through the ship. Endowed with its own momentum, it did a better job of resisting the hyperfiber's tug. And worse, the black hole missed the bow by less than twenty kilometers, tracing out a perfectly perpendicular trajectory. It was close to a dead-on shot, and the damage was spectacular. The Janusian Submaster was dead. Reactors were pierced, and the plunging black hole had traveled through Fall-Away—a vertical chamber hundreds of kilometers tall and filled with some of the most expensive homes on the ship. This time there was genuine carnage. Every two seconds, new casualty lists were generated, while AIs predicted a final count approaching fifty thousand. All dead. Then after the Fall-Away, the black hole had cut through the ship's core, and then the trailing hemisphere, missing twelve cities by nothing before it finally burst back into empty space through the ship's central rocket, increasing the damage to the mangled and still-powerless motor.

But inside that wealth of data and cold conjecture was a notable gap.

Marrow.

Washen rose to her feet.

The image of Pamir stood beside her. With a knowing look, he told her to stay where she was. With a hand composed of compliant photons, he touched her real hand, as if he could hold her in this place.

She sat again, her energies spent.

Pamir took control of the meeting. On Washen's authority, he gave orders and set priorities, then turning toward Aasleen, he asked, "When are we ready?"

The chief engineer flinched.

"Which one?"

"Endeavor," he said, naming the ship's port.

"Eight days," she offered. "And an hour."

The fef Submaster bent his body as far as possible, the raised face declaring, "We have extra hands."

"Hands aren't the trouble," Aasleen explained. "Unless it's too many hands, which is where I am now."

Crash projects were always ugly and inspired, and nothing the engineers could do now would complete the impossible work any sooner. Pamir nodded and moved on. More orders became necessary. In the chaos at Fall-Away, looters were at work, and he ordered Osmium to pull troops out of the reserves. "Whatever you need to bring order and not kill anyone. Understand?"

"Agreed," said a mouth.

Soon everyone in attendance had better places to be, and some new purpose, and that was when Washen took over again. Barely three minutes had passed, but the span felt enormous and eventful. Again, the Master was speaking to the entire ship. Again, Washen peered down the length of the table, long hands pressed with authority against polished olivine, and with a voice that sounded more flat than unperturbed, she told her audience, "Go and do your work. Nothing else." And then a premonition took her, and with a menace that was easy to generate, she said, "This isn't going to be a long war. From here on, everything the polypond has, she's going to be pushing at us now."

THEN THEY WERE back inside Washen's apartment.

Except neither dared come close to a ripe and well-known target like this. What if the polypond sent a spray of tiny black holes at this one place, trying to murder the captains who had always lived in this district? No, they weren't inside Washen's apartment, and they certainly weren't naked in her bedroom. They were at opposite ends of the ship, and the image of hands being held was nothing but a bit of pretend. Yet there was no other place in the ship where a special immersion eye sent its encoded feed. Only in her bedroom, under the olivine sky, could Washen gaze down on Marrow.

In the blackness, iron glowed red and fires burned. But the world was quieter than she had ever seen it, and it was darker, and that despite the passage of the black hole—a nearly perfect shot that had missed the center of its core by less than a hundred kilometers.

"Which is a very big miss," Pamir offered.

She said nothing.

"The prisoner in the middle," he continued. "Tiny as tiny can be, the estimates keep claiming. What are the odds that the polypond could actually hit that kind of target?"

Washen refused to speak.

"She might have a thousand small-mass black holes," he continued. "Give or take, of course. And if she keeps firing them into us, each time more accurately than the last . . . at this current rate, with a sample size of two blasts . . ."

"One in a million," she offered.

Which were bad enough odds to make them feel better. But Pamir was too honest to leave it there. "All she has to do is cut the thing out of its containment," he remarked. "Whatever the prisoner is. A Bleak. Or a Builder. Or the Creation held up." He let go of her hand, adding, "That's what the prisoner tried to do, af- ter all. Before, when it wanted to ram us into that fat black hole."

Washen meant to respond.

Her words were already formed and waiting. Her mouth opened far enough to let out the first tentative sound. Then came an impact that she never felt. A black hole with the smallest mass so far struck within forty-six meters of the ship's true bow—a mathematical point on the hyperfiber hull that was celebrated with a sim- ple diamond plaque now submerged under a hundred kilometers of living ocean.

It was a tiny piece of infinity, but the polypond had accelerated it to one-third the speed of light.

The trajectory was nearly perfect.

As she watched—as her mute mouth hung open and her eyes brightened— Washen saw a flash of light emerge from the hyperfiber directly above Marrow, traversing the sleepy buttresses and cutting through the heart of the iron planet, then emerging on the far side with the same eerie blue afterglow that hung in what was an otherwise nearly perfect vacuum.

If the containment at the core had been disrupted . . .

If the ancient safeguards were failing . . .

If the monster was being unleashed now . . . now could she be here, lying with Pamir on her big undimpled bed?

"We may not have eight days," she allowed, thinking of Endeavor.

"We might not have eight minutes," Pamir grunted. Then with a big laugh, he said, "We might have died already. The universe has been created, finally, and we're just shadows making tiny, unimportant sounds . . . !"

Thirty-five

THE SIX GREAT ports had been named after the children of an otherwise forgotten explorer. Alpha was where humans first slipped inside the ship, and it had always been the jewel, preferred by captains and requested by the most important passengers. Beta was a lesser sister, honorable and always reliable, and in her own fashion lovely. Caprice was where the muscular freighters brought in or removed cargo. Denali had earned a reputation for the illicit, although her main function was to handle objects and wild souls deemed a little dangerous. Endeavor was a quiet clean facility used to house surplus taxis and streakships. While the final port, the obscure and mostly unvisited Gwenth, had been left virtually untouched by a hundred thousand years of human occupation. Its central cylinder was rarely lit and never pressurized, and except for basic repairs made to adjacent hatches and berths, the facility looked as if no one had come to the place since the Builders had packed up their tools and walked away.

O'Layle stepped into a narrow and very deep chamber, and with a nervous little breath, smelled nothing.

Nothing.

It occurred to him that no human being, nor any other species for that matter, had stood where he was standing now. A glow-globe followed him, illuminating the entire room with a soft peach light. The floor was a sheet of hyperfiber older than the galaxy, perfectly clean but dimmed to gray by the pressures of simple time. The flanking walls and the low ceiling were much the same. It took a hundred strides to walk the length of the room, as he was supposed to do; then came a thick pane of diamond braced with hyperfiber strands. The glow-globe went black. O'Layle touched the diamond with a single finger, and only then did he realize that his hand was shaking. Both hands were trembling, and a sturdy pressure was building against his chest. What was he supposed to do? Stand alone in the darkness, waiting for the Builders to return? For a moment, despair got the best of him. He dipped his head, butting it against the cold pane, and his arms crossed on his chest, squeezing hard, forcing his tight little lungs to exhale and breathe again.

"Look."

The voice was directly behind him.

"Ahead," said the voice. "And down."

When could he stop listening to others? When would his soul again be his own? Not yet, plainly. And with eyes that had adapted to the perfect blackness, O'Layle stared down into a chamber vast enough to hold a hundred fully fueled starships.

There, and there, flecks of light moved a little ways, then vanished.

More lights emerged, and one of them rose off the round expanse of floor, making no sound he could hear and no vibration that was transmitted through the thick pane. What he was seeing was beautiful—a sparkling mass of light and uncoiling energy—and as O'Layle watched the object rise, he realized it was intricate and vast, and in the end, utterly ordinary.

A simple tech-wagon sat in the middle of the lights, loaded with fefs and Remoras and scaling its way up an invisible thread.

"What's happening—?" he began to ask.

"Not yet," the voice told him.

O'Layle knew that voice. A name and face swam out of his memories, and then much else with it. Odd. That was the sensation. Prickly odd. A thousand tiny memories began to bubble out of nowhere, and in the middle of it, he said, "Perri," with a soft, almost despairing voice.

"Quiet," Perri told him.

He couldn't obey. "I don't feel right," he explained. "Something's wrong with my head, my mind—"

"Stand still," a second voice growled.

O'Layle didn't recognize that male voice, but it never spoke again. Instead, Perri moved closer to him, if not exactly close, and through acoustic trickery, he whispered into the frightened man's ear. "You're safe," he promised. "You're fine. I brought an old friend of mine."

In the near blackness, O'Layle saw nothing. "I want to help," he said again. "I told Washen—"

"We know."

"What occurred to me," O'Layle muttered. "I was thinking, and suddenly it occurred to me . . . and if it's useful, and I can help . . ."

"But that's an entirely different matter," Perri claimed.

O'Layle shut his eyes, and now the blackness was his own.

"My friend brought some machinery with him—very rare, very elaborate tools—that help with memories. Did you know, O'Layle? The universe has infinite layers, and you exist in some infinite fraction of them. Did you know that?"

"Yes," he blurted.

"And you understand that?"

Rarely, and never with much feeling. He shook his head, admitting, "It's never made much sense to me."

"Nor to me," Perri replied.

O'Layle turned again, looking out through the diamond. No one told him to remain motionless, and the odd prickling in his head seemingly had fallen away. The lights below were softer now, and scarcer. As he watched, two and then two more of the glows folded in on themselves and vanished.

"How long have we known each other?"

Perri asked the question, and then he gave a clear and definitive answer. He named the precise year when they first met, and with a sharp tone, he asked, "Is that right? Or am I mistaken?"

O'Layle started to say. "You're right."

Then, he hesitated.

"No."

"I'm wrong?" Perri snapped.

"It was eighty years earlier," O'Layle confessed. "I had a different name, a different face. You and your old wife—"

"Quee Lee."

"You were attending a party. In the Wealth District, wasn't it? Sure, it was. I haven't thought about that party in ages. If ever."

"What do you remember?"

"Your old wife."

Silence.

"She wandered off to find something unfancy to eat. That's what she said to me. 'Unfancy fare.' And I turned to you and asked, 'So how did you find . . . '"

His voice trailed away.

"How did I find what?" Perri purred with a soft, almost seductive voice. "Tell me what you remember. Exactly."

"'How did you find such a sweet place to park your prick?'"

In the darkness, O'Layle braced himself. The remembered moment came back to him, and with it arrived the memory of a pretty-faced man cracking him in the mouth with a crystal goblet. Suddenly he felt a blow delivered tens of thousands of years ago, and with one hand rubbing his unsore jaw, he asked, "How does this trick work?"

"In certain ways, the mind acts across the quantum universe." Perri seemed to have moved closer than before. His voice was both softer and louder, and with only the barest trace of anger, he explained, "Memories can be enhanced. If the one person that you are can be linked with an infinite number of very similar O'Layles, and if all of you can work together to resurrect forgotten things—"

"I'm sorry."

"No, you're not sorry," Perri told him. "You're just scared for the moment."

And maybe for the rest of my life, O'Layle thought.

"Yes," Perri said. "That's when we met."

"I wish I was sorry."

"Oh, sure."

O'Layle took a deep, deep breath. But he could still smell nothing but emptiness and himself.

"Do you know why you've come here?" Perri inquired.

"No. Why?"

"I have no idea. Washen asked you here." His interrogator laughed for a long moment. "She told me where to find you. I asked about you because I want to pose a few questions to you, while I still had the chance."

O'Layle bristled. "What questions?"

Silence.

There were no lights below him now. But above, moving swiftly and silently, were sparkles and glimmers bright enough to show O'Layle the outline of one of his trembling hands.

"About the long-ago past," Perri offered.

"All right."

"And aliens."

"What aliens?"

Silence.

Again, O'Layle's mind felt the odd cold touch of a trillion fingers. With a quavering voice, he asked, "Which species?"

"I want to know about the aliens that you never think of."

Now the lights above were quietly blinking out of existence, and suddenly every cold finger dove inside O'Layle's helpless mind.

Thirty-six

THE SKIN OF the water was sticky and thick, warm and pleasantly scented—not unlike the aroma of a spent petal from a blooming lilac. Mere lay upon it, on her back, hands folded across her narrow belly and her bare ankles crossed; and to the best of her limited capacity, she listened to the water, feeling for the pulse and tides of the world beneath her.

During the last long while, the pulse had quickened.

Great organs were beginning to move, shifting positions according to some fresh need. The water was gradually warming, and sometimes a jet of fluid caused its skin to ripple slightly. This tiny living dollop—a nameless drop of the great polypond—was making itself ready for something. And Mere was a minuscule twist of life clinging to the creature, stripped of clothes and machinery, helpless in every meaningful way.

"I will show you now."

Her response was to do nothing. She lay motionless, her breathing slow and even, the newborn heart beating lazily while she kept her eyes closed tightly enough that only the slightest hint of light crept into them.

"Mere," said the vaguely feminine voice.

She would do nothing easily or instantly.

"You will wish to see this," the polypond decided. Then with an impatient gesture, it evaporated the lids of her eyes.

The Great Ship filled the sky, and Mere barely recognized what she saw.

"Watch," the voice commanded.

That was her only choice. Her head was suddenly locked in place, her helpless eyes unable to make tears. What she watched was an enormous sphere flecked with vivid colors and slippery bolts of energy. The hull lay hidden beneath a deep, stormy ocean. The only landmarks to survive were the rocket nozzles, but each wore a fresh appendage that had grown out of the water. None of the engines were firing. The ship was drifting, helpless and ensnared. And as she thought about the consequences of that helplessness, a sudden flash of light filled the central nozzle, leaving in its wake a thin vertical trail of ionized matter standing in the rarefied gases that had pooled inside the great nozzle.

Mere's new heart hammered against her new ribs.

The polypond released her, and she stood, only her tiny feet still gripped by the world's skin.

"Why?" she asked.

"You can't hit the target," she assured herself.

Then with a genuine curiosity, she had to ask, "What do you call it? What you think is at the center of the ship—?"

"The All."

"Inside Marrow?"

"The All," the voice repeated.

She mouthed the word, "All," and nodded grimly. Then in a tone of simple confession, she admitted, "I don't know the mathematics, the philosophy. The seventh theory isn't often taught in my realm, and almost never believed."

Silence.

"The universe is unfinished. You claim."

"Do you regard the Creation as being finished?" The voice responded with a tone both reasonable and amused. "Have the stars finished aging? Has every species evolved to perfection? Will another trillion years bring no change to everything that you see and can imagine?"

Mere was positioned behind and to one side of the Great Ship. She could see past its wet limb, out into the depths of the Inkwell. With a finger, she reached at what looked like a simple blue dot, and the dot grew larger, magnified and highlighted until she could see too much: an ensemble of powerful machinery and living limbs steering a sphere of hyperfiber, and inside that sphere, highly charged and held in suspension, was something very tiny and exceptionally powerful. She knew it. Another black hole was being aimed, a careful hand lobbing it at a very tiny target.

"The universe is changing, changing," she allowed. "Everything evolves in every way, yes."

"But what you see is only shadow," the polypond assured. "Shadow and vague possibility, and with each moment, the useful energies of the universe diminish. Stars age. Entropy rises. Matter compresses into pockets of nothingness, while the galaxies ride the dark tides, receding from one another at a rate that only quickens with the next moment, and the next."

As Mere watched, the shepherding machines began to fold themselves up into knots and dive into the sphere, lending their mass to the final weapon. With a tight little voice, she said, "If the All is riding inside my ship . . . if it is anywhere, and real . . . how big is the All?"

"It has no definable size."

"But how large is your actual target?" She pressed a finger and thumb together, adding, "You want to rip it out of its containment. Its prison. So just how large is this nut that you want to crack?"

"Quite small, yes."

"Like a nut?" She held an imaginary walnut in her hand. "Bigger? Smaller? Or do you even know?"

Silence.

"O'Layle knew nothing about it. Just rumors thrown over some half-truths. The specifics, if there were any . . . only the people who lived on Marrow were privy to what was inside . . ."

Living pieces of polypond were now crawling inside the hyperfiber sphere, presumably falling all the way to the black hole, living water and dying flesh accelerating to the brink of lightspeed before vanishing with a quick flash of X-rays that left nothing to see.

Mere pulled her view back to the Great Ship.

"Waywards," she muttered.

"Yes?" the polypond replied.

"O'Layle wasn't the only soul that you rescued. Was he? Of course he wasn't. Thousands threw themselves off the ship. Who else did you find? A little taxi jammed full of odd gray people, maybe?"

She nodded, answering her own question.

"In the center of Marrow, under the hot iron and nickel, is a machine. A prison cell, maybe. Something ancient, whatever it is. I saw the official files, years later. And Washen told me what she knew. The Waywards would weave hyperfiber around gold and lead ballast, and inside refrigerated cabins, they sank down. Down to the prison, down the containment vessel, whatever we agree to call it . . . down where the All is safely and forever entombed."

"There were twenty-three Waywards," the voice allowed, "one of whom happened to have the rank and good fortune to see the All for herself."

Mere nodded, breathing hard.

"But the Great Ship is built to survive," she offered. "It's designed to cross vast reaches, enduring whatever natural hazards it finds. Stellar-mass black holes are rare between the galaxies. But the tiny ones, like you're using . . . the odds of one of them impacting on a target measuring just a few kilometers across . . ." She shook her head. "No, that's too inevitable. The Builders wouldn't have allowed such a porous little prison to be built."

She said, "The All has no size."

Again, with a surging confidence, she told both of them, "You're trying to hit nothing with bombs tinier than my fingertip. It won't work. You can't succeed. In one shadow realm out of a billion . . . maybe . . . but that kind of cataclysm has to happen every day, in some shadow realm . . ."

Then she laughed sadly, remarking, "But we're still here, aren't we?"

The hyperfiber sphere was accelerating, plunging toward the ship with a fierce urgency. The first flash erupted on the leading face of the ship, which was unexpected. Mere shouldn't have been able to see the impact up near the invisible bow. Yet there it was, a fountain of radiant gases; and an instant later, even before her racing heart could fill with blood and beat again, that knob of twisted and highly charged nothingness burst out of the ship's trailing face. Not from inside the centermost nozzle, this time. Not even from somewhere within the forest of other towering nozzles. The black hole missed the core by nearly twenty thousand kilometers, delivering a horrible glancing blow that surely killed thousands before it emerged into space again, leaving in its wake a fierce little pinprick of heat that was already beginning to cool.

"A weak shot," Mere almost said.

But she stopped herself. With a tight quiet voice, she said, "That was intentional. Wasn't it? A nudge to push your target into a slightly better position."

Silence.

But there was something smug and proud in the silence. With a low whisper, she said, "Show me. Out ahead."

The view changed instantly, radically. What she saw was a feed from a sister bud or a machine traveling on a different trajectory. From beside the Great Ship, she could see in every direction, and with an improving deftness, she identified and studied a series of little blue marks set along the ship's course.

Each mark was the same as the others—tiny black holes contained within neat spherical jackets of hyperfiber.

Beyond was what was interesting. Out on the fringe of what was visible—but probably no more than a week or two in the future—waited something else entirely. Mere enlarged what looked like a faint red smear, and after a moment or an hour, she managed to breathe again. But she refused to make any comment. Masking her pain to the best of her ability, the tiny woman forced herself to look in the opposite direction, gazing back into the Coal Sack with these wonderful borrowed eyes.

"You are going to die," she said.

"I am not alive," the polypond responded. "I am shadow and nothingness, and I have never been."

"In every existence, the captains will defeat you," she promised. Never in her wisp of a life had she sounded more human, a boastful brazen and preposterous voice saying, "They'll find a thousand ways to make you fail. To subvert and deny what you want. To make you look silly and stupid, and miserable. And afterward, you will die."

Silence.

"All these millions of years, you've kept this nebula intact. Suns pass near it and through it, but you move the gases and dusts just so. Genius and giant muscles have kept your ocean whole." She paused, enlarging key portions of the dense black Coal Sack. "But that's all shit now," she growled. "Look. Already, the exhaust of so many engines—your engines, mostly—is pushing the dust, making it fall into high-density zones that are tugging at the neighboring dust and gas, and in another few thousand years—not long at all—this home of yours, this strange great body, is going to start collapsing into a hundred new suns. And you will be dead."

Again, the creature said, "But I am only shadow."

"A cowardly, stupid shadow," she said.

The skin beneath her rippled and grew still, its stickiness gone. And a moment later, with a flinch of a foot, Mere caused herself to lift free. The bud's engine had stopped firing. They were close enough to the target. The Great Ship's mass would pull her the rest of the way home.

"Don't lose your hold on me," she whispered.

A purplish tendril grew out of the water, its tip reaching for her, then hesitating.

"Hold me close," she advised. "And when you reach the surface, I think you should try to protect me."

"For what gain? Will you help me?"

"Gladly."

"Then tell me," said the voice. The tendril flattened and turned into a simple mirror, showing Mere herself.

"Tell you what?"

"How will these great captains fight?"

"I do not know," she confessed.

"What are your ship's secret weaknesses? Offer that much."

"Nothing I know is going to be timely or important." Gazing at her own reflection, she shrugged her shoulders. "Sorry."

Silence.

"I don't think you understand," she warned.

Then with a cold voice, Mere explained again, "You are going to die. The captains will fight you until you are defeated. Behind us, your nebula will collapse into suns and new worlds. Your neighboring species feel no love for you, and some of them will hunt down your surviving pieces. Or worse, your pieces will fly apart and becoming separate entities, each with its own name and tiny soul."

"How can you help me?" the voice asked.

Mere laughed.

For a very long time, she made a show of her laugh and a human brashness, then with a wide sharp smile, she declared, "Isn't it obvious? You stupid, silly creature . . . don't you see what I am to you . . . ?"

Thirty-seven

WHILE THE STORIES found their way to Washen—the accelerating estimates of damage and death; the first reports from repair teams; firsthand accounts from a random hundred survivors; plus the black hole's mass and velocity and its precise course—she began to touch herself. First with one elegant index finger and then its mate, she stabbed at her own sides, the strong nails pressing at the mirrored uniform and the yielding flesh beneath. She wanted to suffer an ordinary, endurable pain. The ship was in misery, but all she could feel was a deep cold numbness set on top of the most trivial emotions. She was sad, of course. Grieving and still disbelieving, and in a striking fashion, she felt embarrassed. How could such a thing have happened? The worst moment in the ship's long life, and who was it who was standing on the makeshift bridge?

Embarrassment made her grimace, for a moment. She let her hands press harder, as if trying to bore a hole through her own belly. Then thousands of years of pure habit took hold. Washen straightened her shoulders, and, pulling back her stabbing fingers, she reached for her head, taking the time and finding the perfect poise to adjust the tiny mirrored cap that lay on top.

With a command, she silenced the majority of her nexuses.

With a smooth, almost casual gesture, she captured the Master's eye. "When you are ready," she told the ancient woman. "Explain and reassure, please. And be as honest as you can make yourself."

The Master appeared stern and furious. The gold of her skin glistened with perspiration, and the light in her eyes looked ready to burn. The makeshift bridge was a sketchy affair—a giant chamber full of control stations—but the majority of the stations were unused for the moment. To a casual eye, it almost appeared as if just these two women were trying to guide the ship by themselves.

"I remember my duty," the Master Captain purred.

The implication was: Do you remember yours, Washen?

"Aasleen?"

Distance and a tangle of distractions delayed the voice.

"Yes, madam. My teams are moving," the chief engineer replied with a smooth deep rush of words. "The Khalla District gets first emphasis, once the Beta tank is secured."

The black hole was as massive as a thousand-kilometer ball of iron, and it was smaller than a fat pea, and it had effortlessly bulldozed its way through countless neighborhoods, sucking in matter and scorching what it could not grasp. Plus, it had punctured twin holes in one of the ship's main fuel tanks. An ocean of frigid liquid hydrogen was jetting out from the wounded hyperfiber, the holes too large to heal quickly without help.

Washen gave no reply.

And then Aasleen realized, "But that's not what you want from me, is it?"

Unseen, the First Chair nodded.

"Port Endeavor?"

"This last blow was a nudge, probably." Washen spoke with a firm low voice, dark eyes wandering up and down the long aisles. "The polypond wants to adjust our course, if I'm guessing right."

"Reasonable," the distant voice agreed.

"How close are you to bringing it online?"

"Twelve hours, three minutes."

"If we abandon the port now—?"

"I've got too many bodies in the middle of too much work. That and a forty percent drop in yield, if we go now."

Washen nodded.

"Madam?"

Aasleen had been both colleague and good friend for ages. To hear her say, "Madam," with a tone such as that, with subservience and a skeptical air, caused Washen to pay strict attention now.

"Yes? What is it?"

"Madam," her chief engineer said again. Then with a tight little laugh, she offered, "Engineers know . . . on very rare occasions, a problem sometimes requires a little more heart than cleverness. More words than a guiding touch. If you know what I mean, madam."

WITH A SECURITY detail in her shadow, Washen left the bridge.

A waiting cap-car carried her and the soldiers upward, racing in a bone-bending rush through a vertical highway left empty, by decree and by fear. Long avenues and little cities were tucked into side chambers, each looking similarly stripped of life. All the living bodies on board the ship amounted to a very tiny fleck of matter, and they were widely dispersed now, hunkering down inside apartments and useless bunkers and elaborate hives, everyone trying to remain very close to invisible.

At Port Gwenth, a second team of black-suited soldiers met Washen. In their midst stood Pamir, and with just a glance, he said everything.

Things were a damned mess, he said, and with luck this mess would soon become infinitely worse.

Washen asked about their invited guests.

In crisp phrases, Pamir gave his assessments. He said, "Terrified," and then, "Intrigued." Then with a decidedly pleased grin, he described another guest as being, "Nervously expectant."

It was a brief walk to the first chamber. "Terrified" stood near the doorway, and as soldiers and the two captains strode inside, he made a show of smiling. Then a quavering voice declared, "This is wonderful—"

"Really?" Pamir snapped.

Washen walked past O'Layle. He was forced to run to catch up with her, remarking in near panic, "I felt something. A rumbling nearby."

"It wasn't that close," she countered.

"No?"

"Everyone's pulled out?" she asked Pamir.

"I was the last to leave," he replied.

"Begin," she ordered.

They were still fifty strides from the diamond window. But Pamir gave a nod, using his own authority and a simple coded message.

Washen thought she now felt a distant rumbling.

But no, it was just another black hole. A little one, this time. It had struck within centimeters of the bow, and, carrying its own terrific momentum, it had managed to cut through the ship in less than a tenth of a second.

Damage reports offered themselves.

She ignored them. Before anyone else, she reached the large window, and with both hands pressed against the chilled surface, she looked upward into a great blackness.

"Did I help?" O'Layle asked. "Was any of it helpful?"

She couldn't see anything. And she shouldn't see anything, either. It was too soon and too far, the assorted simulations predicting that nothing would be visible for another minute or two.

"Was what helpful?" she asked.

"My memories."

"Which memories are those?"

The Second Chair cleared his throat. "I let him visit with one of his old friends. Perri, of all people. Perri had a few questions to ask."

"About memories?" asked Washen, puzzled now.

"Long-ago stuff," Pamir reported.

Sooner than expected, there was a flash of light and a hint of motion. Washen refused to look at the scene from any other vantage point. This was where she was standing, and with her own weary eyes, she stared up a vertical cylinder that never before had felt the caress of strong light.

"Is it important?" she wondered aloud.

Neither man responded.

Washen glanced back at them. What was going on?

O'Layle said to Pamir, "I remembered what I could. Which was more than I would have guessed. Honestly, I want to be useful here. Any way I can be—"

Another flash came racing down the interior of the port.

With a weak laugh, O'Layle asked, "What's happening?"

Pamir joined Washen at the window, and with a casually expert voice, he explained, "The polypond feeds herself with fusion reactors strung along a web of superconducting plastics. When that web distorts too far and breaks, the plastic tries to heal the fissure. When the broken ends are close enough, they make some impressive sparks."

The port was suddenly illuminated by a cobalt light, hot and near.

"A hundred thousand web strands are breaking right now," he mentioned to O'Layle. "Your lover is feeling a little battered just now."

Finally, O'Layle stepped up beside them.

"No," he whispered.

Pamir laughed, and said, "Yes."

"You opened the main hatch. Didn't you?"

Neither captain responded.

O'Layle tried to laugh, his expression skeptical and worn-out. Outside the window, a plug of living water and living fire was descending into a perfect vacuum, accelerating toward the port's barren floor.

"You keep saying you want to help," Pamir reminded O'Layle. "Well, we thought we'd invite your dear girl inside for a chat. Give you the chance to tell her what you want to tell her, if you're still willing."

O'Layle stepped back from the window.

Another light arrived with the water—a softer biological glow making the flood look like blood—and while the torrent swept past with a thunderous roar, Washen whispered to the man beside her, "What work is Perri doing?"

"It's something your son got started," Pamir explained.

Then with a hard stare at Washen, he added, "By the way. Now Perri wants to interview you, too. Very, very much."

Thirty-eight

"I KNOW NOTHING," the prisoner had declared.

"Good," said the shadow's voice. "I can't think of any quality more useful than a little innocence."

Then, against its will, using the most coercive means possible, the prisoner was coddled. Three times it managed to kill itself, with toxic metabolites twice, and then with a complete shutdown of electrical activity. But each death was countered by a team of autodocs following the best advice of specialists pulled from a dozen species. Three times, the prisoner managed to burrow into the infinite Nothing, only to be roused and repaired again. After that, every attempt at suicide was anticipated and subverted. Fatal genes were deleted before they could be used. Viruses meant to destroy synapses and cell membranes were deactivated. Then other viruses were introduced into the syrupy blood—newly constructed phages designed to keep the mind both healthy and wondrously, dangerously happy.

Finally, a cocktail of new senses was grafted onto the utterly helpless soul, and with those senses came a little mouth.

"I know nothing," the prisoner declared. "But waste your time, please. Interrogate me as much as you wish."

Its captors wished to soften its will, dispensing visions of a dark watery world and it adorned with wings again. It soared above the world's body, the new eyes sensitive to heat and the newborn mouth able to sing out, parabolic ears absorbing the reflected sounds while a new talent, reflexive and swift, drew sonar images of its cooler surroundings. In many ways, the scene was familiar and endlessly soothing. The captors were clever and eager to show their cleverness. This nonplace was very much like the She, speaking to the prisoner in a multitude of ways, reassuring even while reminding that nothing here was real.

"I am not real," the prisoner called out, believing passionately in its ultimate nonexistence.

Existence was no more than shadow, it remembered.

Only beyond shadow, in that realm yet to be born, would existence and life become something lovely and true.

"I am helping make the real," it vowed.

"Perhaps you are," a voice replied, using the human language. "Let us talk about that a while."

Suddenly the soaring wings had vanished.

In an instant, the prisoner was deposited inside a long chamber, cold and hard and empty save for itself and an assortment of odd bodies, human in shape but otherwise nothing at all like humans. A rubbery face broke into a wide show of plastic teeth, and from between the teeth came the odd, unexpected words. "We have a few little things to say, and then you may ask questions."

"I will ask nothing," the mind declared.

But in the next instant, it felt considerably less sure. The long dreamy flight above the illusionary world had served to distract the prisoner, and horrible things had been done to it. Sample neurons must have been studied and cultured, and fresh masses of brain had been woven together and linked to its existing mind. Unopposed, the enemies had tripled its intelligence, creating a great sloppy mind lying naked in a bath of salt water. Molecular oxygen was supplied by a heavy bluish blood, cobalt-centered and ancient in design, and the blood was pumped by a peculiarly familiar heart. What kinds of toxic memes had been implanted, ready to subvert its most critical beliefs? The prisoner braced itself for the onslaught, but nothing seemed to change. The new mind, built in a rush of wild genius and desperation, was apparently empty. A void. But like any empty neural net, it was hungry, eager for every whiff of newness within its reach.

"What do you intend to say?" the prisoner blurted.

The AI sages smiled together, each expression a little different. Each masklike face hinted at personalities and philosophies shared by no one else. In a fierce rush, they spoke about high mathematics and obscure dimensions. Each entity drew a unique and elaborate image of the universe's creation, and then with the Creation described, each told a hundred different stories about both the present and the most distant futures.

"Nothing is known," they claimed.

Then together, they said, "Everything is known."

Suddenly the prisoner was expert in everything that it deplored. Suddenly it found itself able to think about reality in new ways, and about life, and with a cold terror, it realized that a fresh-born sliver of itself was happy to believe that there were no shadows and everything was real, and what it had been born into was nothing but the crippled dream of a lost child.

THE POLYPOND STOPPED flowing into the port.

Alone again, O'Layle stared out through the diamond window, watching as the turbulent waters managed to slow themselves, connective tissues and mangled organs glowing as they began to heal themselves. Once, a metallic body brushed against the window, glowing fins rubbing against diamond, creating a sound not unlike a child screaming. Then everything went dark outside, and the polypond seemed to do nothing for a very long while.

Twice, the ship shivered as black holes dove through its heart.

And twice, the ship survived the onslaught, again proving its durability to any foolish doubters.

"She doesn't care about me," O'Layle whispered.

Washen had promised to keep watch over him, listening to whatever he had to say, but she didn't find reason to respond now.

"Maybe she doesn't notice me," he muttered.

He wanted encouragement, but none was offered.

What should he do?

With a courage born from simple weariness, he walked forward. Once again, he placed his face flush to the window, and as he felt an electric prickle against his damp skin, he saw motion. He watched a pair of wide eyes opening, emitting a deep blue light that illuminated a familiar face.

The face, womanly and beautiful, pressed against the thick pane, and in response, the window began to melt away and vanish.

Riding the pressure of many kilometers of living water, the face flowed inward, forcing itself inside the long chamber and then stopping. If the polypond wished, she could flood the room in an instant, crushing O'Layle's body to a scattered scum. But she chose not to come farther. Perhaps she knew that the captains had taken every precaution. All she could accomplish was O'Layle's death, and until that served a clear function, it would not be worth the effort.

The face grew a woman's body.

An endless spine reached back into the polypond, and a voice born from some great neural mass said, "Hello, my old friend."

O'Layle couldn't help but smile.

"Do you know what your captains are attempting?"

He said, "I think so."

"Do you know how many chambers like this are occupied? By souls like yourself? By scared little voices?"

He had no idea.

"Thousands," she assured.

The beautiful face showed a dismissive scorn. And a deep voice added, "The captains and passengers are pleading with me. They wish me to stop doing the only thing that can matter to me."

O'Layle swallowed.

With a slow hand, he reached for the face. Its surface was hard and very warm, composed of a diamond hybrid or an odd ice. Either way, it was too stubborn to explode into his room.

"What does your little voice wish to tell me?"

He couldn't remember anymore.

"After all of our time together," she continued, "I can't believe you could offer one original thought now."

O'Layle saw the insult. In reflex, he straightened his back, squared his shoulders, and said, "I abandoned this ship. I was wrong, but that's what I did. I was afraid and stupid, and then I was lost."

The glowing blue eyes brightened.

"In the middle of nothing, my fears grew worse," he continued. "I was this scared little man, and there was nothing around me but emptiness. The cold. And so I began to talk, to scream . . . anything that I thought might help save me . . . to save a life that had told lies from the womb, practically . . . but no lie as big as the lie that I gave to you . . ."

With a tight little voice, he laughed.

"I would have said anything to save myself," O'Layle admitted. "I was this little monster inside a ball of hyperfiber, and with every mouth at my disposal, I claimed to know great things. I promised everything to whoever might hear me, and who would come rescue me . . .

"And if you think about it, maybe that's what the Great Ship is. Someone's ugly little lifeboat, maybe. Maybe?

"And this thing that you're trying to set free at the core . . . maybe what it is . . . maybe all it is . . . it's just some little scared son of a bitch, like me . . . a natural liar and a coward . . . a pretender trying hard to make himself look important . . ."

He hesitated.

Suddenly, the face changed. A shifting set of expressions passed across the hard surface, and the first hint of alarm appeared in those bright blue eyes.

"I was trying to make myself look important," O'Layle repeated.

"That's what I was doing," he said. And then he touched the hard cheek of the face, adding, "And that's what you've been doing all along, too, I think. Alone and crazy, and loud, and full of shit . . . !"

THE AI SAGES had stopped talking.

The prisoner was thinking about everything it had learned, and by every means, it denied the mathematics and their consequences. Then in the middle of this grand internal debate, it felt itself changing again. Without warning, a neural tether merged with its swollen form. Working swiftly and with a grand delicacy, a second team of autodocs had linked it to the main polypond herself. Plainly, the captains hoped this new knowledge would infect the great living ocean. A change of mind would precipitate out of a few ethereal equations, and the war would finish with a whimper. It was such a foolish, self-deceptive plan that the prisoner, now linked with the she, could afford to be amused, enjoying all of this considerable talent and badly wasted energy.

The rubber-faced machines were leaving the long room.

Berating them with a harsh long laugh, the prisoner declared, "This won't win anything, you know. Not even two moments of doubt, in the end."

Through the prisoner, she asked, "What can you possibly tell me that I haven't conceived on my own? With millions of years and all of my resources . . . what do machines like you offer me that can feel even a little new . . . ?"

With a roar, both prisoner and polypond declared, "The universe is empty."

They claimed, "The universe is waiting to be born.

"You should be helping me," they roared with a mocking tone. "Not fighting me. To have the Creation arise from your actions . . . because of your cold hands . . . wouldn't that be a wondrous beginning and the perfect ending . . . ?"

From between the mock-human bodies, a new body appeared.

The prisoner kept speaking, throwing insults and encouragements while its own mind was being purged and reconfigured by the living ocean. Then the words slowed to nothing. The polypond had abruptly fallen silent. Using the eyes grafted onto the coddled prisoner, the ancient alien watched with interest as a strange little alien dragged itself forward on a pair of long, leathery wings.

"What are you?" the prisoner asked.

Then with the same mouth, the polypond said, "No."

Only the new alien and the polypond were inside the long chamber. With a much-practiced motion, the winged creature managed to pull its head up high, displaying a belly covered with little hooked feet.

A mouth lay among the feet.

In translation, the voice sounded flat and a little scared.

"Hello," the newcomer muttered.

The mouth clenched for a moment, and the feet pulled in against the belly, and then the mouth opened again.

"I know nothing perfectly," the creature cautioned. "But there are some good reasons to think that I am . . . maybe, maybe probably . . . that probably I am one of your little sisters . . ."

Thirty-nine

"YOU STUPID, SILLY creature," she said. "Don't you see what I am to you . . . ?"

Nothing. Apparently that's what Mere was. Her brazen words were followed by a prolonged silence and a perfect stillness. Watching the sky display, she continued to observe their long plunge into the Great Ship, and she secretly doubted if she had done even a little good. Then came the sudden violent slurp of water in motion, the world beneath her pushed aside by a whalelike mass. What resembled a pair of jaws rose high on both sides of Mere, and out of reflex, she hunkered down, throwing her sticklike arms around her bowed head.

In an instant, she was swallowed.

In another instant, the excess water had been purged, and she found herself collapsing on a cushioned bed, the wet air hot enough to burn, a great invisible hand shoving her downward, face and belly against a dense slick fat, the pressure almost suffocating her.

The whale was a small shuttle, she guessed.

The shuttle was changing trajectories, fighting the Great Ship's enormous pull as well as its own momentum. Mere breathed in gasps and low sobs. When she had the energy, she managed to whisper, "We are much the same." And with the next breath, she added, "In some ways, identical."

"Are we?" said a close, curious voice.

"But what it is, what everyone assumes you are . . ." she began.

The acceleration increased, splintering the frailest of her little ribs.

"You are not," Mere said, gasping with a wrenching pain.

"What am I not?"

"Gaian."

The hull began to scream, a few first breaths of atmosphere racing past. She listened to the roar and listened for any other words. But the shuttle remained mute, diving steeply into the newborn atmosphere. Turbulence shook both of them, and the gee forces again pushed her deep into the glistening white-as-milk fat. Then the noise fell away into a lesser rumbling. Bruised arms lifted. Hands too small for a child closed into limp fists. Quietly, she wept, breathing with the tightest little breaths, and when the miseries didn't lessen, she realized that for the first time in her life, she had a mortal's body. The polypond had resurrected only the most ancient of her flesh, DNA and proteins dancing slowly, slowly and desperately trying to heal her myriad wounds.

"What am I?" the voice wondered.

With a sob, she said, "I do not know. Not exactly."

"But I am similar to you, you think?"

"In a fashion—"

"Then what precisely are you?"

She told her story. With a gasping voice, in crisp, measured phrases, she explained how she had been born between the stars, alone. She described her solitude and the slow painful progression of light-years and the centuries. But her oblivion ended with a world and a living people, and that one, long, painful blessing continued to bring joy beyond measure as well as rich gifts of memory and belief.

Mere paused, and the shuttle began to split and deflate.

Within moments, the heat shield and flesh were ripped apart by an armored beak, and she found herself sitting on the narrow back of a very long avian—a giant albatross in form, but with its long wings folded into tough stubs and some kind of jet supplying thrust. They were flying across a brutally rough sea, barely high enough to avoid the tallest waves. Some kind of demon-door surrounded her, keeping the air motionless. Into that enforced stillness, she said, "You weren't Gaian. And you aren't. What the captains and I assumed from the first . . . we didn't understand your history . . ."

"There is no history," the polypond replied.

"Because every history is valid, or so claim the shadows." Mere made herself laugh. "Every past is genuine and ignorable. Isn't that what you believe?"

Silence.

She said, "Interesting."

The sea beneath her was jammed with moving bodies and swift, brightly lit machines. Sprays of iridescent vapor rose high on either side, and pushing through the demon barriers and antinoise baffles were hints of thunder and titanic screams.

"I had stars to watch," Mere continued. "My starship was nearly dead, but I could look out at a universe full of light. While you . . . you were drifting through the black cold depths of the nebula, alone . . ."

Again, silence.

"Your blessing was the ship that you were riding inside. I think. I think." She nodded with a growing certainty. "It was intact, for the most part. It possessed a fully equipped recycling system—a biosphere in a jar, in essence—and if its engines were dead, at least you didn't have much momentum to fight. You were drifting. Do you remember? Not well, I think. It was millions of years ago, after all. And you were a tiny, lonely, and possibly insane mind. Who knows how much of what you remember are only delusions?"

"I remember everything."

"Delusions," she repeated. "Hundreds and thousands of years of daydreams and madness. And then without warning, you found what?"

"Many beginnings," it argued.

"No. Just one. Probably a lump of tar and ice, which was more than you needed." She paused, breathing softly while holding her ribs. "You were a single organism equipped with a talented array of machines, and with the machines' help, you survived. You prospered. Or at least, you managed to replicate your on-board reactors, and you re-formed your little world in some fashion. But without any other species with which to work . . . with nothing but your own clinically clean body, its narrow genetics and finite number of cells . . . you gradually, very gradually, managed to invent something that approached a genuine biosphere . . ."

The jets beneath her gave a kick, the avian streaking faster across the tumbling waves.

"Gaians are rare," Mere admitted. "But they always emerge from living worlds. Inevitably, they are compilations of many species. Animals and plants, microbes and fungi. Every Gaian I know of, and those very few that I have been lucky enough to meet . . . they share traits. They are self-centered. Self-obsessed. But they aren't gods, nor do they pretend to be. Because gods require worship, and worship is not possible for them. They are so utterly self-possessed that the praise and fear of another entity, small or giant, simply cannot interest them. And the praise of their own pieces . . . well, that's like me expecting my own thumbs to deify me . . ."

She laughed.

"You had a little world," she said. "You were alone, and you were insane—impoverished in every sense, and probably for tens of thousands of years—but written in your own genetics was the compelling, irresistible need to be with others. You were a social organism. I'm guessing. And following the whispers of your genes, you eventually hit upon the idea of cloning yourself, introducing little tweaks and odd mutations to make each one of you serve some increasingly narrow niche.

"Instead of a Gaian twisting a million species to serve one great function, you caused a single organism slowly to grow complicated.

"Alone, you began to fill your sky.

"With sufficient tools, this could happen. Not quickly and never neatly. I imagine there were some early disasters and ugly little wars between disagreeing groups of clones. But eventually, you developed tricks and the essential hardwiring to keep all of your increasingly far-flung pieces joined in spirit. In soul."

An enormous wave rose up before them, then with a great slow motion, it receded, revealing a round region of ocean that was different—a zone marked by agitated white foam spread across dark, almost black water.

The avian tilted its head and rose higher.

"In the end," Mere claimed, "there is not much of a distinction. Between what you are and what a Gaian would be. But I'm not talking about ends. Not now, at least. Beginnings. That's what I keep coming back to."

The avian tucked in its wings, accelerating upward.

"You believe in a universe that isn't quite real. That isn't finished, and that has no lasting consequence. Which is a horrible thing to believe, I think. Most of the souls I know are rather like me. Not you. Which makes me wonder: Why are you so considerably different?

"It's not enough, blaming your impoverished beginnings. If I was in your place . . . if I had been born in a starless black, and if I had stumbled on this odd awful theory before any other . . . well, maybe I would have believed it. But later, when I learned about other species and the stars . . . I'd like to think that eventually I would have let doubts sink in, and found hope . . . I would have let the past become something real, full of consequences, and the future would look like a realm where I could live and live happily . . ."

The white foam had dissolved beneath Mere. For kilometers on every side, the water was calm and dark, like ink in a great bowl.

She was flying above one of the ship's main ports. Had the alien breached the hull? Or were the captains responsible?

To the best of her abilities, Mere didn't betray her fears.

Instead, she calmly said, "No."

Shaking her head, she said, "In another fashion, we couldn't be more different."

The avian had attained the high reaches of the atmosphere. Beyond the demon-doors, the air was thin and cold, while beneath lay a great deep realm as black as the sky.

"You weren't born alone," she said, with a plain, certain voice.

Then with a grim, sorry nod of the head, she added, "I think there was somebody else. Or many others. I think your oldest memory . . . the single image that drives to this moment . . . is that someone very much like you said to you, 'You are banished. You are not fit to live with us. We banish you for all time.'

"Those others sent you wandering in the nebula, alone.

"You were a child still, or nearly so. And you still remember enough that the memory aches, and it sickens you, and of course you'll cling to any theory or lame belief that promises you that every awful thing in your past has no consequence."

Mere shook her head, telling the sky, then the water, "If you are sufficiently clever and perfectly ruthless, you have the chance to obliterate everything that has hurt you. You will erase a past that you won't let yourself believe in, but that you cannot, despite all your cleverness and muscular beliefs, ever get free of . . . !"

Forty

"I DO NOT know you well, sister.

"The utter pure and perfect truth is that what I know is what the great captains have learned about you. In painstaking detail, they have studied your genetics and the repeating structures inside your cells and organs, your tiny bodies and great. They have teased apart what has been borrowed from aliens, separating it from what seems to be yours. And what they have found—what they have shown to me and explained in some detail—are similarities and stark parallels between your vastness and my little self. We are not the same species, no. Too much time and too many circumstances have been crossed. Your brilliant reinvention of yourself has erased much of what you were. But like me, you possess a cobalt-based blood and a five-carbon sugar metabolism. Like me, your mind is wet and elegant, born inside young tissues set between our largest limbs. We are profoundly conservative souls. In our details and even with the broadest sweeps, we hold true to our natures. Out of all the possible bodies to weave, you have a reflexive need to produce bodies very much like mine. Modified, yes, but true to their origins, and even now, they dance in the lung-wet atmosphere above your great body . . . like the grin worn by the happy human apes, you cannot help but show your truest, oldest self to others . . .

"You know me not at all, sister.

"In your presence, I am a baby. Twenty thousand years ago, as this ship counts time, I was born as a finned larva swimming in an ocean world. Oooloo, we call our home. Ooloo is our name. We are a modest species, free of age but not so durable as most, happily scarce and free of ambition. But we are not innocents, and we are not afraid of the company of others. For as long as our history flies, we have produced heroes who gladly abandoned their home skies, riding with the visiting star-travelers to see what else there is to be seen, sending home songs and images and elaborate scents harvested from a thousand worlds, experiences the rest of us can still enjoy today, and embrace.

"This ship we ride upon and within . . . what do you truly know of it . . . ?

"I was a baby by every measure when we first heard the Great Ship singing from between the stars. It still lay in the distance, but closing. Using old machines and timeless tricks, we built a tiny starship, and in a race that cares more

of form than speed, a thousand babies sought the honor of the journey. I finished second in the competition, which was worse than last. But as happens
sometimes, luck took a role. The winner was killed in an accident that was not
an accident, and I survived an equally unlikely disaster. Then it was learned that
the Ooloo who finished third had conspired against both of us. Guilty of murder, he was sentenced to the ritual doom given to any despicable soul: his wings
were chopped free, and his still-living body was saddled with weights, and while
I was riding off on my great adventure, he was dropped into the ocean, plunging
into the black depths where his wingless form would live out its life alone, slithering about in the deep black mud, subsisting on detritus and his own endless
misery.

"I know you, my sister.

"When I arrived in this place, my first friend was a great captain. Washen welcomed me and explained her essential laws to me, and in payment for my passage,
she took title to a dry little world that orbits our sun. Perhaps to be made into a
new home someday. And with many thanks, she accepted the full, unabridged history of the Ooloo, including every account from that ancient time—that very
brief period—while my species actively sought to plant their own colony worlds
across the universe. About that time, I knew little. I know much more now.
Washen visited me recently, asking about a grand mission to another watery
world. A colony was to be established. And by all accounts, it was a successful
colony. But we eventually lost interest in far-flung possessions, and our citizens returned home. It was during that long unhappy voyage that a baby was conceived
and born. While the starship skimmed along the wispy edges of a young nebula,
the baby died suddenly. His slightly older, possibly jealous sister was blamed. The
records are thorough. Even today, the trial survives as a digital record, untouched
by the millions of years. Washen explained how teams of AI scholars, working at
the brink of lightspeed, had noticed similarities between that family's genetics and
your own. Certain coding sequences remain true today, woven into thousands of
your oldest genes, including an odd and useless mutation in your cobalt blood, and
what is certain is that the death of the youngster was either an accident or a malicious murder, and that the homebound citizens could accept nothing that
smacked of leniency. They ordered the girl's wings cut away—tiny wings barely
half-grown—and in a ceremony honorable and cruel, they lashed the criminal
into a suit of metal and threw her into the depths of the black nebula.

"Her survival was quite unlikely. But plainly, you did survive. Which cannot be
explained, not by any record brought here by me. No. No, I can only assume that
a parent, or perhaps both of your parents, stole supplies from the ship's stores. A
fusion battery, I imagine, plus enough recycling equipment to keep you alive for
thousands of years. And that is why you could survive at all. The illegal and immoral charity of grieving parents saved a little girl—saved you—and then you
were dropped into the blackness and made blind. Across the thousands of years,

you forgot your past life, and I can only imagine how awful your existence must have been.

"You should know me, my sister.

"I have always tried to be the honorable Ooloo—a worthy emissary representing my tiny species—and in that vein, I must tell you this:

"If I could, I would strip away your wings a second time.

"Seeing what you are doing now, and knowing the awful thing that you are attempting, I would if I could happily chop off every last one of your wings and toss the miserable pieces of you not into any blackness, but into a blaze of fire. Not into a cold endless gloom, but into the kind of brilliance that burns, blinding you in that more perfect and eternal way . . . !"

Forty-one

THE AVIAN STRUCK the black face of the water, its body splitting apart, organs tumbling loose, and all of its pieces dissolving in the next wild instant.

Mere was grabbed and nearly crushed. Fractured ribs were twisted and shattered again, cutting into spongy lungs and the soft wet muscle. But she refused to scream. Holding her mouth closed against the fantastic pressures, she felt herself suffocating. But her new flesh was too weak to endure more than a few moments without oxygen, and she wouldn't let herself believe that even one breath waited outside her increasingly blue lips.

A monstrous force yanked her down and down.

Then despite all of her effort and focus, a single bubble emerged from her mouth, laced with carbon dioxide and other toxins, rising off her face and shattering into a thousand tiny bubbles that were lost instantly among the swirling waters.

Moments later, a second bubble escaped.

Through squinting eyes, she saw the precious air shoot out of her mouth, abandoning her with the most shameless panic. She saw her own arms dangling upward, their flesh pressed tight against the sketch work of bones, the weight of so much water and blood and meat and mind threatening to crush her.

A third bubble started to emerge.

And then, feeling the fire in her chest and too much exhaustion, Mere let the last of the air spring free, carrying with it a sad, long, sorrowful wail.

The air exploded upward, and stopped.

She was staring at a puddle of gas, silvery and buoyant and very beautiful. What had she ever seen that was so lovely? Nothing. As she dipped into unconsciousness, she was marveling at the beauty of a little woman's final breath as it danced lightly just out of reach.

Her eyes closed.

The bubble expanded and reached down, covering her outstretched hands and the long frail arms, elbows emerging and then her hairless head and the quiet face and a small but always sturdy body with the tiny breasts and the long fat nipples meant for a much larger woman. That body slumped and fell. Obeying some final command, it refused to breathe. But a fingerlike object pushed through the wall of the chamber, poking her; and then it delivered a second poke, along with a burst of blue electricity.

Mere coughed.

She threw up water and blue, oxygen-starved blood.

Before she was completely conscious—even before she could remember where she was and why she was—a familiar voice said, "Listen."

Again, she threw up.

"Do you hear me?"

A look of understanding swept across her face. First, Tilan-style, with the mouth pulled wide and the tongue displayed. And she gave a human nod, weary but relieved.

"Listen," the voice said again.

"I am—"

"Nothing."

"What?" She couldn't hear what was being said. She had to swallow, purging the water from deep inside her ears, and even then there was a numbing buzz that swept away every other sound.

"I am tiny," said the voice.

The creature was screaming at her, desperate to be heard.

"Tell them!"

"You're tiny," Mere whispered.

"And vast."

She nodded, understanding exactly how those two statements could be equally true.

"What is tiny might believe," the voice declared. "But what is vast will not listen to you or to them, and it will not accept what it hears."

"Eventually—"

"No," the polypond interrupted. "There is no time for things that are eventual."

Mere dragged her bony knees to her chest, shivering. Outside the newly made chamber, water was roaring past at a spectacular speed, or she was diving deeper, and while she stared through the transparent wall, she glimpsed something that looked like a tall window behind which stood an assortment of people.

"It cannot be stopped," the voice warned.

"You can't end it?"

"Nothing can," the polypond moaned.

Then with a mixture of deep regret and utter pride, she explained, "I foresaw everything that was possible. I knew you might trick me, or even that you might, in some small fashion, convince me I was wrong. And so what I did—what is vast about me, and all that is small—what I am has worked hard to fashion one good weapon that would survive every doubt.

"Tell them that the weapon cannot be stopped, and if you please, explain that a small piece of me feels remorse.

"Please, will you tell them, please . . . ?"

Forty-two

A SINGLE FINGER lifted into the gray light, and with an expression that seemed both curious and exhausted, Aasleen stared at the finger's broad tip, saying, "No," with a voice that was dry and undeniably old. Then a moment later she said, "Not yet," with a palpable disappointment. Then after another brief pause, with a grim certainty, she said, "No."

She looked awful. Washen's chief engineer hadn't slept in weeks, or washed, and judging by the sharpened cheeks and the narrowness of the neck, Aasleen must have given up eating, too. Just standing was a burden for the woman. Standing before the First Chair, she rocked gently, shifting her fading weight from one exhausted leg to the other and back again. One last time, she said, "Not yet," then suddenly, almost unexpectedly, the weary face brightened. Infinite burdens lifted, at least a little, and a voice younger by a hundred thousand years quietly declared, "Now. We're ready."

Washen nodded.

To the Master Captain's image, she asked, "Do you agree, madam?"

The golden face appeared a little better rested, and in certain ways, almost confident. Was it her true face, or was the Master enhancing her appearance? Washen had time to pose the question; the woman was standing on the opposite side of the ship, far enough removed to delay any response by a full luxurious second.

"Agreed," the Master finally replied.

The ceremony was finished. An order already crafted and agreed upon was left in the First Chair's hands. The final decision was hers, and what surprised her was the ease with which she said, "Go."

Aasleen was a projection, but physically closer. "Port Endeavor—?"

"Go."

The first trace of change came across the nexuses, alarms wrapped around raw data, and that was followed a half moment later by images captured by a circle of immersion eyes. A hatch older than the Earth was opening, its hyperfiber cap separating along a thousand fissures, bending with the hidden hinges, then folding backward with an ease and elegance all the more astonishing because of what lay on top. One hundred kilometers of life squatted on the hatch, pressing down with pressure enough to crush steel and flesh. Water exploded downward into the waiting vacuum. With an expert eye, Washen picked out the shapes of key organs and fusion stomachs and the elastic bands and walls that always weaved their way through the polypond's body. At Port Gwenth, the body had flowed unimpeded down the great shaft. This time the polypond made adjustments, strengthening the banded tissues and doping its fluids with smart gels, the ocean dropping slower this time, then slowing further, bowing downward in the middle while the edges clung stubbornly to the slick gray face of the shaft.

This time, the alien intended to move slowly, cautiously.

"Good," Washen whispered.

Closed, the hatch covered hundreds of square kilometers. Even at full speed, the retraction required ninety-one seconds. Eyes emerged from the alien's leading edge. The darkness beneath would appear cold and apparently empty. Probes and bioluminescent markers were dropped, and for a while they found nothing but an enforced vacuum and a familiar, probably reassuring chill.

Then the first warning came.

Aasleen's projection had vanished, and the Master's. Now Pamir showed himself, standing inside another portion of the ship. He was near Denali, inside one of the auxiliary bridges. With a keen amusement, he said, "Look. Our guest is beginning to worry."

The only visible response from the polypond was a shimmering deep inside the body, bluish and faint.

Someone else said, "Now."

Aasleen.

And then the shimmer vanished. Suddenly and everywhere, the belly of the polypond turned white. Washen's view showed only the upper edges of the port, and even if she knew what was to come, the fierce glare took her by surprise. An instant later, the first jet struck, its rising plasma boiling the water and shattering the freshly made steam, then stripping the electrons from the screaming nuclei. The carefully crafted strength of the body was obliterated. Gels vanished. Membranes and carbon fibers surrendered. The sluggish flood turned into a torrent, and then the plunging water met a greater flood rising upward to meet it.

A hundred engines were firing.

And then another hundred joined the wildfire.

Through a tiny, heavily shielded eye, Washen looked downward. The project—

a crash program with the emphasis on the ancient word "crash"—had involved the ship's engineers and technicians. An army of them had fabricated hyperfiber braces and buttresses, testing them on the run, and then fastening to them the most potent engines held in storage. A fortune in starships had been stripped of their muscles, and fuel tanks had been ad-libbed, and a lake of liquid hydrogen had been lifted from the deep tanks, using adapted pumps and empty tunnels.

Again, the Great Ship had an engine.

True, it was a clumsy, low-powered engine. But Washen felt the sluggish kick, and she allowed herself to smile, just slightly, which caused Pamir to shake his head, warning her, "It could all fall apart."

But it wouldn't. Aasleen was too smart, and Pamir was too lucky. And for all of her fears and her consumptive gloom, Washen couldn't see any way that their enemy would be able to counter this very simple response.

Nor fight what was coming next.

Wanting to feed her pleasure, she asked her companion, "How's your work moving?"

"Along," he allowed.

"The timetable?"

"Holding."

Again, Washen looked upward. The cumulative thrust of the stardrives—a carefully layered thrust meant to enhance its power and give its owners many options—was shoving up into the dying water. In principle, one hundred kilometers of liquid *anything* could resist the power and heat for a long while. But the boiled water kept turning into plasmas that expanded with a useful vigor, struggling to find any means of escape. And there was no place to go, save upward. The increasing thrust of the rockets gave the fire no choice, and despite the hundreds of cubic kilometers of water pouring in from all sides, only a tiny portion of that white-hot plasma could be quenched.

A scalding bubble formed and lifted, pushing away.

A second, much larger bubble grew in its wake, and feeling the insistent shove of the engines, it rose faster, merging with the first bubble before both of them vanished from view.

Washen allowed herself a small laugh.

AIs had dreamed of this moment, and their dreams weren't too far removed from the truth. It wasn't the third bubble that won out, or the fourth. The polypond was swift enough and clever enough to put up a struggle, at least long enough that Aasleen called the First Chair, warning her, "We're going to have breaches."

There had been too many little hatches to secure inside the port. Without time or enough hands, they had no choice but to risk a thousand fires scorching hallways and the nearby avenues.

"Thrust?" Washen asked.

"Ninety-four percent," said Aasleen. Said a myriad of AIs and alert nexuses.

Throttle back, or throttle up? Washen posed the question, but she didn't need to give either command. The next bubble of plasmas not only pushed to the surface, but it pushed down against the fierce pressure of the engines. In an instant, a wide cylindrical hole had been cut through the polypond, and the rising jet—a great cumulative body, stable and relentless—burst out into space.

A millimeter at a time, the ship responded.

With measurements exact and heartening, Washen felt them slowly, slowly changing course. The next black hole would have to match this new trajectory, and none of these bits of degenerate matter could hope to strike the ship's center. And for as long as the engine blazed, the polypond was being injured—maimed, seared, cooked, and slowly changed into a lifeless vapor hotter than a sun.

Washen reached for Pamir.

The empty air let her hand pass. Then with a harsh little laugh, Pamir's image said, "Hey. Do you want to see something really incredible?"

An alarm was sounding.

Suddenly an AI sage was calling to her by name.

"What—?" Washen began.

Then, she saw a face.

She saw her.

"Mere," said a tangle of voices, surprise and amazement mixed with a thousand flavors of doubt.

YET EVERY TEST claimed the same result.

"As far as I know," said the tiny creature, still naked and dripping, "I am she. And nothing more."

Mere had appeared at Port Gwenth, emerging inside the chamber where the imprisoned and now-enhanced polypond mind had recently met with its long-lost Ooloo sister. Mere and the mind were at the room's far end, still isolated by a series of demon-doors and sniffers and sleepless tools that killed everything dirty or suspicious. The polypond mind had fallen into what, for lack of a better word, looked like sleep. The woman needed rest, but she insisted on standing as close to Washen as possible. She was in pain, but it wasn't just the misery of her wounds that made her wince.

"You need engines," she muttered.

An autodoc was examining her flesh and broken ribs, measuring her against an ocean of data reaching back thousands of years.

"You have to dance," Mere said, then she broke into a hard, aching cough.

Her immortal genes had been stripped away, or she had died and been recanted with just her human genes. Washen nodded, and with a genuine satisfaction, she told the creature, "We have an engine now."

"Yes?"

The First Chair explained what had happened, but only to a point.

"That's not enough," the woman interrupted.

Was this Mere? Really?

"It's not close to enough," the tiny woman gasped.

Washen straightened her shoulders, and with a stiff, almost offended voice asked, "Why not?"

Mere told her.

And Washen quietly absorbed the news, always reminding herself that they didn't know if this was truly her old friend or if any of these terrible words could be trusted. This drama might well be nothing but a calculated deception, the polypond throwing a trusted face and voice at the First Chair, trying to illicit some wrongheaded reaction.

"Did you hear me?"

Every word, yes.

"Washen?"

That was who I am. But who are you?

Then in a dead language, in Tilan, the little creature said, "Kill this body and look at my brain. If you doubt me—"

"No," Washen said.

The First Chair stepped backward, and paused.

To nobody, she said again, "No."

Pamir was standing beside her now, as a projection. And the Master Captain had appeared, along with Aasleen and Conrad and Osmium, and in another moment, the rest of the surviving Submasters. She ignored them. Consciously, she searched the available nexuses, finding the correct eye—one of the security eyes sewn into this chamber's wall—and she looked herself from that narrow vantage point.

Aasleen looked tired, but Washen looked considerably worse.

Where that woman was thin, the First Chair was thinner. And with a voice that couldn't sound older, she whispered, "All right then. I believe you. I believe."

Forty-three

WHEN PAMIR WAS more criminal than captain, this had been one of his favorite haunts: Port Denali. The place had always worn a delicious reputation, boisterous and crude yet unexpectedly beautiful, rich with obscure species and dangerous humans who went about their little business with minimal supervision from the Powers-on-High. But change was the basic currency of the universe, and now Pamir was one of the greatest Powers, and his old friends and lovers had been scattered about the ship, the pure selfishness that had infused the port with its purpose now replaced by more impressive, infinitely more focused energies.

Brigades of harum-scarums were scattered across the glassy gray floor, and between them and hanging high above were starships. Tired old vessels from alien worlds, mostly. Machines just swift enough and durable enough to carry their wealthy passengers to the Great Ship. Each was being dismantled and the best of its pieces were being reassembled, then hoisted up into the lacework of hyperfiber being cobbled together far above. In another few weeks, with luck, this could have become the ship's second ad hoc rocket. Or with a little more work, and with the harum-scarums at the helm, this peculiar fleet of scrap and inspiration could have taken the war back up to the surface again.

But weeks might as well be forever, Pamir reminded himself.

Osmium stood in the shadow of one tiny ship. Eyes like black glass stared off into the distance, while an internal eye watched the latest news. "The probes launch in another moment or two," he reported.

Pamir climbed off the little cap-car.

Osmium closed his glassy eyes. Then the eating mouth made a vulgar sound, and the breathing mouth said, "I do not know."

"What don't you know—?"

"She is my old wife, or she is something else." Mentioning Mere, he touched his groin through his mirrored uniform—a gesture fond and honest. "She is telling the truth, or she is lying. Or perhaps the truth lies somewhere between."

As they spoke, a series of little probes were being shunted along several converted hallways leading to Port Endeavor. The probes had been prepared in advance, and then in a final frantic moment, they had been reconfigured. Their missions were narrowed, and every sensor was given the same small portion of the sky to study. But they were ready now. Hatches were thrown open, and finger nukes shoved both probes and their jackets of low-grade hyperfiber out into the maelstrom, and even as the hyperfiber began to shred and turned to dust, the machines were lifted, spinning out past the polypond's boiling self, streaking away from the ship and into the quiet and the cold.

The first data would arrive in moments.

Pamir felt his stomach tighten. A long hard look at his half-built fleet made him want to scream, giving a voice to his rage.

Osmium made a hard, injured sound.

Then with an almost human ache, he said, "She might not be my once-wife. But the little creature is telling the truth."

"Now we know," Aasleen declared.

And then she fell silent.

Once again, the Submasters joined the Master on the auxiliary bridge—each one of them an image made real enough to capture their mood and infect their neighbors. The mood was worry and resignation and anger and determination, and running beside every other emotion, a genuine curiosity. Now they knew what was coming, but what did they know? Washen interrupted Aasleen's concentration, saying:

"Details."

In a breathless rush, Aasleen explained what they were seeing. Some of the probes had failed, and others were destroyed by the polypond's weapons. But thousands of images were descending from the survivors, showing what looked to be a ribbon—a lovely silvery ribbon of lace, thin but opaque, and a little bowed at one, two, no, three points along an outer edge that never ended. The ribbon was more than a thousand kilometers wide and probably not much thicker than a hand, and it formed a perfect ring that was a hundred thousand kilometers in diameter—larger than the Great Ship by a factor of two—and it was a circular structure that was sturdy enough to spin, making a full rotation in just under ten seconds.

It was rotating at a tenth the speed of light.

In a breathless rush, Aasleen said, "This is something you design in school, as a baby engineer. This is the kind of machine every good student dreams up and assembles in the mind and as a simulation, and your teacher gives you a passing grade, nothing more, and she tells you, 'But of course no species has time or the need for this sort of contraption.' And you put your plans in a drawer somewhere. If you even bother to keep them. There are probably a trillion drawers in our galaxy filled with these kinds of ridiculous dreamy schemes, and honestly, I never believed I'd ever see any one of them made real."

More details emerged. The hyperfiber was at least equal to the Great Ship's best. The three bends along its length were generated by static charges and the subtle tugs of barely visible threads, and inside the center of the ribbon was a substantial mass—reactors and control nodes and probably some potent engines, too. The subtle bends in the ribbon were new features. Each bend grew more pronounced by the moment, and every captain understood what was happening: The great wheeling ribbon was being turned, repositioned to bring itself back in line with its very close target.

"Now we know," Aasleen said again.

The Master asked, "What do we know?"

"How the polypond dismantles entire worlds," the chief engineer replied. An appreciative smile came before a polite scorn. "We always assumed patience. Some kind of slow organic dismantling of the massive bodies that happened to fall into the nebula. But she doesn't work slowly. That's one of the lessons here. What she does . . . she builds a cutting implement . . . an enormous hyperfiber blade . . . then spins it up and pushes it close enough to its target that the planet's own gravity brings it close, letting it slice home . . ."

She fell silent for a moment, her mind wrapped around the images.

"You can't just cut a world to pieces," she admitted. "It's not that simple. Gravity would pull each piece back into the main body again. But of course, a blade doesn't just cut. It heats. The energy of its momentum is transferred into the target, and if you're cutting wood or steel, or a continent and the mantle beneath . . . the object of your abuse begins to gather up the energy, and everything melts in a relatively short period . . . in just a few centuries . . ."

Again, her voice faltered.

Aasleen had to feel confident about her numbers. When she was sure, she said with authority, "The blade would fall into the core, and then the polypond would yank it out again. And speed it up again. And let it fall again. And up again. And after enough of that business, the target would be a radiant drop of vaporized stone and metal, and by charging up the ribbon's surface . . . oh, sure . . . the polypond could start lifting out whatever tastes useful, carrying it up into space . . ."

"But you're talking about dismantling planets," the Master began.

Pamir's image stood next to Washen's. They glanced at one another, anticipating what would be next.

"Our ship isn't just rock and iron," the giant woman reminded everyone. And then, even as she sensed her mistake, she said with an almost hopeful voice, "Even the highest grade of hyperfiber—even moving at relativistic speeds—won't be able to cut far into our hull."

Every Submaster was studying the data.

"The blade would degrade and shatter," Aasleen agreed. "Of course, madam. Ever since apes made the first cutting tool, the blade's hardness has always been a problem that confounds and inspires us."

Along the edges of the great ribbon, at regular intervals, Pamir saw the regular marks of a telltale feature.

He said, "Shit," under his breath.

The Master Captain noticed. A vast hand reached for a point on a display, enlarging it until the image began to blur. The blur was critical. Another probe had sent a tiny burst of laser light at this point of interest, and the light had struck an elaborate bundle of machinery whose only function was to continually replace itself, bringing up new matter from a buried reservoir jammed with raw ingredients and relentless instructions.

"Shit," said every Submaster, in a fashion.

"Those early black holes . . . the ones that the polypond threw into us . . . they were extras, apparently. Or she wanted to measure our guts, acquiring a better feel for her target." Aasleen touched the same display, remarking, "If your saw is no tougher than the plank that you wish to cut, then you need to strengthen it. Glue bits of broken glass onto a cotton string. Or diamond dust fused to a steel blade.

"Or maybe, if you are very patient and exceptionally determined . . . and vast . . . you can impregnate your saw with a thousand tiny-mass black holes,

highly charged so they can be controlled, and placed evenly along the blade's leading edge . . . ready to slice into our hull, or anything else, working their way down
and down . . ."

PAMIR ABANDONED THE meeting.

Still unaware of the disaster, the harum-scarums continued to work, following
a schedule and a broad menu of plans that could not have been more useless.
Through a minor nexus, he kept tabs on what was being said. Of course the Master doubted that such a machine could ever work. And Aasleen answered every
complaint with a response that couldn't help but sound like gushing praise for
their enemy. And Washen was talking to the empty image standing next to her,
saying, "We need one good option."

"There are none," Pamir replied.

Then in a loud voice, he called out, "Osmium."

The Submaster was still standing beside him. But it took a breath or two before
Osmium shook loose from the others. He closed down the nexus linking him to
the meeting and stared at his companion, puzzled, then curious, watching the motions of the ape's fingers.

On the hull of a half-dismantled starship, dust had collected. It was a thick dust
made of human skin and alien skin and scrap hyperfiber and other rich hints left
behind by the vanished multitude. Pamir was drawing in the dust. With a desperate energy, he invented unworkable or outright fanciful solutions—most involving
detonating the starships inside every port, leaving the Great Ship tumbling and
gutted by their own hand.

"Not that way," Washen whispered.

She was using a security eye, watching over his shoulder.

"Then you draw something better," he growled. With a flattened palm, he began to wipe away his enormous drawing of the ship. Then he hesitated, muttering, "We need some other engine."

"It won't happen soon," Aasleen interrupted.

Every Submaster was watching over his shoulder.

"The blade's falling on us now," the chief engineer reported. "Within the
hour, it makes contact—"

"Here," Washen interrupted.

With the projection of her hand, she took hold of Pamir's hand, leading a fingertip as it drew a few elegant lines inside his rendering of the ship. Then with a
hard and flat little voice, she explained what she meant.

Hearing the idea, Aasleen said, "Maybe. Maybe."

"How did you dream up this improbable?" Pamir snapped.

With a tone as mystified as anyone's, Washen admitted, "I do not know." Her
phantom hand bled into his, and again, with a quavering voice, she said, "Honestly, I don't know where this came from . . ."

Forty-four

"THIS IS WHAT will happen."

In a multitude of languages—as sound and as scent, flashing photophores and tactile caresses—she began her warning. And then with a mixture of ripping pain and the gravest concern, she paused. For a long moment, the great golden face was tight and slick, the wide eyes glistening with tears too stubborn to roll. Her mouth lay open, the pink meat of the tongue pushed between the extraordinarily white teeth, and billions of passengers and crew listened for the steady wet inhalation of the Master's next breath. This will be awful, they knew. Very few could imagine what was next, but even the most peculiar species, isolated and unfamiliar with human ways, could sense that whatever followed would be horrible, and probably all of them would die.

"This is coming," the Master Captain said. And then she showed them something impossible. She shared the most recent data about the blade's size and density, its velocity and point of impact. "A degree port of the bow," she described, and then after another deep breath, she added, "In another twelve standard minutes."

Spellbound, her audience tried to absorb the news.

"Our finest armor is thickest at the bow," she reminded them. But before anyone could take comfort in that fact, she said with a brutal confidence, "Our hyperfiber will be sliced apart by the revolving black holes. That much is certain. A white-hot fissure will open up, and before the wounded armor can flow back on itself, the polypond's blade will cut into the plasma. Its rapid spin will increase the damage. We think the blade carries a profound electric charge, and most of our simulations show a flattened jet of superheated matter carried away from the ship. The loss of mass will be trivial, but of course, that is not the point."

She paused again.

Breathed, again.

"We've dubbed the contraption the Sword of Creation. With each passage, its black holes will continue to acquire mass and destructive capacity. The hyperfiber behind them has been carefully shaped to accomplish this one task. The polypond intends to cut through the heart of our ship. In regions that are rich in rock and air, the damage zone will expand. Blast effects and cave-ins will obliterate everything in a zone as much as twenty kilometers wide. Which is why I have ordered a complete evacuation of the following districts . . ."

"Why run?" many asked themselves. "There's no escape, so why prolong the misery?"

And then, as if she had heard their doubts, the Master interrupted her own thorough listing of doomed places. For an instant, something of the old cockiness reemerged. She had evolved into a complicated figurehead. Virtually everyone on board knew her personal history and the endless rumors. Washen was the real queen now, with the other Submasters wearing their own vast roles. But still, the

Master was the face of the ship, and she was as much its voice as anyone. When she told everyone, "This is not finished," they heard and smelled, saw and felt more than just her words. This was the face that every sentient soul could read at a glance, and a single glance provided just enough encouragement. Hundreds of thousands began retreating, even as the same face told everyone else, "Remain ready. At any moment, you may need to flee, too."

Then with a sigh and another sad shake of the head, the Master reported, "If nothing changes, the Sword of Creation will reach Marrow in a moment less than two hours. And a few minutes later, the swollen black holes will begin to strike whatever sits at the center of that mysterious world. And at the very least, we will have the rare honor of learning what precisely it is that is down there."

Then with a broad and weary smile, she added, "I have had many honors in my life. But this is one distinction that I would most gladly avoid."

Forty-five

"THE KEENEST BLADE is the blade never felt."

Mere said the words in Tilan, then human, and finally in their original harum-scarum. Then she glanced at the face of an old-fashioned timepiece that Washen had only just given her—a round machine full of humming parts wrapped inside a dull silver case—and she carefully counted the seconds until impact. For a multitude of responsible reasons, she was being held in quarantine. Her new body was being tended to by an intense little autodoc. Stripped of every kind of nexus, she was reduced to watching events as they were projected into the longest wall of her chamber. But at least the feeds were immediate, uncensored and honest. Probes in high orbit above the ship watched the Sword from every angle. Straight on, the great machine was a delicate vertical shimmer—a taut line vibrating under some great pressure—and then the vibration would relax slightly, and the looming threat would suddenly vanish against the black of the nebula. But probes watching from one side or another saw an enormous ribbon of silk, perfectly round and possessing the illusion of stillness. Without features for an eye to follow, the mind couldn't tell that the Sword was turning. And even with its enormous size, it looked remarkably insubstantial next to the Great Ship—like a child's throwing hoop about to strike the indifferent face of a great wet stone.

The autodoc told her, "Relax," and laced her shattered ribs with a healing agent. "And exhale now. Please."

Mere blew out, wincing with the pain.

"Inhale now. Please."

The pain diminished noticeably, or she was too distracted to notice.

Beneath the Sword, the newborn sea was churning. Suddenly a narrow band of water developed a crease, fibers and gels and dams of woven hyperfiber forming a double wall that instantly began to pull apart. It was a reflex, she imagined. The polypond was fully prepared to die, yet its own flesh instinctively fought to save itself for another few minutes. Spending vast sums of energy and concentration, the entity dug a deep valley in its own flesh, exposing the original hull of the ship. For an instant, Mere could see the once-flooded telescopes, crushed by currents and the pressure, and the slick gray-white face of the deep, utterly useless armor. Then the Sword plunged into the breach, and for a long amazing instant, it hovered.

Rockets were firing at the hub, tweaking the Sword's angle one last time. Then they abruptly stopped firing, some point of perfection achieved. Like a woman pulling a dagger into her own chest, the ship's gravity yanked at the blade, and a scorching white light filled the screen.

A gentle tremor passed through Mere.

Was it the impact, or a personal nervous flinch?

"Do not move," the autodoc advised. Then with a different voice, it assured her, "You will survive, darling, and so will the rest of us."

Mere didn't believe the words, but she couldn't help but embrace the sentiment. She watched the screen, and the machine watched, too, with its extra eyes, and after a while, one of them said, "Astonishing."

The word was inadequate, but every word would be. With each second, one hundred tiny black holes swept through the strongest matter known, gouging and cutting and setting the wreckage into churning motion, the quasi fluid rising into the sharp edge of the blade itself, feeling the carefully sculpted charge that grabbed hold of it and flung it outward. The jet formed a single stream, white and intense, and ethereal, and lovely in a horrible fashion. Tens of kilometers of hyperfiber were swiftly sliced away and left useless, and as the Sword cut deeper, it slowed its descent again. Rockets fired and fired harder, and the blade held its pace, and some critical point was achieved. Achieved, and obvious. Suddenly the white stream of plasmas was tainted with traces of yellow and amber, then a vivid burst of deep red. The black holes were burrowing through granite and basalt, and into atmospheres and water, too.

The autodoc had stopped working. Every glass eye was focused on images still thousands of kilometers removed from this place, and the spider-thin hands held delicate instruments up high, and a voice that could never sound anything but utterly confident asked, "What will we do? What will the captains do? How will Washen defeat this thing?"

A distinct, undeniable vibration caused the chamber to shake.

"She'll destroy the Sword," Mere offered. "Or knock it free and outrace it. I would guess."

Neither spoke for a moment.

Then with a vaguely skeptical tone, the machine asked, "Is any of that possible?"

And then it dismissed its own question. "Every illness has its cure," it declared. "How can I believe anything else?"

FIVE MINUTES MORE.

The tremors grew worse by the moment, insistent, then rough, then the roughest blows were punctuated with hard, sharp rumblings. Great explosions and little collapses sent vibrations traveling through the meat of the ship, many of them skimming along the base of the hull, arriving at Port Gwenth along with a growling groan that was felt more than it was heard.

Mere sat alone. Her frail little body had been patched as far as possible, and the confident yet terrified machine had hurried off, giving the excuse, "I have other patients who need me more." Which was fine. Was best. When hadn't Mere preferred solitude? But even as she told herself she was fine, a new voice found her. Soft and prickly, it said, "Hello," then, "I was looking for you." And Mere couldn't help but feel genuine relief, turning in her seat, a hundred little aches meaning nothing and the sight of a human face—even this human's face—winning a small but cherished joy out of her.

"Hello," he said again, the pale yellow eyes growing larger. "My name—"

"O'Layle," she interrupted.

He hesitated. For a moment, he glanced at the images on the long wall, and then he forced himself to step closer, asking, "Have we met?"

"Never," she promised. Then she looked straight ahead again, studying the endless cutting and the vivid colors streaming out of the wound now. "But I studied you and your transmissions from the Blue World—"

"Oh, you're the one they sent into the Inkwell. In secret."

She nodded, not looking at him now.

"That's why we're in quarantine together," he continued. "I heard about you. A little while ago, one of the captains explained . . . that the polypond spat you back at us . . ."

Already Mere was growing tired of this man.

"We're much the same," O'Layle continued, stepping close to her. Staring at the images of carnage, he said with a quiet, awed voice, "Both of us lived with her. As part of her."

In a fashion, she thought.

Then he knelt, altogether too close. He insisted in pushing his face beside hers, remarking, "Both of us have served the alien. Each in our own way, naturally."

Somewhere along the narrow lip of the Sword, an ocean was struck. Hydrogen was stripped of its electrons and thrown into space, a vivid white line marking the obliteration of billions of liters. Watching, Mere wished she were blind. Closing her eyes, she felt the ship shaking even harder now. Then the voice beside her named an alien species, and with a low laugh, he asked, "Do you remember them?"

"The !eech?" Mere said, "Yes, I do."

"You are sure?"

"I studied them. Before they came on board, I went to their world and lived with them—"

"Because that's what you do. With difficult species, yes." His voice was happy, almost giddy. "You don't know me, but I have heard much, much, much about you."

Shut up, she thought.

Then Mere opened her eyes, concentrating on the wall, on the deepening gouge being chiseled into the heart of the ship. How much longer before the Sword hit the core? Glancing at the new watch that filled her hand, she whispered, "Forty-two minutes."

O'Layle didn't hear her, or he simply didn't care about the time that remained. What he needed to say was, "I knew them, too."

"Who?"

Then he said the name again. He clicked his tongue in a clumsy fashion, and then said, "Eech," afterwards. "!eech," he told her. And with a delight that was boyish, pure and nearly sweet, he boasted, "They once hired me for a task. A very important job. This was aeons ago, of course. But I should have remembered. I guess they must have done something to my mind afterward . . . some kind of selective amnesia . . ."

"Why are you telling me this?" she blurted.

But O'Layle wouldn't answer her directly. More than forty minutes remained until the ship and possibly all of Creation was obliterated, and he invested a full two minutes boasting about the sums of money that he had been given and how he had been fooled. "After I did my job, they convinced me that it was an inheritance," he offered with a low laugh. "It was so much money that it took me a thousand years to spend it, and all that time, I couldn't remember that I earned it. I lied even to myself, telling others that it was a gift from a dead old friend—"

"The !eech went extinct," Mere interrupted.

O'Layle winked at her, nodding.

"On this ship, at least," she said, struggling to recover the details for herself. "Thousands of years ago, they suddenly vanished."

"Oh, I know all about that."

The tone should have scared her, but her soul didn't have room for any more fear. Mere shook her head, one hand physically shoving at the much larger man. Then with a cracking voice, she asked, "Why are you telling me this?"

"They've been asking about it," O'Layle said. "About the !eech. Asking me these sharp little questions. Prying at my head with fancy memory-enhancing tools. I truly hadn't thought about that species in the last hundred centuries—it's remarkable how much I had forgotten—but now it's pretty much come back to me again."

"What did you do for the !eech?"

He kept smiling. "They needed someone to help. You see, they had taken some sort of vote and decided . . . well, as you say . . . long ago, they suddenly became extinct . . ."

"You did that?" she spat.

He rolled his shoulders. Like an evil child, he said, "They were desperate. I remember that now."

"You murdered the species?"

"If a species wishes to die," O'Layle countered, "then it isn't truly murder. Now is it?"

With both hands, she shoved at him. But the man refused to move, gazing at her with a look of pride and growing consternation. Finally, with a wounded voice, he asked, "What kind of monster do you think I am?"

Even as the ship fell apart around them, he had to tell her, "I didn't have to kill any of them. I just had to make them seem dead to the universe. You see? That's what I'm trying to explain."

Forty-six

VERY LITTLE HAD been brought to this obscure place. Half a dozen brigades of soldiers had brought their field weapons to help with security, and a team of engineers was working feverishly to complete the setup, and there was an ensemble of small machines wrapped around the single object that those machines had been built to serve. The First and Second Chairs also just arrived. There was no point in hiding any longer. What happened here, in a matter of minutes, would determine whether or not the ship survived. Washen and Pamir found themselves standing side by side, hands touching for a moment, then falling apart, and one of them repeated the word, "Improbable," while the other nodded agreeably, allowing herself a slender smile and a determined sense of genuine confidence.

The facility had no name, only a complex designation describing both its location and purpose. What they stood inside was a few hectares of mothballed controls and warmed air set deep inside the ship, on the brink of the cold iron core. Above them, visible through insulating sandwiches of diamond and aerogel, was a much larger chamber—a spherical volume a little less than a hundred kilometers in diameter. It was one of several dozen auxiliary fuel tanks that had never been used. Each tank was filled with vacuum and darkness, and each lay equally deep inside the ship, but separated from the six primary fuel tanks. It was inevitable that one of these empty tanks would lie directly between the ship's bow and Marrow. And as such, it became the best last place to fight.

The engineers clustered at one end of the big room, but the bulk of their work happened inside a long piece of adjacent plumbing, robots and AIs moving in graceful blurs, assembling a delicate device from stock parts. There were complications, always: Parts failed to mesh, and little corrections had to be made to plans barely an hour old, and there were constant tremors running down through the ship's meat, the shaking growing harder by the moment. Aasleen stood among her engineers, asking questions and offering unsolicited advice. Finally, the team leader turned to her, saying, "Madam," with a sharp voice. "We know exactly what we are doing here. You are not as qualified as I. And if you don't leave us alone, I will pull off your head and shit in your neck. Madam."

Chastened, Aasleen joined Washen.

Gazing straight upward, they saw nothing. Again, blackness ruled the universe, and a bitter sucking cold ran through the black, and for a slender exhausted moment, Washen found herself wondering:

What if the polypond is right?

If the Creation was something aborted or delayed . . . and if freeing the mysterious passenger, the prisoner in the center of Marrow, could wipe away this endless night . . . then how awful was the crime that they were committing here today . . . ?

Washen swallowed her doubts and closed her eyes.

Into that self-imposed darkness, a voice spoke.

"Mother," he said.

For an instant, she assumed Locke was elsewhere. She left her eyes closed, opening one of the last of her working nexuses. But the only presence waiting there was the Master herself.

"News?" the woman inquired.

"None," Washen admitted.

"Then why pester me?" she snarled. And as the nexus closed again, Locke said to his mother:

"Here. Look here."

He stood behind her. She hadn't noticed his arrival, and as she turned to face him, a reflexive anger took hold. Why would her only child set himself in this very dangerous place? She came close to scolding him, then relief pushed the anger aside. Quietly, without hope, she said, "We are going to win here. Now."

The small man nodded dutifully, saying nothing. He was dressed like an AI sage, except for a Wayward belt tied around his waist, the brown leather looking peculiar against the milky white toga. Like everyone in this place, he was exhausted. A few deep breaths were necessary before he had the wind to admit, "I have been trying to find you and talk—"

"I've always kept a nexus open to you," she interrupted.

"To your face, Mother."

The deadly tone made her focus.

To his face, she asked, "What is it?"

"I know who they are now," he began.

"Who they are *now*?"

"As you guessed, like I imagined . . . for billions of years, and maybe since the beginning, they've been following in the ship's wake . . ."

To Washen, it felt as if a fist of stone had been driven into her belly.

"They were chasing after our ship," Locke continued. "But they were a long distance behind, and I don't think they knew their target's location. Not precisely, no. But then we fired the big engines—for the first time ever. We changed our trajectory, not once but thousands of times." He lifted a flattened hand, and, using the fingertip of his other hand, he showed what he imagined must have happened. The Great Ship dove into the galaxy, tracing out an elaborate and highly publicized course partway around the Milky Way. While the other ship, following at some considerable distance, had several options open to it.

"That second ship could have dropped close to the old white dwarf, just as we did," said Locke. "But it would have been noticed, and I don't think its crew wanted to be seen. And besides, they still would have been left far behind us. If their goal was to catch up to us—"

"But they couldn't do that," Washen interrupted. "We've been over this and over this." She shook her head, using her own flattened hand and fingertip to describe various trajectories into the Milky Way. "I don't see how anyone could close a gap as large as what we're talking about . . . tens of thousands of light-years behind us, maybe . . ."

"But what if this other ship . . . ?"

Locke started to pose another question, then paused. The floor was shaking, the entire ship vibrating now, an epic force moving closer to them by the instant.

Pamir looked straight up.

Aasleen stared at the Wayward, her eyes wide and glassy. "But if these pursuers had a streakship," she began.

"Or its equivalent," Locke agreed. "A swift vessel, but very limited. Too tiny to carry the sensors necessary to pinpoint exactly where the Great Ship was. Coasting at the ship's velocity. No extra fuel to make endless course corrections." He nodded, reminding his mother, "Hammerwings fly slowly when they hunt. Only when they see their prey for certain do they accelerate to full velocity."

The shivering floor quieted for a moment.

Then the drumming grew worse than ever, threatening to knock everyone off their feet.

"They couldn't see their target until we ignited the engines, until we gave it a voice. We made the Great Ship boast about its merits and future course, and by then humans had control, and what would be the most reasonable course for something that is very swift but small?"

Pamir dropped his gaze. "Get ahead of us," he offered. "Wait for us along the way, somehow . . ."

"They'd have to be exceptionally patient," Aasleen warned.

Then with her next breath, she admitted, "But they've already invested a few billion years in their pursuit."

Humans would never comprehend that kind of fortitude.

"I've been thinking this through," Locke continued. "If I was small but very quick—and if I didn't know where the Great Ship was, but I had a fair idea about its velocity—I would match its trajectory to the best of my ability, then I would wait, and watch, and wait. For as long as was necessary. And when I saw the Great Ship fire its engines for the first time—a tiny flicker thousands of light-years ahead of me— I'd know that someone had finally found it and claimed it for themselves. And that's when I would spend all of my reserves. I wouldn't try to catch the ship straightaway. I probably don't have the resources to take it back from its new owners. But I could decipher the ship's future course, and if I burned every gram of fuel to jump ahead, diving into the galaxy at a point along that course, and there find a likely world . . ."

He hesitated.

"What?" Washen snapped.

"I'd find an empty world and then play an enormous game," Locke explained. "I would build up my numbers, invent a history and then use that history to fool the captains . . . I would beg for a small berth on this vast, precious ship . . . and after an appropriate interval, I would quietly vanish from the captains' view . . ."

The floor bucked suddenly.

A thousand silent alarms told Washen the worst. Then in the next moment, the team's lead engineer declared, "We've got to load and calibrate; then we are ready. Ready!"

The first thin trace of light appeared directly above them.

Locke glanced upward and quietly said, "The !eech."

But the Submasters had no time left for oddities and old histories. Suddenly they were hurrying off to stations where they could help orchestrate the final battle. Even Washen had to say to her son, "Not now. In a few minutes, maybe. But I can't listen anymore, darling."

Locke found himself standing alone.

The band of light above him was brightening. The polypond's ultimate weapon was biting into a sudden emptiness. But he paid little attention to the mayhem, his mouth closing for a moment while the eyes wandered in no particular direction, then the mouth parted again, and to nobody he said, "But this is what is most interesting. I think."

He explained, "They left just enough of a trail to be followed. Just enough that I could envision their existence and find their marks and follow them until I am absolutely sure that they exist."

He paused.

Again, the floor shivered, and he glanced up at the descending blade, and in the barest whisper, he said, "Of course. Whatever they are, whatever they desire . . . they want very much to be found . . ."

Forty-seven

THE CAP-CAR WORE a dozen burly coats of the finest hyperfiber, but the protection was far from adequate. "We're being seared alive," 'Osmium remarked, as they lifted into the blue-white glare. With gamma radiation punching its way through the armor and through their bodies, he told his companion, "We are cooking like a meal," while his eating mouth made the rudest possible sound.

"Closer," Pamir insisted.

Dying bones ached as they rose higher.

"Tracking now," he said.

In any given nanosecond, the car knew its position to within the diameter of an iron nucleus, and its body was sprinkled with delicate lasers that were nearly as precise. Whispery beams measured the outer edge of the Sword, while others mapped each of the black holes. An ocean of data was accumulated in moments. As the Sword cut deeper into the empty fuel tank, more of its surface lay exposed, stroked by light and memorized in withering detail. Another three cap-cars, similarly equipped and flying toward other vantage points, did the same relentless job. Harmonics were measured. Warps and points of strength were identified. The polypond's weapon was stable but eroding. Elegant mathematical maps were built and tested, discarded and built all over again. In less than forty seconds, a single AI overseer—there wasn't time for teams of machines or human involvement—decided that it could predict where the next region of greatest stability could be found, and it marked the nanosecond when its weapon could be unleashed. And then, finding itself with almost four seconds to wait, it decided to signal the captains, using a cheery voice to sing, "Hope."

They were hovering thirty kilometers from the Sword's superheated edge. Pamir's body was dying, and his mind wasn't far behind. He heard, "Hope," and for a sloppy instant, he couldn't remember the word's significance. Hope for what? Turning to the harum-scarum, he meant to ask, but Osmium put a hard hand to his face, steering his eyes back to the main display.

A golden flash appeared below them.

Pamir remembered: A minor conduit led down into a useful loop, pristine and full of nothingness. The engineers and their robots had built a simple but powerful acceleration chamber inside that loop. Minutes ago, an object no bigger than a fist had been introduced—a sphere of hyperfiber adorned with immersion eyes and tiny thrusters, all laid over a sphere of iron and busy machines, which in turn covered another paper-thin sphere of hyperfiber. At the center of that was a highly charged, rapidly spinning black hole—the same tiny black hole that the fef had brought aeons ago as a gift to the captains. Smaller than a pinprick and containing the mass of a small mountain, the hole was launched along a precise line, its velocity tweaked endless times during that microsecond ride toward its target.

Oblivious to the danger, the Sword continued to roll through the heart of the ship, cutting and consuming while its powerful frame absorbed every new stress and the cumulative damage.

One of its teeth emerged from the ripped stone above—a swollen but still tiny black hole held tightly in place—and the tooth passed above the captains' last hope. They missed each other by five kilometers. A last course correction was attempted. To the brink of what was possible, the aim looked perfect. And then just before it struck the target, the black hole's electrical charge was bled away, leaving it perfectly neutral.

At a fat fraction of lightspeed, the Sword was struck, a pinprick of nothingness diving into its very thin edge.

Human eyes were too slow to watch.

Nothing changed. As the cap-car descended, streaking for cover, Pamir saw the wild razor light continue to lengthen, cutting into the middle of the fuel tank. In the duration of a heartbeat, their weapon had already done all of its damage and left the ship behind, racing out into the Inkwell now, and eventually, escaping from the Milky Way. But even the most hopeful models predicted a delay of ten or twelve seconds. They had cut the Sword at its strongest point. Strength had a predictable flat surface. Far narrower than the hyperfiber ribbon, the black hole would burrow into its meat, leaving behind a channel of plasmas and empty space. As the black hole ate, it grew. As it grew in mass, the damage would increase, and a multitude of instabilities would rise and rise again.

Most models promised fifteen seconds, give or take.

The cap-car dove into an empty conduit, crush-webs grabbing at the burnt bodies inside.

Through tears, Pamir stared at the flickering images.

Fifteen seconds became twenty.

Became twenty-five.

No model predicted such a long wait. If the Sword could spin around once and again, showing no sign of catastrophic failure, then none would come. They hadn't done enough damage. Improbable meant unlikely. Why did anyone bother to believe that they had a real chance at making this work?

A voice said, "Bad aim, it looks like . . ."

Washen.

There wasn't time for a second shot. What they needed was a long stretch of empty space—a vacuum surrounded by known masses and predictable forces—and that had been lost. The vast radiant blade continued to descend, slicing and carving until one of its awful teeth bit into the tank's floor, ripping apart the place where the Submasters had gathered.

Where Washen had been.

Pamir called to her.

Silence.

The tube around him began to vibrate. He and Osmium were nearly ten kilometers from the cutting zone, and they were at risk. But of course, everything was ruined and doomed, and only habit caused Pamir to tell his companion, "We need to run some more."

The harum-scarum laughed.

Then Washen's voice dropped down on him. Through a nexus that was rapidly failing, she screamed, "No. Not this ship. No!"

She sounded like a furious, red-faced, and utterly powerless child.

In despair, she wailed, "Not my grandchildren! No—!"

Then every nexus failed; every sound became a perfect silence.

Pamir took control of the little car. He considered sloughing off the brutalized armor. But he thought again and started to move them deeper into the ship, following the conduit, pushing toward the closest pumping station.

Osmium continued to laugh with both of his mouths.

Pamir glanced his way.

Then a weak, sorry laugh leaked out of him, and Pamir started to say, "Quite the day—"

The cap-car slammed into a wall and halfway disintegrated. Shards of armor plating and engine parts flew ahead and fell to the floor of the little tube, and the car's cabin fell on top of the wreckage and slid to a halt. And then again, with an even greater violence, the pieces picked up and moved.

Or the pieces were utterly still, and it was the ship that was moving.

Both answers presented themselves to Pamir; and then he wasn't thinking about anything at all.

SALVATION

"Well, well. Life lurks behind those eyes, I see."

The life behind the eyes slowly absorbed its surroundings. Tree limbs lay shattered and strewn about, white wood bleeding sap and the air stinking of sugary water and chlorophyll. Closer was a face. A human face, apparently. Perri slowly focused on the face, and after some groggy considerations, he decided that it was a human face, but not a normal one by most measures. Indeed, what was perhaps the oddest kind of creature was kneeling beside him, holding a rusty shovel in one hand, smiling happily with a face that was probably not much more than a hundred years old, and ancient beyond all measure.

The luddite gave his battered ribs a poke with the shovel. "Back to your wits yet, are you?"

Perri coughed, then admitted, "No."

"You were looking for something here. Remember? Tracking some odd bug or worm or something . . . some species that owed you money, you told me . . . though I still don't believe you, of course . . ."

"What happened?" Perri muttered.

"The hillside decided to join the valley floor."

He dimly recalled the avalanche beginning—

"And you were carried along for the ride." The ancient face had a bright, almost boyish grin. "Remember that?"

Perri had ridden into this obscure cavern inside a cap-car, yes. He recalled racing through, trying to beat the Sword before it cut the cavern in two. At the end, what he wanted was to return to his wife, to hold Quee Lee once more before the polypond either won or lost. And this was the only possible route—a deep cavern, isolated and happy because of its isolation. Its twin rivers fed into a sea that drained nowhere but up, offering a thousand routes leading to the ship's upper reaches. To Quee Lee's front door, and home. But Perri had stopped for a few moments. Why? He had seen something, or something had seen him—

"We spoke," he recalled. Dredging up pieces, he said, "I asked you about an alien."

"You caught a whiff of something," the worn face reminded him.

A biological cue, yes. An instrument riding on his car had inhaled a fleck of dust that triggered an alarm. Somewhere in the last one or two thousand years, a creature that may or may not have been an !eech had crossed this ground.

"You were looking for your bug," the luddite said.

Perri nodded and weakly sat up.

"Whatever it was . . . you thought it might have climbed up that wall, into one of the Old Caves . . ."

"It hadn't," he replied. Then with a sad shake of the head, Perri added, "It was a spurious trace. My machine's fault, and mine."

"I don't trust machines myself." Something about that statement was terribly humorous. The old boy threw down his shovel and laughed for a long while, stopping only when Perri had recovered enough to stand on his own.

"The Sword's already gone past," Perri observed.

"While you were coming out of the Caves, yes."

"Is that what started the avalanche?"

"Hardly."

Off in the remote distance, the cavern came to an abrupt end. A strong glassy wall stood where there should be nothing but bright air and white clouds. The Sword's fantastic motion and the wild energies had created an alloy of molten hyperfiber and gaseous rock. What remained could be kilometers thick, chaotic and impermeable and very tough. The new wall looked cold and rigid, but distances were misleading. Perri assumed that the Sword was now slicing into Marrow, reaching for whatever lay at its core, that irresistible marriage of purpose and fire carving out the heart of the ship.

"How long ago?" he asked.

"Did that machine pass?"

"A few minutes?"

Another laugh filled the air. "No, no. It's been ages longer than that. You were dead ten different ways, and I found you and unburied you, and now I've been watching your goo turn back to fake flesh—"

"How long?"

"Thirty hours, nearly."

Perri didn't know what to say.

But his savior could guess the next questions. With a nod and a yellowy grin, he explained, "Someone managed to turn the Sword at the last moment. The captains, or somebody, convinced that damned machine to twist sideways and miss the core, cutting its way out the trailing hemisphere and off into space somewhere. To die, we can hope."

Washen had done it, thought Perri. Against very long odds, she had managed to save the Great Ship.

He said as much, almost cheering.

The luddite preferred amused silence.

For the first time, Perri tried to walk.

His savior watched him and smiled, and after Perri's first careful steps, he asked, "Anything feel a little odd?"

"Everything does," Perri replied.

Then he hesitated. "What am I supposed to feel?"

" 'Every man is as heavy as his burdens,' " the man sang out, quoting some old luddite text.

"What do you mean? My weight?" Perri bent his new knees and then stood again. Then he stared at jumbled rocks and the raw, exposed hillside, and with a building astonishment, he asked, "What triggered the avalanche?"

"The ship."

"How?"

"Well, the whole great gal was moving." The old face broke into a wild, raucous laugh. "Like never before, the ship shook and twisted, and quite a bit more than that, too . . ."

Perri considered the words.

" 'Every man is as heavy as his burdens,' " the man repeated. "After the shaking stopped, something about this world felt different, and I wanted to know what. I may be a primitive man, but I'm not stupid. It only took me a full day and a hundred tests to decipher—"

"What's changed?"

"Everything has grown heavier," the luddite proclaimed. "I've checked my conclusion on three scales, testing my own body as well as known masses. Over the course of the last thirty hours, I have become more robust by a little less than half a kilogram."

"What do you mean?" Perri sputtered.

Then, "I don't believe you."

The luddite took no offense. With a shrug and a big wink, he simply said, "But that makes perfect sense. If this ship of ours is accelerating now."

Accelerating how? The engines were dead, and the ship was sliced into two pieces, and Perri hadn't heard so much as a hum out of any of his waiting nexuses since he came back to the living—

Oh, shit.

He dropped to his knees, as if struck in the belly.

"I'm not the oldest fellow in the world," his companion admitted. "And I'm not the brightest by a long ways. But judging by the evidence, I'd say . . . and with a certain amount of confidence . . . that after a very long sleep, the Great Ship has found her true engines, and she is once again, at long last, under way . . . !"

O'Layle sought her out, and with a mixture of astonishment and giddy pleasure, he reported, "The guards are talking about leaving. And they might leave the doors open for us, unless they do not. In either case, I think we can slip out before long."

Mere nodded.

"You look well," he lied.

She still had only a mortal body repaired in haste, and she remained far from healthy. Rebuilding her immortal genes would take patience and talent, neither of which she had at her disposal just now.

"What's wrong?" her companion inquired.

Mere stared at him with huge wise eyes.

"We weren't obliterated by the polypond," O'Layle reminded her. "We beat the creature in the end—"

"And she is sitting on our hull still."

"And here we are, still completely alive. Which is why I don't see the need for gloom."

"The ship is accelerating," she replied.

"Slowly," he countered.

But at a considerably faster rate than anything known before. Mere could have told him that much, and she could have spoken for days about the consequences of this one unexpected event. Even at their best, the Great Ship's engines were weaklings next to this kind of energy production. But then again, maybe what they had always considered to be the *engines were nothing more than maneuvering rockets. Had anyone ever bothered to won-der—?*

"The ship still functions," O'Layle continued. "We have good air and clean water, which is a testament to the machine's capacity to endure." Then he threw out his chest, adding, "We both know something about enduring, I think."

Mere was weak. When she stood up, as she did now, she could feel the slight but insistent tug that was trying to pull her sideways. It occurred to her that this was as much acceleration as the ship could endure without disrupting lives and the flow of vital fluids. Gravity still dominated, but those inside the leading face would feel heavier than before. Those under the trailing face would feel lighter. And those like her, standing near one of the ports, would feel a delicate hand always shoving them sideways.

"Where are we going?" she asked.

O'Layle laughed at her.

"But there is a better question," he warned.

Mere looked down. In her hand, slick and a little heavy, was the timepiece that Washen had slipped to her. Just a few days ago, it happened. Yet the event seemed very distant now, while a million other, far better days felt as if they had ended just half a moment ago.

"Who is in charge now?" she asked.

"Precisely," he gushed.

Mere looked up. She breathed in and held the breath, and after a long moment, she asked, "Have you seen any captains?"

"Not one."

"Who then?"

"No one. Myself, I have only seen our guards."

"Tell me."

He had to smile, enjoying the suspense. Then with a little tip of the head, O'Layle told her, "They are being spotted, here and there. Back from extinction, and looking the place over, I'd imagine. Now that they're the ones in charge—"

"Who?"

"They haven't given a name yet," he admitted. "But then, the !eech were never the most outspoken of souls."

Mere absorbed the news.

"But isn't that the best news?" O'Layle had to ask. "You and I . . . we know this species, and we have worked well with them, in the past . . . and probably in the future too, I would think . . ."

A narrow finger opened the silver lid of the timepiece, great brown eyes staring at the moving arms and silent numbers. Then after another little while, Mere put on a smile, and she lifted her gaze, and quietly, she said, "So tell me. How exactly can we slip out and away?"

"Contingencies," Pamir said. Then with a rumbling tone, he added, "Two centuries of making ready, modeling and planning, and we still didn't imagine anything quite like this."

His companion refused to respond.

No matter. He led her down the hallway, on foot, watching the back of one of Osmium's favorite sons. It was only the three of them slipping into Port Alpha. The rest of the security team were elsewhere, making their presence obvious. At a juncture with another hallway, they paused. No one else was visible. Two sealed doors and a hundred meters of open floor were all that remained between him and his goal now.

"Twice," the woman muttered.

"I know."

"I have lost the ship two times now."

Pamir showed her the barest hint of compassion, then swept it away with a glare. "We lost it for you, this time. Washen did. I did. But if you think any of us could have predicted this mess . . ."

The mess remained too enormous to measure. But clearly, the Great Ship had survived the polypond. Others had taken hold of the helm, and by incomprehensible means, they had twisted the ship slightly. Feeling an irresistible pressure, the damaged Sword was warped, and with twenty Earth masses bearing down on its cutting edge, its blade had slipped sideways. In the end, it cut the Great Ship into two unequal pieces, doing untold damage in the process. But the core and Marrow were spared. And in any other scenario, that would be a good enough reason to celebrate.

But in the midst of one attack, another enemy had risen. And with an ease that terrified every captain, the nexuses were disabled, while the reactors and pumps, and the waste disposal and environmental controls, were each being stolen away by quick hands that still refused to show themselves.

Reaching the first door, Pamir paused. Using a simple radio transmitter, he said, "Status?"

"We still have control," Aasleen said through a clutter of static.

"I need a door opened."

"Isn't it?"

Pamir turned to the harum-scarum. "Burn it open!"

"We'll expose ourselves," the Master warned.

"We're pretty damned exposed as it is," he countered. Then to the soldier, he said, "Burn it, and anything or anyone that gets in our way."

That door and the door standing behind it were obliterated. Running through the smoldering mess, Pamir led them out onto the floor of one of Port Alpha's secure berths. The vessel looming over them was a strange contraption, resembling a submarine more than a starship—a heavily armored machine ready to burrow its way through long stretches of dangerous water. Only after it passed through the polypond would it shuck off that exterior. Inside was a streakship, fully fueled and in perfect repair, with a small picked crew and an AI pilot that Pamir knew well. The AI spoke across a shielded radio channel, telling his old friend, "Hello. Welcome. Another journey, is it?"

"Not today," Pamir replied.

The Master walked heavily, her significant bulk not only useless but taxing. Yet despite her own anguish, she began to run, broad legs swishing, almost matching Pamir's near sprint.

"I'm staying behind," he told the pilot.

"But why?"

"I'll do more here."

The AI accepted that judgment without comment. "Then what is my mission?" it inquired.

"Someone has stolen our ship," he replied. "It is human property, by law and rights, and my species needs to be warned. Who else should deliver that news but the unseated Master?"

There was a pause—an eternity for an AI.

Then the voice said, "Agreed."

The trio had reached the sealed vessel. A single hatch blossomed open, and feeling all of her weight, the Master Captain bent low and began to climb inside. Again, with a mournful voice, she said, "Twice I have lost this ship."

"And twice in the past you have taken it," Pamir replied. "For yourself, for humankind. For the Milky Way."

The golden face nodded.

Silently, the open hatch began to melt at the edges, flowing back together again.

A moment later, for no apparent reason, the lights inside the berth died away, and from the Port's control came a sputtering, sloppy voice saying, "Hurry, hurry. They're coming, we've got to launch now . . . !"

Near the ship's center, a seamless night had been born.

Contingencies continued to play out, relentlessly and in every corner of the universe, and who could count how many plans were unfolding?

Washen had given up trying. What remained, for now and maybe for always, was the belief that the Great Ship had been built by wise minds, and it was meant to be an enduring, perhaps everlasting creation. And wrapped around that belief was the hope, probably innocent and flawed . . . but still the keen perfect hope that for all of its problems, Marrow was meant to serve as the castle's keep. Desperate good warriors could make a final stand here, and maybe they could try to take back the sky, eventually.

Years ago, spurred by imagination and inner voices, Washen had ordered a narrow and secret tunnel to be reopened, reaching almost all the way back to Marrow. In the last few days, using equipment at the bottom of the shaft, she and a few selected companions had finished the excavation, and in another few minutes, with more luck, they would collapse everything that lay above again.

That would stop no one from following, of course. But then again, whoever was in charge of the ship had been on board for millennia, and none of them had taken so much as a stroll across the world below.

The world below.

Washen's long legs hurried, carrying her and her pressure suit down a set of temporary *stairs. The stairs had been cut into the wall of the hyperfiber tube, leading everyone to a place that Washen knew well—a place she had barely left in any fashion but physically.*

Just where she had left it, an old-fashioned timepiece waited.

Robots had carved it out of the hyperfiber, leaving it only a little damaged. She picked it up and clung to it, then she turned and looked down. The world beneath was black, save for the patches of volcanic fire and burning forests and soft, colored glows that could mean nothing but human life.

A voice behind her said, "Mother."

She forced herself to look at the others.

"There's news," Locke reported.

"A general broadcast," Mere added, one tiny hand holding out a view screen linked directly to the rest of the ship. It was the same secure line that Washen had set in place here to eavesdrop on her grandchildren, and she didn't trust it anymore, either. But for the moment, she allowed it to work.

Aasleen reported, "The new rulers are saying, 'Hello.' "

Washen held the screen against her chest, unwilling to look just now.

Moving like smoke, Mere came up beside her and paused, looking down at the swollen odd world and the darkness. The buttresses had fallen almost entirely asleep. Yet they remained strong enough that despite the ship's acceleration, Marrow had not moved. Plainly, the Builders had imagined this contingency, too. When would Washen ever become less than amazed with these vanished souls?

"Cut the dome open," she ordered.

With quick energies and a blunt precision, the diamond barrier beneath them was punctured in one small spot. Air began to fall downward, creating a soft little wind that was heard more than felt.

"Seal up," she told everyone.

The suits were secured and pressurized, and heavy packs full of supplies and twin chutes were pulled against their backs.

Everyone wore a silver timepiece on his or her belt. Washen had handed them out at the end, just to these few. Each little device held directions to the meeting place and a specific time, and everyone who had not come was now left behind.

Pamir?

She kept looking for him among the dark figures. And he kept on avoiding her gaze, having made his decision to remain elsewhere.

The wind continued to sing.

Finally, almost as an afterthought, Washen looked at the broadcast from the world above. A creature that was very nearly flat, armored and segmented and wearing a pair of trilobite-style eyes, was telling the surviving billions, "The captains could not save you. But we did, and we will protect you. Great things are coming, my friends. Great things!"

Mere said the alien name.

!eech.

Washen shook her head, but it was Locke who corrected her. With a soft touch against the shoulder of her suit, he said, "No, no. That's just an invented name, we think."

"Then what are they?" Aasleen asked.

"The Bleak," said Locke.

Said Washen.

With that, she turned away, leaping for the hole and passing through it.

Then she began to scream.

But it wasn't a fearful scream. Not at all.

It was the full-throated, wonderstruck shriek of a girl who until now, until this moment, had forgotten just how much fun it was to fall.

About the Author

Robert Reed is the critically acclaimed author of eleven science fiction novels, including *The Remarkables, Down the Bright Way, Black Milk, The Hormone Jungle, The Leeshore, Beyond the Veil of Stars, An Exaltation of Larks, Beneath the Gated Sky, Sister Alice,* and *Marrow.*

Reed is also a prolific writer of short fiction, having been compared to both Ray Bradbury and Philip K. Dick and nominated several times for the Hugo Award. His short stories have appeared in *Asimov's Science Fiction Magazine, The Magazine of Fantasy & Science Fiction, Science Fiction Age,* and many other magazines. *The Dragons of Springplace* is a selection of his prestigious short work. He was the Gold Award winner of the first Writers of the Future contest.

Cutting-edge hard science fiction coupled with strong characters and intricate plots is Reed's forte. He, his wife, Leslie, and their daughter, Jessie Renee, live in Lincoln, Nebraska.

25.95

| FIC | Reed, Robert. |
| Reed | The well of stars. |

$25.95

DATE